When You See Me

When You See Me

Lisa Gardner

C

CENTURY

3 5 7 9 10 8 6 4

Century
20 Vauxhall Bridge Road
London SW1V 2SA

Century is part of the Penguin Random House group of companies
whose addresses can be found at global.penguinrandomhouse.com.

Penguin
Random House
UK

First published in Great Britain by Century in 2020

www.penguin.co.uk

A CIP catalogue record for this book is available from the British Library.

ISBN 9781529124392 (hardback)
ISBN 9781529124408 (trade paperback)

Printed and bound in Great Britain by Clays Ltd, Elcograf S.p.A.

Penguin Random House is committed to a sustainable future
for our business, our readers and our planet. This book is made
from Forest Stewardship Council® certified paper.

MIX
Paper from
responsible sources
FSC® C018179

For my own beautiful mamita, even though she shares entirely too many potty-training stories at writing conferences. Thank you for believing in my novels, Mom, even before I did. Love you!

When You See Me

PROLOGUE

M Y MOTHER LIKES TO HUM. *She stands at the stove, stirring this, tasting that, and humming, humming, humming.*

I sit in a chair by the table. I have a job. Grate the cheese. It's an easy job. The queso blanco crumbles to the touch. But I'm proud to do my part.

My mother says you do not have to be rich to eat like a king. It's because she loves to cook so much. Everyone comes to my mother's kitchen for her homemade salsa or special mole sauce, or my favorite, the little cinnamon churros dipped in chocolate.

I am five years old, which is old enough to stir the chocolate as it melts on the stove. Lentamente, my mother says. But not too slow, or it will burn.

Melted chocolate is hot. I stuck my little pinkie straight into the pot the first time, because I wanted a taste. First, I burned my finger. Then I licked at the thick chocolate and burned my mouth. My mother shook her head when I started crying. She used her apron to wipe my cheeks and she told me I was a silly chiquita and I must grow stronger and wiser so I do not stick my hand into bubbling pots. She brought me an ice cube to suck on and let me sit at the table and watch her fuss and hum over the steaming pans.

I am my mother's chiquita. She is my mamita. Our special names for each other. I love watching my mamita in the kitchen. When she's there, she's happy. No shadows on her face. She stands taller. She looks like my mami again, and not the sad woman who leaves in the morning in her dull gray maid's uniform. Or worse, the scared woman who sometimes comes home in the middle of the day, shoves me in a closet, and tells me I must be very quiet.

I always listen to my mami. Well, once I didn't. I ran after a brown puppy because I wanted to pet his ears and the car roared by me so fast I felt the wind in my hair. Then my mother grabbed my arm and screamed at me, No, no, no, bad, bad, bad. She spanked me and that hurt. Then she sat in the red dirt and cried and rocked me against her and that hurt worse, like I had both a tummy ache and a chest ache at the same time.

"You must listen to me, my love. We have only each other. So we must take extra care. You are mine and I am yours, always."

I wiped my mother's cheeks that day. I lay my head against her trembling shoulder and promised to always be good.

Now that I'm five, I walk to the school by myself, then come home by myself. I'm alone all afternoon, which is our secret, my mami says. Others might not like it. They might take me away.

I don't want to be taken away. So I'm a brave girl and I come home and turn on the little TV and watch cartoons and wait. Sometimes I draw. I love to color and paint. I'm always careful to clean up afterward. My mamita has a hard day, scrubbing and cleaning after others. Each day she leaves in a sharply pressed uniform with a crisp white apron. Every evening she returns exhausted, wrung out. And those are the good days. Sometimes, she comes home sad and scared, she must shed her drab uniform, pull on a colorful skirt, and head straight to her kitchen so she can smile again.

It's nighttime now. We are having burritos with slow roasted black beans and shredded chicken. It must be a special night, because we don't always get chicken. Meat costs more and we must be smart about such things.

But my mother is happy and stirring the beans, while the tortillas warm in the oven. Our kitchen is small but bright. Red tiles, green and blue paint. Pieces of pottery from my mother's mother, who she had to leave a long time ago and will never see again. But my mother was blessed with these pieces so that her mamá would always be with her, and one day, with me, as well.

"You don't need many things," my mother likes to tell me. "You just need the right things."

I hear howling in the distance. The coyotes in the desert, singing to one another. The sound makes my mother shiver, but I like it. I wish I could throw back my head and make the same mournful cry.

I practice my mother's hum instead. Then, I play my favorite game.

"Mamita," I say.

"Chiquita," she answers.

"Bonita mamita," I say.

She smiles. "Linda chiquita," she answers.

"Muy bonita mamita."

"Muy linda chiquita."

I giggle, because we are a pack, a little pack of two, and this is us, howling at each other.

"You are a silly chiquita," she says, and I giggle again and steal a piece of queso blanco and swing my feet beneath the chair with delight.

"Dinner," she declares, pulling out the tortillas.

The coyotes howl again. My mother crosses herself. I think I'm glad that I am hers and she is mine, forever.

———

THE BAD MAN COMES AFTER *dinner. My mother is at the sink, washing. I stand on a stool beside her, drying.*

He knocks, heavy and hard. At the sink, my mamita freezes. The shadows come back to her face, but I don't understand.

I just know that she's scared. And if she is scared, so am I.

"The closet," she whispers to me.

But it's too late. The back door bursts open. The man is there, filling the space. Our kitchen, which has always been perfect for a pack of two, is now tiny.

No place to hide.

I see his dark shadow as he lurches into the room, a giant, massive form, who appears more beast than human.

"What did you do?" he asks. He talks to my mother directly. Not yelling. His voice is cold, calm. It makes me tremble and want to cross myself.

"N-N-Nothing," my mother tries.

She's shaking too hard. I know she's lying and the Bad Man knows it, too.

"Did you really think I wouldn't find out? Did you really think you could outsmart me?"

My mother doesn't answer. I stare at her a long time. Her face has gone blank, but in its smoothness, I realize whatever the man is accusing her of, she did it. And he found out. And now, something awful is going to happen.

We are a pack of two. I want to reach for her hand. I want to be a brave girl for her. But my legs are shaking uncontrollably. On my little stool, I can't move.

Abruptly, my mother sets a pot into the sink, cutting the tension with a loud clatter. "Would you like some dinner? Burritos. Please, let me make you a plate."

Speaking of food, her voice calms. She moves slightly, placing herself between the man and me.

"Sure," the man says, but there is something in his voice that makes me tremble again.

I wish desperately I were in the closet. But I can't duck in there now. Can't go anywhere without him seeing. And some part of me, stubborn, foolish, stick-your-finger-into-hot-bubbling-chocolate stupid, doesn't want to go, and leave this man-beast alone with my mother.

She picks up the plate I have dried. She moves smoothly to the stove, where there are leftover tortillas and cold beans. She takes her time. Tortilla. A spoonful of beans. A sprinkle of queso. Folding the burrito. Placing it back in the oven. Finding the salsa, delivering it to the table.

"Beer," the man says.

My mother crosses to the tiny fridge, removes one of the beers tucked in the back.

She appears very composed, except for her hands, constantly crumpling her bright red skirt.

"Sit with me," the man says after she removes the burrito from the oven.

"I must finish the dishes—"

"Sit with me."

My mother sits. She shoots me a quick glance. There is something in her eyes, something she's trying to tell me. Standing on my stool, I don't understand. I don't know where to go, what to do. We must take care, she said. But I don't know how to take care of her now.

I just want this Bad Man to go away, and for my mother to be alone with me in the kitchen again.

The man eats his burrito. Bite by bite. He drinks his beer. He doesn't speak, and the silence makes my tummy hurt.

As the last forkful is scooped up, delivered to the Bad Man's mouth, my mother exhales slightly. Her shoulders slump. She has made some kind of decision, but I don't know what.

The man glances in my direction.

"She's very pretty."

"She's a baby," my mother states coldly. She stands up. "We'll go outside."

The man raises a brow. "Feisty, aren't you?"

"You want to talk? We go outside."

"I don't know. I like your kitchen. It's very cozy in here. Maybe you should clear this table. We could show your daughter what you're really good at."

My mother stares at the man. Suddenly, she marches around the table, straight toward him. He flinches, caught off guard, and I'm proud of my mamita for making the Bad Man recoil. She hits his shoulder with her body as she passes, hard, pointedly. Then she grabs the back door and flings it open. Before the man can react, she's outside.

At last he stands up. He pauses, stares at me a long while. I don't like the look in his eyes.

"What's your name, girl?"

I open my mouth, but nothing comes out. I am still shaking too hard.

My mother calls from outside.

He gives me a final glance, then moves for the doorway. "Stupid girl," he mutters.

I'm holding the dish towel. Alone now in the kitchen, I stare at it, wish I had something to dry. Wish the night would go backward and I could be sitting at the table, grating cheese and listening to my mother hum.

Then, more noises. The man, his voice angry and booming.

My mother. No, she says, over and over. Defiant, then stubborn, then pleading. A crack, a smack. I flinch. I know those sounds. He hit her. She speaks again, but her voice is so low I can barely hear it. I just recognize the tone. Broken. The Bad Man has hurt her, and my mamita is broken.

The angry voices stop. Everything stops. The silence scares me worse.

We are a pack. We have only each other. We must take care.

I carefully step down from the stool. I walk to the open doorway. I head outside.

My mother is on her knees. The man stands before her. He is holding something. A gun. He's pointing a gun at my mother's head.

I don't think. I bolt. I race to my mother, a blur of little arms and little legs. I fly like the wind, I want to believe. I hurtle myself into her arms.

As my mother screams, "No! Get away! Run, chiquita, run!"

She throws me from her, even as I try to clutch her arms. She tosses me behind her. "Run," she yells again. "Run!"

I see the tears pouring down her cheeks. I see the terror in her eyes.

I don't run. I can't.

I hold out my arms for my mother. We are two. We must take care—

The Bad Man pulls the trigger.

Later, I will dream of this, night after night. Later, this one moment will be all I have left. The last time I spoke. The last time I listened to my mother's hum. The last time I held out my arms for the person who loved me.

Now, the bullet tears through my mother's throat. A spray of red. Her hand, belatedly coming up.

Then the bullet continues on, slamming into my temple. I fly back. I land on red dirt. Dazed, hurt, confused.

The Bad Man walks over to me. He reaches down, feels my neck.

"Huh," he says.

Then, right before I pass out, the Bad Man lifts me up. I don't fight him. A sheet of blood coats my eyes. I stare through it at my mother's fallen form. And I feel the burn of the bullet that has gone from her to me. That has brought the last of my mamita into me.

Our pack of two is no more.

CHAPTER 1

W ATER."
    "Check."
"Granola bars."
"Check."
"Apples. PB and J sandwiches."
"Check, check." Janet paused, looked up from the day packs opened on the B&B's quilted bed. "How much water?"

"I'm going to say two bottles apiece," Chuck replied. He was lacing up his hiking boots, banging his heel against the hardwood floor to ensure a tight fit.

"It's really hot out," Janet hedged. They'd fled Hotlanta for the weekend, heading north into the mountains only to discover the humidity was marginally better here than in the city they'd left behind. Just what they needed: a heat wave in Appalachia.

Chuck considered the matter. "Better throw in three bottles apiece. We definitely want to stay hydrated."

"Sure," Janet said, trying to keep from sounding sarcastic. As if they knew what they were doing. As if Chuck's hiking boots hadn't just come from a sporting goods superstore, while both backpacks had been dug out of the dusty bowels of his parents' garage. Janet hadn't even bothered with real boots, sticking with her tennis shoes. Chuck had already warned her about rolling an ankle on the trails. Seriously, she'd just wanted a romantic weekend at a B&B. She and Chuck had been dating nearly a year: short enough that they were still making the effort, long enough that a getaway weekend sounded fun.

But hiking? That was Chuck's idea of a good time. Personally, she would've gone with room service and sex, but given the way her boyfriend was now clomping around their quaint room with blatant hiking boot satisfaction, *that* wasn't happening. Maybe at the end of the day. Assuming either of them could still move.

"You have the map?" she asked him now, as she was a city girl and knew it.

"Yep. Trail is marked. Four miles round-trip, one-thousand-foot elevation gain. We can do this." He stopped long enough to waggle an eyebrow at her, offer a reassuring kiss.

She acquiesced while leaning all the way into him. He could be charming, with his mop of brown hair, thick lashes, and dark puppy dog eyes. And he was fit, an up-and-coming ADA who burned away his courtroom frustrations running half marathons. Given how much she enjoyed every inch of that runner's body . . .

Fine, she would hike. For love, people had done worse.

She stepped back, hefted up the first pack, grunted a little at the weight.

"We're going to earn those water bottles," she said.

Chuck swung the second pack onto his own back as if it were nothing. "We got this," he said.

"Promise to carry me?"

"I don't want to use up all my strength. I still have some plans for us, end of day. I've heard the views are excellent from the trailhead.

But I'm kind of wondering"—he leaned closer, whispered in her ear—"if sex on a mountaintop won't be even better."

"Sweaty and pine needly," she told him, but he had her attention now. Hiking. Huh. She didn't even like gyms. But the great outdoors, coupled with the promise of the right reward . . .

"We got this," she agreed hoarsely. Then, after fighting with the straps of her pack, she followed her lanky, cute-as-sin boyfriend out the door.

First mistake: Chuck set the pace. He was a cardio freak, and steep winding mountain trails were no problem for him. Janet was gasping almost immediately, and transitioning from romantic thoughts to murderous plots. One woman on the jury, she figured. That's all she'd need to be acquitted of Chuck's impending demise, if he didn't slow down for his obviously suffering girlfriend.

Second mistake: Chuck wore new boots. One mile up, he developed a hitch in his stride. Shortly after that, he was wincing.

Janet worked as a vet tech, which made her the medical expert even when it came to humans. Meaning she was the one who had to forcefully halt Chuck's determined death march, sit his ass on a boulder, and demand that he remove the boot.

The heel of his left sock was already spotted with blood.

"Gee," she couldn't resist saying, "so much for my crappy tennis shoes."

He glared at her, and she could tell he was also making the transition from sex to bodily harm. Some things sounded like more fun than they really were. Hiking, Janet had already decided, was one of them.

She had Chuck gingerly pull off his extra-thick hiking sock. Even sitting in the shade, they were both drenched in sweat and breathing hard. Janet was never leaving air-conditioning again.

She rummaged through her pack till she found the first aid kit, another purchase still bearing tags. She inspected the bare-bones offerings. Neosporin and Band-Aids it was.

Chuck flinched when she touched his heel, then made little whimpering noises in his throat. So much for the take-no-prisoners assistant district attorney. He considered himself to be the intense one, while she was his breath of fresh air.

She hadn't the heart to tell him he had no idea how much courage it took to help wounded animals, and just how tough you had to be to realize when medical intervention wouldn't be enough, and that last, final step was all you could offer the sweet, trusting eyes staring back up at you.

She let him have his man pride now, trying not to sigh too loudly as she gently dabbed the antibiotic cream on his raw heel, then covered it with a Band-Aid. Not a perfect fix, she already knew, as his stiff boots would continue to rub.

"We should go back," she suggested.

"No way. Not this close."

"We still have a mile to the summit, not to mention the hike back down."

"I can do it. It's just a blister."

"Didn't you once say blisters are the worst enemy of the long-distance runner?"

"This isn't a long distance."

"You're crazy."

"That's why you love me."

"I thought it was the puppy dog eyes."

"I don't have puppy dog eyes!" He was already working his sock back on.

"Puppy dog hair?" she suggested, giving up the battle she already knew she would lose. She returned the first aid kit to her pack, looking off in the distance as he slid his foot back into his boot. He was gritting his teeth, hard.

Janet rose to standing, watching Chuck lace up his boot, then hobble about as if he were magically all better.

She retrieved her water bottle from the side pouch for a long drink. It didn't help. She was hot, sweaty, and completely done with the great outdoors.

CHUCK RESUMED THE HIKE. HE was going to destroy his own foot, no doubt about it. Would rub off all the skin and be in pain for days to come. And she'd get to hear about it. Again and again. Like the man-flu, except for feet.

New objective: Get to the top, take in the view, snap a selfie, retreat. Then, never speak of this day again.

Chuck's limping grew more and more pronounced. Janet trudged along, waiting, waiting . . .

"I want a stick," Chuck announced abruptly.

He stopped and she nearly ran into him.

"A stick?" she said.

"Like a walking stick. I think it will help."

"Sure." Because a wooden staff would stop his foot from rubbing against his brand-new boot?

But Chuck was now a man with a plan. They'd come to a turn in the trail. A slightly flatter spot, but up this high, the trees were shorter and Janet didn't see much in the way of fallen branches. Chuck shrugged out of his pack. She followed suit, grateful for the break even if she didn't completely understand the mission.

They set their packs beside a boulder, then Chuck took the first step off the trail, heading deeper into the shade of the trees. Janet wasn't sure she liked this, but found herself following.

There were low leafy shrubs everywhere; Janet hadn't a clue what anything was called. But a thin path seemed to wind between the underbrush. Chuck hobbled forward, eyes peeled for the right stick, branch, something. Janet kept casting glances back where they'd left the trail.

Isn't this how people died? Wandering off trail, never to be seen again?

Chuck came to a small clearing. The ground was flatter and rockier here. They were definitely off the beaten path, this area covered in layers of decaying leaves. It smelled of mold, Janet thought, crinkling her nose. But ahead was a huge, broadleaf tree and around it, yes, a scattering of debris.

Chuck limped to the base of the tree. Started looping around. Janet stayed put, one eye still on the exit route behind them.

"Hey, look at this!"

Chuck emerged from the other side of the tree trunk, carrying a bleached-out stick.

Janet frowned. "Isn't that too short?"

"Yeah, yeah. But just look at it. The silver gray tone, and it's so smooth." He ran his hand along its length. "Not a trace of bark and so perfectly weathered. But still hard as a rock. I wonder how long this stick has been here? How many years to achieve this perfect degree of fossilization?"

He was closer to her now, that grin back on his face. Like a dog with a toy, she thought. Which is when she got her first true look at his prize.

"Chuck . . ."

"What?" He came to a halt beside her.

"That's not a stick."

He hefted it up. Long, weathered, and smooth, just as he'd described it. With two distinctly round knobs at the end.

Janet did not want to say what she had to say next.

"What?" he demanded again.

"Chuck, that's a bone. A femur bone, if I had to guess. And given the length and width, not any animal I know of. Which leaves . . ."

Chuck dropped it. And there went Janet's romantic weekend, as her badass boyfriend began to scream.

THINGS TAKE TIME, LONGER THAN most realize. First the local sheriff's department had to hike in and secure the scene. Then the state's forensic anthropologist was summoned to confirm that the remains were indeed human and begin the painstaking task of exhumation.

Sketches were made. Dirt sifted for trace evidence. The search zone widened as it became clear scavengers had been raiding the site and not all pieces of the skeleton remained intact. Smaller bones were recovered farther off. Many more remained missing.

Eventually, the forensic anthropologist and the heavily weathered skeleton journeyed back to Atlanta and the comfort of the lab, where the bones were given their own box and a case ID number. Several experts, not to mention some grad students, stopped by to check it out. Everyone was impressed by the quality of the find. No one had immediate answers.

More weeks passed. Then a couple of months, given the case backlog.

Finally, progress. A local artist reconstructed the face using modeling clay. Photos were taken. Images loaded into a nationwide database—and at last, a possible match. The forensic anthropologist conducted additional studies, cross-referencing age, gender, then the presence of an old childhood injury (broken arm) to the corresponding humerus. Confirmation was made, and finally the skeleton had a name.

Which was when SSA Kimberly Quincy received the call, as her name was flagged in the missing persons case file. According to the forensic anthropologist, the remains of Lilah Abenito, missing fifteen years, had been recovered in the mountains of Georgia. Cause of death, undetermined, but injuries to the hyoid bone were consistent with strangulation.

Kimberly hung up the phone. Absorbing. Thinking. Absorbing some more. She'd been waiting for this call for so many years, it felt faintly impossible. But at long last, Lilah Abenito had been found. Which meant . . . ?

Kimberly took a deep breath in, long breath out. Then she knew exactly what to do.

CHAPTER 2

FLORA

I DATED ONCE. PJN. PRE Jacob Ness. I remember brushing out my sun-streaked hair till it glowed California gold. Then I'd line my lashes in deep purple and go heavy on the mascara to bring out the gray depths of my eyes. A wisp of a dress. Thin spaghetti straps, a hem that barely brushed mid-thigh. Why not? I'd spent my childhood running around the wilds of Maine and I had long, graceful legs to show for it.

In those days, I was a girl on fire. I didn't just enter a bar, I sauntered: bright, shiny, the life of the party. I was young and arrogant. And stupid. Dear God, so stupid. Even now, eight years later, I wish I could go back and have twenty seconds alone with my younger, stupider self.

But no such luck. So instead, bright, shiny me headed to Florida on spring break. And like tons of pretty college coeds, I donned my wisp of a dress and headed out with my bestest buds, all almost as golden and giggly as me, ready to rock the palm trees. We downed tequila shots. We shimmied across peanut-strewn floors. We spurned good-looking guys for downright sexy ones.

Then . . .

I danced myself away from the protection of the bar lights. Into the shadows of the sparsely populated beach, listening to some song only I could hear in my tequila-soaked head.

And Jacob Ness, who later told me he'd been watching me for hours, snatched me off that beach. Yanked me right out of my life, my pretty girl bluster, my young and glorious ways. He came. I disappeared. And for the next four hundred and seventy-two days, I learned about an entirely different kind of existence. One involving a coffin-sized box and the whims of a vicious predator who'd always wanted his own personal sex slave.

Again, if I could just have twenty seconds alone with younger, stupider me . . . But there are some mistakes you never get to take back. And there are some experiences there is no returning from.

There is *what was*. And now there is *what is*.

But I still miss that girl sometimes. Especially on a night like this one.

WE MEET AT THE RESTAURANT. Keith knows better than to ask to pick me up at my apartment. It's silly, really. The guy is such a computer nerd he can probably hack the DOD. No doubt he has my address. Hell, probably a blueprint of the entire town house, for that matter.

But I need my illusions, and at this phase of our "relationship" he's willing to give them to me. Tonight's attempt at dating will take place at a popular rib joint in Boston. The kind of place known for its huge portions and sketchy neighborhood. Hipsters need not apply. Tourists definitely wouldn't survive. My kind of place.

Last time I agreed to dinner, Keith took me to some establishment that was clearly five-star pretentious with starched white table linens and twenty-nine pieces of silverware. Even wearing my nice hoodie, I didn't exactly blend in.

Keith did the requisite, "You're beautiful anywhere you go, in anything you wear."

I debated how much damage I could inflict with the four available knives, particularly the fish knife, which was a new and interesting implement. Not terribly sharp, but then again, you didn't need a razor's edge when targeting eyeballs. For that matter, the butter knife had a heavy silver handle, perfect for bludgeoning. Then there were the crystal glasses that could be smashed into jagged edges, or fine china plates which could be hurled as deadly Frisbees . . .

We left shortly after that.

I adhere to a certain style. I call it urban disenfranchised. Basically, steel-toed boots and dark-colored cargo pants topped by any number of hoodies. Some of my sweatshirts have words on them—a logo or print. All have been washed so many times they can no longer be read.

I don't spend money on clothes, not party dresses or even new hoodies. I did recently invest in a new butterfly blade. The steel handles, when folded together like a closed fan—or wings of a butterfly— are etched with the most amazing dragon design. Flick of a wrist, the handles flip open and back, the blade appears, murder and mayhem ensue. I love my new blade, spend hours at night, flicking, unflicking, tracing the amazing craftsmanship, then flicking, unflicking, all over again. Tonight, the butterfly knife is wedged in the top of my boot. It's one of the main reasons I came out. I wanted to see how walking around with the concealed weapon would feel.

Because dating . . . A girl like me, with a guy like him . . .

Keith Edgar is a self-employed computer analyst. He's also a true-crime enthusiast who considers himself to be one of the foremost experts on Jacob Ness. I met him in December, only because I needed some information on the life Jacob led before he found me.

At the time, I'd assumed Keith would be some basement-dwelling dweeb who drooled over crime scene photos the way others drool over porn. He'd be bat-blind, moonfaced, and with a fetish for Doritos and energy drinks.

Instead . . .

He's tall, with a lean athletic build, thick dark hair, and impossibly blue eyes. He favors Tom Ford suits and—in the middle of the night, when I'm thinking about things I don't want to think about—I'm guessing Calvin Klein briefs. He's incredibly smart and can analyze a police report or a predator profile almost as quickly as I can.

My current theory is that he's either the first good thing to happen in my life in a very long time. Or he's a serial killer.

Which is one of the many problems with nights like tonight. I honestly can't decide. And I don't know if that already tells me something about him, or yet more things I don't want to know about me.

Now, sitting at the table at the edge of the crowded rib joint, I count the exits. Front, back, kitchen door, which probably also has a rear egress. Three. I would prefer five.

Across from me, Keith watches me tap my fingers against the sticky wood tabletop and shakes his head. "Four," he corrects, having already deduced my line of thinking. "The men's room, at least, has a window large enough for escape. You'll have to check out the ladies' room on your own."

He nods in the direction of the restrooms. They are located on the opposite side of the bar, which is positioned like a circular bull's-eye in the middle of the floor. Annoying layout if you ask me. Six steps to dart left, half a dozen to escape right, given the obstacle smack-dab in the middle. Still, more exits are more exits.

"I'm thinking of the short ribs in the chipotle maple glaze," Keith says brightly, picking up the menu.

"You're a brave man to wear cashmere to a rib joint."

I earn a brilliant white smile. Serial killer, I think again.

"Flora, most would consider me a brave man just for sharing a table with you."

Endearing, too. Dammit.

"I bought a new knife," I say.

"For my side dish, I've picked sweet potato fries. And you?"

I scowl at him. "Cole slaw."

"Seriously? No one chooses slaw over fries. Now you're being contrarian."

I scowl harder.

He waggles his smartphone. "I can bring up studies if you'd like: Slaw versus fries and those who lie about their innermost desires. Don't make me go all nerd on you. You know I'll do it."

He would, too. Charming, endearing, and smart. Bastard.

I return to studying the menu. I'm anxious and uncomfortable. My hands, holding the menu, appear foreign to me. My nails clipped short, no buff or polish. My palms ridged in calluses. I have practical hands, I tell myself. Capable hands. But practical and capable for what?

I still don't know what to do with a man like Keith. Who's obviously interested in me, but also patient and understanding. Sometimes, he even says exactly the right thing, except instead of making me feel better, it makes me suspicious. He's too knowledgeable, too understanding.

They say Ted Bundy was very persuasive, as well.

"Ribs and sweet potato fries," Keith says.

"Chicken and slaw," I counter.

"Anything to drink?"

I shake my head, point to my water. I rarely drink. He'll order a beer, but generally only one. A consideration for my abstinence or because he's just as big of a control freak as me? This is what dating is supposed to be all about. Getting to know each other. Determining the answers to these questions. Who is he really? Who am I really? And even more intriguing, who might we become together?

I swear to God I'm sweating through my T-shirt and I've already lost my appetite. Serial predators I can handle. This evening, on the other hand, might be the death of me.

Once upon a time, there was a beautiful girl named Flora who laughed and flirted with all the boys. And now?

My phone vibrates. Saved by the bell. I yank it out of my pocket, desperate for the distraction. A moment later, however . . .

I glance up at Keith, frowning.

"You have to go?" he asks. He doesn't bother to mask his disappointment.

"We both have to go."

"Both?" He sits up straighter, clearly intrigued.

I hold out my phone to show him the text. "Sergeant D. D. Warren. She wants to meet both of us. Immediately."

Keith throws cash on the table, grabs his leather jacket, and rises to standing before I can even push away from the high top. In his face, I see the same spark I feel in mine. The thrill of the hunt.

He really is perfect, I think.

And find myself reassured by the subtle pressure of the new blade pressing against my lower leg as I follow him out of the bar.

SERGEANT D. D. WARREN IS A Boston homicide detective. She has short, curly blond hair, crystalline blue eyes, and a razor-sharp jaw. No one would call her beautiful, but she's striking in a cool, slightly dangerous sort of way. The first time I met her, she struck me as a woman who suffered no fools and took no prisoners. She hasn't disappointed me yet.

Even though I was a Boston college student when I was abducted, D.D. never handled my case. My kidnapping fell under FBI jurisdiction. Instead, I met D.D. five years after my safe return, when I'd given up sleeping and moved to Boston to hunt predators.

Our initial meeting involved me standing bound and naked over a would-be rapist I'd just annihilated with chemical fire. D.D. wanted to discuss my questionable approach to crime fighting. I wanted the record to show that he'd started it.

I wouldn't describe our relationship as an easy one, but a year ago she asked me to serve as her confidential informant. I think she's slowly but surely trying to convert me to her side of law and order. Honestly, her job involves way too much paperwork, I argue it's only a matter of time before she joins me in the world of vigilantism. We may both have a point.

I don't have many friends. Like a lot of survivors battling PTSD, I don't do trust, sharing, or confidence in others. But I would count D.D. as at least a respected associate. And there are times, as cranky as she can be, that I think she almost likes me. A little bit.

Nine months ago, we worked together to solve a domestic homicide. D.D. had recognized the shooter—the pregnant wife—from a case she'd worked sixteen years prior. I'd recognized the victim—the husband—as he'd once hung out in a bar with my kidnapper, Jacob Ness. Both D.D. and I had questions we needed answered.

Along the way, I learned some uncomfortable truths.

Fact one: Jacob Ness, who I'd killed with my own hands, was a suspect in six other missing persons cases, investigations that would most likely never be closed due to the fact he was no longer around to provide information.

Fact two: Jacob Ness, who I'd officially refused to discuss with law enforcement agents upon my rescue, had probably led a much fuller life of evil deeds than even I'd suspected. This life involved networking on the dark web, utilizing computer skills Jacob had no obvious way of knowing. He'd also had access to some kind of cabin where he'd held me in the beginning of my captivity and maybe had kept others, as well. And yet, the FBI could never identify where this location might be—we took to calling it the monster's lair—which once again suggested a level of forensic sophistication out of line with his background.

Fact three: I'd thought I knew everything there was to know about the evil, awful terrible man who'd held total control over every breath I took for four hundred and seventy-two days. I was wrong.

Enter Keith Edgar. Given his computer skills and self-proclaimed expertise in the subject of Jacob Ness, he'd been a logical source to contact for more information regarding Jacob's larger criminal history. That Keith happened to look like Ted Bundy was purely a coincidence, or so I told myself.

Working with Sergeant Warren and FBI SSA Kimberly Quincy, Keith and I had been able to finally determine Jacob's username and password for the dark web. This enabled Keith to start tracing some of Jacob's online activities from eight years ago and even solve a murder. The FBI had shown their gratitude by taking away the computer. SSA Quincy had mumbled some trite apologies at the time—FBI policy, FBI forensic techs, FBI blah, blah, blah.

I'd been extremely annoyed. Keith had been devastated. But not too much, which made me wonder how much information he'd copied/memorized/mapped before Quincy had snatched his toy away. Computer geeks can be very resourceful, and definitely aren't ones to bother themselves overmuch with federal statutes.

In the months since, I've never directly asked Keith what he did. I figured he wouldn't tell me, being the protective sort. While at the same time, if he did make a bombshell discovery, I'm sure I'd be the first to know; he'd just never mention his source.

We work together well. Which is what I keep telling myself, as the Uber driver drops us off at BPD headquarters. Even this time of night, the glass monstrosity is ablaze with lights.

Keith and I don't speak. We head inside where D. D. Warren is standing in the lobby, already waiting for us. By her side is a small travel bag.

In that moment, I know.

Beside me, Keith knows, too.

"They've found something," he breathes.

"They've found some*one,*" I correct.

And whoever she is, I'm already very sad and very sorry for this poor woman whom I never met but with whom I will forever share a bond.

Both of us once met Jacob Ness.

And neither one of us ever truly came home again.

CHAPTER 3

D.D.

BOSTON SERGEANT DETECTIVE D. D. WARREN was in love.

She'd never meant for it to happen. In fact, once upon a time her life had fallen into three carefully planned phases: work, work, and work. She indulged in the occasional all-you-can-eat buffet, because a girl needed a hobby. Or maybe that was her shoe fetish. But either way, she'd spent the majority of her adult life happily kicking ass and taking names. Some of her fellow investigators found her obsessive, if not prickly. Not her problem. Following an on-the-job injury, she'd become a supervisor of homicide—technically a step up, though the truth was that D.D. was happier in the field than behind a desk. Her former squad mates, Phil and Neil (and now petite, perky, pain-in-the-ass Carol), had finally gotten used to her hands-on ways.

Today's phone call from SSA Kimberly Quincy—inviting D.D. to join a major taskforce that was re-opening several cold cases attached to an infamous predator—was the stuff of policing legend. D.D. should be thrilled, giddy, dancing in her brand-new smooth-as-butter black leather boots. Except, of course, she'd fallen in love.

She'd had to return home. Alex, her crime analyst husband who taught at the police academy, totally understood the demands of her job. He'd been the same way once. Now, at this phase of life, he could afford to slow down, admire her zeal, and smile at her in such a way that stated *I told you so* without him ever having to utter the words.

What had brought her low? Totally captured her heart, then ripped it from her chest, so that every day she had to leave it behind? They had a son. Six-year-old, hyper, adorable Jack. Who raced around the house in Avengers pajamas with his favorite canine sidekick, Kiko. Jack jumped, their spotted rescue pup jumped higher. Jack sprinted across their fenced-in yard, Kiko ran faster. Jack wasn't into shoes, but Kiko certainly loved to gnaw on an expensive pair of heels, which Jack then quickly hid under beds and behind sofas, anything to cover for his partner in crime.

Jack was silly, wild, and way too charming for D.D.'s or Alex's mental health.

Which made it so hard to stand in the family room and state, "Mommy has to go away for a few days. Probably a week."

Jack approached it smartly: no immediate waterworks. Instead, he'd played the brave young man. Head up, shoulders back.

"Okay, Mommy. If that's what you have to do to catch the bad guys . . ."

While his lower lip trembled. Then, suddenly flinging himself sideways, he wrapped his skinny body around Kiko's seated form.

"At least I still have you, girl. I know *you*'ll never leave me."

He aimed a single glance over his shoulder to see if D.D. had caught the show.

Leaning against the wall, Alex broke into mild applause and congratulated Jack on his performance. Which made both D.D. and Jack glare at him with uncomfortable similarity.

"Your mom's gotta go," Alex chided their son. "Now give her a hug and stop auditioning for Broadway."

Eventually, with a dramatic sigh, the six-year-old had forced himself to his feet. He gave his mother a pat on the back.

"I will miss you," he declared stoically. "Please text."

"How much TV is he watching?" D.D. demanded of Alex.

Her husband shrugged. "So many superheroes, so little time."

"I will be home as soon as I can," D.D. told her son.

"Sure," Jack sniffed.

D.D. found herself turning to the dog—honestly, the shoe-eating canine—for moral support. Kiko gave D.D. her back.

"Well then," D.D. said, addressing her husband. "Will you at least take my calls?"

"Always," Alex assured her. "I'll even accept FaceTime."

"At least someone still loves me."

Alex put an arm around her shoulders. "The heartbreak of little boys," he murmured in her ear.

"Parenthood ain't for sissies," she mumbled against his shoulder.

He kissed her softly. "You know he'll get over it in another minute. Go get 'em, slugger. We're both proud of you."

"Three to four days," she muttered. "Seven tops."

"Federal taskforce?"

"Yep."

"Gonna catch a bad guy? Maybe even bring some poor lost person home?"

"I hope so."

"Then don't worry about us. Your menfolk will be fine. Though I make no promises about too much TV or Frosted Flakes for breakfast."

D.D. shrugged. "I like Frosted Flakes for breakfast."

"Perfect, we'll blame you."

Which is how D.D. found herself back in her car, travel bag beside her, returning to BPD headquarters with one more awkward conversation to go. Love, such a complicated and powerful emotion. Able to topple the strongest among us, to waylay the unsuspecting, and to wriggle deep inside a woman heretofore laser-focused on her career.

It all made sense till Flora Dane sauntered into BPD headquarters with Keith Edgar at her side. One look at the tightness in her shoulders, the bounce in his step, the way they both glanced at each other while trying *not* to glance at each other, and D.D. was forced to remember the other half of love. The part that didn't bloom and grow. The colder, starker truth that love could cost you everything.

And often did.

D.D. LED FLORA AND KEITH to the homicide division's suite upstairs. Both had been there before, and while D.D. would like to say the bump up to sergeant meant she could now host meetings in her massive office, she could barely stand with a fellow detective in the closet-sized space. Instead, D.D. led Flora and Keith to the glass-doored conference room, which—like the rest of the building—resembled an insurance company more than an urban police force. For that matter, the homicide unit had blue carpet and cubicles that screamed staid corporate job. Some of the detectives had strewn crime scene tape and blood spatter photos all over their padded gray walls just to keep their sanity. Humor was an investigative necessity.

"Here's what we know," D.D. started without preamble. "Skeletal remains were discovered two and a half months ago in the mountains of Georgia."

"Georgia," Keith interrupted, giving Flora a meaningful glance. Both Flora and D.D. glared at him.

"Outside the town of Niche," D.D. continued, "which is some quaint little community that exists to house and feed hikers doing the Appalachian Trail. Too small a town for that to be Jacob's home base." She eyed Flora pointedly.

"He'd stand out," Flora filled in. "A long-haul trucker with a raging drug habit and a lack of personal hygiene. Not ideal small-town material."

"Exactly. The body, however, was identified as Lilah Abenito—"

Keith abruptly pulled his laptop from his bag, fired it to life. Notes, of course. Now D.D. remembered. Keith spent all their encounters pecking away at his computer like some rabid chicken. The man practically lived hardwired. She often wondered what Flora, who had a strictly hands-on approach to problem solving, thought of having a techie boyfriend.

Keith got his laptop booted up. D.D. continued: "Lilah Abenito was declared missing fifteen years ago. She is one of the first victims connected with Jacob Ness. Given the find, FBI agent Kimberly Quincy is forming a federal taskforce to investigate Lilah Abenito's murder, and look for further evidence of Jacob Ness's past activities."

"What do you know so far?" Flora asked. She hadn't taken a seat, but was standing in the conference room, gripping the back of a chair.

"Not much. But now that this case has been declared a priority, given its connection to Jacob Ness, everything will be revisited, including the forensic anthropologist's initial findings. While us task-force members"—she looked at Flora and Keith—"will be heading to Mosley County. Our job is to re-examine the gravesite—and all trails, communities, and activities around it."

"I'm guessing this tiny town isn't off a major freeway," Flora said.

"No. Up in the mountains and off the beaten path. Certainly not off the kind of roads a long-haul trucker such as Jacob Ness would be traveling for work."

"An old grave makes it harder to find evidence," Keith was musing out loud. "On the other hand, fifteen years ago Ness's crime spree was still in its infancy. Means he probably wasn't as refined about covering his tracks. He hadn't perfected his technique."

"This is a unique opportunity," D.D. agreed. "SSA Kimberly

Quincy has invited us all to join the taskforce. Which, I don't have to tell you, is quite an honor for two civilians."

"She needs me," Flora said flatly. "No one knows Jacob like I do. No one else survived to tell the tale."

"I didn't do so shabby tearing about his computer in December," Keith echoed. "Certainly I learned more in forty-eight hours than the FBI did in six years."

They were both right, and D.D. knew it.

"We'll head to Atlanta tonight," she informed them. "First task-force meeting will be bright and early in the morning, and our work starts immediately after that."

Keith didn't speak. He simply shut his laptop and rose to standing, clearly having made his decision.

As for Flora, D.D. knew there was never any doubt. Wherever Jacob Ness went, now as before, Flora Dane followed. It was both an impressive show of strength and a sad testimony of survivorship.

"You have the tickets?" Flora asked.

"Our Delta flight leaves out of Logan, nine oh two P.M."

"We'll see you at the airport."

CHAPTER 4

DO YOU HAVE A NAME?
  I can almost remember mine. It hovers on the edge of my memory. I lost it the night the Bad Man came, and the gun exploded. Then my mother was gone, and my words went with her.

  I see a picture. Hazy, shimmering around the edges. Sometimes I get a fragrance, like a flower. Other times the image dims, becomes silvery like the moon. Then I can hear my mother's voice, soft and low. Humming. Walking around the house, washing our clothes, stirring the pots on the stove, she was always humming. Sometimes, I try to hum again. I place my hand against my throat, feeling for the vibration. I have a memory of sound, of words, of lips that worked and a mouth that spoke. But no matter how much I focus on my mother's hum, will her happiness into my throat, I can't make anything come out.

  The Bad Man came. My mother told me to run but I didn't. And our pack of two is no more.

Girl. That is what they call me now. Girl, do this. Girl, wash that. Girl, come here. Girl, go away.

I picture the bad people as black shadows with narrow eyes. The men, the women, they all appear the same to me: a mass of darkness I walk among every day, fetching this, tending that. I keep my head down, my feet silent as I hobble through the halls, dragging my weak leg behind me.

I have a scar. Long and searing across my temple into my hairline. And my left eye and the corner of my mouth droop, my face appearing slightly melted. But I don't mind my scar. In the middle of the night, I trace the thick ridges with my finger over and over again. This is my mother. The last piece of her I will ever have. Like the special pottery she had from her own mother. You don't have to own many things, you just have to have the right things.

"Run," my mother said.

But I didn't. I turned. I reached out my arms for her.

The crack of the bullet. My mother falling, myself falling.

The Bad Man standing over me.

Girl, fetch that.

Quiet as a mouse, I do, I do, I do.

I HAVE MY ROOM. A *tiny closet with a thin sleeping pad and two threadbare blankets. I sleep in my clothes, because once I didn't and I was sorry. Besides, the bell might ring. Don't be slow, never be late. Follow the rules and in return, I get pieces of plain white paper and boxes of beloved crayons. I can't talk or read or write, but I can draw. Pictures, images, symbols. If I am not washing, fetching, tending, I draw.*

Some are beautiful, and I hide them under my sleeping pad, though they always disappear sooner or later. I imagine shadow beasts gleefully feeding sheets of bright color to roaring flames, delighting in their power to rob the world of one more speck of light. But I draw more images of green grass, and blue sky, and red and blue tiles, and fountains that bubble with the sound of laughing children because I believe my pictures can sing, even though the beasts don't hear them. And the monsters can feed the fire as much as they want, because I always have the pictures in my head, and I can repeat them again and again.

A girl must take her victories where she can find them.

Some of my pictures make me cry. Or maybe I'm already crying when I pick up the crayons, and the colored wax weeps with me. I don't let these drawings survive. I color the paper black. I scribble so hard the paper tears, the crayon breaks. Still I rub, rub, rub till the very floor trembles with the force of my agony.

Then I tear up the page into the teeniest, tiniest pieces. Bite-sized. And I take all that sadness back inside me, cleaning the floor, sweeping up the shredded bits of wax, because I don't want to leave any trace of my pain behind.

I don't want the bad people to know that much about me.

Girl, you are stupid, they say.

I don't nod. I don't acknowledge them. I let them believe what they want to believe.

Shadows can hurt. They can rob the world of light and ooze into all the cracks and crevices. But no shadow can last forever.

People are coming.

They murmur urgently.

I listen harder. I try to hear more. I can't learn any details, but something has changed. A discovery in the mountains, something bad for the shadow beasts—so, maybe good for the rest of us?

People are coming. That much is clear. And the Bad Man is concerned.

I must ramp up my own efforts. Tiny little stolen moments in the *bathroom, staring at my reflection above the sink, using my fingers to smash my lips, pull on my tongue. Move, roll, speak. I squish my lips into a perfect rosebud and try to exhale. Puh, puh, puh. I hold my palm in front of my lips, waiting to feel the expulsion of air. But I get nothing.*

People are coming and all these years later, I'm the same Dumb Girl I've always been.

I know what will come next.

Screams in the middle of the night. Sounds from girls who will never make another sound. I feel it, too — something here, then gone, like a tear in the universe.

At night, I huddle deeper in my closet. Waiting for the door to open. Knowing soon it will be my turn. And I try, because I have to try. Because somewhere way down deep, I am my mother's daughter and I feel her inside of me, as surely as the bullet lodged in my skull.

I get out my pieces of paper. I try to picture those awful lines I see on other scattered documents. If I could just arrange those shapes in the proper order, form words, sentences, meaning. They're a code everyone understands but me. The right sequence unlocks language, except I just can't seem to manage it. The lines run away from me. They have minds of their own, and won't stay where I put them.

I try to start simply. Names. I want to write the names of the other girls because everyone has a name. Everyone but me, but someday I will get mine back. Until then, the least I can do is remember, make a record of all those who've been lost. Maybe these people who are coming, they will care, they will help. If only I could talk, write, grunt.

So I struggle, trying to force my clawed hand to grip the crayon, drag down, across, into the shape of these mystery letters. But I can't get it. The lines grow blurry. Then they dance, bounce up and down on the paper to prove I don't own them, I don't understand them at all.

In the end, I draw. Elaborate, vibrant scenes with hidden patches of darkness. The girls that were. The spaces where they will be no more. Late into the night, I draw and I draw and I draw.

So many to remember. I can feel the house shudder around me and I know that it mourns. It's only a house, and not a bad one. Just an old home that never asked for any of this.

The house and I cry together. Then, when I'm done, I hold up the paper. I memorize each line, color, whorl. This patch of pink, this blur of green, this smile of blue. These new dark shadows.

People are coming.

I need words, letters, something. But all I have is this. The pictures of my pain. Slowly I start shredding. The teeniest, tiniest pieces. Bite-sized. Dots of pink, green, and blue. Larger pieces of red and black.

Then the real work begins. Chew swallow chew. Chew swallow chew.

I consume it all. No record of the girls, no trace of my defiance left behind. Just bits of names, now taken inside me, to carry alongside my mother's dying breath.

I need a better plan.

I need to act.

Soon.

People are coming.

CHAPTER 5

KIMBERLY

SSA KIMBERLY QUINCY HAD TRACKED killers, taken down art forgers, and tackled government corruption. Her father, Pierce Quincy, had been one of the Bureau's most legendary profilers, meaning she had both pedigree and reputation on her side. Still, leading a multijurisdictional taskforce was its own kind of challenge. Like herding a pride of lions.

She had fellow agents in the room, plus a county sheriff. And now, adding to the party, a Boston cop, a kidnapping survivor, and a true-crime enthusiast/computer analyst. The agent in Kimberly was slightly annoyed; the investigator in her was genuinely impressed.

Kimberly had been the agent who'd finally identified Jacob Ness as a serial predator, and led the raid on the motel room where he was holed up with Flora Dane. In a career full of memorable moments, Kimberly would never forget that day. The way Jacob Ness, eyes and nose streaming from the tear gas, had tended to Flora first, wrapping her face in a wet towel. Tenderly. Right before he handed her his gun. And Flora used that gun to blow out his brains.

Flora had then turned and stared at the incoming SWAT team with the blankest face Kimberly had ever seen. There was reading about the effects of long-term trauma, and there was seeing it up close and personal. It had been nearly an hour before Kimberly had gotten Flora to respond to her own name. That hour had been one of the longest of Kimberly's life, when she'd feared they hadn't rescued a woman after all, but only a shell of one.

The Flora who stalked into the room now, assessing the law enforcement occupants with an upward tilt of her chin and a defiant glare in her eyes? That woman was a far cry from the blood-spattered ghost Kimberly had pulled from the motel room. But Kimberly knew that while the girl might be stronger, she was still PTSD personified. As Kimberly had discussed with Boston sergeant D. D. Warren earlier by phone, she wasn't sure if including Flora in this investigation was a good idea or not.

Then again, Flora hadn't just survived Jacob Ness, she'd studied him, adapted to him, and even, in a matter of speaking, befriended him. She was his legacy, and in the days ahead, the entire taskforce would most likely need her insights to get the job done.

D.D. now ushered Flora and Keith to two seats. She took the third at the end of the table, closest to Kimberly. The trio had arrived in Atlanta shortly after midnight, though none looked worse for the wear. Fortunately, the recently built FBI field office was within miles of a Marriott, making for a short morning commute.

Kimberly cleared her throat, then started handing out the binders she'd been up all night preparing. Introductions were made, including for Flora and Keith. Whatever the other law enforcement officers thought about having two civilians in their midst, they were professional enough to keep it to themselves.

Kimberly got down to business.

"As many of you are aware, most serial predators have two lists:

their official victim list and their so-called asterisk list—victims law enforcement believe predators may have killed but have never been able to substantiate, often because we lack human remains. Hence statistics such as Ted Bundy murdered at least thirty women, but maybe killed as many as a hundred. Why the discrepancy? Because we can't prove the rest.

"In the case of Jacob Ness, whom you all know operated in this area and was ultimately ambushed in an FBI raid in a motel room outside of Atlanta, we've definitely tied him to multiple rape and murder cases. But following his death, he's remained a person of interest in the cases of six missing women. All fit his victimology and timeline of operations. But none of these bodies have ever been recovered, leaving us with open cases and plenty of questions.

"Which brings us to ten weeks ago, when skeletal remains were found off a hiking trail in the small mountain town of Niche, Georgia. The forensic anthropologist positively identified the body as Lilah Abenito, one of the women believed—but never proven—to be a victim of Jacob Ness. I think we all understand the importance to her parents of having answers once and for all. To have their child be more than a name on some infamous predator's asterisk list."

Kimberly waited a beat.

"What we do know: Lilah was a seventeen-year-old Hispanic female first reported missing from Alabama fifteen years ago. The actual circumstances of Lilah's disappearance aren't well documented. Her parents were both illegals and waited several days before contacting authorities. Her father worked at a local diner as a dishwasher; her mother took in laundry. According to them, Lilah wasn't one to get into trouble. Serious student, no known boyfriend. She was supposed to walk straight from school to her job at a local nail salon. She never made it. Forty-eight hours later, her parents filed a report. Local police conducted a rudimentary investigation without results."

Kimberly glanced around the room at her makeshift taskforce, most of whom were rapidly flipping through the reports she'd photocopied last night. The initial investigation's findings were part of the binder. It was neither the best nor the worst inquiry Kimberly had ever read. Clearly, the police had been inclined toward labeling Lilah a runaway, though her parents had denied it vehemently, and follow-up with her classmates had not revealed any signs of trouble on the home front. From an FBI point of view, with knowledge of a serial predator operating in the vicinity, the investigation was cursory at best. For the knowledge the local LEOs had at the time . . .

"Fifteen years ago," Kimberly continued now, "social media was still in its infancy. So, given what we're accustomed to being able to learn about a teenager in this day and age, there's hardly anything on Lilah. Her parents claimed she was a good girl, looking forward to attending community college in the fall and becoming the first member of her family to graduate. Except, one bright sunny afternoon, she disappeared. Until ten weeks ago."

Kimberly paused again, let everyone absorb. Kimberly believed in personalizing cases, had learned it firsthand from her profiler father. The victim had to matter—because God knows that in the weeks and months to come it would cost them all significant pieces of their personal lives to pursue justice.

"How did Jacob Ness become a suspect in the disappearance?" D.D. spoke up first.

Flora Dane, Kimberly noticed, remained completely expressionless. They could've been discussing the weather. But Kimberly didn't doubt that Flora was registering every word.

"The age and gender matched Ness's known targets. Also, the town where Lilah disappeared is near a major truck stop."

"Her abduction occurred within Ness's preferred hunting grounds," D.D. translated.

"Exactly."

"Cause of death?" Flora spoke up. She stared at Kimberly balefully.

"Unknown. The forensic exam was limited by the lack of any remaining soft tissue and the fact that many of the bones are still missing."

"You don't have the full skeleton?"

"Scavengers, unfortunately, wreaked havoc with the site, given the shallow burial. Looking at what was recovered, Dr. Jackson identified a broken hyoid bone, which can be a sign of strangulation. However, in a girl that young, the hyoid bone often isn't fused yet, so Dr. Jackson can't conclusively rule that as COD."

"He preferred knives," Flora said. Every investigator was gazing at her now. Flora kept her stare on Kimberly.

"True. But remember the timeline. If Lilah Abenito was indeed one of Ness's victims, her disappearance fifteen years ago would mark her as one of his first."

"He beat his wife. Raped a teenager. She wasn't his first."

"First kill," Kimberly amended, keeping her tone as matter-of-fact as Flora's.

The Mosley County sheriff raised his hand. "Hank Smithers here. I've read about Jacob Ness. I understand your point that this girl disappeared from his known hunting grounds. But there are two locations for us to be considering. The second, where her body was dumped, is in my neck of the woods to the north. We're talking more mountains than highway. How do you figure that?"

"We don't," Kimberly said honestly. "That's one of the questions we need to answer. Now, Miss Dane"—Kimberly nodded toward Flora—"in her statement regarding her own abduction, thought she was initially held in a mountain cabin. It's possible Ness has a connection to northern Georgia, Mosley County, whatever. We've never been able to identify that cabin, and as you can imagine, we'd like to."

"The remains were found off a hiking trail," Keith interjected, frowning. Kimberly had watched him flip through the binder. From what she could tell, he'd scanned the entire contents in a matter of minutes. "How far up the path?"

"More than a mile."

"Incline?"

"Six hundred foot altitude gain. Trail gets significantly steeper after that."

Keith turned to Flora. "He strike you as a hiker? Because I've never read about him doing any physical activities, not even high school sports."

"The Jacob I knew was a fat, out-of-shape addict. I can't imagine he was magically fitter eight years prior."

"Hauling a body one mile uphill is no mean feat," Keith added.

"You're assuming he was carrying her," Kimberly replied blandly. "For all we know, Lilah was alive when she walked up that trail."

"He led her to the location he wanted, then killed her," Flora stated. "Now that sounds like Jacob."

"Or he had help." Keith, looking at Kimberly again.

She nodded slowly. "It's important to note what we *didn't* find in the grave. Clothing. Shoes. Physical restraints. None of that. The body was laid out in the shallow grave unbound and completely naked."

"Forensic countermeasures," D.D. interjected. "He removed any objects that might yield evidence."

"That's certainly a possibility. To be clear, Jacob didn't take those steps with his other known victims?"

"No, he just dumped them, bloody clothes and all." Flora again.

"Maybe that means she was special," Keith spoke up thoughtfully. "First victims, there's often a personal connection to a serial preda-tor. Meaning Jacob took extra precautions because he had more to fear if someone found the body."

"All reasonable assumptions," Kimberly said to the taskforce.

"But just that—assumptions. We don't want to get too far ahead of ourselves. While there's good reason to consider Jacob Ness a prime suspect in Lilah Abenito's abduction and murder, we don't *know* that he did it. We don't *know* anything at all, which is a huge injustice to her and to her parents, who all these years later, are still waiting for their daughter to magically come home."

"There's more than one serial killer running around the mountains of Georgia?" Sheriff Smithers drawled sardonically.

"We need to take things one step at a time," Kimberly agreed, "and keep an open mind."

Kimberly gave the room a moment to process. When none of the taskforce argued with basic investigative protocol, Kimberly cleared her throat and moved on to the next pertinent part of the briefing. Basically, bringing everyone else in the room up to speed on a conversation she, D.D., Flora, and Keith had started nine months ago in Boston. And a scary discussion at that.

"We recently had some developments regarding Jacob Ness's recovered laptop. The computer initially appeared devoid of data. Further analysis by our techs revealed Ness had taken steps to automatically clear his computer activity on a daily basis—a much higher degree of sophistication than we expected from a man with limited formal education. Recently, however, Miss Dane and Mr. Edgar helped us identify Ness's username and password, unlocking a host of dark web and cloud-based activity on the laptop. It's clear now that while Ness was a loner in real life, on the internet he actively sought out and participated in forums with members who shared his own predatory instincts. The question is, did any of these virtual partnerships result in a real-world relationship?"

Kimberly nodded toward one of her fellow FBI agents, a striking twenty-eight-year-old woman with glossy black hair. "Su Chen," Kimberly addressed the agent directly, "is one of our best computer analysts. She's been studying Ness's laptop for the past few months."

Keith sat up straighter, as if eyeing the competition. Kimberly admired the hostile glance Su sent his way before picking up her notes.

"The identification of Jacob Ness's username and password have been pivotal." A slight nod toward Flora and Keith. "The good news about online forums is that they're searchable; once we have a username, we can trace much of the subject's online activities. Unfortunately, the web is a steadily evolving environment. I haven't had luck identifying any particular group from seven years ago."

"What about posing as Ness online, waiting for one of his former associates to contact you?" Keith asked immediately. Kimberly understood the question; nine months ago Keith had used that strategy to assist with another homicide investigation. They had been fortunate that Ness had used a pseudonym for his online activities, meaning many of his dark web contacts didn't realize he was a serial killer who'd been killed in an FBI raid years ago.

"I'm in ongoing virtual conversations with two different subjects at this time," Su replied coolly. "So far, their interest is purely porn, which I'm guessing was their previous relationship with Ness. Given the seven-year gap, I'm sure other participants are wary of Ness's sudden reappearance, so success might not be overnight, but I have faith in the strategy."

"Can I study the laptop again?" Keith asked.

"What do you hope to find?" the computer expert asked.

"What could a second pair of eyes hurt?" Keith countered.

Agent Chen studied her civilian counterpart for a moment or two. "I will see what I can do," she said abruptly.

Battle of the nerds, Kimberly thought. "Other questions?"

"What next?" the sheriff, Hank Smithers, asked.

"We go to Niche," Kimberly replied. "Expand the search grid around the first set of remains."

"You think there might be others," the sheriff said.

"Jacob is a suspect in the disappearances of five other women. Lilah Abenito isn't the only victim, just the one who was found first."

"Shh . . . rimp," the sheriff muttered, editing his curse nicely.

"There may indeed be more graves," Kimberly continued. "Also, the forensic anthropologist is working on narrowing the time of death to give us a tighter investigative window. Meaning recovering additional pieces of the skeleton would help."

Sheriff Smithers nodded. "I can get us a dog team, as well as local searchers. There are people in the area who know those woods like the backs of their hands."

"Perfect. Then, computer aside, we're looking at old fashioned groundwork. Checking property records. Circulating Ness's photo. Fifteen years is a long time—"

"Not in my county," the sheriff interrupted. "What it lacks in size, it makes up in memories." He glanced at D.D. "I'd work on that accent if I were you. And for the love of God, don't mention you're from the North."

Kimberly honestly couldn't tell if the man was joking or not. But she figured D.D. didn't care one way or the other.

"If Jacob was in the mountains, how'd he get there?" Kimberly continued now. "Does he own a vehicle we've never discovered to go with this property we never found? Does he have an associate, maybe a personal connection in the area who helped him out? We need to be flashing Jacob's photo to motel owners, bartenders, retail clerks. If he was staying in a local cabin, he'd have to come to town for food, booze, drugs. Before, we were searching northern Georgia. Now, we have a town. Let's hope that leads to the break we've been waiting for. Any questions?"

No one raised a hand. With a final nod, Kimberly closed up her binder, signaling the meeting was over. She'd just risen to standing when Flora spoke up.

"How sure is this Dr. Jackson that the remains belong to Lilah Abenito? You said the skeleton isn't even complete . . ."

"In addition to facial recognition, Dr. Jackson was able to match a childhood injury from Lilah's medical file to a healed break on the skeleton."

"Okay," Flora said.

Kimberly eyed her suspiciously. "What do you mean by that?"

"I'm going to meet Lilah Abenito," Flora announced. "Best place to start, right? With the victim?"

Then, without awaiting permission or approval, Flora got up and left.

CHAPTER 6

FLORA

D.D. DRIVES. THE RENTAL CAR is in her name and I wasn't going anywhere without her, that much was clear. Keith sits in the back. I could tell he was torn about joining us, his concern for me warring with his desire to track down that agent and get his hands on Jacob's laptop. But in the end, he chose me. Should I be flattered?

No one speaks. We stare out our windows, study the bright sky and the miles of concrete that seem to be Atlanta.

I was here once before. In a local hospital after the raid on Jacob's motel room. Then I was debriefed at the FBI field office, which wasn't even this field office but a tall, black glass monstrosity that looked like Corporate-R-Us. At least the new brick campus appears governmental. But none of it feels familiar. None of it triggers . . . anything.

I'm still a mountain girl. Which makes the next part of our day—heading north to search hiking trails for human remains—all the more difficult to take. The woods should be a place of respite.

Now all I can think about is Jacob marching some poor girl up a trail to her own death.

THE FORENSIC ANTHROPOLOGIST IS DR. Regina Jackson. She is a brisk black woman, not surprised to see us, so apparently SSA Quincy phoned ahead. She wears dark blue Crocs, turquoise scrubs, and a white lab coat. She shakes our hands and studies us as hard as we study her. I don't know much about forensic anthropology, just what I've seen on TV. I'm surprised by her surgical scrubs and wonder if we've interrupted a dissection.

Then, I can't help but stare at her thick black hair, pulled back in a tight bun, for any bits of flesh, fragments of skin. Keith is equally wide-eyed, but then, he treats all meetings with real-world crime experts with the wonder other people reserve for star athletes. Prior to meeting me, most of his experience with investigations came from searching the internet for articles on cold cases. Now he's a regular at BPD headquarters, sitting in on FBI meetings and shaking hands with a forensic anthropologist. Should I be concerned he's attracted to me for the company I keep?

We clear security, then Dr. Jackson leads us down the kind of long sterile hall that I associate with hospitals, morgues, and government buildings. The floors are polished concrete, the walls painted cinder block, the hanging lights fluorescent. By end of day, everyone must have massive headaches.

She pushes through heavy double doors into a larger, colder space. In the corner, I spy the entrance to what appears to be a small office. Dr. Jackson's name is next to the door, but she doesn't head for it. Instead, she cuts a straight line past several large stainless-steel tables—for bodies, for bones? On our right are rows of metal bookshelves filled with what appear to be extra-long shoe boxes. Every box is the exact same color—cream. All are labeled with scrawled black numbers.

Case numbers. For the bones inside. Dozens and dozens of sets of remains.

Again, the three of us proceed in silence, the only sound the clack of D.D.'s heeled boots against the floor. On the far wall is a span of pale wooden cabinets with a solid surface countertop. More workspace, I realize, as the full array of tools, papers, and clutter becomes clear. Then, sitting in a small pool of cleared space: Lilah Abenito.

Her reconstructed face stares at us like a chiseled bust. Dark sightless eyes bore into me. Long brown hair, heavy brows, graceful jawline. As one, we slow.

She is young, I think. Beautiful. Innocent.

She is everything Jacob loved to destroy.

DR. JACKSON EXPLAINS THE FACIAL reconstruction methodology to us: "We are fortunate to have a local artist, Deenah, whom I consider one of the best around. She's a sculptor in real life, and while I love science as much as the next expert, I believe her when she says all skulls want to reclaim their skin."

She glances at us, and I realize she's serious. It makes me finger my own cheeks. Does my skull love my skin? Beside me, I realize Keith is doing the same. We both shudder simultaneously.

"The first step," Dr. Jackson continues, "is to place markers along the skull to establish tissue depths for the forehead, cheeks, jawline, etc. Once the markers have been placed—which takes weeks of careful measurement—Deenah fills in around each marker with clay."

Dr. Jackson regards us matter-of-factly. "We always use earth-colored clay and brown eyes. In theory, bones don't tell us coloring, so brown is considered neutral. In the case of Lilah, however, given her Hispanic heritage, the coloring probably is accurate.

"The last step is photographing the results. Deenah takes the final photos herself. Proper lighting is important, and the skull must be shot from several angles. The photos are always taken in black and white—because, again, we can't be sure of coloring. The images are then loaded into the nationwide database of missing persons. In this case, we had a hit within a matter of days. Lilah Abenito." Dr. Jackson's voice softens as she says the name and I realize this process is personal for her. She and this artist have worked together to bring this skull back to life. And in doing so, hopefully grant this girl some justice and her family some closure.

"Once we had a name, I requested Lilah's full case file, including medical records. I found a notation regarding a fractured left humerus, which I was able to match with a healed fracture in the same place on the remains."

"In other words, you're certain this is her," D.D. states.

"As certain as it gets in this kind of work."

"But you don't have a cause of death?"

"The remains were discovered fully skeletonized. Unfortunately, there are many CODs that bear no impact on bones. Asphyxiation. Drug overdose. Poisoning. Even exsanguination. As long as the blade didn't hit bone upon entry, there would be no indicator of the initial wound, or the act of violence that led to death."

"Can you tell if she was . . . tortured?" I'm not sure how to ask the question. "Signs of cutting, knife work. Maybe not major damage, but something more subtle?"

"Assuming the blade struck bone," Dr. Jackson says, "yes, we would find evidence. And assuming we had the bone in question. Unfortunately, we're still missing significant pieces of this skeleton. For example, most of the rib bones are still unaccounted for. At this time, there are more things I don't know about these remains than I do."

"Signs of sexual assault?" D.D. again.

"I would need soft tissue to make that determination."

"But it's possible she was kidnapped and raped?"

"Physical restraints can leave markings on a skeleton, especially if utilized long-term." Dr. Jackson flickers a glance in my direction and I realize she knows exactly who I am. Of course she does. I rub my right hand self-consciously. I still have pale scars around both my wrists. There were times, especially in the beginning, when I struggled so hard it certainly felt as if my shackles cut to the bone.

It's an unsettling thought. I've always known that Jacob lives in my head. But to think he's still in my bones, that even if I live another fifty years, when I die and my flesh falls away, I will still be a girl who was kidnapped for four hundred and seventy-two days . . .

Keith's fingertips whisper across my elbow. As usual, he has followed my line of thinking.

"What about fingertips?" I hear myself ask. "Any evidence of trauma?" Say, endless months clawing against the locked lid of a coffin-sized box?

"I have no phalanges for analysis. Small bones are the first to be snatched by predators. Some might be tucked away in nearby animal dens."

"That'll be a fun search effort," D.D. mutters.

Dr. Jackson shrugs. "You want more information, bring me more bones. As it is, I was able to run tests on lipid degradation in the right tibia's bone marrow to estimate a postmortem interval of fifteen years."

"She died fifteen years ago?" I ask uncertainly.

Keith chimes in, "Lipid degradation?"

"It's a fairly new analysis for establishing time of death in fully skeletonized remains. We know lipids remain in bone marrow for decades. So after taking a biopsy of the marrow—a bone plug removed from the tibia—I analyze it using a high-resolution mass spectrometer to determine the amount of lipid breakdown. The result: I can say with some degree of certainty this girl died fifteen years ago. Can I state she was buried then, as well? No. But given the condition of the bones, that's a fairly safe assumption."

I nod slowly, then return to studying Lilah Abenito's reconstructed face.

If what Dr. Jackson is saying is true, then Lilah Abenito was dead before I ever headed off to college, danced naively on a Florida beach, and woke up screaming in a pine box. But I feel a connection to her. Whether we have all the answers or not, I already imagine she gazed into Jacob's leering face, flinched at the feel of his greasy fingers, recoiled at the stench of his body.

The room is closing in on me. I curl my fingers into fists, force myself to focus. They're looking at me. Dr. Jackson, D.D., Keith. Waiting for me to cry, to break down, to scream wildly—something.

But I don't want their pity.

And I won't give Jacob the satisfaction.

"What can you tell us to help us find more of the remains?" I ask Dr. Jackson.

"Dogs," she states immediately. "I have a lab filled with millions of dollars' worth of equipment, and I can tell you none of it works as well as a good dog's nose. I've witnessed canines hitting on hundred-year-old remains. What they even smell, none of us can tell you. At that point, there's no organic matter left; the bone is little more than a dried sponge. But the dogs always know."

"Approximate search area?" Keith asks.

She shakes her head. "Impossible to tell. The search bias is to head downhill, as it's easier to walk. When looking for a skull, which rolls, that might help. But we have the skull. We need vertebrae, ribs, phalanges, and plenty of animals head up to stash their treasures, not down."

"In other words, hike up." D.D. sighs.

"I've found bones in hollow trees," Dr. Jackson offers. "A decaying log makes a great den for all sorts of small animals, which is what you want to be looking for."

D.D. frowns. "What do you do, knock on surrounding trees or something?"

"Exactly."

D.D.'s eyes widen.

"Have you ever been in the woods?" I can't help but ask her.

"I've hiked." D.D.'s tone is defensive. I realize for the first time that the sergeant isn't just an urban detective, but a genuine city slicker. I turn toward Keith.

"And you?"

"Um, I think I have a picture of a tree somewhere. Maybe a screen saver."

"Oh my God, I'm the only one here with wilderness experience."

"We can't all grow up in Maine," D.D. grumbles. "That's why it's Maine."

I feel a renewed sense of responsibility. "Anything else?" I ask Dr. Jackson.

She studies me for a long while. "Examine the topography. Look for signs of water runoff. You'll want the dogs to trace any and all creeks, as small bones can easily wash downstream. Pay particular attention for debris dams, which may have captured some of the bones. At this stage, they'll resemble small, weathered sticks, so expect to wade into the water, get up close and personal. Finally, check for predator activity, signs of animal dens. In the beginning of decomp, raccoons are the worst. They'll even crawl right into the chest cavity to gnaw on the ribs, let alone the damage they do to hands."

I once burned a man alive. But this conversation is making me queasy.

"Small rodents—rats, mice, squirrels—steal bones once they're dry. Chances are, many of the missing phalanges and ribs are in nests.

So again, you can't just study the ground. You need to look all around, get a local wildlife expert if you can. Someone who can track small game. I once worked a search where we recovered an arm and half a rib cage from a coyote's den. That kind of find could make a huge difference for us. I'm assuming you have a search team?"

She glances at D.D., who nods.

"Standard protocol applies. Lay out the grid, work the grid. Then . . . listen. This line of work." She turns back to Lilah's graceful face. "Bones talk. And all children just want to go home again."

CHAPTER 7

D.D.

D.D. WAS A NEW ENGLANDER to her core. The only time she'd previously spent in Georgia was flying through the Atlanta airport. Now, she followed the rental car's GPS, heading north from the city into the mountains.

"Our first major town will be Dahlonega," Keith rattled off from the back, staring at his phone. "It's considered the gateway of the Appalachian Trail and—incidentally—in eighteen-twenty-eight, the site of the first major gold rush in the United States. The phrase, 'There's gold in them thar hills'? That's originally from Dahlonega."

"Okay," D.D. said, as clearly someone needed to answer, and since leaving the forensic anthropologist's office Flora had given up speaking.

"Dahlonega is known for its historic town square, surrounding vineyards, and luxury spas." Keith looked up from his phone. "Any chance we're staying in Dahlonega?"

D.D. laughed. "Welcome to real policing. We stay in economy inns, live on pizza, and are proud of it."

"But I'm not really a cop . . ."

"You may go wherever you please," D.D. assured him. "But don't expect us to call you with all the exciting case developments you'll be missing."

Keith sighed heavily.

"According to SSA Quincy," D.D. continued, "the local sheriff—"

"Smithers," Keith interjected. "Took office twenty years ago. Active in D.A.R.E. and teaching educational classes in the school system. He's also very proud of his Hunter's Safety Certification program as well as firearms education for civilians."

Computer nerd *and* a know-it-all.

"Sheriff Smithers volunteered his office as taskforce headquarters," D.D. continued. "It's in the center of the county, near Dahlonega, with some hotels nearby. He's working on reserving a block of rooms in a local motel as we speak. I imagine we'll learn more when we get there."

"But ground zero is a good fifteen, twenty miles from Dahlonega," Keith began, having no doubt traced it out on the map.

"Understood, but if you look up the little town in question, it's barely a speck on the map. Apparently, it has a general store, some quaint B and Bs, local restaurants, and that's it."

"Niche, Georgia," Keith promptly rattled off. "Located almost two hours north of Atlanta, it's at three thousand feet and boasts cool mountain air, quaint storefronts, and access to the AT. With a population of three thousand, its primary industry is tourism, though there's a growing retirement community based on quality of life, natural beauty, and small-town life."

"Road access?" Flora finally spoke up. Her gaze was out the window, looking at the scenery, ostensibly, but probably still seeing Lilah Abenito's reconstructed face. God knows D.D. was.

She hadn't known what to think about Flora's desire to "meet" the victim. In D.D.'s opinion, Flora shouldered way too much blame when it came to Jacob Ness's reign of terror. And D.D. was never sure how much of Flora's vigilante streak was truly due to a desire to feel safe, versus a need to serve penance.

"Dahlonega is at the end of a major highway, GA Four Hundred. What we're on now," Keith said. "After that, we're traveling rural routes. Some of them quite steep and windy. For example, Route Sixty we'll be taking to Niche."

"Does any of this look familiar?" D.D. glanced over at Flora.

The woman shrugged. "All roads look alike to me. We've passed several truckers, so it's possible Jacob followed this route. Mostly, however, he worked east–west, not north–south."

"According to Ness's trucking logs—"

"You've read his trucking logs?" D.D. interrupted Keith.

"You haven't?"

"Never mind."

"Highways Twenty and Eighty-Five were more likely occurrences. And if he was hauling north–south, Highway Seventy-Five makes way more sense than Georgia Four Hundred."

"Do you ever remember being in a smaller vehicle, say, a car or truck?" D.D. asked Flora.

"I don't remember anything immediately following the abduction. One moment I was dancing on a beach, the next . . . I was in a box in a dank basement. When he announced we had to go, he had his rig parked outside. Not with a trailer attached. Just the cab."

"What do you recall about the outside of the house?" Keith leaned forward from the back seat.

Flora shook her head. "He blindfolded me so I couldn't see much. Just narrow gaps above and below the fold. I had an impression of towering trees. And the air was cool against my cheeks. The mountains. I was definitely in the mountains. It reminded me of home."

"Niche is known for hiking trails lined with wild mountain laurel. It can also have some snow in the winter. All in all, that's not so dissimilar to the wilds of Maine."

Flora didn't say anything.

"When he was driving out, did you notice any town signs, road markers, anything?" Keith pressed.

Flora finally twisted around to look at him. "I was in a box. Even in his rig, he'd built a custom pine box just for me."

"He had his rig," D.D. spoke up, focusing the conversation. "That's good to know. It's been seven years since your rescue, but Jacob Ness was big news, especially around here. I'm sure many people still remember him, and might be reluctant to speak up when showed his photo. It seems to be human nature not to want to get involved. On the other hand, flashing around a photo of a big rig— that's much more innocuous and might get us somewhere."

Still sitting forward, with his shoulders nearly between the two front seats of the rental car, Keith nodded.

D.D. slowed as civilization appeared ahead. She made out an open square, lined with pretty trees, park benches, and squat redbrick buildings with crisp white trim. Very scenic, very quaint.

"Dahlonega," Keith announced from between the seats.

No kidding, D.D. thought. She made a right-hand turn, braked for a pedestrian in the crosswalk, then further scrutinized their surroundings.

"We take the road to the left, which is north to Niche." Keith again, while Flora continued her intense window-staring.

"Wrong. We stop. Eat lunch. There. Diner!" D.D. pulled into a parking space with renewed enthusiasm, while Flora finally roused herself.

"No! We have to get to Niche, meet up with the sheriff, start the search." The girl sounded slightly wild.

"What time is it?" D.D. asked.

"Just after two," Keith provided.

"How many more hours before sunset?"

Keith studied his phone. "Five hours, forty-seven minutes, give or take."

"Grid set up? Volunteers logged in? Canine team delivered?"

Now both Keith and Flora stared at her.

"Today is prep," she explained to them, one hand on the door handle. "Debriefing in Atlanta this morning, now setting up mobile HQ and getting organized in Niche. In other words, the action starts tomorrow. In the meantime, we spent half the night flying, slept only a handful of hours, and—speaking for myself—had only a banana and four donuts for breakfast. Feed me now, or I'll kill you both."

Flora and Keith climbed obediently out of the car.

"Besides," D.D. said as she led them into the diner. "We have our own plans to make."

SHE LET THEM GET SETTLED. Coffee and water all the way around. Keith inquired about some weird egg-white omelet with spinach and feta; total waste of a diner, if you asked D.D. Flora said she wasn't hungry. D.D. planted the menu back in front of her.

"You will order. You will eat. You are part of a taskforce now, and you owe it to the rest of us to pull your shit together and keep functional. Got it?"

Another wide-eyed stare. "I'll take oatmeal," Flora told the waitress standing at attention.

"Honey, it's Georgia. How 'bout some grits?"

"Sure."

"She'll take fresh fruit and yogurt with that," D.D. spoke up. "As for me, I'll have the Hungry Man special, two eggs over easy, sliced ham, buttered biscuits, and anything else you can squeeze on the plate."

The waitress beamed in approval. D.D. knew how to do diners right.

"What do you mean we need a plan?" Keith asked the second their waitress left.

"I mean a taskforce is a beast. Many opinionated individuals, many kinds of expertise, and many moving parts." D.D. planted her elbows on the table, dead serious now. Flora seemed to be coming out of her funk.

"Tomorrow, the search for additional remains. Do we help?"

"Of course!" Flora said immediately.

"For the sake of argument, how much experience do you have searching for bones?"

"At least I know the woods," Flora grumbled.

"True. And if you want to be there, I won't stop you. But I can tell you now, the most valuable members of the search team will be the dogs. You heard Dr. Jackson. So what do *you* bring to the table?"

"Eyes. Feet. An understanding of where to look, after talking to Dr. Jackson."

"Information we should definitely share with the team," D.D. agreed.

"I don't get it," Keith spoke up. "What do you want us to be doing?"

D.D. studied him. "What did you want to do most this morning?"

"Analyze Ness's laptop," he said immediately.

"Exactly. Because you have skills. Because you made more progress tracing Jacob's internet footsteps in two days than the FBI did in seven years. You should be on the computer. But tomorrow you'll head into the woods?"

Keith flickered a glance at Flora. Wearing his leather jacket and dark green cashmere sweater, he stood out in the diner. Too upmarket metro for this neck of the woods. What he had to wear into the forest, D.D. was guessing, would be even more fish out of water. Yet, she gave the man credit. Based on the look he was giving Flora, where she went, he would follow.

"You want to search, we can all search," D.D. conceded. "But we don't want to be just more bodies on the taskforce. We need to add value. As in, what can we do, what might we know that no one else does?"

Now she stared at Flora hard.

"You want me to walk around the town of Niche," Flora said slowly. "See if I recognize anything. Except, I never saw the town." Her voice picked up. "I just went from that stupid basement to that ꜱᴛᴜᴘɪᴅ rig . . ."

The waitress had returned with the bowl of grits. She glanced at Flora nervously. Flora sat back, let the bowl of corn mush be set before her. Next came the fruit. Then the yogurt. Flora glanced at the food, didn't appear optimistic.

"You will eat," D.D. reminded her again, as the waitress walked away. "Or I will stick you on a plane back to Boston."

That earned her a glare. Which was good. Angry Flora was more workable than sad Flora.

D.D. let her get down the first bite of grits. Flora made a face.

"Add maple syrup," Keith said. "Or honey."

"How do you know?" she asked him.

"I read."

"About grits?"

"When flying to Atlanta . . ."

Flora narrowed her eyes at him, but picked up the maple syrup. The second bite seemed to go better.

"You may not remember the town," D.D. said now, "but you still might be linked to it. I think that's what you and Keith need to work."

"Hey, I thought I was laptop guru!"

"Unfortunately, you've lost the laptop to that much prettier FBI agent. Besides, remember what she said. You may have found Jacob's password and username for the dark web, but unfortunately you were about half a dozen years too late. We need something more—or at least, something current."

"Stupid pretty FBI agent," Keith grumbled, which earned him a second glance from Flora.

The waitress appeared with his egg-white omelet and D.D.'s Hungry Man.

D.D. took in her overflowing plate and hummed in approval. She hadn't been this happy in days.

"So," she continued, picking up her fork, diving in. "You're still computer dude. Just don't worry about Jacob's laptop, at least not yet. And remember, there are two things we're looking for."

"Bones," Flora spoke up, moving on to the yogurt.

"And Jacob's cabin where you were first held. Now, are any of us particularly qualified to locate skeletal remains?"

They both shook their heads.

"I think you and Keith should go around with the picture of Jacob's rig and quiz the locals. You"—she stabbed her fork at Flora—"can see if they recognize his truck. While Keith can look for signs that someone recognizes you."

"You think someone in Niche might know me." Now Flora had given up on her food completely.

"There must be a reason Jacob came to the mountains. This isn't on any trucking route, we haven't found any houses in his name. Which brings us back to . . ."

"He had help," Keith provided. "An accomplice, or at least a friend."

D.D. nodded. "That's a theory worth pursuing, especially now that the police have discovered another body linked to Jacob's MO."

"He's not from here," Flora said slowly. "All his family ties are in

Florida. Yet he brought me to the mountains, and probably Lilah Abenito, too. So why northern Georgia? Why this town, this place?"

"And who can answer these questions for us?" Keith concluded.

"Strategy," D.D. announced, around a mouthful of biscuit. "The trick to surviving a taskforce is to pick your path, play to your strengths, and no matter how much the committee gets in your way, accomplish real work. We didn't come here to play well with the feds. We came here to learn anything and everything about Jacob Ness. Are we clear?"

Flora and Keith nodded at her.

"I still want to go into the woods tomorrow," Flora said quietly.

"Why?"

"I just . . . I need to see. I need to know."

"Torturing yourself doesn't accomplish our mission, Flora."

"I know. But I keep thinking about what Dr. Jackson said. All children just want to go home. If I could find anything, even a single rib, bring that piece of her home . . ." Flora stared at the table. "I need this."

"Okay. Tomorrow we play with the taskforce. Then—"

"We go rogue!" Keith burst out.

D.D. stared at him. "You are entirely too excited about that."

He smiled. "It's the company I keep." Then he flickered another glance at Flora that made D.D. shake her head.

CHAPTER 8

THE MOTION CATCHES MY EYE. *Furtive movements. Someone trying to do something unseen. I can't help but glance over.*

Immediately, the girl glares at me.

She has a small paring knife tucked against the skirt of her uniform. At her scowl, I quickly look away. At the opposite end of the kitchen, Cook bustles away, pulling trays of food out of the fridge to prep dinner. Soon I will begin my kitchen duties: fetch this, tend to that. Right now, I finish pulling scalding hot plates from the still-moving conveyor belt of the commercial-grade dishwasher. You must unload quickly, before the plates reach the end and crash to the floor. In the beginning, the steaming dishes would burn my fingers and I would slow from the pain. Then things would break, earning me even greater punishment. Now, after all these years, I don't feel the heat.

The girl wanders over, trying too hard to look innocent. Cook glances up. I want to shake my head at the girl, tell her to stop, but that will only call more attention. Instead, I focus on my work, the row of shiny white plates, lined up on their edges, marching toward me.

"You saw nothing," the girl hisses in my ear as she wanders by. She sounds cruel, but I understand. She is very beautiful. With smooth almond skin and thick black hair. This life, these people . . . beautiful only makes things worse.

Cook is watching both of us. The help aren't supposed to converse. Then again, it's me. How much conversing can a Dumb Girl do?

I want to tell this girl to put the knife away. I want to describe to her the first time I managed to sneak a knife out of the kitchen. How [illegible] some damage, or at least go down fighting. Instead, in the blink of an eye, the butter knife had gone from my hand to his. I never even saw him move. So much effort and risk on my part. Preparing myself mentally, determining how to sneak a knife out of the kitchen, starting to plot the next stage of my escape.

Then the Bad Man was standing in my doorway.

And a moment later . . .

It was done. Just like that. I don't know if I even opened my mouth to grunt a protest. One minute I thought I was so smart. The next . . .

Sometimes, I think the Bad Man knows things before we do. Like he's not human. This is why I need my name. So my mother's love can help me, because surely nothing on this mortal earth can defeat a man who moves like smoke and punishes like an anvil.

That day, the Bad Man had pulled out his own weapon from the sheath of his boot. Not a butter knife at all, but a hunting knife: smooth on one side, serrated on the other.

I remember staring in mute horror as he took my hand and gently extended my arm toward him. Then, using his blade, he started to draw on the clean brown skin of my forearm. Blood welling up, forming fine red lines while I hissed and trembled and did everything in my power not to flinch. His knife carved sinuous patterns into my flesh. Mesmerizing. Beautiful, even.

We both stared. Bound by the winding forms and the knowledge that if I jerked away, that sharp ugly blade would gouge into my arm, sever my arteries, and destroy the first pretty thing about me.

Later, he said I should thank him for turning my arm into a work of art.

I wear long sleeves now. But at night, I still trace the ridged lines. And right or wrong, I can't help but admire the pattern. I am a Dumb Girl with a shattered temple, scarred hairline, and distorted eye. There's nothing attractive about me. Except for the intricate scroll-work on my right forearm, a road map of his power and my pain.

Now this beautiful girl with her big dark eyes . . . He won't make her pretty. He'll carve away an ear. Take an eye. Draw a crude V down her cheek or create thick ridges in her neck. He'll steal her loveliness from her. I've seen him do it, heard the girls scream, caught the evidence of his handiwork later, walking slowly, brokenly down the halls.

Cook lets me wash the knives unsupervised now. She knows I'm defeated. She knows there's nothing to fear from a weak, brain-damaged thing like me.

But I can't tell my story, deliver these warnings to the girl, standing here.

Instead, I risk a single look under my lashes. I try to beam out: "I know. I'm afraid, too. You're not alone."

And just for a moment, the beautiful girl falters.

She will die tonight. We both know it. The stolen knife is too little, too late. Not a last stand, but an admission that all is lost. Sometimes fear is like that: It leaves you with nothing but the desire for it to be done.

The girl is trembling now. My eyes have said too much. She crosses herself, and from across the room, Cook barks, "You two! Back to work."

But the girl is shaking too hard.

I try to soften my eyes, to be the blank stare they all expect, instead of the dark knowing that floods through me too often these days. I wish I could ask her name. I would add it to the list in my head. A name is such a precious thing. Everyone should have at least that much. A single marker to carry, leave behind, be remembered by.

And maybe my gaze is more powerful than the rest of me, because suddenly she whispers, "Stacey. Stacey Kasmer. My family—"

Cook slams both hands against the stainless-steel table. "Don't make me come over there!"

"—live in this tiny little town, you've never heard of it. But if you should see them . . . get out . . . and I don't . . ."

She can't say the rest. We both know change is in the air. Bad things have always happened here. But now, with People Coming, it's all happening faster. Too fast.

"Tell my parents I'm sorry," she whispers furtively. Then bursts out loud, "Stupid Girl! Grab that plate before it falls!"

Belatedly, I grab the teetering dish, as powerfully built Cook, who likes to wield cast-iron pans, broom handles, and marble rolling pins, comes stalking over.

The knife is gone, tucked beneath the girl's skirt. We're not allowed pockets, so I have no idea where she's placed it. I'd secured mine in the waistband of my underwear, which the Bad Man must've figured out, because after carving swirling patterns in my forearm, he took away my panties for the next six months.

Cook arrives. She grabs the girl's shoulder, shoves her back. Then cuffs me hard. I'm not expecting it. I stumble against the sharp edge of the dishwasher, feel it gouge into my belly. Before I can recover, Cook delivers another stinging blow, then for good measure, slaps the other girl, as well.

"Back. To. Work."

The beautiful girl drops into a curtsy. I wonder what she had been in another life. A dancer? Cheerleader? Or just a girl with ambitious dreams? Most arrive older than I was. I don't even know how I got here.

But others . . . Some, I think, come looking for jobs. But there are also girls who speak languages none of us understand. I don't think they choose this place at all. They never stay long. They are the Ones Who Can't Be Seen.

Though I try to see them. I try to see everything.

The girl—Stacey—turns away. Her footsteps aren't completely steady. Hopefully Cook will think she's merely cowed from the blow. She makes it three steps, four, five.

Then I see it. A drop of blood. Turning into a trail.

A clatter.

The knife. It's fallen from her skirt. Bounced onto the floor.

Belatedly I glance at Cook. Maybe she didn't see it. Maybe I can scoot over, cover it with my own foot . . .

But Cook is staring right at the knife, the blood, the girl, who is no longer walking, but swaying slightly in place. Cook once again crosses her thick arms over her chest.

"Stupid girl," she mutters.

I get it then, as with a little sigh, Stacey's arms go up, her body goes down . . . She collapses to the floor, lying there, dark eyes open, in the growing pool of her own blood. She didn't bother to wait till later. Or till they found the knife, snatched it from her, did something worse. Because they know everything, anticipate our every thought, then shred us down to the bone.

But this . . . Slicing open the artery in her own leg. Not even the Bad Man can stop this.

Stacey doesn't make a sound. Instead, as I watch, the light in her eyes dims and dims.

A final breath, then she is gone. Frantically, I glance around. I want to see it. Her soul leaving her body. I want to watch it go up, up, up. I want to believe it sails high above us. Maybe she's already halfway to heaven. Maybe she'll find my mother, and my mother will fold this poor, pretty girl into her arms, and whisper that she's safe.

Is that her soul? That smudge of purple in the corner of the room? Is a soul purple? Or maybe the color depends on the person, because when I see my mother, she is always silver to me. I honestly don't know. I just want to believe. I need something, anything to cling to, as the pool of blood nears my feet.

"Clean up the mess," Cook grumbles. She turns back to her cooking prep.

The episode is over. A girl is dead, but our servitude continues.

I turn off the laboring dishwasher. I finish stacking the sterilized plates.

Then I make my way carefully to the girl's fallen form. Stepping around the spot of blood, this line, that pool.

I crouch down and gently close her eyes. Her dark sooty lashes rest against pale, pale cheeks.

The Bad Man will come, haul away the body, with a single toss over his massive shoulder. I will mop up the blood. Just another day in the life.

But for now, this single moment.

I purse my mouth. I wish again for the power taken from me so many years ago, that I could move my tongue and lips and form a single word.

Instead, inside my head, where I know all things, where I'm stronger, wiser, and braver than I'll ever be in this world, I whisper, "Stacey."

I hold on to her name. And vow once again to make them pay.

CHAPTER 9

KIMBERLY

KIMBERLY HAD MARRIED AN OUTDOORSMAN. Mac was a special agent with the Georgia Bureau of Investigations and was already teaching their two daughters to hunt, fish—wrestle with bears, for all she knew. Kimberly herself was a runner. She liked jogging the long winding paths around the commercial park where her office was located, or if she was feeling exotic, racing down rural roads.

She wasn't a huge fan of mountains. The names in Georgia didn't help. Blood Mountain. Slaughter Creek Trail. Not to mention that the last time she'd been in the area, pregnant, chasing a serial killer, Blood Mountain had more than lived up to its name. She and Mac never discussed it. In their line of work, there were always a few cases that stuck with you. Blood Mountain was Kimberly's. On the bad nights, Mac would say, "That one again?" and she'd say, "Yes," then they'd both let it be.

You accepted. You moved on, best you could, and on the few nights Kimberly suffered the nightmares, she lay awake afterward and instead of trying to shove the memories back in the box, she took them out, let the ghosts play awhile. She remembered the boy, the last look on his face, because no one else would, and he deserved that much.

Given that personal history, scenic Dahlonega made her shudder. She kept her hands on the wheel, driving directly to the sheriff's department. It was situated along the left side of yet another historic town square. The requisite green space occupied the middle, populated with park benches and broadleaf trees waving delicately in the light wind. The sheriff's office, clearly a newer addition, was a squat gray building adjacent to the courthouse. It looked more like a prison than a law enforcement agency, but maybe in these parts it served as both.

Kimberly opened the front door, was hit with a blast of air-conditioning, and forced herself to proceed.

Just because tomorrow morning she'd re-enter the Appalachian Trail in search of bodies for the second time in her career did not mean history was repeating itself.

An older woman wearing a pink sweater set smiled from the receptionist's desk. She was surprisingly tall and broad shouldered, a solid physical presence that no doubt helped with unruly visitors. Her real height was hard to distinguish, given that she had ash-blond hair pulled in a bouffant bun that appeared immune to heat, humidity, and the forces of gravity. Kimberly stuck out her hand. The woman answered with a firm grip.

"Francine Bouchard. Call me Franny. Everyone does."

"Thank you. I'm—"

"Supervisory Special Agent Kimberly Quincy of the Atlanta FBI. Of course. The sheriff's been expecting you."

"Do you know everyone who walks through the door?"

"Honey, around these parts, it's impossible not to. Water, tea, coffee?"

"Just the sheriff, please."

"Speak of the devil," Franny drawled, then nodded her head down the hall, where sure enough, Sheriff Smithers had just appeared.

A big burly guy, he looked every bit the Southern cop to Kimberly. He had a broad ruddy face, with creases in the corner of his eyes from a life spent outdoors, as well as an easy smile. In this neck of the woods, he probably wore many hats and worked long hours—whatever it took to get the job done. All good in Kimberly's opinion, given they'd be working close in the days and weeks ahead.

"Survive the drive?" the sheriff asked now, walking down the hall to greet her.

"Always beautiful in the mountains," she half lied.

"Water, coffee, tea? Franny can set you up." He nodded to his receptionist, who standing was indeed almost as tall as the sheriff, yet still managed to look exactly right in her sweater set and delicate gold necklace. The art of the Southern woman, Kimberly thought, because God knows she'd never mastered it.

"Water," Kimberly conceded this time. "Thank you, ma'am."

Franny produced a bottle of water from the minifridge behind her. Another beaming smile, polite head nod, then Franny resumed her seat, attention already on the computer monitor in front of her, while Sheriff Smithers led Kimberly back to his office.

The sheriff didn't occupy a huge space. The tight quarters offered glimpses of linoleum floor dominated by an oversized 1980s pressed-wood desk piled high with stacks of files. The sheriff gathered up the papers, looked around for a new spot to stash them. At last, he dropped them on the last clear spot on the floor.

"Sorry. Not much time for organizing lately," he muttered. "Or for that matter, any place to put anything. We outgrew this space about twenty years ago. Sadly, the county doesn't agree. We're supposed to be a quaint tourist area. No crime in the mountains, right? Unfortunately, no one told the drug dealers that."

Kimberly got it. Voters, especially in rural communities, liked to think bad things only happened in big cities. Whereas most drug dealers would tell you the very lack of population is what made small towns excellent for meth labs, growing farms, and import/export opportunities. Not to mention addicts lived everywhere and came from all walks of life.

But Kimberly and the sheriff weren't paid to argue with their budgets. They were paid to get the job done, regardless.

Sheriff Smithers planted himself behind his massive desk, half obscured behind the debris. Kimberly took a seat across from him.

"Got us a dog team," he announced. "Two shepherds from a buddy who does search and rescue. Experienced cadaver dogs, have flown all over the world, or so I'm told."

"And they were available on such short notice?" Kimberly asked.

The sheriff shrugged. "Good news. No current tragedies or natural disasters to pull them away. Handler's name is Dennis. He says his dogs need to go first. Too many humans running around pollutes the scent. Not that they can't find it—he was firm on this point. But it's more work and the dogs'll tire faster. Given the size of the search area—"

"Understood."

"It'll change our timeline for the human volunteers," the sheriff continued. "I can't even have them outlining the search grid, because again, that'll contaminate the area."

Kimberly nodded.

"So I figure me and one of my deputies will head up with Dennis at oh dark thirty tomorrow. Two hours later, the rest of you can follow."

"I'd like to hike up with the dogs."

Smithers shrugged. "You can, but bear in mind, the search crew needs a voice of experience. I got one good deputy. I don't have two."

In other words, the sheriff was suggesting they divide and conquer. He'd handle the canine efforts. She'd handle the human efforts. Dogs moved way faster—and deeper—into the woods than the humans could. Fair enough, Kimberly figured.

"You have a checklist operator?" Kimberly asked. Keeping track of all the searchers was half the battle. Kimberly hadn't done such detailed fieldwork in a bit. But being the one who now read all the reports, there was nothing worse than a massive search area where half the grids went untended or un-annotated. Details mattered, and tomorrow would be an intense exercise in logistics.

"Franny, my receptionist." Smithers jerked with his chin toward the front of the building. "She's good. Grew up in these mountains, knows everyone's business, and exactly how to put the overexcited, not to mention the just plain stupid, in their place."

"She appears formidable," Kimberly agreed. "She's okay with having to manage her own neighbors? That can't be easy."

"It won't be a problem. I've known Franny for nearly thirty years, starting when I was just a deputy. She worked as a waitress at my favorite diner. Got herself knocked up. Probably by some married tourist, but she never said. Back in those days, being a pregnant teen wasn't easy, especially in these parts. But she kept her head high, no matter the gossip. Did her job. Managed nosy friends and judgy neighbors just fine. Unfortunately, her baby didn't make it. Stillborn. Within a matter of weeks, Franny was back at work, pouring coffee, clearing tables. Next time I was in, she looked right at me. 'Sir,' she said, 'I reckon I've made enough mistakes for a lifetime. Now I'm ready to work hard, build a life. What do you suggest?' I told her to get her GED, then come find me. And she did."

"Impressive," Kimberly agreed.

The sheriff nodded, leaned back in his chair. "I was thinking we should start the searchers at the bottom of the trail tomorrow. Sure, the body was found a mile up, but nothing saying there aren't bones to be found further down. Don't want us to get tunnel-visioned."

"The killer wouldn't want to dump remains too close to civilization. But the raccoons probably aren't so worried?"

"Exactly."

"How many people?"

"Three dozen. Mostly from around the mountains. Some are experienced search and rescue, we get lost hikers often enough. Of course, you'll have a few coming for the show."

She knew what he meant: people drawn by the sensational nature of a body in the woods.

"But we got some solid hiking guides, local hunters. They know this area. Where humans and animals are prone to wandering."

Sounded good to Kimberly. She rose to standing. "I'll meet you at the trailhead, five thirty."

Smithers nodded. "I read about your father," he said abruptly.

"Everyone knows my father."

"Big shoes to fill."

"Then it's good I have a solid head."

"And the Boston detective and two civilians?"

"I've worked with them before. They'll pull their weight."

"Even the vigilante?" he asked dryly. "I might live in the sticks, but I got Google, you know."

Kimberly had to laugh. "Flora's intense. But she knows things no one else knows. And if this case does tie to Jacob Ness . . ."

The sheriff nodded slowly. "The thought of him, operating in my backyard. Maybe even living here, because that's what you think, right? That maybe he had some kind of cabin, safe house in these woods."

"You're a smart man, Sheriff Smithers."

He considered her shrewdly. "As much as it turns my stomach to think of a man like Ness prowling my county, the alternative . . ."

That it wasn't a stranger at all, but a local who'd buried Lilah

Abenito's body. Someone who knew the area and had ties to the community. A neighbor, given an area this small. Maybe even a friend.

Kimberly didn't offer him any words of comfort, because in that case, there would be none to say.

Instead, she extended her arm. A final handshake, and they were done.

CHAPTER 10

FLORA

I CAN'T SLEEP. I HARDLY do even when I'm home. It's one of those things the docs tell you will pass. Night terrors, insomnia, an over-pumped adrenal system that keeps me constantly on edge. One day it will ease. I'll sleep an hour more here, an hour more there, till eventu-ally, *voilà*, I'm a real person again.

It hasn't happened yet.

I pace my hotel room, roaming from cheap chair to funky curtains to minuscule kitchen banquette. I try sitting on the edge of the bed. Then standing next to the window. Lights on. Lights off. TV on. TV off. Up, down, and around again.

SSA Quincy had met us at the budget lodge, where we had to wait our turn behind the proverbial family of four. The father already ap-peared frazzled as he searched through his wallet for the right credit card, while the harried mom was frantically trying to herd two small children who had no intention of standing still. The older girl kept dashing behind the check-in counter, making the clerk yelp. I caught the boy, age five or six, eyeing my right boot as if he already knew about the butterfly blade.

I pegged him as a future serial killer, but then, I've never been good with kids.

When we finally stepped up to the counter, Kimberly flashed her FBI creds and the motel attendant regarded us even more suspiciously than the evil kids. Every time I looked at him, I wanted to reach for my butterfly blade.

Play well with the locals, Kimberly had told me. I swear that woman sees everything.

Over dinner, she'd reviewed process for the morning. Dogs would go first, then humans. We'd be assigned a search grid and a dozen little orange flags. Work our area, stay hydrated, check in frequently.

It sounded simple, the way she said it. Yet, I already understand there is nothing simple about the day ahead.

I want to be in the woods already, tapping some hollow tree and magically producing Lilah Abenito's fingers, ribs, vertebrae. Or maybe a femur, with the hand-carved message *Jacob Ness was here.* I want answers, even as I understand there's never going to be anything adequate enough to explain what happened to Lilah. To me. We exist in rarified company—two girls who one day met a real live monster. Except I survived.

Now I'm back in Georgia, waiting for something to feel familiar. To turn a corner of the road, or walk into a restaurant and experience a sense of déjà vu. I feel I should know something. I *need* to know something. Or once again, Jacob wins.

I hear a noise from the room next to me. The sound of a door opening, then closing. Footsteps in the hall. Soft. Discreet. The steps of a person who doesn't want to call attention.

I cross to my door immediately, on high alert. I have the chain fastened, as well as the dead bolt deployed, but compared to my system at home, this is nothing. Cheap locks for a cheap room.

I pull out my butterfly blade from the waistband at the small of my back. I'd had to check my luggage to bring it and the rest of my toys to Atlanta. D.D. had scowled at me. She'd known why I couldn't carry on my tiny bag. You'll be surrounded at all times by armed members of law enforcement, she'd muttered tightly. But we both knew I wasn't going to budge on the subject. I'd checked my bag. And upon arrival, unpacked my knife, flipped it open, shut, open, shut, open, then folded it up neatly, like closing a fan, and slipped it in my pocket.

Now, I flick open the blade as twin shadows appear in the beam of light beneath my door. The shadows pause, solidify.

Someone is standing outside my door.

Keith. Who, given tomorrow's adventure, probably also can't sleep. Who swore he knew everything about me, including my insomnia. Who claimed he cared, maybe enough to offer . . . what? Conversation? Solace? Distraction in the middle of the night? Or maybe more, some kind of physical interlude to keep our minds off more serious matters?

I could open my door. Reach forward, unfasten the chain, release the bolt, swing open the door until there was nothing between us. He would enter my room.

And then?

This is what other girls did. Other people. Take comfort where they could find it. A few moments of oblivion to balance out their turbulent lives.

Was sex oblivion to me? I didn't know anymore. Once I'd been an active, healthy teenager. I certainly hadn't gone off to college a virgin. But those days, that girl . . . She feels so long ago. Not even a memory of my life, but a film reel from someone else's. Surely I never flirted shamelessly. Never coyly tossed back my hair. Never dug my fingers into a man's shoulders and urged him closer, faster, harder.

My breathing accelerates. Maybe I'm not as immune as I think.

The twin shadows remain. The person in the hallway clearly working as hard on his courage as I am on mine.

I raise my hand. I place it against the hard plane of the cheap wooden door, moving slowly, careful not to make a sound. I close my eyes. And for a moment, I let myself imagine:

Keith's hand, splayed on the other side. Keith's palm connecting with mine. Our fingers touching.

Deep breath in, deep breath out.

Then I take my hand away, and walk back to the bed, where I lie on my side, and stare at the light limning the doorframe until the twin shadows finally shift, then fade away.

I HIT THE MOTEL LOBBY thirty minutes early. Keith is already there, looking like an advertisement for *Jogger's Monthly*. Black running tights, topped by some wicking shirt in electric blue, further covered by a long windbreaker with a million zippers, snaps, and light reflecting strips. His tennis shoes complete the ensemble, base black with swishes of silver and blue.

Clad in my uniform of bulky cargo pants, a faded cotton T-shirt, and worn Gap sweatshirt, I look like I'm about to board a subway, while he looks like he's about to hit the start line of the Boston Marathon.

Which makes my lip twitch. I giggle, then snort. Because honest to God, neither of us looks like any kind of search and rescue volunteer. Keith must've gotten it, too, because a moment later, he starts chuckling, as well.

"Welcome to the dream team," he says, crossing over. "Coffee?"

"I'll take a gallon."

He leads me over to the meager breakfast offerings. Basically fresh coffee, a small basket of fruit, then anything that comes from a cellophane wrapper. I snag blueberry Pop-Tarts.

I'd just made my way through the first mug of coffee and one of the pastries when D.D. careered into the small lobby, looking bleary-eyed and cranky. For a city slicker, she's still dressed better than us—gray outdoor pants, topped with a dark blue fleece embroidered with *BPD* on the upper left corner. She even has a backpack, with both sides sporting bottles of water.

"Coffee, black," she grunts. Keith doesn't question, just starts pouring.

"Why do you have outdoor clothes?" I ask her. "You said you didn't do mountains."

"Training exercise." She takes the mug from Keith, downs the first half in a single gulp, even though it's steaming hot. "Department keeps us outfitted."

"Should I have a backpack?" I eye her supply of water, and start feeling nervous all over again.

"They'll give you a light pack at check-in. Gotta carry marking flags, map, water, maybe a compass."

I stare at her. "I don't know how to read a compass."

Keith raises a hand. "I have an app on my phone."

"Of course you do." D.D. downs the second half of her mug, holds it out for more. I wonder if we should just give her the pot.

"Food?" I ask.

This cheers her up. She paws through the slim pickings, selects two packages of Pop-Tarts, an apple, and a banana. One package of Pop-Tarts and the apple go into her day pack. The rest she tears into.

My lack of a backpack is bothering me more and more. I stick the remaining pair of Pop-Tarts into the front pouch of my hoody, then add an apple. I look like a kangaroo, but I tell myself fashion has never been my crutch.

Keith disappears, reappearing with a lightweight runners pack, with strings spooling over his shoulders. He adds fruit, two bottles of water.

Then that's it. We have a runner, a thug, and a detective. The dream team indeed.

D.D. heads for the car, and Keith and I follow.

THE DRIVE TO THE TRAILHEAD is short enough. The volunteers are already pouring in, and D.D. has to work for parking. We follow the flow of humans—a mix of male and female, young and old, all more appropriately dressed than we are—to the check-in table, where SSA Quincy, in an FBI windbreaker, is clearly in charge, along with some older woman who is wearing a sheriff's department fleece with the same aplomb other women wear cashmere.

D.D. checks us in. She doesn't make small talk with Quincy. Given the long line and level of activity, now is not the time. On the table, Quincy has spread a huge map that is broken into brightly marked squares: the search grid. To the side, I see the key. Neon pink belongs to Nate Marles, bright green to Mary Rose Zeilan. Team leaders, I figure.

Quincy hands us a small map with notations. Our first assignment. I check it out on the larger map. We're about a quarter mile up from where the body was first found. This disappoints me till I remember what the forensic anthropologist said—many predators like to retreat with their treasure to higher ground. So maybe this will be a good place to find a raccoon's den or an abandoned squirrel's nest. I need us to find something. Make some kind of difference.

At the next table there are cases of water and piles of bananas, then boxes of mesh gear bags filled with tiny surveyor's flags.

"One bag per search team," Quincy is saying now, voice brisk as the line builds behind us. "Should you see anything you think might be relevant, you stop and take out a flag. Write your grid coordinates in Sharpie beneath the flag number. Then mark the flag on your map and call it in to your team leader. Got it?"

"Got it." D.D. almost sounds chipper.

"Run out of flags, send one of your teammates down for more." Quincy glances up, takes in Keith's outfit, pauses slightly. "Send him. He looks fast."

Keith doesn't bat an eye. "Like the wind," he assures her.

Now D.D. is smiling, too.

"Pace yourself," Kimberly warns. "Eyes open. Step steady. Good luck."

Quincy looks behind us to the next guy. We move down the line of tables and finish picking up gear. The older woman from the sheriff's department takes our names a second time, checks us off a list, and that's that.

Up into the woods we go.

I DON'T MIND THE HIKING. I jog almost daily, though not in fancy clothes like Keith's. But a woman who lives in my constant state of hypervigilance has to run endlessly just to burn off steam. Plus lift weights and scamper along buildings and swing my way around abandoned structures. I can't reason my anxiety away by admonishing myself that the worst will never happen. Because the worst thing did happen to me, making all fears real, all terrors genuine. So I roleplay my way through it. I find an old warehouse, I get myself untrapped. Samuel, my FBI victim advocate, first told me about the technique—easing anxiety by building strength—but I don't think he expected me to take it this far.

Now, looking at the towering trees all around us, with a thick undergrowth of leafy green bushes—I think someone mentioned mountain laurel—it occurs to me all the new escape models I could be prepping for.

I keep moving. D.D. and Keith have no problem with the pace. Apparently, we're all crazy.

No one speaks. We hit the one-mile mark. Shortly afterward we come to a small clearing, where another law enforcement type is standing with a clipboard. He checks us off as having survived this far, and gets serious about how to find our particular section of the grid.

He and D.D. talk for a few more moments. Keith, I notice, keeps looking behind the guy, as if there's something he's trying to see deeper in the woods. Then I get it. This is ground zero, so to speak. Where the hiker went in search of a stick and found a bone instead.

I look down the hill where we just came. And for the first time, I feel uneasy.

That climb was nothing for me. But Jacob? Jacob who sat behind the wheel all day and lived on fried food and was famous for his week-long drug- and alcohol-fueled benders . . .

I can't picture Jacob here at all. Does that mean he never came to these mountains? That he lied to me about the Georgia cabin? Or does that mean I don't know him as well as I thought I did? That he kept secrets even as I surrendered every last bit of me?

"It's okay," Keith says.

I realize I'm standing with my hands fisted.

"He didn't win. You're the one who's about to help a murdered girl go home again. You got this."

"Stop looking inside my head," I mutter.

"Then stop being so easy to read."

I scowl, but being pissed at him has made me feel better. Which is probably what he intended. Keith always seems to know me too well. Which is the reason I don't trust him at all.

D.D. has our coordinates. We resume climbing.

BY THE TIME WE REACH our assigned area, we've shed our outer lay-ers. We can hear things from time to time, other searchers in the woods, but we don't see them. Each area is that large, given how much ground we have to cover.

"The body searches I've done," D.D. says, "we stand in a line, walk forward at the same pace and prod the ground with a stick. You're looking for softness, signs of recently disturbed earth. This is totally different from that. I'm not even sure of the best approach. It's going to be hard to look beneath every leaf for small, random bones, so I'm liking Dr. Jackson's advice: Let's look for animal activity. Knock against some hollow trees, investigate fallen logs. Maybe we'll get lucky." She pauses. "This is where we leave the trail. It's important that we stay together. Keith, time for your magic compass app. We don't want to become the next thing the search party has to find."

Keith pulls out his phone. We're all sweating. It's cooler in the shade of the woods, but I now eye those same shadows skeptically. The trail had been easy to follow. Wide, nicely carpeted with fall leaves. Now we face clumps of giant mountain laurel clogging up the sides. There are gaps here and there.

D.D. picks one. Keith and I muscle our way through behind her.

On the other side, the woods are more open than I'd imagined. The trees spread out, the ground cover a mix of leaves, fallen debris, rocks, and scraggly bushes that don't get much sunlight.

The earth smells loamy. It tugs at me. Memories of my mother's farm, of a childhood spent running around forests not so dissimilar to this one. I always felt most at home in the wild. It's been a long time now, though, since I left for the streets of Boston.

"Um, we should probably pick a line and walk it," Keith suggests. "I say we head due west, straight across our grid. When we reach the coordinates on the other side, we'll shift north, then head back due east. Like vacuuming a carpet."

"Works for me," D.D. says. "Remember, Team Roomba: stay together."

We all start walking. I find myself trying to look up, down, and around all at once, which leads me to seeing nothing at all. I try to re-focus myself. First, eye level—looking for signs of nests, animal activities—then looking high.

It gives me some sense of discipline, but doesn't lead to instant results.

Keith finds two nests. D.D. works a hollow log. Still nothing.

"You know there's a good chance we won't find anything," D.D. says an hour later, after informing us it was time for a water break. The day is getting warmer. Though we're moving slowly through the woods, my cotton T-shirt is now plastered to my skin.

"We're talking a few dozen small bones spread over half a mountain. Most searchers won't find anything. We just have to hope that some do."

I nod. I know what she says is true. Still, if we do all this and come up empty . . . I can't take the idea of failure. I can tell by the look on Keith's face he's thinking the same thing, too. He didn't don his ridiculous running outfit to return home empty-handed.

We sip a little more, then cap our bottles, get back to hunting.

There's a big tree up ahead. I can already see part of it has been bored away, maybe from a woodpecker or some other animal. I feel my pulse quicken even as I rise on my tiptoes and, turning on the flashlight function of my cell phone, shine it in. No tiny eyes peer back at me. I reach in, pat around lightly. Downy feathers, leaves, and something slightly more substantial. A pile of twigs. Bones?

We're not supposed to touch anything. But then again, I can't flag what I can't inspect. I find another small stick on the ground, and use it to poke around the hole until I find what I'd felt earlier. Slowly but surely, I use the twig to drag the item toward me. Closer and closer . . .

I pull a little too hard and it plunges from the opening onto the ground. I gasp, jump back, then immediately crouch down. It looks like bones. So many tiny, tiny bones.

I've done it. I've found . . .

"A mouse skeleton," Keith says. I glare up at him, then poke the pile a bit more.

Dammit, the bones *are* too small, and now that he's mentioned it, they do form more or less the shape of a mouse.

"Probably an owl's den," he says. "Looks like the guy had a good dinner."

I scowl. "Don't owls swallow the entire thing? Produce owl pellets or something like that?"

Keith blinks at me. "Oh. You might be right."

"Score one for rural education," I tell him. "I once found one of those pellets at the local nature park, so whoever left behind these remains wasn't an owl. But you're right, they appear to be mice bones."

Just then we hear something. Barking in the distance.

D.D. jogs closer. "Sounds like the dogs made a discovery."

The barking goes on and on.

"Kind of a big discovery." D.D. reaches for her phone just as it starts buzzing. She glances at the screen. "Quincy," she informs us, then places it to her ear.

"Yeah. Got that. Dogs made a hit. What? You're sure? Okay. We're headed over."

She punches off the call, turns to us with renewed intensity.

"The dogs found missing bones," Keith says instantly.

"No. The dogs found another body."

For a second, none of us speak. None of us can speak.

"There are more?" I ask softly.

"At least one more grave. Quincy wants us to go help."

"A dumping ground," Keith exclaims. "We've found a serial kill-er's dumping ground." He sounds excited. I know he can't help himself.

But just for a moment . . .

I am sad. I am scared. I am lost.

I am one of those girls all over again.

"You can go back to the hotel if you want," D.D. tells me gently.

As if I really could.

I shake my head. I turn back toward the direction we came from. Keith makes some adjustments to his compass. Then as one, we move toward the dead.

CHAPTER 11

KIMBERLY

T HINGS WENT A LITTLE DIFFERENTLY than expected," Kimberly Quincy said into the phone.

It was nine P.M. She was finally back in her motel room after one of the longest days of her career. She'd spent the past few hours in conversation with her supervisor, plus the taskforce team. Now, she needed fifteen minutes of sanity before the next round of logistical planning. Through the phone, she could hear her girls chattering away in the background. Nine P.M. was bedtime. No doubt they were taking advantage of Mac's distraction to launch one last misadventure.

The sounds of real life. Kimberly could never decide if such normalcy was the most beautiful or most disconcerting noise after a day such as this one.

"You find more bones?" Mac asked from their home in Atlanta.

"Bodies. We found more bodies."

A pause. "Girls," he said to their daughters. "Go pick out something to read. I'll be back in a sec."

"Last time you tried that, they beat each other with the books instead."

"But it did wear them out," Mac countered.

She heard a click. A door closing. Mac retreating from the girls' adjoining rooms in order to head to the master for a moment of privacy. She closed her eyes. Let herself picture it. Their modest ranch-style home with its open family room, overstuffed sofa, jumbled floor. One bedroom awash in purple (Eliza's). A second room adorned in shades of blue (Macey's). Both filled with an assortment of sports trophies, stuffed animals, and well-thumbed reads. Then there was her and Mac's space, where the bed was never made and family photos lined most surfaces and the treadmill sat in the corner where it was genuinely used during the hot, humid days of summer but served as a substitute clothes hanger the rest of the year.

She kept meaning to paint an accent wall in the bedroom. And to organize the closet and tidy up the master bath. But the truth was, she never had that kind of time, and probably wasn't even that kind of person. She and Mac lived for their family and their jobs. Which she liked to think made them perfect for each other.

"From the beginning," Mac said.

"The cadaver dogs found three more bodies."

"*Three* more?"

"At least. We dug down enough to unearth three skulls, but withdrew to wait for the forensic anthropologist, Dr. Jackson. Maybe there's more underneath? I don't know. Best we could see was a tangled mess of bones." Kimberly's hand shook slightly holding her cell phone. "A mass grave, Mac. When was the last time you heard of a serial killer burying three victims at once?"

Mac didn't answer right away. She didn't expect him to. She still didn't know what to make of the day's discovery and she'd had hours to ponder it.

"How old is the grave?"

"The remains appear fully skeletal. We'll need to wait for Dr. Jackson and her team for additional details. I'm wondering about the shallow burial. Most things people want to keep secret, they bury deep. But all four of these bodies were barely interred. Meaning our perpetrator is someone who knows the area well and was confident the graves wouldn't be discovered? Or didn't have the time or strength to dig a full grave? Flora says Jacob Ness wasn't the fittest guy around. I don't know."

"Are the new bodies also female?"

"We have to wait for Dr. Jackson for proper exhumation. She was adamant her team and only her team handle the grave site. At this stage, soil, bug exoskeletons, flora, and fauna, all of it will matter. We're not the right people for the job."

"But you're betting female," Mac guessed.

"The skulls appear small, which would be consistent with female. Also, I have to believe this grave is related to Lilah Abenito's, and she was a teenage girl. I don't know. Are we seeing what we want to see? Have I approached this case all wrong from the start? Honestly, I've never felt so stupid, and I'm supposed to be leading this taskforce."

Kimberly sighed again. Sitting on the edge of the bed, she rubbed her temples, where she could feel a budding headache.

"You called for reinforcements?" Mac checked.

"Marshall agreed to activate ERT." Marshall was her boss, and the Evidence Response Team was the FBI's elite group of specialists who assisted with particularly involved evidence collection. Kimberly herself was a member. Sometimes ERTs assisted in jurisdictions that couldn't afford to have evidence techs of their own, or lacked the FBI's lineup of sophisticated toys. Other situations, such as plane crashes or mass casualty events, simply demanded greater resources. Kimberly's Atlanta team had been called to work the Pentagon site after 9/11. One of her instructors had talked about raking the debris for days to recover a single gold wedding band. The look on the wid-ow's face, she said, when they were able to give at least that much of her husband back to her . . .

Kimberly's instructor had passed away five years later. Cancer. Most likely from exposure to hazardous chemicals at the site. FBI agents often talked about having a call to serve. Very few civilians understood just what that meant.

"You doing okay?" Mac asked softly now.

"I'm struggling," Kimberly admitted. "With how to manage this mess—the amount of people to supervise, the pressure for immediate answers to horrific questions . . ."

"You think the graves are Jacob Ness's handiwork?"

"I think we'd be lucky if that was the answer. Old dumping grounds from a deceased predator."

"Fits expectations while minimizing fear. And given you didn't find any new remains, works with the timeline of a guy who's now dead."

"We know serials don't magically quit," Kimberly considered out loud. "And to the extent all the bodies we've currently found are fully skeletonized, I would guess we've made a fresh discovery of an old crime. That fits the timeline for Ness, while making for a compelling narrative: Ness started off kidnapping girls near or around his truck-ing route. He brought them back to the relative quiet of the moun-tains, then dumped the bodies. Until he built up the confidence and resources for longer term abduction scenarios, such as what he did with Flora."

"What does Flora think of the new discovery?"

"She's . . . troubled. Could Ness have killed and buried four young women? Absolutely. But Jacob hiking up a mountain, wandering through the woods while carrying a corpse . . . According to her, not in a million years. He was the laziest kidnapper who ever existed."

"Could Jacob have driven up to a different trailhead, then hiked down to where you found the bodies?"

"That's a good question. We haven't had time to scope out the full network of trails up here. Everyone wants answers now, of course. If only it were so simple."

"Yep."

They both fell silent for a moment. Kimberly leaned her head against the wall and listened to the steady rhythm of her husband's breathing, as familiar as her own. No more sounds of their daughters, meaning Eliza and Macey had either settled in for the night or, more likely, were engaged in some kind of criminal conspiracy. She should let Mac go. Let him return to his responsibilities while she tended to hers. But she wasn't ready yet. She needed this. A moment of calm in the storm.

"Wasn't Jacob Ness known for his binges?" Mac asked at last. "Drinking, drugs, that sort of thing?"

"Yes."

"Could that be what the three girls represent? Homicidal rampage? Ted Bundy certainly had his infamous night where he attacked an entire sorority."

"Bundy was frenzied that evening. He struck and moved on. That's easier than transporting, then dumping three bodies in a single grave."

"Which brings you back to wondering about an accomplice. Someone with local ties, who drew Jacob to the area. In that scenario, three girls isn't so implausible."

"Want to come to Niche, Georgia? The locals keep eyeing us with suspicion, and the mountains are dotted with skeletal remains, but other than that, what's not to love?"

"Oh no, you got this. Besides, all cases get worse before they get better. It's the nature of the beast."

"True." She shook out her shoulders, sat up straighter. Time to get to it.

"Call if you need to talk. Even in the middle of the night. I don't mind."

"The joy of our jobs."

"The key to our marriage," Mac corrected gently.

Kimberly smiled. "Love you."

"Love you, too."

"Mac, the girls have left you alone for a very long time . . ."

"Pray for me," he agreed.

Kimberly smiled again. She touched her lips with two fingers, as if she could send her husband a kiss across cellular towers. As if she could feel the brush of his lips in return.

Then, she went back to work.

CHAPTER 12

D.D.

D.D. DRAGGED FLORA AND KEITH to the county sheriff's first thing in the morning. The building's conference room would be serving as command central for the original taskforce. Given yesterday's discovery of additional remains, a mobile command post had been set up at the base of the hiking trail to coordinate the bone experts and other forensic specialists who would be scouring the mountainside.

Kimberly and D.D. had spoken late last night. Given the explosion in size and scope of the investigation, Kimberly had requested that D.D. partner with Sheriff Smithers on local interviews, as Kimberly would need to supervise the exhumation of the newest grave. A big ask, and a nice show of trust from a federal agent for a city cop not even in her own jurisdiction. Which just went to prove how understaffed their taskforce was. In fact, D.D. suspected Kimberly knew D.D. intended to drill the locals one way or another. This way, the feebie probably figured she'd have some control over the situation.

Like others hadn't tried and failed to manage D.D. before.

D.D.'s mood was downright cheerful walking into the squat

municipal building. Shuffling behind her, Flora looked like she hadn't slept a wink, Keith either. But what else was new?

Personally, D.D. loved this phase of a major investigation. Gearing up for battle. Here are the knowns; here are the unknowns. Now marshal the troops and get it done.

The sheriff wasn't in the conference room. D.D. recognized two FBI agents from their original taskforce meeting. One was directing local officers to various stacks of paperwork, while attaching a giant map of hiking trails to the main wall, front and center. D.D. guessed blown-up maps of Niche and the surrounding towns would go up next. Plus the murder board, photos of each victim, what was known. Then a basic whiteboard for organizing group discussion.

The second FBI agent seemed to be the designated IT guy. The tables had been moved into a standard U-shaped configuration. Now he was distributing laptops at discrete intervals while referring back to his own computer, where he would then type furiously away. Most likely, the agent was establishing a secure network for all the task-force computers, rather than utilizing the sheriff's system. It was a better way of managing all the data and ensuring chain of custody of sensitive docs. Welcome to the new age of policing, where the issue wasn't getting information but managing the deluge of data. From witness statements to hotel records to restaurant credit card receipts, they'd be drowning in docs by the end of the day. D.D. appreciated the FBI had better tricks for managing the madness, given their expertise in major cases.

D.D. waved hello to the overworked agents, earned curt nods in return as both remained on task. Then, given the level of chaos, she exited from the room—Flora and Keith still trailing behind—and headed down the hall.

If *she* were the sheriff, she'd be taking refuge in her own office, away from the bedlam. After a few tries, she found his office.

"Sheriff Smithers."

The sheriff had indeed been leaning back in his chair, feet up, eyes closed. Now he bolted upright, feet dropping with a thud to the floor, his hat falling from his head.

"Uh, uh . . ." He clearly recognized her, but was too befuddled to remember her name.

D.D. took pity on the exhausted man. "Sergeant D. D. Warren from Boston PD. Call me D.D. And you remember Flora Dane, Keith Edgar."

The three of them could barely fit in the office, given the small size and piles of paperwork. The sheriff looked around belatedly, as if he should offer them a seat, but couldn't figure out how.

He gave up with a deep sigh. "Ah hell."

"It's okay. There are more important things going on right now than housecleaning."

"Got that right."

"SSA Quincy asked me to meet with you this morning, coordinate the interview efforts."

"Yes, ma'am. I spoke to her last night." He looked past D.D. to Flora and Keith. Neither had said a word. Sleep deprivation? Shell shock from a sad case that had already taken a sadder turn? D.D. didn't know, but she turned and eyed them expectantly.

Keith managed to extend his hand, mutter a greeting. Flora just stared at the sheriff. The flatness of her expression didn't bode well. The woman had retreated deep inside herself. Maybe a protective measure. Maybe honing her homicidal impulses.

"With all due respect, ma'am"—the sheriff eyed D.D.—"those two are civilians."

"Guilty as charged," D.D. agreed.

"Can't have civilians conducting official interviews."

"Agreed. Not to mention, talking really isn't Flora's strength." She arched a brow at the silent woman. She got nothing back. Definitely not good.

"Did Quincy review with you her initial goals?" D.D. turned back to the sheriff.

"Yes, ma'am. Identify town leaders, influencers—"

"Busybodies," D.D. offered helpfully.

"Business owners," the sheriff continued dryly. "Get the lay of the land."

"Are there neighbors who give them the willies, known town crazies?"

"I already pulled the names of everyone with a criminal record, ma'am. Got officers assigned to pay them a visit. 'Course, not the easiest line of questioning—what were you doing fifteen years ago? Now, we can flash around photos of Jacob Ness, but who's gonna admit to knowing a monster like that?"

"They probably won't. But you can ask their neighbors if they ever saw anyone matching Jacob's description visiting the area. I'd also ask about his rig. Identifying a vehicle feels safer than getting involved with a known rapist."

The sheriff nodded.

"Is there a town leader? Minister, mayor, who might be a good guide to the local population?"

"There's Mayor Howard. Um, Howard Counsel. He and his wife, Martha, own the historic B and B on Main Street. One of the grand old summer homes. As close to fancy as we get around here."

"Wraparound porch, rockers everywhere?"

The sheriff nodded. "That's the one."

"We should definitely pay him a visit."

"We?"

"You and me. If he's the mayor, he'll want a show of respect. Two uniformed officers asking him questions will only rile him up. Two leaders from the taskforce, including the county sheriff, stopping by for a friendly chat to update him on what's going on in his town . . ." D.D. paused.

The sheriff nodded, getting the gist of what she was saying.

"He'll appreciate the attention," she finished, "and of course we'll ask him some questions while we're at it."

"Mayor Howard and his wife . . . their families go way back in these parts. I don't know how open they'll be to outsiders, but they'll want to see this matter quickly resolved. A sensational murder case, well, it's unseemly. Not to mention bad for business. They aren't going to want our taskforce lingering."

"Perfect. Are they early risers?"

The sheriff shrugged.

"Doesn't matter," D.D. decided. "After the excitement of yesterday, I doubt anyone is sleeping anyway. Let's go."

The sheriff blinked. "Right now?"

"No time like the present."

The sheriff reached down for his hat, still looking a bit frazzled. "I'd like to change my shirt," he said.

D.D. realized for the first time that the sheriff did appear quite wrinkled. As if he'd slept in his uniform. Poor man. "We'll step outside. I'll give Flora and Keith their assignment. Then all of us can get cracking."

"We have an assignment?" Keith asked.

"Absolutely." She ushered them out the door into the hallway.

"What?" Keith asked, as she closed the office door behind them.

In answer, D.D. studied Flora. The woman remained distant. But maybe a task would rouse her out of her fugue state.

"Right now, we're spinning in circles. Is this Jacob's work or not Jacob's work? Yes, he could murder four girls. But no, he probably couldn't handle disposal of the bodies."

Flora nodded, still appearing a million miles away.

D.D. sharpened her tone. "We need to know once and for all if Jacob was in this town. A final, definitive, *yes he was part of this*."

"I told you, I was in a box. I never saw—"

"You never saw, you never heard," D.D. interjected curtly. "But what did you *do*? Come on, Flora, earn your keep. You're not here for decoration."

Flora's nostrils flared. She eyed D.D. mutinously, but at least there was some fire in her eyes.

"I don't get it," Keith said.

D.D. kept her attention on Flora. "What did you do when you were held captive? What did you experience? Think, Flora. Nine months ago when you did the memory exercise, what did you use as triggers?"

The woman suddenly blinked. She straightened, engaged for the first time all morning. "I ate," she said softly. "Jacob, when he returned, always brought food. Lots of takeout. Ribs, wings, burgers, pizza. The greasier the better."

D.D. nodded approvingly. "I'll be the first to say, this assignment pains me, if only because I wish I could do it myself. But we all have our crosses to bear. So I'll be a good doobie and tackle the mayor, while you and Keith identify all the local restaurants that have been in business for the past ten years and then . . . eat. Order every item on the menu if you have to. You want to keep dining around until you find something that, I don't know, tastes like a match."

Flora stared at her.

"It's not enough to search for establishments that have been open ten years," Keith spoke up briskly. "We need ones where the head cook has remained the same, as well, as chefs influence the style of food prepared."

"Sure."

"I can google a list of restaurants for Niche plus surrounding towns, then prepare a spreadsheet listing length of operation, hiring date of head chef, opening date for owner/operator."

"Great."

"I'm not sure my palate is that refined," Flora interjected. "Or my memory that good."

"You're not trying to identify the secret ingredient in the special sauce, Flora. You're just searching for a sense of déjà vu."

Flora nodded slowly. Her flat affect was gone. Now she appeared . . . younger, nervous. Scared that she would discover a dish that reminded her of Jacob? Or more terrified she wouldn't, and the man, what he did to her, what he might have done to others, would forever remain a mystery to her?

Coming to Georgia had been a brave move on Flora's part. D.D. respected it. She even felt for the woman. But she kept her expression firm and her expectations clear. Coddling had never worked when it came to Flora. An impossible challenge, on the other hand . . .

"All right," Flora said abruptly. "We'll do it. Dine our way through town. How hard can it be?"

Keith squeezed her shoulder, which was answer enough.

Behind them, the door opened, the sheriff appearing in his fresh shirt.

"Touch base end of day," D.D. instructed. She made a shooing gesture with her hands. Flora and Keith belatedly turned and headed down the hall.

"Where are they off to?" the sheriff asked.

"Two crazy kids in love? Who knows?"

CHAPTER 13

KIMBERLY

KIMBERLY MET UP WITH HER ERT team shortly after five A.M. They gathered in the motel's lobby before coffee had been brewed and cellophane-wrapped pastries tossed into the basket. They were a good team, experienced and detail oriented. Kimberly trusted each member with her life, and had done so the last time they'd retrieved bodies from a mountain in Georgia.

Supervisory Special Agent and Senior Team Leader Rachel Childs was their designated circus master. The five-foot-nothing redhead had grown up in Chicago and had a set to her jaw that discouraged dissent. By contrast, Harold Foster, a six-foot-one beanpole who towered above her, was their designated outdoorsman. He'd hiked the entire length of the Appalachian Trail before heading off to college and was eager to do it again. He was also well versed in flora, fauna, predatory wildlife, and poisonous snakes. Kimberly had a tendency to hike close to Harold—when she could keep up with him.

Harold and Rachel had brought two more agents with them.

Franklin Kent, whom Kimberly had never met but had a voice

that reminded her of the bayou, was as well-equipped as Harold, so another with mountain experience.

Finally, Rachel introduced Maggie Sharp, who appeared to be lugging their survey tool for crime scene mapping. A walking IT department.

They all exchanged pleasantries. Kimberly explained the two graves and the role of Dr. Jackson, the forensic anthropologist who would be in charge of the exhumation. The ERT, meanwhile, would assist with establishing the grid, working the outer perimeter, and, yes, retrieving any additional scattered bones.

They split into two which would to the trailhead. Kimberly and Harold went ahead to set up mobile command at the base of the hiking trail and meet up with Dr. Jackson. Which put team leader Rachel in charge of coffee and snacks—arguably the most important task.

As Kimberly and Harold reached their destination, Dr. Jackson pulled up in a white ME's van, and Kimberly made the introductions. She'd only worked with the forensic anthropologist a couple of times, but Kimberly already appreciated her no-nonsense approach. This morning, the woman wore loose-fitting clothes and hiking boots. Kimberly noticed a pile of coveralls in the back of the van, which were quickly loaded into a pack. Then there were buckets, trowels, sifters, tarps.

Kimberly was beginning to wonder if they should consider a horse or a donkey to assist with transport when the rest of her team appeared and wordlessly started absorbing supplies into their own packs while attaching various buckets to various hooks all over their bodies.

Then they were off. Harold took the lead, Rachel not far behind. Kimberly had given both coordinates, so she wasn't worried.

She took an easier pace, falling beside Dr. Jackson. The older woman was doing great, given she probably spent most of her life in a lab. But the mile-long trail was steep and it didn't hurt to take a couple of breaks.

"When I told you to find me more bones," Dr. Jackson grumbled, "I didn't mean this."

"Did you look at the pictures I sent you?"

"Of course."

"We stopped digging once we saw the top of the skulls. I didn't want to do more harm than good."

"Finally, some words of common sense from a fed."

"It does happen," Kimberly assured her.

"You're fishing. You want me to tell you things you know I can't yet tell you."

"I want to know the age of the grave site. Sooner versus later. Have we stumbled across something old, or something ongoing?"

"The skeletal condition is one vote for old. But I'll have to get the remains back to my lab to tell you more."

Kimberly nodded, accepting the verdict as they continued their ascent.

The first burial site had already been worked thoroughly a month ago. Given the need to recover more bones, however, Rachel assigned Harold and Franklin to continue examining the area in case they'd missed something. Harold was famous for covering miles of mountainside in a single step. Kimberly didn't know what Franklin was famous for yet. The agent seemed to be focused, dedicated, and completely self-contained. A puppy and a panther. It would be an interesting day for both of them.

She led the rest of the team up to the site of the new mass grave. Two deputies had been assigned overnight watch. They rose gratefully to their feet as Kimberly and her crew emerged from the dense underbrush.

"Morning, ma'am."

"Hot coffee?"

"Yes, ma'am!"

Kimberly had learned early in her career it was the little things that got the job done. Now, they all took a moment to unload their gear, unpack bags. They made sure to stay well clear of the grave to prevent cross-contamination, though Kimberly could tell everyone was anxious to get a look.

The deputies were dismissed back down the mountain to get some sleep. Eventually, two new ones would arrive. It never hurt to have an oversight crew, keeping their attention on any approaching threats—whether coyotes or gawkers—as the forensic team's efforts would be focused on the dirt.

Rachel directed her team to get set up. Maggie unpacked the Total Station, an instrument first used by survey crews to create 3-D models of major roads and traffic patterns, then adapted to render 3-D images of complex crime scenes. As Kimberly had already related to Mac, the remains were not laid out in a neat and orderly fashion. Instead, best she could tell, the bodies had been tossed in together. Then, over time, as flesh and sinew gave way, the remains had collapsed in on one another.

Back in the lab, Dr. Jackson would carefully rebuild each skeleton, while digital images from the Total Station would be used to preserve information from the original scene.

Once they had their supplies sorted out and organized, Rachel consulted with Dr. Jackson on the plan of attack. In spite of what people sometimes assumed, the FBI's Evidence Response Team's main goal was to *collect* evidence, not to analyze it. None of them were forensic experts, though some, like Harold, had developed areas of interest over the years.

Dr. Jackson had donned coveralls over her hiking ensemble. She now passed out additional garments, and they all suited up, grimacing at adding an extra layer of clothing over their sweaty gear.

Birds chirped in the distance. There was a nice wind in the trees as Dr. Jackson stepped gingerly over the lines and made her way to the middle of the grid. Kimberly already knew what she would see: a slight depression in the earth, next to a mound of dirt. Lay people assumed the mound was the grave. Not true. The depression was the grave, the mound of dirt was the earth the killer had dug out of the ground, then left to the side after dumping in the bodies. Over time, decomp reduced the mass in the grave, causing the earth to settle, and creating a distinct pattern all crime scene techs learned to identify: one mound plus one depression equaled one unmarked grave.

Or in this case, one unmarked grave with three rounded skulls already peering out from the loose soil.

Dr. Jackson picked up the first trowel. They got to it.

CHAPTER 14

FLORA

CAN'T EAT ANOTHER BITE. You do it."

"Me? I don't think that's the point."

"Please, I double-dog dare you to tell me these ribs taste any differently than the ones before them, or the ones before those."

I glare at Keith, my eyes daggers of contempt, until he has no choice but to rise to the challenge.

"Double-dog dare. Well, if you're that serious." Keith gamely picks up a knife and fork, slices off a bite of barbecued meat.

"Who uses a knife and fork to eat ribs? Authentic experience. Come on!"

"You're very cranky," he informs me, but sets down the silverware, picks up the bone with his fingers.

"I have good reason to be cranky."

"And yet, what does it change?"

I glare at him again. He shrugs a shoulder, then takes a delicate bite of pork and chews thoughtfully. "I would say these ribs have a tad more vinegar than the ones before. Or maybe it's a hint of cloves."

"You are making that up!"

"Yes. I am."

Keith sets down the bone. I can't help myself, I half sigh, half explode in exasperation, throwing myself against the back of the booth.

"I hate this."

"I know."

"I don't remember. I was too busy being grateful for food, any kind of food. I was scarfing and inhaling and chewing like a goddamn animal. I didn't notice sauce, or flavor or seasoning. I was fucking starving and I ate like a starving woman."

"I'm sorry."

"Oh shut up."

Another shrug. I want to scream. Or tear out my hair or rip apart this booth. I want to run so far, so fast, that this awful food and those awful memories can never catch me and I'll never have to think about Jacob again.

Keith had identified two restaurants in Niche that had the same owner-operators for the past ten years. A diner and a pub. So we'd started there, the owners trying to protest it was too early to be serving dinner, me staring them down until the entire menu suddenly became available. It was creepy how easy it was to select entrees. Oh, Jacob would love this, Jacob would like that. Like picking out food for an old friend, or long-lost lover. Which brought back other memories, the chili dog in St. Louis that exploded down his shirt after the first bite and I burst out laughing before I could catch myself. Then froze, thinking he'd smack me, except he started laughing, as well. He'd ordered two more and we'd eaten them greedily at the truck stop, talking about nothing in particular, enjoying our time in the sun.

Who enjoys a sunny afternoon with their own rapist?

And yet that was Jacob, too. He wasn't a monster all of the time. Or maybe he realized that the moments of normalcy made his monstrousness all the more frightening.

D.D. had given us her rental car. After hitting the two establishments in Niche, we'd driven south to Dahlonega, which had many more restaurants. We'd been eating, I don't know, forever. Ordering plate after plate while fellow diners stared. My stomach ached. My head hurt. I wanted to vomit, though whether from food or memories of Jacob . . .

"They remodeled Columbine High School the summer after the shootings," Keith offers up. He's pushing the ribs around on the plate with his fork. "The administrators knew it was important to wipe out as many traces of violence as they could so the student body could move on. And they understood that meant not just patching bullet holes, but instituting a whole redesign, especially one that changed up the library, where so many were killed."

I nod absently. Keith likes to talk. Sometimes I pay attention, sometimes I don't.

"But the principal argued a new look wasn't enough," Keith continues. "They also needed to change the fire alarm tone, which had gone off for hours that day. Just the sound of those notes sent himself and the students back into a state of panic." Keith paused. "They also removed Chinese food from the cafeteria menu."

He looks at me. "That's what the cafeteria had been preparing for lunch that day. Chinese food. No one could take the smell anymore. Again, it led to immediate panic attacks. Poor Chinese food. It probably was a lunch many used to enjoy."

I stare at him.

"I understand you're overwhelmed," he says softly. "I know thinking about Jacob, remembering anything involving Jacob, has to be excruciating."

I don't say a word.

"But Sergeant Warren, what she said is true. We process information through all of our senses. We make associations through all our senses. From building design to the fire alarms to cafeteria food. You may not have seen much when you were first kidnapped. But you experienced a lot. You processed way more than you know. And with a little time and patience . . ."

"I'll magically know if I've been here before?"

"Or you'll be able to confirm once and for all that you weren't."

"My memory isn't that good. My senses are not that refined."

"Or your safeguards are just that high."

"I'm not trying to avoid this!"

"Flora, no one blames you for not wanting to take a trip down memory lane. Sergeant Warren is asking the impossible of you and she knows it."

I'm horrified to realize my eyes have filled with tears. I'm going to cry. Goddammit, I refuse to be this weak.

"What if I told you it all tastes right? What if I said, every single thing we tried . . . Yes, Jacob could've brought that to the basement. Every meal is exactly the kind of thing he would've liked. And I know that, because I lived with him that long, I got to know him that well."

"Okay," Keith says.

"Okay? There's nothing okay about this!"

"You're here. He isn't. You won. He lost. Everything is okay about that." Keith reaches across the table and takes my hand. "You're here with me. And that's very okay."

I want to tell him he's wrong. That I never feel like I won. That mostly I just endured, and I hate myself for that, too. For the days I didn't fight. For all the times I fell upon Jacob's offerings of food and greedily devoured them. Shame. I think of Jacob and to this day, I feel shame. It follows me everywhere I go, even sitting at a booth in a tavern staring at barbecued ribs.

"Let's go," Keith says.

"Where? Isn't there another pub we're supposed to hit?"

"You're full, I'm full. We're done."

I stare at him curiously. "So now what?"

"We take a page out of Sergeant Warren's book. We launch our own investigation."

"What are we investigating?"

"ATVs."

"What?"

"Forget Jacob for a moment. There's no one in the world who can physically lug four bodies up a mountainside. I barely made it up that trail yesterday and I can run for miles."

I nod slowly.

"Meaning there has to be another way, maybe even a whole differ-ent path we haven't identified yet. Personally, I'm favoring a four wheeler-accessible trail. Think about it; it's not just getting a body or bodies to the site, but also shovel, pickax, other supplies. The area is too heavily wooded for a truck, which leaves us with an ATV."

I nod again. While I've been lost in my dark thoughts, Keith has clearly been using his head, and his logic makes sense.

"Where to start?" I ask.

"I Googled a nearby ATV rental company. They must have trail maps, right? Not to mention local knowledge. Because it might be that the trail doesn't exist anymore, which is why we didn't see imme-diate signs of it. But maybe there was something people used fifteen years ago, that sort of thing."

I don't speak right away. Instead, I study this serious man sitting across from me with his Ted Bundy good looks and relentlessly curi-ous mind. I realize I'm no longer angry, I'm no longer ashamed. I'm intrigued.

Keith is right. There has to be some other way to access the burial sites than just hiking. And who better than us to figure it out?

Slowly, I nod my agreement.

Hand in hand, we slide out of the booth and head for the door.

CHAPTER 15

D.D.

HOWARD AND MARTHA COUNSEL OWNED and operated the Mountain Laurel B&B. The pale lavender Victorian sat on the corner of Main Street, with a broad wraparound porch decorated with lush hanging baskets and half a dozen rocking chairs. On this beautiful September morning, the veranda looked perfect for sitting out front with a mug of coffee in one hand and a book in the other.

Which made it interesting that the porch was completely empty. Though, it was only shortly after eight. Crime had a tendency to get people like D.D. out of bed early. She forgot sometimes how the rest of the world lived.

Sheriff Smithers mounted the front steps, grabbed the bronzed door handle, then gestured for D.D. to enter first. The front door opened to a grand entryway. Sweeping staircase in front, lovely pale green and yellow sunroom to the left. A tinkling bell had marked their arrival. Now a smartly dressed older woman in a dove-gray skirt and elegant pin-striped blouse appeared from a hall behind the staircase. Her heels clacked against the marble floor as she made her way briskly to the giant cherrywood desk that served for guest registration. When she spied the sheriff and D.D., her steps slowed.

"Sheriff Smithers." The woman halted in front of them, blue eyes curious.

The sheriff was holding his hat before him. Now he extended one hand in greeting. "Mrs. Counsel. Good morning, ma'am. Sorry to disturb you so early. This is Sergeant D. D. Warren, a member of the taskforce investigating the remains found in the mountains. As you've no doubt heard—"

"You found another body yesterday," Mrs. Counsel answered for him. "Maybe more, if the rumors are to be believed."

The sheriff didn't confirm or deny. For now, they were trying to keep the news under wraps to keep the media from descending. How long that strategy would work was a good question. But all investigations hoped for a little luck.

"Is Howard around?" the sheriff asked. "We thought the mayor might appreciate an update."

"Absolutely." Mrs. Counsel extended a hand to D.D. "Please, call me Martha. I'll fetch my husband. We can meet in the front room." She gestured to the room on the left. The walls appeared to be papered in a pale green lattice pattern, while the floor was covered in a sage green carpet with butter yellow roses. An eclectic mix of old tables were positioned around the space; no doubt where the B&B guests enjoyed breakfast, afternoon tea, late-night brandy.

"Coffee, tea?" Martha asked now as she led them to a larger table in the corner.

The room was currently empty, which D.D. found interesting. For a tourist town, the inn seemed lacking in visitors.

"Do you have many guests?" she asked, as they arrived at the table and the sheriff pulled out a chair for her.

"We have four couples right now. But it's the middle of the week. This time of year, the weekends are busier. It's too late in the season for thru-hikers, and families are tied up with school. We will get a lot of couples, day hikers, and some families on the weekend, however. Let me get Howard. I'll be right back. Coffee?" she asked again.

"I would love some," D.D. said, while the sheriff nodded gratefully.

"You ever been on a taskforce this big?" D.D. asked Sheriff Smithers as Martha clacked out of the room.

"No, ma'am."

"Go home tonight. Sleep in your own bed. This is going to be a marathon, not a sprint."

A young Hispanic girl appeared in the doorway. She wore a pale blue maid's uniform, the skirt cut modestly below her knees, sleeves reaching to her wrists. Her dark hair was pulled up tight in a bun, while on her shoulder she balanced a massive tray topped with a silver coffee service.

The girl crossed the room slowly. She moved with a slight limp, as if dragging her right leg behind her. As she drew nearer, D.D. could make out a shiny scar at the edge of the girl's hairline and noticed the left half of the girl's face drooped slightly, as if she'd suffered a stroke.

The girl stopped at the table beside theirs. She carefully lowered the tray, then without a word, set about pouring coffee from the silver pot into two delicately flowered china mugs.

"Good morning," D.D. said.

The girl glanced up slightly. Her gaze fell on the sheriff's uniform and her eyes widened. She didn't say a word, just kept on pouring. She slid the first cup before D.D., the second before the sheriff. Then placed sugar and cream in the middle of the table.

"I see you've met our niece," a new voice boomed into the room. A distinctive-looking older gentleman with a cream-colored linen suit and mint-green bow tie strode into the nook, Martha by his side. Mayor Howard, D.D. would presume.

Immediately, the serving girl took a step back, placed herself in position against the wall, and stared at the floor.

"She doesn't talk," Martha provided, her arm looped through the mayor's. "She suffered a dreadful car accident when she was young. Killed her mother, left her mute and brain-damaged, poor thing."

"Shouldn't she be in school?" D.D. asked, still puzzling over such a young girl dressed as a maid.

"No point," the mayor said dismissively. "She can't read or write. The area of the brain that processes language is damaged beyond re-pair. The doctors were very blunt on the subject. There's nothing to be done. But we've taken her in, of course. Family is family."

And free help is hard to find, D.D. thought uncharitably. She looked over at the wall, but the girl remained expressionless. It was hard to tell if she'd registered the conversation, much less understood it.

The mayor pulled out a chair for his wife, placing her next to the sheriff. He rounded the table to take the seat next to D.D., where she noticed he could look the sheriff in the eye.

"I take it the rumors are true; you found another body yesterday," the mayor drawled at last.

D.D. sipped her coffee, let the sheriff do the talking.

"Yes, sir. We found additional remains, not far from the origi-nal site."

"Oh my goodness." Martha covered her mouth with her hand, glanced at her husband with concern.

Mayor Howard sighed heavily. "Another girl? That's terrible. Sim-ply terrible."

"How do you know it's a girl?" D.D. asked.

"Isn't it always?" He eyed her guilelessly.

D.D. couldn't figure him out.

"Where are you from, dear?" he asked her now.

"Boston."

"But you're here, part of some taskforce, searching through my woods. Now how did that come to pass? A Boston detective on a Southern taskforce?"

"I have relevant experience," D.D. said blithely. She was saved from further reply by the mayor's wife.

"Was this new body . . . also a skeleton?" She whispered the final word, as if it was something shocking and terrible. Maybe it was and D.D. had just been doing this too long.

"We're still conducting our investigation, ma'am. The forensic anthropologist is on-site as we speak."

"Oh dear. All this sad, sordid business. Right here. In our own backyard." Martha eyed her husband in distress. "And just in time for fall hiking season. Oh dear, oh dear."

"Have you learned anything more about the first girl?" the mayor asked Sheriff Smithers.

"Only that she'd been there for quite some time."

"How long have you been mayor?" D.D. spoke up.

"The past ten years," Howard replied evenly.

"And before that?"

"My daddy. The Counsels have a long history of service to this town."

"Do you hire a lot of young girls?" D.D. glanced at their "niece," who still stood unmoving next to the wall.

"Of course," Martha huffed out. "Especially for the busy summer season. As you can tell, our town is small. During boom seasons, we must bring in outside workers. But all of our employees are legal, if that's what you're asking, and we have the paperwork to prove it."

D.D. nodded thoughtfully. What the Counsels said made sense. On the one hand, Niche was a quaint small town where the full-time residents probably did know one another by name. On the other hand, for significant portions of the year, the workforce was transient and the area flooded with tourists. Getting a bead on all those people, going back fifteen years, would not be easy.

Which brought her to the locals, as good a starting point as any. She rose abruptly. "Excuse me, I need to use the restroom."

"I'll show you—"

"No need. I'm sure your niece knows the way." Before anyone could blink she had the girl by the elbow and was guiding her away from the wall and out of the room. The girl stumbled slightly and D.D. forced herself to slow down, walk calmly. Just another woman in search of a toilet.

She could feel the girl's arms tremble beneath her fingers, but the girl didn't—couldn't?—say a word.

Out of curiosity, D.D. removed her hand once they'd left the room and waited to see what the girl would do. The girl didn't make a run for it. Instead, she turned left, entered the hallway behind the staircase, then a moment later limped to a door marked *Ladies*.

D.D. studied the young maid. So the girl could understand things, she just couldn't communicate. Which made D.D. think she wasn't nearly as impaired as the Counsels claimed.

"Are you okay here?" D.D. asked softly.

The girl locked her gaze at a spot past D.D.'s shoulder. Didn't make a sound.

"Can you speak?"

The girl's lips pursed. For a moment, it appeared as if she were trying to whistle, make a noise. But nothing came out. She resumed staring at the wall.

"Can you type?" On impulse, D.D. dug out her cell, then pulled up a text message screen. She indicated to the tiny letters. "Pick one. Type what you want to say."

The girl looked at the phone, then took it gingerly from D.D.'s hands, turning it over. She seemed genuinely curious. Eyeing the letters, the blinking cursor. Her fingers fluttered across the screen, almost in longing. Then she shook her head, appearing genuinely frustrated, and handed the phone back.

A full minute had passed. Much longer and Martha would appear to see what was keeping them.

"I think you know things," D.D. tried again. "Much more than you let on."

The girl inhaled slightly, which D.D. took to be a yes.

"When I go back, we have to ask the Counsels some questions. I'd like your answers, too."

Brown eyes widened in alarm.

"No, no, there's nothing to be afraid of. This is what we're going to do. Stand where you usually do, arms by your sides. When I ask questions, show one finger for yes." D.D. held up one finger. "Two for no. What is yes?"

Shakily, the girl raised a single finger.

"No?"

Two fingers. D.D. knew it. The girl was plenty smart. Her "family" was taking terrible advantage her.

"Do they hurt you?" D.D. asked gently.

The girl didn't move.

"Are you scared?"

Nothing.

"It doesn't have to be like this. Even if they're your family and they've told you that you have no place else to go, that's not true. I can help you find options."

To be honest, though, D.D. wasn't sure just what those options were. She didn't have jurisdiction here, let alone understand the available resources for displaced kids. But the sight of such a young girl already forced into a life of servitude because of—what, a childhood injury? The cop in D.D. was offended—not to mention the mother in her.

Almost as if reading her mind, the girl slowly held up two fingers. Followed quickly by a faint shake of her head. There was something in the girl's eyes. Not fear, D.D. thought. More like stubbornness.

The sound of heels clacking across the marble foyer. D.D. quickly pocketed her phone. She and the girl turned as a single unit and headed back down the hall where Martha was already waiting for them.

The woman eyed D.D. suspiciously. Then regarded the girl even more harshly. When neither said a word, she pivoted on one heel and led them back to the sunroom.

THE SHERIFF WAS STILL TALKING to the mayor, keeping his comments brief. D.D. pulled her chair way out, the rude Yankee who didn't know how to sit ladylike at a table. From this position, she had a clear vantage point of the mayor, his wife, and their niece, who was once more standing at attention against the wall.

Time for the real questions.

"In cases like this," the sheriff said, "it's best to keep an open mind. We don't want to get ahead of ourselves."

The mayor and his wife nodded encouragingly, as if they understood they were about to be taken into some grand confidence.

"Of course, we do have a suspicion."

More supportive nods.

"Do either of you recognize this man?" Sheriff Smithers withdrew a photo of Jacob Ness. Not the best photo, D.D. thought, as it had been taken during his first arrest for beating his wife over twenty years ago. He was a hard-looking thirty even back then. Clearly a lifelong smoker, drinker, drug abuser, he stared into the police camera sullenly, his lip curled in a faint sneer.

Martha stifled a gasp. "Why, that's Jacob Ness. Of course we recognize him. He kidnapped that college student. What was it, five years ago? He's a monster!"

"The college student was from Boston," the mayor filled in, eyeing D.D. with renewed interest.

D.D. took the photo from Smithers, made a show of positioning it on her knee, where it just so happened to be turned in the direction of the wall.

"Have you seen him around here?"

"Isn't he dead?" Martha asked. "I thought the police killed him. Are you saying he did this?"

"Howard, Martha." The sheriff held up a calming hand, regaining their focus. "These graves are old. Whatever happened here, there's no need for immediate alarm. Having said that, something terrible happened in our own backyard. We need answers. And we owe it to the victims to get justice."

"Do you have any recollection of ever seeing this man in this area?" D.D. prodded again. "Doesn't matter if it was seven, ten, fifteen years ago. Just, did you ever see him here?"

"Absolutely not!" Martha answered first. "And we would know. We followed everything that happened in the news, the FBI raiding the hotel, saving that poor girl. Why, if we had ever seen that man in our town, you can believe, Sheriff, we would've rung you immediately. Thank heavens a man such as that never passed through our community!"

"What about this vehicle?"

Next the sheriff produced a picture of the cab from Ness's big rig. This time both of the Counsels shook their heads.

"Other loners that spring to mind?" the sheriff pressed. "Maybe the kind of neighbor most try to ignore but everyone's a little nervous about?"

The Counsels exchanged glances. Their shoulders had come down. If they were shocked before, considering a known serial rapist had passed through their community, they seemed more comfortable now. Back to the local misfits. All towns had some.

"There's Walt." Martha brushed the back of her husband's hand, as if for confirmation. "Walt Davies. He lives in his own cabin above the ridge. An old family camp. He keeps mostly to himself, one of those off-the-radar types. We only see him when he comes into town for supplies. Let's just say he's not the most sociable . . . or hygienic . . . man."

"I've never considered Walt dangerous," the mayor spoke up, frowning. "I'd guess he runs some moonshine. Hell, maybe has his own herb business, if you know what I mean. But he's never done anything untoward. Most of us leave him well enough alone, and he returns the favor. Having said that, Sheriff, I doubt he takes kindly to government types. Before paying a visit to his homestead, I'd take some precautions."

Sheriff Smithers nodded his head at the warning, made a note. "Anyone else? Maybe a guest you see regularly, but who doesn't quite fit? No hiking boots or interest in the great outdoors, keeps mostly to himself?"

Martha waved a dismissive hand. "Many of our guests are loners who keep to themselves. They come to the mountains looking to get away. They have their own thoughts, their own problems. And they appreciate us letting them be."

"Do you have guest records going back fifteen years?" D.D. asked.

The mayor looked at his wife. She shrugged. "I'd have to check. We installed our new computer system . . . I'd guess ten years ago? But I can look."

"We'd appreciate any and all records you have," Sheriff Smithers assured her.

"Going back fifteen years? That's thousands of names, Sheriff."

"I know."

Martha sighed, as if resigned to her fate.

"Great." D.D. rose to standing. "We'll be back tomorrow for the records."

Smithers blinked at her abrupt tone, but didn't correct her as he also climbed to his feet.

"Thank you for the coffee, ma'am." He nodded to Martha, shook hands with Howard. D.D. didn't bother. She was already halfway out of the nook. Sheriff Smithers hastened to catch up.

"What was all that about?" he asked huffily as he finally reached her outside. D.D. didn't answer right away, but waited till they were farther down the street.

"I think they're lying to us."

"About what?"

"Plenty of things. Their niece for one thing."

"That poor girl—"

"That poor girl understands plenty."

The sheriff frowned, caught her arm. "Did you talk to her? That why you grabbed her for the ladies' room?"

"She can't speak. That part seems true. But that doesn't mean she can't communicate. And she hears just fine. When you were running the Counsels through the round of questioning, I asked her to participate as well. One finger for yes, two fingers for no."

The sheriff stared at her. "She could do that?"

"Yep. And get this, when you showed the picture of Jacob Ness—"

"Hang on. Ness died seven years ago. Even if he'd been around right before then, that girl would've been only a little kid herself."

"Little girls have eyes and ears. Especially ones who get to spend their lives standing at the edge of a room, waiting to serve more tea."

The sheriff still appeared uncertain. "She answered? When I showed the picture of Jacob, she answered?"

"She held up three fingers."

"Three fingers? I thought you said it was one or two?"

"I know. Which proves just how smart she is. Her answer wasn't yes or no. I think she made up a new code on the spot: three fingers for maybe."

"That doesn't tell us anything."

"It tells us she knows more than the Counsels believe she knows.

And it tells me I'm going to find a way to speak to her again. Alone. That girl needs us, Sheriff. I don't know exactly what's going on around here, but the discovery of these remains, it's a beginning, not an end. And we'd better catch up fast, because you know what happens when old skeletons suddenly come to light? People get scared. Then new bodies have a tendency to drop. Something happened here. Something very bad. Real question is, is it over yet?"

CHAPTER 16

FLORA

I EXPECTED A KID AT THE ATV rental company. Instead it's an old guy in a green flannel shirt, worn jeans, and sturdy hiking boots. He glances up when Keith and I walk through the door, takes in Keith's obviously upscale urban wardrobe, and appears to do some quick math. Probably doubling the rental price for the cute tourist couple.

I thought Keith would start with the subject of maps. Instead, he smiles, lays on the charm, and plays the part of naïve out-of-towner with more money than common sense.

First question from owner-operator Bill Benson: Have we ever driven a four-wheeler before? We both shake our heads.

Okay, one ATV or two? Bill eyes me dubiously. He appears old school, as in women should be seen not heard, and definitely have no place operating any kind of motorized vehicle.

Keith wants to know about the ATVs first. Sizes, models, how comfortable for two. Hey, if we wanted to bring blankets, a picnic basket, does Bill have anything with storage, that sort of thing.

Bill takes us out back to peruse his inventory. A standard ATV can definitely hold two of us just fine. Or, given the scenarios both Keith and I are running through our minds, one driver plus one body strapped behind the driver. Three bodies seems a stretch to me, and I have no idea where you'd put a shovel, but then I see a compact trailer parked to the side, obviously meant to be attached to the rear of one of the ATVs. Probably intended for hauling leaves, lawn clippings, that sort of thing. But also perfect for dark deeds done at midnight. I can tell by the look on Keith's face that he's thinking the same.

Keith inspects each four-wheeler. He settles on one that looks exactly like all the others to me. And finally we get to the matter of where to ride.

Bill walks us back inside, where he unfolds a map of the surrounding area. There aren't just ATV trails, there are hiking trails. Dozens, if not hundreds, looping all over the place. The myriad of dashed and solid lines reminds me of the subway map in Boston, except much more complicated.

"Now then," Bill is saying, "these dashed lines are hiking only. Stay clear, not just because you don't want to be running anyone over, but because most are too narrow. You could a hit a tree, really ruin your day."

"The ATVs look pretty hardy to me," Keith says. "What if we wanted to do a little off-trail exploration?"

"Oh, the machines are tough, all right. And this time of year, you don't have to worry about mud. But you get off the trails and you start destroying plant life. People don't take kindly to that. Besides, underbrush is dense in these parts. Bushes, mountain laurel, smaller trees. You can get stuck or lost plenty easy."

"We're actually staying over by Niche, but I didn't notice any rental companies over there."

"No, sir, we're the only providers in the area."

"So, if we wanted to rent the ATV for the day, explore closer to our hotel?"

Bill eyes Keith suspiciously. I stay quiet, studying the map and wishing it made more sense. I may have grown up in the woods, but I never used any kind of guide to roam my own backyard. I simply headed out, following deer paths, animal trails. I never knew where I was going, and yet I never felt lost. The more I roamed, the more the woods were my home.

By contrast, this overhead view of a mountain range, with solid lines for ATVs and dashed lines for hikers and curved lines for grade, seems like an overly complicated maze, designed not to show the way, but to get everyone hopelessly lost. I finally pinpoint Niche, then identify the dashed line indicating the trail we'd hiked up yesterday to the first body. How far up the dashed line we'd gone, how far off the trail the first body was, let alone the others, causes me a second round of confusion.

"What is this ATV trail?" I ask abruptly. I'd found a solid line that seems to be following some ridge above where we'd found the bodies. I study the map's scale again, trying to understand distance from one point to another.

"That's Laurel Lane. Some pretty views in the spring," Bill offers. He looks at me, then Keith, then me again. There's no way he hasn't heard about the discovery of bodies in the woods yesterday. And given the location of the Laurel Lane trail in relation to the search efforts . . .

"We're part of the taskforce," I give up. "We came in with the FBI yesterday to assist with the search."

Beside me, Keith nods.

"You don't look like FBI."

"I'm a computer analyst," Keith volunteers. "I have experience calculating search areas."

Bill grunts, seeming to accept Keith's job description. Then his gaze goes back to me.

"I'm a victim advocate," I say.

"A victim advocate? For bones?"

"Everyone needs a voice."

Bill arches a brow.

I lean forward, whisper quietly. "As I'm sure you've heard, we found another grave yesterday."

Bill appears intrigued in spite of himself.

"You ever travel Laurel Lane? Roar along on your ATV, enjoying a sunny day? Ever imagine what was in those woods? How close you might've passed to those poor dead bodies, each and every time?"

Bill swallows thickly.

"Hiking with a corpse is tough," Keith speaks matter of factly. "The taskforce has been discussing it, and most likely the killer used some mode of transportation to haul the bodies to the burial sites."

"How . . . how many girls?" Bill asks roughly. He drops his voice. "I heard a dozen."

"Do you know this area?" I ask.

"Yes, ma'am. Like you said, been on that trail many a time."

"Could you get a truck on that path?" Keith asks.

"Too narrow. And like I said, the underbrush is thick along there. Not to mention, some times of the year, all rutted up. Be a risky trip."

"How busy is this trail?" Keith points to Laurel Lane.

Bill shrugs. "This time of year, weekends are our bread and butter. But weekdays are quieter. You never know, though. Daytime," he ventures, "would be tricky for, um . . . well, what you're talking about."

"The ATVs have headlights for nighttime rides," Keith says.

"Not the best, though. After dark, most riders wear headlamps, or you can clip on additional lighting. If you were going off trail, you'd definitely want some assistance."

Keith takes the map. His gaze is thoughtful, as if all the squiggly lines speak to him. Clearly, he doesn't want to give away too much information regarding the location of the graves, and yet there's plenty the map alone can't tell us.

"It looks like Laurel Lane is part of a whole network. You can access it from a number of different trails. How do locals do it? Trailer in the ATVs to one of these parking areas, then take off?" Keith asks.

"You can," Bill agrees. "But plenty of folks just head out their front door. There are dirt roads not on this map, which connect with the ATV circuit. Some locals even have their own personal paths they've bushwhacked, leading to the network. Four-wheelers are popular around here. Lots of people own 'em, and they want to just take off, not be messing around with trailers."

"You could trailer us in, though?" Keith asks.

"That's generally what we do with groups. You pick the area, I take the ATVs, get you started. I can guide you, too, if you'd like." Bill's gravelly voice picks up. Talk of murder might make him uncomfortable, but clearly, the chance to be part of the action . . .

"Basically, you're saying this map doesn't show everything?" Keith presses. "There are dirt roads, personal paths, lots of other things going on which only the locals know about?"

"We don't like to give away all our secrets," Bill deadpans.

Keith doesn't seem to know how to ask what he wants to know next. I don't either. We'd walked the woods around the first burial site for hours yesterday, looking for animal dens and scattered bones. We'd never seen anything close to a trail.

"If there was a path, say, over a decade ago," Keith muses finally, "but maybe it hadn't been used for a while, how would we find it?"

"You don't."

"We don't?"

"The mountain takes back its own. The woods don't want to be cleared or groomed. Hell, it takes four different ATV clubs to keep these marked trails accessible. Work is constant and ongoing. Ask any landowner. You want to keep your yard, you gotta *keep* your yard."

"So an old trail . . . would just return to the wild?"

"Yes, sir."

In other words, Keith's theory about an old, locals-only trail may be right. Or maybe even more personal than that—a trail once made by one person and known only by that person. Except this section of the Appalachian Trail was part of the Chattahoochee National Forest, not private property. So anyone who'd blazed a private path off the known byways would have to be someone with access. Maybe a park ranger, or local guide? It feels to me like the more we learn, the more the truth spins away.

"What do you think?" Keith asks me.

I understand the issue. We can't keep asking questions without giving away too much. Were the graves accessible from the Laurel Lane trail on an ATV? There's only one way to find out.

"I get to drive," I say.

"Deal." Keith pulls out his wallet. "We'd like to rent one ATV with transport to Niche. We'll also need a map and helmets. Oh, and any kind of insurance you got. Maybe, make that double."

CHAPTER 17

KIMBERLY

As KIMBERLY QUICKLY LEARNED, EXCAVATING a mass grave was like emptying a bathtub one scoop of water at a time, keeping the water level even as you slowly brought it down.

Dr. Jackson liked to talk while she worked. "Now, if this were an archeological site, we'd start at the edge and dig ourselves in. But when you work a burial, you need to protect the grave itself, including the walls of the original pit which may yield tool marks we'll want for evidence later. So what we're going to do is start right in the middle. We'll scoop off shallow amounts of dirt into buckets. Buckets will then be poured through a coarse sieve, then a fine sieve. Hopefully that will yield some interesting tidbits—buttons, jewelry, bits of fabric. A shell casing would be nice. But we also want flora, fauna, seed pods. We don't know what we don't know, so at this stage, anything left in the sieve is considered evidence."

Kimberly nodded obediently, organizing their small crew into the human chain. Dr. Jackson took the lead, patiently removing shallow slices of dirt. Kimberly came next, holding up the bucket to receive each scoopful. Full buckets were passed down for sifting. Empty buckets passed back for refill.

Maggie roamed around them. Setting up the Total Station in select spots. Shooting data before bringing the toy to the next site, different angle.

The work was tedious and hot. Before long Kimberly could feel the sweat beading along her brow. She had to take a break and tie a handkerchief around her hairline. Dripping bodily fluids into a crime scene would definitely be in poor form. She noticed the others having to stop to do the same.

This graves, like the first, was not especially deep. Nor did it turn out to be particularly wide. Within a matter of hours, Dr. Jackson had fully exposed a tangled riddle of bones. Without the skulls for reference, Kimberly wasn't sure she would've known she was looking at three bodies. It might have been six, maybe a dozen.

It was . . . heartrending. Three people reduced to a single cluster of bones.

Dr. Jackson called for a water break. The woman had a kerchief around her head and her neck, both heavily stained with sweat. When the forensic anthropologist straightened, Kimberly could hear the woman's back crack, could see her wince.

"Definitely not in the lab anymore," the doc said grimly, extracting herself carefully from the grave.

"Have you worked a mass grave before?" Kimberly asked as they headed to the edge of the woods, where the rest of their team had already gathered in the shade and were greedily sucking down liquid.

"Too many times. Rwanda. Central America. Many forensic anthropologists donate time working international cases. The countries where some of the worst genocides have taken place don't have the resources to process their own sites. They rely on the international community to lend a hand."

"I thought . . . I thought it would be easier to make out each body,"

Kimberly said. She noticed the others were eavesdropping shamelessly on their conversation.

Dr. Jackson shook her head. "Mass killers don't like to work any harder than they have to. Some even make their victims dig their own graves. In this case, looks to me like one small ditch was carved into the earth. Which, given the amount of bushes and tree roots, couldn't have been an easy task. Then, the bodies were dumped in. Over time, the skeletons collapsed into the jumbled pattern we're seeing here.

"Now, there are a couple of factors we can already consider. We've removed most of the dirt from the grave, and there's still no trace of clothing."

"Like the first grave," Kimberly said.

"Exactly. I've also noted the first pelvis. Definitely female. Based on a quick glance, I would guess they all are." The forensic anthropologist sighed heavily.

Kimberly nodded, taking another swig of water and feeling those words like a weight in her chest. Four murdered girls. All dumped on one mountainside, and dead so long not even a memory of flesh remained. Good God, what had been going on around here?

"Can't tell you time since death. That'll take some quality time with my mass spec back in the lab. Clearly, we're looking at older remains, but are these two sites five years apart, a few years apart, a few months apart . . . that's going to take some analysis."

"Three bodies in one burial site is unusual for a serial predator."

"Can't say I've run across that before myself. We already got an interesting find in the first sieve, as well."

Kimberly hadn't worked the sifting process so she looked at the doctor.

"Appears to be a slender piece of plastic tubing," Dr. Jackson explained. "The size and diameter reminds me of medical equipment, say a cannula used for an IV."

"Seriously?"

"Again, this is premature. But we also found a dirt-covered strip of adhesive. Like the kind used to tape an IV to the back of a patient's hand."

"There are possible medical supplies in this grave? No clothes or signs of restraints but *medical supplies?*"

"Like I said, gotta get back to the lab."

Kimberly stared at the doctor. She honestly didn't know what to make of such findings. A mass grave had been strange enough. But a mass grave where one of the victims may have received medical treatment?

Kimberly heard a sound in the distance. A low splutter, building into a throaty growl as it grew closer. Instantly, she and the rest of the team were on their feet.

Closer. Louder. Roaring. Clearly some kind of vehicle approaching where no vehicle should be.

Kimberly drew her sidearm.

An ATV came crashing through the bushes. Two riders, both wearing helmets, pitched forward as the vehicle careened sideways then lurched to a sudden stop. Kimberly lined up her Sig Sauer on the driver just as the person opened her visor and Kimberly found her gun pointed straight at Flora Dane's forehead.

CHAPTER 18

D.D.

"ARE YOU TELLING ME that didn't bother you?" D.D. asked.

Sheriff Smithers had just pulled into Niche's town office. Now he killed the engine, stared at her. "What?"

"That girl. The way the mayor and his wife treat her. She's just a kid. She should be in school, not working as a maid."

"In Georgia, school is mandatory from six to sixteen. Now, that girl looked old enough to be a teenager to me. Could be she already graduated from some special school, or that she's homeschooled. You don't know what you don't know. And Mayor Howard and his wife . . . they've done a lot for this community. You can't just assume the worst."

"I can, too," D.D. muttered, as she popped open her door. She didn't like Mayor Howard or his wife. Everything was a little too perfect. She was always suspicious of people whose houses seemed more like set pieces than real homes. And everything about that grand inn, from its wraparound porch outside to the silver coffee service inside . . . it smacked of pretense. Look here, not there. Admire appearances, then move along before peering beneath.

"There must be a record of the girl," D.D. said, joining the sheriff on the steps of the town office. "You realize we don't even know her name?"

"I'll make some inquiries," the sheriff offered, "but I can tell you there's no real dirt on the Counsels. Any legitimate misdeeds would've already crossed my desk. For that matter"—the sheriff nodded his head toward the administrative building—"Dorothea, the town clerk, knows everything about everyone. Better yet, she likes to show off she knows everything about everyone. You want to know more about the mayor and his wife, she's the one to ask."

D.D. perked up. "Meaning we can kill two birds with one stone."

"We were due for a break sooner or later."

THE NICHE TOWN OFFICE WAS small, looking more like a white double-wide to D.D. than a traditional government building, but then the town was so tiny maybe this was all it needed.

They walked into the middle of the squat space. To the right was a large open area with chairs lined up against the wall. For town meetings, D.D. would guess. To her left was a raised counter, marking the clerk's office. An older woman with silver-framed glasses on a long glittering lanyard stood up from her computer to greet them. She wore a pink turtleneck, though D.D. would've thought it too warm for such things.

"Dorothea." The sheriff reached out a hand.

The older woman batted her heavily mascaraed eyes. She had a mass of platinum blond hair arranged in a French twist, and the too-thin build of a woman who'd spent her entire life denying herself dessert for the sake of her girlish figure.

D.D. held out a hand. She didn't get the same lingering look as the sheriff, but Dorothea was polite enough.

"Sure you heard about the excitement yesterday," the sheriff began. He'd taken off his hat as soon as they walked through the door. Now, he turned it in his hands. D.D. was starting to recognize his routine: The sheriff liked to approach his constituents with folksy charm. Hat in hand, literally, just one of the neighbors, asking a few questions.

As Dorothea nodded, D.D. decided the sheriff might be onto something. You attract more flies with honey than vinegar, as the saying went.

She'd never been particularly good at that approach, given her own blunt, take-no-prisoners style. She smiled now, forced herself to slow down, make eye contact.

Dorothea appeared momentarily uneasy, so maybe D.D.'s expression wasn't quite as neutral as she hoped. Probably, even things like smiling took practice.

"We're interested in some property records," the sheriff said.

"Well now, Sheriff, of course I want to help. You know I do. But I have a responsibility to this town and the privacy of its citizens."

"Tax rolls are public domain, Dorothea. Nothing to worry about. We just need to dot some i's, cross some t's. This is gonna be a very big investigation and we want to put our best foot forward. Show these Yankees"—he grinned, elbowed D.D.—"we know what we're doing."

So that's how it was going to be. Dorothea beamed at the sheriff. D.D. stopped with the smiling, returned to her more traditional role as bad cop. Or as the case might be, stern Northern cop.

"Which property records, Sheriff?"

"Well, that's the thing. We don't exactly know. I'm guessing we're going to need you to do some fancy database searching. Not that I imagine that's any problem for you."

Indeed, Dorothea had already returned to her computer, hands hovering over the keyboard.

"We want to go back . . . I'm gonna say, fifteen years." The sheriff nodded, as if that number sounded good enough. "Let's say homesteads that include at least an acre."

Dorothea gave him a look. D.D. was guessing, given the rural location, at least an acre was pretty common for property around here.

"Now, this is the trick—we're curious about property that's changed hands. Maybe the owner died, something like that."

Nodding. Fingers flying across the keyboard now.

"How many is that?" the sheriff asked after a minute.

"I have two dozen."

"Any properties showing a cabin deep in the woods? Or removed from its neighbor?"

Dorothea frowned at the sheriff, then consulted her list. "Ten or so."

"I'll tell you what, just download them all. That'll be good."

The sheriff glanced at D.D. She added: "What about any proper ties that have been foreclosed on? Regardless of lot size, location."

"That gives us four or five more."

"We'll take those addresses, as well."

Dorothea nodded. Hit a button. The printer fired to life.

"I heard you found bodies," Dorothea whispered at last, looking at the sheriff and placing extra emphasis on the s at the end of the word.

"Skeletal remains," the sheriff confirmed soberly. "Nothing for immediate worry. But violent crime is violent crime. We'll be getting to the bottom of this."

"Young girls? Many of them?"

"We're still conducting our investigation."

"Does that ring any bells for you, Dorothea?" D.D. asked, because she saw a gleam in the woman's eyes. The town gossip. Of course she wanted to be in the know. "Are there many girls that pass through here?"

Dorothea hesitated, glancing at the sheriff. He nodded slightly, as if granting permission to speak to the outsider. Dorothea turned to D.D. "During the summer season, this place is crawling with new faces, including plenty of girls suited for waitressing, hospitality, and the like. But come winter, business drops way off. Most businesses cut down, the kids head back to school. Winter, we're a sleepy town in a lot of ways. Without the hikers . . ." She shrugged.

"True," the sheriff agreed. He took the stack of property records from Dorothea and thumbed through them, as if already bored.

"It's a beautiful main street," D.D. commented. "I especially love the Mountain Laurel B and B run by the mayor and his wife. What a gorgeous Victorian."

"One of the true prized jewels of the town!" Dorothea warmed immediately. "That property was originally built in eighteen-thirty as a summer home for a rich Atlanta family. They had four daughters. One, Martha Counsel's great-great grandmother, married locally and stayed on. That house has been in the family for generations!"

D.D. nodded. So the hotel belonged to the missus, not the mister. Interesting. "I just met the mayor and his wife. Such a shame about their niece."

"Oh, they take good care of her. Poor thing. To have been in a terrible accident. Girl was left simple, you know."

"What's her name again?" D.D. asked.

Dorothea blinked. "Why, I don't recall. She's very quiet and it's not like you see her out and about."

"She's not allowed out?"

"I didn't say that!" Dorothea frowned at D.D., clearly not liking her attitude. "Girl can't talk. That's not exactly who you send to run errands."

"Of course," D.D. conceded. "She reminds me of someone I once knew, that's all. And you're right, such a tragedy. When was the accident anyway?"

"Ten years ago, maybe?"

"The girl's been living with the Counsels that long?"

"Well, when I first met her she was an itty-bitty thing. And Lord, the scar back then. Seemed to be half the poor girl's head." Dorothea eyed D.D. reproachfully. "They've done right by her."

"Family protects family," D.D. agreed.

"The Counsels take care of this whole town, always have. You're here for the fall. That's a good season for us. Lots of hikers, tourists, people eager to spend money. But December, January, February? Those are lean months. Not all families have the resources to make it through. The Counsels keep eyes and ears out, they don't boast, but if they hear about anyone who needs a little extra help . . . Let's just say, grocery bills have been known to be magically paid. Property taxes caught up. Even medical bills cleared. Around here, neighbors look out for neighbors. And Howard and Martha are good neighbors."

"You ever meet Martha's sister? The one who died in the accident."

"Oh, Martha doesn't have a sister."

D.D. paused. "I thought the girl was her niece?"

"Well, that's what she says. Martha was an only child. She means the girl's mother was like a sister to her. Or don't you have such things up North?" Dorothea smiled thinly.

One point to the older woman with the glittery lanyard, D.D. thought. Though it would explain the girl's obviously Hispanic heritage, while Martha looked about as white bread as they came.

"Do the Counsels have children of their own?"

"No." Dorothea's voice dropped. "Though I know they tried very hard in the early days of their marriage. They just weren't so blessed."

"How sad for them. And how fortunate they were willing to take in an orphaned child."

Dorothea beamed again, clearly pleased that D.D. was finally recognizing the Counsels' sainthood.

"Are there other full-time staff at their B and B?" D.D. asked. "Just out of curiosity."

"A cook. An assistant. You would have to ask them more."

The sheriff cleared his throat. D.D. got the hint.

"Thank you so much for your help. And the property records," D.D. said.

While the sheriff added, "A pleasure as always, Dorothea."

"You're going to figure this out, right, Sheriff? It breaks my heart to think of some poor souls buried in our own backyard."

"We're on this, Dorothea," the sheriff assured her. "We'll find the answers, get these girls some justice."

"If you need any other help . . ."

"Of course."

Dorothea turned to D.D. more sternly. "We're a good community," she said, as if daring D.D. to deny it. D.D. merely smiled, and starting to understand the rules of engagement, went for a point of her own.

"Of course. But bad things can happen everywhere. And the woods around here clearly aren't as safe as they look."

CHAPTER 19

KIMBERLY

TASKFORCES MUST BE FED. WHICH made Kimberly incredibly grateful to Franny, Sheriff Smithers's receptionist, checklist operator, and all-round extremely tall den mother. By the time Kimberly and her crew had trudged back down the mountain, it was already nearly eight P.M. Kimberly took a much-needed shower, then headed straight to the Mosley County Sheriff's Department for the evening debriefing, where she discovered her fellow investigators already camped out in the conference room enjoying what appeared to be an entire buffet of homemade casseroles.

"From the ladies of the First Congregational Church," Franny said, appearing at Kimberly's elbow. "They know how hard you people are working and wanted to show their appreciation. You must try the chocolate trifle. Patty makes it every year for the fall cook-off. It's the best."

Sure enough, across the room D.D. was standing over a giant glass bowl containing what appeared to be layers of chocolate pudding and whipped cream. The detective was licking a spoon, and wearing an expression that probably shouldn't be viewed outside of a bedroom.

"Is there lasagna?" Kimberly asked. "I smell lasagna." She'd been on her feet for fourteen hours and hiked up and down a mountain half a dozen times. If there was pasta in this room, she'd earned it.

"Third tray from the right. And don't worry, we have more where that came from."

Franny bustled off to shift more platters, distribute more plates. Kimberly decided this was already the best taskforce meeting she'd ever attended. Which was good, because they had a lot of ground to cover.

She ate. Shamelessly. Then went straight for the trifle, even though D.D. glared at her and made a sound suspiciously like a growl.

"Call dibs on the bowl," the Boston detective said.

"Rock-paper-scissors."

A fresh glare from D.D.

"Not gonna help you," Kimberly informed her. "I have two daughters who practice that look on a daily basis. Besides, I spent the day exhuming skeletons. You?"

"Fine. I get the brownie platter."

"Deal."

"Why isn't Flora eating?" Kimberly asked presently, leaning against the wall beside D.D., savoring the trifle. There were little chocolate chips. And toffee. Heath bar crunch maybe? "Or is that a symptom of PTSD?"

"She ate all day."

"She ate all day?"

"We'll get to it. Your day?"

"We'll get to it." After one more scoop of trifle, Kimberly decided.

"Where are your ERT people?" D.D. asked.

"They stayed at the hotel; they're beat and have to be back at the site at oh dark thirty tomorrow morning. But I have the report on what we found."

"Dr. Jackson?"

"Same deal. She's jonesing for her lab, not a meeting where all she can say is 'wait for my report.' We have at least one more day of field work, then the team and Dr. Jackson will return to Atlanta. In the meantime, we have discoveries to discuss."

"I have a new lead," D.D. said. "She's underaged, can't speak, read, or write, and apparently suffers brain damage from a childhood injury. But I have a feeling about her."

Kimberly arched a brow.

"After the meeting," D.D. murmured. The detective had her gaze on Sheriff Smithers, sitting across the room and apparently devouring taco salad. "This town, the locals . . . I have some concerns."

"You mean you're not falling for Main Street's quaint charms?"

"Not after learning what's buried in the mountains."

Kimberly couldn't argue with that. She cleared her throat, indicating it was time to get started. And just like that, the room fell to order.

Kimberly took up position front and center. "All right. First off, a big round of applause to the ladies of the Congregational Church for this amazing dinner. A huge step up from a taskforce's general diet of pizza, pizza, and pizza."

Everyone clapped enthusiastically. Clearing platters, Franny paused, blushed, fidgeted with the delicate gold cross she wore around her neck.

"Now then, we have several efforts to catch up on. I'll go first with the report from the second burial site."

Kimberly waited a heartbeat. Investigators hastily shoved aside plates, booted up laptops and tablets.

"The second grave revealed three more sets of skeletal remains.

Dr. Jackson was able to confirm all three are female. At least two are teenagers and one prepubescent."

"How young?" D.D. spoke up, her tone expressionless.

"Nine or ten."

Silence.

"No clothing was recovered from the grave," Kimberly continued evenly. "Though we had a few unexpected finds, including a short piece of plastic tubing, a strip of adhesive tape, and a pair of latex gloves."

Keith's hand fired into the air, and Kimberly nodded for him to speak.

"You're going to test the gloves for prints? And the inside? As well as touch DNA?"

Look who'd once more spent some quality time with Google, Kimberly thought. "All evidence will be subject to a complete forensic exam. For immediate consideration, Dr. Jackson is theorizing that one of the bodies may have had IV tubing taped to the back of her hand at the time of burial."

"But that would mean the person had received medical attention," Flora said slowly.

"It's possible."

"Jacob wasn't averse to needles, but medical assistance? I was lucky if he tossed a couple of aspirin my way."

"The presence of an IV seems outside of Jacob Ness's purview," Kimberly agreed. "Still, evidence is evidence. The tape may yield DNA, something to help identify victim or perpetrator. In the meantime, Dr. Jackson will conduct a full analysis on each set of remains. She knows we need answers soon."

"Does the doc think the second burial site is from the same time frame as the first?" Sheriff Smithers asked.

"In her own words, that's not an unreasonable conclusion, but will require additional testing."

"The first skeleton," Sheriff Smithers continued now, "Lilah Abenito."

Kimberly nodded.

"She wasn't from around here. She went missing from Alabama. Meaning these other girls, they might be from elsewhere, too. Makes sense, if you think about it. Four local girls going missing all at the same time would call attention. But if they're from different places . . ."

"We're going to need to pull missing persons records for teenage girls, nationwide, going back fifteen years, maybe even twenty."

"That's gonna be a lot of names."

"We have some work ahead of us, no doubt."

"COD?" D.D. spoke up.

"Nothing obvious. Again, Dr. Jackson hopes to learn more back at the lab."

"Asphyxiation," Keith murmured.

"Highly possible. We did get one break. This newest grave yielded several seed pods that were most likely interred with the bodies. Based on a preliminary analysis"—Thank you, Harold, thought Kimberly—"we assume the bodies were buried early spring. So that at least gives us a start on a more exact timeline."

"Except we don't know which year," Keith spoke up.

"We're starting fifteen years ago, working around that. Now tell us about your efforts today," Kimberly addressed Keith and Flora.

"I ate," Flora said.

"So I heard."

The entire taskforce regarded Flora curiously. The woman cleared her throat, sat up straighter. She appeared defensive, but maybe that's the best a survivor could do, surrounded by a room of professional law enforcement types.

"Jacob liked food. Lots of food." Flora looked around the room, at the empty aluminum casserole pans. It was hard for Kimberly not to feel guilty. "Sergeant Warren recommended I try out some of the local establishments, see if any of the food tasted familiar. But, um, I just don't know. It was too long ago. I don't remember enough." The woman sat back abruptly. Kimberly had a feeling there was more to it than that. She waited, but Flora didn't speak again.

"You and Keith did make one major discovery for the day." Kimberly nodded at Keith to do the honors.

"We worked on the logistical issue of getting four bodies up a mountainside, while also having to consider carrying an assortment of tools for digging a grave," Keith rattled off. "It seemed to us, having already hiked up and down to the grave site a couple of times—"

Around the room, people nodded.

"—that wasn't the most feasible way of accessing the area. And certainly not something one of our suspects, Jacob Ness, would even attempt."

More nodding.

"Upon further investigation, an ATV seemed the most likely mode of transportation. So we approached a local dealer, established there is at least one trail running just above the grave sites that would yield easier access, and then, well, we rented a four-wheeler. Sure enough, we arrived at the second burial site pretty quickly."

"You nearly ran over the second burial site," Kimberly corrected.

Neither Keith nor Flora said a word.

"Which did prove your theory," she grudgingly allowed. "And I appreciate your thinking. Hiking up bodies, tools, and now if we consider one of the victims may have been sick and/or incapacitated enough to require an IV . . . an ATV does make more sense as a mode of transportation."

"We also learned many of the locals own ATVs and even groom their own private trails," Keith said. He looked at Sheriff Smithers. "So it may be our perpetrator didn't even come from the main road, but accessed the byway from a path on their own property."

"Four-wheeling *is* popular around these parts," the sheriff considered. "I can have one of my deputies check it."

"Which brings us to your day," Kimberly transitioned, turning focus to the sheriff and D.D.

"We interviewed local leaders and the town clerk," the sheriff reported. "Reached out to local hotels on generating whatever reports they could on guests going back fifteen years. Timeline is an issue. The biggest property in Niche, the Mountain Laurel B and B, which is run by the mayor and his wife—they got a new computer system ten years ago, so they can't even tell you who was around before then."

"Shrimp," Kimberly murmured, remembering the sheriff's discreet oath from their first meeting.

"Exactly. Um . . ." The sheriff cleared his throat. "We got one name to chase, Walt Davies. Apparently an antisocial type. Lives alone in the woods and prefers it that way. Possibly brews his own moonshine and/or grows his own dope. Which will add to the tensions if a bunch of uniforms suddenly show up on his property."

"Moonshine and weed?" Flora spoke up.

The sheriff nodded. Flora sat back, eyes narrowed in thought. The sheriff cleared his throat, continued on: "I'll assign a couple of my boys to pay him a visit tomorrow. Local deputies, which hopefully will appear less threatening than, say, the feds. Either way, sounds like we should approach with caution."

"You want to call in reinforcements? SWAT?" Kimberly asked evenly.

"Nah. I'm afraid showing up with the cavalry will start a war. I think we should try out some local charm first. Proceed from there. We got a list of other properties from the town clerk that fit our parameters as possible cabins Ness could've holed up in eight years ago. We should assign a couple pairs of investigators to check each location in person. Don't know if you want to be part of that?" The sheriff looked at Flora.

"I wasn't outside, so looking at exteriors, I won't be any help. But the basement . . . I might be able to recognize the basement. Especially the brown carpet. I spent a lot of time studying that carpet."

"How many properties?" Kimberly asked.

"Eighteen."

She nodded. "Okay, send out pairs first. If there are some that are particularly promising—say, set back enough from neighbors and have a basement with brown carpet—Flora can review the finalists."

"I think we have to look harder at the locals," D.D. spoke up.

Kimberly gestured for the detective to continue.

"When we spoke to the town clerk, Dorothea, she mentioned business around here is seasonal. Spring and summer is super busy with hikers—meaning sure, someone like Jacob or another predator could appear or disappear without anyone taking note. Now, you're saying you believe at least one of the graves is from the spring. Combining that with the ATV info"—D.D. nodded toward Keith and Flora—"I think that smacks of local knowledge. Who would know where to bury the bodies when the trails are crawling with thru hikers? How to access that area with maximum privacy? And have access to an ATV that doesn't draw any notice?"

"You don't think it's Jacob?" Flora spoke up quietly.

D.D. shrugged. "I haven't ruled him out. But four bodies, three in one site . . . This is different. This isn't lone-predator activity—at least not any kind of lone predator I've ever heard about."

Keith nodded vigorously.

"I think we're back to our first theory," D.D. continued. "Murder as a team sport."

"Why the IV?" Kimberly pushed.

"I have no idea."

"Where's the closest hospital?" Kimberly asked the sheriff.

"There's a couple," Sheriff Smithers offered. "Nothing too close, though."

"I wouldn't go straight to hospitals," D.D. volunteered. "I'd start with people with medical backgrounds. Nurses, EMTs, a retired doctor, even a vet. An IV isn't that difficult, right?" She turned to the sheriff. "Is that something Dorothea could help us with, being the town busybody and all?"

Sheriff Smithers nodded. "I could ask her."

"Where do you get an IV?" Keith asked.

"Medical supply company," said Kimberly. "Online retailer. I asked Dr. Jackson. Tubing, cannula, medical tape, those items are easy to come by."

"Especially around here," the sheriff added. "In the mountains we always have some survivalist types, and they keep a fair amount of medical supplies on hand. You know, for the coming plague and all."

More nodding from around the room.

"All right," Kimberly said. "This is the plan. Tomorrow, teams of two visit our list of properties. Sheriff, you're in charge of those efforts."

He nodded.

"Sergeant Warren—"

"I'll continue interviewing locals," D.D. immediately spoke up. She gave Kimberly a measured look, and belatedly Kimberly got it. The girl—whomever it was D.D. had met today, she planned on going back. Kimberly didn't get it, but she trusted D.D.'s instincts.

"Okay. We need to start running the lists of hotel guests, such as they are."

As expected, her fellow agents nodded. Crunching massive amounts of data was any FBI agent's bread and butter, and exactly who Kimberly would want to do the job.

"And, um . . ." She turned to Keith and Flora, then realized she really didn't know what they should be doing. "Eat more?" she suggested.

"No, thank you," Flora said.

"I think we should walk around," Keith said. "Visit stores, other establishments. Team sport, right?" Keith glanced at D.D. "Let's see if anyone recognizes Flora. Or if her appearance . . ."

"Spooks anyone?" D.D. filled in, with a pointed look at Keith.

"Exactly."

Kimberly shrugged. They were civilians, so she could hardly give them official tasks. "Scare away," she ordered.

Then hoped the words didn't come back to haunt them.

CHAPTER 20

H E'S BACK.

I don't need to see him to know the Bad Man has arrived. The house tells me. It holds its breath, hunkering down in the growing dark, already fearing the worst.

I sit on the mat in my tiny room, knees tucked against my chest, arms wrapped tight around my legs. I stare at the door, wearing my old summertime uniform that leaves my scarred forearm completely exposed.

The most beautiful thing about me, he had said, as he'd cut the intricate pattern into my skin.

I wonder if tonight I'm the one he'll come for. Because when the Bad Man visits, someone must pay the price.

I think of the blond police lady who came by this morning. She talked to me. She wanted to know if I was safe. She even held out her bright, shiny cell phone, as if to help. I know phones. I see other people use them. Even young children, their fingers flying across the surface, picking and arranging boxes of squiggly lines that hold meaning to everyone but me.

I don't understand the shapes. Small kids do. But not me.

Footsteps. Heavy thuds from down the cold, stone-tiled hall. Moving fast, with purpose.

I pull my legs in tighter.

The blond lady said I didn't have to stay. But she doesn't understand and I don't have enough fingers to tell her everything. She and the kind-eyed sheriff are looking for some man who apparently has already come and gone. I vaguely recognized his mean look, or maybe I've just seen too many men like him. With expressions that promise pain.

The man in the photo they showed is a bad man. But he is not the Bad Man.

I don't know how to tell the pretty blond police lady that, any more than I know how to move my lips and work my throat to share the full horror of this place or list the other girls who are long gone but still need me to deliver their names back to their families.

I have a duty. Like my mother. Run, she tried to warn me. I ignored her. But still, she tried. She was strong and brave. She stood up to the Bad Man. Performed some small act of rebellion that brought him to our home that final night. I've spent years wondering about it. It used to make me angry—why couldn't she have done nothing, just continued with our little lives in our little house?

But now, with my own time winding down, realizing more and more that I will never leave this place, I understand her need to make some kind of stand. To feel, for one moment, like someone who mattered. Because the Bad Man loves to make us less. To dance his blade across our skin until we scream. Then he smiles, and admires his handiwork. And leaves even me whimpering, as I clutch at my ravaged arm.

My mother had a patchwork quilt of lines across her back. As a child, I would trace them with my finger. She never said a word. Now, of course, I wonder.

Thump. Thump. Thump. The footsteps, much closer now.

The house holds its breath.

He's here. Standing on the other side of my door. His hand closing on the knob. One twist. The door will open. One step. He will loom before me, blade by his side, smile on his face.

Just like that, it will be my turn.

I should offer him dinner, I think wildly. Fix him a plate. Will he remember my mother? Recall that night? Or are we all alike to him? Just girls, disposable in the end?

I have to bear the pain, I remind myself. I will close my eyes, fist my hands, scream if I must. And then . . . it'll be done. I'll be gone. And my soul—will it be the color purple like Stacey's, or silver like my mother's? It will rise up, bring me to my mami and we'll be a pack of two, again. Mamita and chiquita. Because I belong to her, and she belongs to me, and not even the Bad Man can keep us apart forever. I have to believe that.

I stare at the door.

Bear the pain.

Bear the pain.

Bear the . . .

Thud. Thud. Thud.

Footsteps. Starting up again.

The man, moving on, away from my door, farther down the hall.

I stop rocking. Hold perfectly still. If not me, then who?

I think of my mother again.

I know what I have to do next.

I CAN'T TALK OR TELL stories or whisper to some well-meaning police lady the full truths of this house. But I can slide slowly down the basement hall, quiet as a ghost, dragging my weak leg behind me. I am nothing, I tell myself. Just a small voiceless girl. And just like that, I vanish.

This time of night, the guests sleep obliviously on the floors above. I used to wonder at their blank, smiling faces in the morning. But all these years later, I understand. No one sees what they don't want to see. And no one (except the blond lady?) has ever wanted to see girls like me.

I pass by closed doors. Some may have occupants, huddled in corners, biting their lips against their building terror. There is at least another maid down here, Hélène, who often works with me. There are other girls, however, that come and go. I don't know anything about them, don't even know if any of them are here now.

The Bad Man disappears around the corner. I move faster, the stone floor cold against my bare feet. My worn uniform is too thin for these tunnels, which are dimly lit and carved deep into the earth. This is the part of the house guests never visit. It is the realm of Bad Things and Bad People.

Monsters are real and they live in the bowels of the earth, where the darkness feeds their appetites and breeds their rages. But I don't know how many fingers to hold up to tell the blond police woman that, so I do this instead.

A pair of heavy wooden doors looms ahead. Old and solid. Like this house, these mountains. I have been in this room before. I know it smells of candle wax and blood. I know it's the house's very core and the house itself wishes it didn't exist. The day the Bad Man carved up my forearm, then left me curled in a pool of my own urine, I dreamt of pulling burning logs from the monstrous stone fireplace inside this room, then flinging them around this space.

The house would applaud, I think. It would smile as its walls caught flame. It would whisper "thank you" as it collapsed on itself and became no more.

But this room is fashioned from more stone than wood. The house might go. This awful centerpiece will never burn.

The Bad Man disappears through the partially opened doors. I place my hand against the wall beside me. I will my body to disappear into the shadows. And because the house is my friend, I can feel it wrap itself around me, offer what protection it can.

I hold very still, then hear the Bad Man's voice.

"What the hell do you mean by this?"

The answering voice trembles, then finds itself. Mayor Howard. The master of the house. Of course, the Bad Man knows differently.

"The sheriff came by today. Some Boston detective, too. They're asking questions—"

"Let them."

"It's not safe." A woman's voice now. Mistress of the house. Except once again, the Bad Man knows differently.

"Did they ask to search this place?"

"Of course not. They have no reason—"

"Exactly."

"But they're showing pictures." The master again. "Jacob Ness, his rig. Rumors are his last victim is here, too, Flora Dane."

"Ness is dead."

"People may still remember—"

"Then they can rat out a dead man. Who cares?"

"The police are everywhere." The mistress, her voice shrill. "Federal agents, local officers. We've been talking to others—"

"Excuse me?"

The mistress falters. "I'm just suggesting . . . The police have discovered at least two of the graves. They're pulling records, conducting interviews, even learning the trails. We need to stop, think—"

"Shut. Up. You do not think. You do not consult others. Need I remind you exactly how this works?"

"Please." The master's voice, lower, placating. "Just consider.

This has been a good arrangement. For you, for us, for everyone. It's all been extremely fortuitous—"

"Profitable."

"Surely it doesn't hurt to take a small break. Just till the risk lessens."

Silence. The Bad Man thinking? The Bad Man considering?

"When will the police attention lessen?" he asks at last. There's a tone to his voice, a silky smoothness that suddenly makes the hair stand up at the nape of my neck. I have heard that note before, in another room far, far away from here. "As you say, the town is crawling with investigators. They've found bodies. They're not just going to go away."

"We could give them what's left of the cabin." The mistress, less shrill, more tentative.

"No."

"But you said . . . rat out the dead man."

"It won't work."

"Why not?"

"Because she's here. And if she sees, she might remember. Then it won't be about one dead man."

"I mentioned Walt Davies." The master again. "You know how he is. Shoots first, questions later. With any luck, they'll fill him with lead, then we can lay all of this at his feet."

"You idiot. Then there will be even more police in the area."

"If we could just take a break." The mistress pleading. "Even for a couple of weeks. Until the immediate attention dies down."

"It doesn't work like that. You know it doesn't. But I think you're correct." A small rustling sound. The Bad Man shifting around the room. "The best way to get the police to leave is to provide them with the answer they seek."

"No." The voice is so soft this time, I'm not sure who's spoken. A noise. I can't place it. Then again: "No. Please no."

"They're looking for a monster," the Bad Man murmurs. "Yes, absolutely. Let's give them one."

Fresh goose bumps. I'm in my mother's kitchen. I'm in the basement hall. I'm a little girl. I'm a voiceless servant.

I am frozen in terror over what is going to happen next.

"No, no—"

"Shhh . . ."

"NO!"

A gurgle. A sob. A scrabbling sound, like claws against stone. The house shifts uncomfortably around me. I can almost hear its mournful sigh, as I step out of the shadows and force myself toward the heavy wooden doors. As I peer through the cracked opening, into the room.

The Bad Man stands tall, a terrible, hulking form.

The master cowers at his feet.

The mistress, on the other hand . . .

The Bad Man has moved behind her. He holds a bloodred rope in his hand. A sash, I realize, from the mistress's embroidered silk bathrobe. He has the tie wrapped tight around her neck, lifting up, up, up, her neck at an impossible angle.

I stare at her. I watch as her face goes purple. As she twitches and shakes and trembles, the incredible strength of the Bad Man lifting her all the way off the floor. He is not human. No one who can do that can be human.

I don't look away. I force myself to bear witness as she finally gasps. Her head sags forward. The monster releases her, and just like that her body crumples to the floor.

The master is still hunkered low, crying pitifully.

I feel a curious sense of relief. That she is gone, that the Bad Man has finally turned on one of his own. Yet I'm shivering uncontrollably.

The mistress, the almighty mistress, is dead. And the Bad Man killed her as easily as snapping a twig.

"*Get up,*" *the Bad Man orders the master.*

Will he kill the master next? Good God, what will become of the rest of us, if there's only the Bad Man left?

I back away then. Turn and flee awkwardly toward my room, gulping for breath. But it's not air I need. It's words. Words and letters and sounds. Something, anything to communicate, because the police lady will be coming again, and this time . . .

I need to think. I need to plan.

The end is coming, but not like I thought it would.

Run. I hear my mother's voice.

I want to be a little girl again. I want to hold out my arms and have my mother scoop me up and hold me close. I want to hear her voice murmur my name. I want to be our pack of two, mamita and chiquita.

I want things I can never have.

Because the Bad Man took them from me.

I duck inside my room just in time to hear the heavy wooden doors groan open, then footsteps once more hit the hall. The Bad Man. Not even a break in his stride as he passes my room, heads upstairs.

The house shudders into silence.

I remain leaning against the wall of my tiny room, breathing hard. One finger for yes. Two for no. Three for maybe. And four fingers? Five?

There must be a way to communicate. There has to be a way to confess all to the blond detective who offered help. I must find it.

Because the end is coming. And name or no name, voice or no voice, I'm going to make the Bad Man pay.

Or die trying.

CHAPTER 21

D.D.

D.D. RETIRED TO HER HOTEL room to spend the rest of the evening researching brain injuries and speech impairment. She felt she'd barely fallen asleep when her phone rang.

"Wake up," Kimberly announced.

"Huh?"

"Sheriff just called me. We got another body."

"*What?*"

"The mayor's wife. You interviewed her yesterday morning, right?"

"What time is it?"

"Just after four."

"In the *morning?*"

"Meet you in the lobby in fifteen. There's no way Martha Counsel's death isn't related to our investigation. Grab coffee. Get hopping. We have a long day ahead."

THE SHERIFF WAS ALREADY WAITING out front when Kimberly and D.D. pulled up to the Mountain Laurel B&B. His uniform was wrinkled and

D.D. would bet he'd once again spent the night in his office. He nodded somberly in greeting, then led them up the front steps.

"According to the mayor, he woke up shortly around three to an empty bed. He went looking for his wife. He called nine-one-one the moment he found her. Dispatch contacted me directly. I arrived first, secured the scene. No one has touched anything."

The lobby was ablaze with lights as they entered. They were at least a good hour from sunrise, D.D. thought, and the inn still held the hush of middle of the night. She looked around automatically for the mayor's "niece," but didn't see any sign of the girl anywhere.

Mayor Howard was sitting in the green and yellow sunroom, staring at the table blankly. He wore a white, monogrammed bathrobe and appeared to have aged a hundred years. Red-rimmed eyes, haggard expression. If he was acting, D.D. thought, then he was one of the best she'd ever seen.

As she watched, he went to take a sip of coffee. The delicate porcelain cup shook so badly, he spilled half the contents before setting it down again.

"Down the hall, third room on the right," the sheriff instructed Kimberly and D.D. "I'll stay with him."

D.D. and Kimberly swapped glances, then followed his instructions. D.D. still didn't understand what they were going to discover, but it clearly wasn't good.

Third door on the right turned out to be the end of the hall. In the mental map D.D. was creating in her head, this room occupied the back, right corner of the historic home. Perhaps the former master bedroom, she thought, as they walked into the sweeping space.

A massive canopy bed occupied the middle of the room. And there, dangling from the top of the wooden frame, hung Martha Counsel, clad in a long white nightgown and open red silk bathrobe, her body swaying slightly from some unfelt breeze.

Neither Kimberly nor D.D. spoke a word. They entered the room. Walked around the bed.

The method of hanging appeared to be a red silk sash, probably the tie from the woman's bathrobe. Judging by appearance, Martha had fashioned the noose around her neck, attached the other end to the wooden canopy frame, then climbed onto the king-sized bed and . . . What? Stepped off?

Had she clutched at the silk as it pulled taut? Struggled to regain a toehold on the bed to ease the strain?

D.D. moved close enough to study the woman's hands without touching. She didn't see a mark on them. Same with the elaborately made-up bed. The green embroidered comforter appeared perfectly smooth.

As if Martha hadn't suffered any doubts or second thoughts. She'd simply gotten up in the middle of the night, left her husband's side, and come here to do what she felt must be done. But why?

"There's a note," Kimberly murmured. She nodded toward the bedside table. D.D. crossed to where she stood.

"'Forgive me the harm I did,'" D.D. read out loud. "'I was selfish to live at another's expense. God have mercy on my soul.'"

D.D. glanced at Kimberly. "Who types a suicide note?"

"Someone with bad penmanship?" Kimberly shrugged. "Or too emotional to write?"

"I don't like it."

"I'm not exactly thrilled either. Which is why we'll be having the medical examiner conduct a full inquest."

D.D. looked around the room. "No sign of a struggle," she murmured. "And not a mark on the body. I mean, silk noose aside."

"And the inn's guests are still asleep in their rooms. Which would seem to indicate no loud arguments or violent disturbances."

"Look at her neck," D.D. said, indicating toward the body. "You can see some bruising along the edges of the bathrobe tie, consistent with hanging."

Kimberly nodded; she looked as conflicted as D.D.

A suicide felt too neat and tidy. And yet, a cursory exam of both the room and the body didn't reveal anything obvious to counter the notion. Sometimes the simplest explanation was the right explanation. Detectives just didn't like it.

"You ever walk in on a hanging where a loved one didn't try to cut down the body?" Kimberly asked now.

"No. First instinct is always to get the person down. Then again . . ." D.D. indicated to Martha Counsel's bloated purple face. "She's clearly past saving."

Kimberly nodded, pursed her lips, walked around the room again. "I don't like it. But I have no good reason not to like it."

"Agreed."

"I wonder what she meant about being wrong to live at another's expense." D.D. shrugged.

"One way to find out. Come on, let's deal with the husband." Kimberly led the way back down the hall to the sunroom.

D.D. thought she caught a flash of movement. A person, disappearing down the hall, but it was too fleeting to be sure. She wondered again about Martha's niece.

Was the mayor really the kind of guy to brew his own cup of coffee? Somehow, she doubted it.

Howard was still sitting at the table. The sheriff was positioned across from him. Neither man was talking.

"Is there someone we can call for you?" Kimberly asked, her voice surprisingly gentle considering her skeptical tone earlier.

The mayor looked up blearily. "She was my world," he said.

D.D. walked behind him, brushing his shoulder. She thought she caught a whiff of whiskey, but couldn't be sure. "Fresh coffee?" she asked.

He had to turn the other way to answer her, which gave Kimberly the chance to lean closer for her own inspection. Divide and conquer. Policing 101.

"I'm fine, thank you," the mayor said. His voice sounded hollow, a faint shadow of the sure figure he'd been just the day before.

"More people will be arriving," D.D. said calmly. "Officers, evidence techs, the coroner. It's only a matter of time before your guests wake up and start asking questions, as well."

"Evidence techs?" Howard echoed.

"Perhaps I could fetch your niece to help. Which room . . ."

The mayor finally roused himself. "No need. I just . . . there's a button. Push the button." He got up abruptly, crossed to the far wall, where D.D. now noticed a swinging door that probably led to the kitchen. There appeared to be a panel beside it, for summoning the hired help. The mayor pushed a black button. Then without saying another word, or awaiting a response, he returned to the table.

"Do you believe your wife killed herself?" Kimberly asked softly.

"She hasn't . . . she hasn't been herself. Not since." The mayor swallowed heavily. He picked up his coffee cup. Once again, his hand trembled so violently he had to set it back down. "Not since the discovery, a month ago," he whispered.

"The discovery of the first grave?" Kimberly clarified.

"Yes."

"How was Martha not herself?" the sheriff prodded softly.

"She seemed distracted. Upset. And at night . . . she used to have a single glass of sherry. But lately . . . I knew something was bothering her. I tried to ask. I did!" The mayor glanced up abruptly, his eyes wild. "But she wouldn't talk to me. She wouldn't!"

The connecting door at the other end of the room suddenly swung open. The girl appeared, wearing her blue maid's uniform and bearing a silver coffeepot. Her eyes fell immediately on D.D. She paused infinitesimally, then recovered herself, moving forward as if nothing was amiss. She dragged her right leg slightly, and her face appeared as pale and bruised as the mayor's. Had she seen the body? Did she know what her "aunt" had supposedly done?

Or was she once again just the hired help? Summoned to serve and knowing better than to question it?

Now, she wordlessly topped off the mayor's coffee cup, while studiously avoiding D.D.'s gaze. She set the pot in the middle of the table, then turned back toward the kitchen.

"Poor thing," the mayor said, looking right at D.D. "First her mother, and now this."

"We'll want to question everyone who was present this evening," D.D. started, before the mayor's harsh laugh interrupted.

"Ask her questions? She can't answer. How cruel can you be? Besides, she doesn't know anything. When I first found the body . . . I started screaming. She came. Cook, too. They may be staff, but we are also family. We all need time to grieve."

With the mayor's attention fully on her, D.D. had no choice but to nod. She would love to force the issue, follow the girl directly into the kitchen and play their one-finger-for-yes, two-fingers-for-no game. But the truth was, the girl was a minor and her uncle ostensibly her legal guardian. D.D. had no grounds to pursue the matter without Mayor Howard's explicit permission.

The girl disappeared through the swinging door. She'd had her left hand down by her side, but D.D. couldn't tell if she was holding out any fingers or not. With all eyes watching, D.D. forced herself to focus once more on Mayor Howard.

"Why do you think your wife was off?"

The mayor didn't answer right away, staring instead at the fresh steam rising up from his coffee cup. "Martha was born with only one kidney," he said presently, his voice rough. "Twenty years ago, that kidney started to fail. Martha went on the transplant list, but you know how it is. So many who need organs, so few that are available."

Across from the mayor, the sheriff nodded encouragement.

"We looked . . ." The mayor cleared his throat, glanced up. "We looked at foreign options. Traveling overseas where for a price such surgeries can be performed. But before long, Martha was too sick for even that."

The sheriff nodded again.

"Martha knew a local doctor. A friend from childhood. Dr. Gregory Hatch. He had a practice in Atlanta. He said he could help her."

"How?" Kimberly prodded.

The mayor fingered his coffee cup. He wouldn't look at them anymore. "Martha told me not to ask too many questions. She said it was better if I didn't know," he whispered. "But Gregory, he got privileges at the health clinic just north of here. And Martha paid him a series of visits. Testing. Lots of testing." The mayor smiled grimly. "You can't really hide that. Then, she went away for a month. To a wellness clinic, she said. Of course, we both knew she was lying.

"But she was my wife and I loved her. And I wanted her to live. So when she gave me a bunch of paperwork to fill out for a 'designated donation,' I didn't argue."

"You donated a kidney to your wife?" Kimberly interrupted.

"I filled out paperwork that said I was donating a kidney to my wife," the mayor said slowly. "But I couldn't. I wasn't a match. I knew that. She knew that. As for the paperwork . . ."

"Your wife got a kidney," D.D. filled in. "This Dr. Hatch did the operation."

The mayor finally looked at them, his eyes red rimmed and exhausted.

"She came home with meds, lots and lots of meds. You'll find them in the bathroom. Anti-rejection meds. She still takes them faithfully. And she's been healthy ever since."

No one spoke right away. Finally, Kimberly did the honors. "Mayor Howard, where did your wife get the kidney?"

"I don't know."

"But it wasn't from you."

"It wasn't from me."

"But she got a transplant, performed by this Dr. Hatch."

"He saved her life."

"I remember a Gregory Hatch," the sheriff spoke up. "Didn't he pass away . . ."

"He died eight years ago," the mayor supplied.

"When did he perform the operation?" Kimberly pressed.

"Around fifteen years ago."

D.D. glanced at Kimberly. According to Dr. Jackson, Lilah Abenito had been killed fifteen years ago. Then there was their mass grave, which included at least one skeleton with signs of medical care. Yesterday, D.D. and the sheriff had told the mayor and his wife that the threat to the community was old. They'd even mentioned that the remains were skeletal. But they'd never been so specific as to say the first grave was from fifteen years ago. That was the kind of detail investigative taskforces kept to themselves.

Meaning, if Martha had connected the dots between her transplant operations and the graves in the woods, she had to have some idea where her kidney had come from. Or, at the very least, what had happened to her donor in the end.

I was selfish to live at another's expense.

Was that what they had stumbled upon, then? An illegal organ transplant scheme? Such things happened. As the mayor had said, the demand for organs was high, the supply low. Black market economies had developed from less.

"My wife was a good woman," the mayor stated now. "She cared about the community. Whatever happened, whatever she did . . . Fear can make a person desperate. She did her best to make up for her sin. You can ask anyone. She performed so many good works, helped out with so many families during the lean times, gave and gave and gave . . ."

The mayor's voice broke. On the table, his hands trembled violently.

The sheriff reached across, patted the man's shoulder awkwardly. D.D. didn't know what else to say. She moved away from the table, her gaze once more on the swinging door that connected to the kitchen. For the first time she noticed what appeared to be a small slip of paper. Dropped by the girl when she'd brought the coffee?

D.D. drifted closer to the doorway. She was aware of the mayor's attention shifting, the man studying her. He definitely didn't want her too close to his niece, that much was certain. And suspicious? D.D. leaned against the wall, made a show of getting more comfortable. Just an overworked detective, already on her feet too long and it wasn't even six A.M.

The sheriff spoke up. The moment the mayor focused on him . . .

D.D. bent down, snatched up the folded paper, then covered the motion by elaborately retying her shoe. When she stood back up, the mayor was frowning at her, but appeared to be none the wiser.

Noise from the front of the inn now. The ME's van finally arriving. D.D. shoved away from the wall to do the honors.

She waited till she was back in the lobby, out of sight of the mayor, before inspecting her find. The scrap of paper was tiny, ripped from a larger piece and folded several times. Smoothing it open against her palm, D.D. could make out what appeared to be a simple picture.

A single image. Black. Distorted. Ominous. With red fire for the eyes and hulking shoulders.

A monster.

The girl had drawn a picture of a demon, then dropped it on the floor for D.D. to find.

Meaning what?

The ME and his assistant knocked on the front door. Still puzzled, D.D. led them to the rear bedroom, and to the body of a woman who'd made her last confession.

CHAPTER 22

FLORA

NOT BEING MUCH OF A sleeper, I spend most of the night pacing. Shortly after four, I hear a commotion in the hall and come out of my room in time to catch D.D. exiting hers. She provides me a brief update of the situation at the mayor's place, then she and Kimberly disappear out the motel doors to do their policing business, leaving me behind.

It still takes me another hour to find my courage.

I wish I could explain it, even to myself, but I can't.

Take on a known rapist? Check.

Walk down a dark alley where a suspected predator snatches his prey? Check.

Race into a burning building to confront a killer, save a pregnant woman, track an arsonist? Check, check, check.

Knock on the door of the handsome man staying in the room next to mine . . . ?

I pace the deserted lobby. Roam the tiny dining area, which at this time of morning doesn't offer lights, coffee, or even Pop-Tarts.

Finally, back down the hallway I go, telling myself I'm brave, I'm strong, I'm a survivor.

I'm shaking by the time I reach Keith's door. I get my hand up to knock. I think of my friend Sarah, who's gone back to college and now has a boyfriend. I think of the way her face lights up when she talks about her life. From surviving to thriving.

She did it. I can do it.

I'm still standing there, frozen with my fist midair when the door swings open. Keith appears, fully dressed and not looking surprised to see me.

"Kimberly and D.D. left," he says.

I belatedly pull down my hand. "There's been a death. Mayor's wife. Hanging."

"Suicide or murder?"

"That's what they're trying to figure out."

Keith frowns at me. "What does that mean for us today?"

I take a deep breath. Will he think I'm crazy? Then again, Keith has been remarkably adaptable so far.

"I want to rent an ATV again," I tell him. "I want to visit the guy they were talking about last night—the loner, Walt Davies."

"The guy who shoots cops on sight?"

"We're not cops."

Keith arches a brow. "We're trespassers. A guy who shoots cops probably shoots trespassers, too."

"Then we're trespassers who will need to talk very, very fast."

Keith doesn't say no. He considers me for a moment instead. "Why?"

"I don't know. I need to do something. And this . . ." I frown, I don't know how to put it into words. Ever since I heard Walt Davies's name last night, it's been stuck in my brain. Because I heard it before? Or because I have a thing for crazy loners?

I say at last, "Yesterday, D.D. had us trying out local food looking for matches. But Jacob had other appetites."

"Drugs and alcohol," Keith fills in.

"Exactly. If this Walt Davies guy is the local supplier of moonshine and dope, there's a good chance Jacob would've sought him out. Especially given Walt's reputation as the town outsider. All the better in Jacob's world."

"Makes sense. But the sheriff said he was going to send two deputies to talk to the guy. So again, why us?"

I give him a look. "That was before this morning's suspicious death. I bet any officer who's slept more than two hours is now assigned to that scene. So why not us? We can't help out at the inn, but as civilians, we might be the right choice for talking to the local paranoid schizophrenic."

"And just like that, I'm worried again."

"In or out?"

We both know the answer. Keith is Keith. He will follow me anywhere, even down to Georgia and up a hiking trail to a grave.

"The ATV rental won't be open for another few hours," he says at last.

"Then we'll go to the diner."

"Our last meal?"

"That's the spirit."

He smiles. Quickly, so I don't have time to think about it, I stretch up and kiss his cheek. He turns his head just enough to meet my lips with his. I don't pull back. We stand there, lips to lips, in suspended animation.

Slowly I draw back. His blue eyes are darker now, harder to read.

"I'll get my jacket," he murmurs.

OVER BREAKFAST, KEITH WORKS HIS computer magic while I pick my way through a bowl of yogurt. It's easy enough to identify Walt

Davies's address, then look it up on Google Maps. Next, Keith pulls up the network of ATV trails to identify the closest connector.

I can't decide the best strategy for approaching a man who's been described as an anti-government survivalist. Head straight down the driveway, hands in the air? Or approach from the rear, getting the lay of the land?

Keith gives me a condescending look, then boots up Google Earth. "You want recon? This is recon."

I obediently *ooh* and *aah* as his laptop screen fills with images. I value the internet as a tool, but I'm a hands-on girl, more prone to footwork than keyboard strokes. Still, Keith is good

First thing we learn, Walt Davies doesn't just have property, he has *property*. The lot appears to be a good twenty acres tucked away from everything. And he doesn't have only a house but a compound. We make out four structures almost immediately. A medium-sized cabin that's probably the main residence, an even larger detached building that could be an oversized garage or a barn, and two small dots we guess are sheds.

"That's a lotta space for one man," I say, studying the property layout while forcing myself to swallow more yogurt.

"Family land," Keith provides immediately.

He is humming slightly as his fingers fly across the keyboard, a nerd in his element. He'd ordered another egg-white omelet. I wonder if I could really be in a relationship with someone who eats such annoyingly healthy food.

I wonder if I could really be in a relationship.

"Main cabin dates to nineteen-oh-five. Here we go: wellhead." He taps a faint spot on the overhead view of the property. "Obviously septic, as well. Generator." He zooms in, panning left then right. "Chickens. So maybe that second building is a barn for goats, small livestock. I have a feeling this is a guy who takes off-the-grid-living seriously."

"What's that?" I point to a series of lines that zigzag through the deeply wooded lot. While Google Earth is handy for a broad over-view, the image gets distorted when Keith zooms in for close-ups. At least to me it does. Again, Keith appears in his element. I wonder if he has Google Earthed my address, or done street view, or whatever else there is that allows one person to spy on another without ever leaving his sofa.

"I think they're trails," Keith says, considering. "Maybe ATV, but some of them appear pretty wide. Maybe for tractors or heavy equipment."

"They go every place. Logging?" I guess.

But when Keith pans back out, it's clear no trees have been cut down, at least not recently.

"Why so many access points to one set of buildings? And all leading to different trails, byways?" I look at Keith. He is frowning, playing around with different perspectives of the property, frowning harder.

"I don't know," he says at last.

I don't either, and it makes me suspicious. I finish my last bite of yogurt, remembering D.D.'s words that I have to take care of myself.

"I don't want to ride up to the front door," I tell Keith.

He waits.

"This guy, he's the local recluse, right? If we approach directly, even assuming he doesn't shoot us, he's not going to magically let two complete strangers wander his property."

I want to see what's in those buildings. I want to understand what's going on with all these roads and entrances and exits. Then, I want to talk to Walt Davies.

"Stealth it is. All right, let's determine our point of entry."

BILL BENSON, THE ATV GUY, doesn't question our second-day rental. He accepts Keith's credit card, asks if we need any help identifying more trails, then appears genuinely disappointed when we decline. In a small town like this, it's probably street cred to have an inside track on a murder investigation. Or maybe just having firsthand knowledge as to what the outsiders are up to. I can't help but think that the minute we leave, he'll be at the local watering hole, disclosing all.

While Bill roams the shelves behind him to select the right helmets for us, I wander the tiny rental space. The requisite framed first dollar is hung above the rack of local attraction brochures, while next to it are haphazard groupings of more personal photos. A group shot of a dozen people, posing in front of their four-wheelers. Maybe one of the ATV clubs. I can just make out a younger version of Bill second to the left, but no one else looks familiar to me. Then there's Bill posed in full hunter's garb, rifle still in hand, as he beams beside the massive buck lying prone on the ground. A young kid kneels at the buck's head, also cradling a rifle.

"My son," Bill announces proudly, coming up to hand me my helmet. "First kill."

"Okay," I say because, being a hunter myself, who am I to judge?

Keith joins us, eyeing the photo more squeamishly.

"Is this your family?" he asks, pointing toward the posed shot of a family of three. Younger Bill stands to the left, son in the middle but now a lanky teen a full head taller than his father. Which leaves the dark-haired woman sitting in the wingback chair in front of them as the wife and mom.

"She's beautiful," I say to Bill.

"Thank you," he says. "We've been married nearly forty years now. How the time flies."

There is something in his voice that makes me give him a second glance. Wistfulness? Resignation? I glance at the portrait again. The woman is very pretty, but almost hauntingly so. I realize now she's not looking at the camera so much as through it. There is something about her eyes, a little too vacant, as if she's sitting for the photo shoot but still isn't there. I wonder if it was her idea to hire the photographer, capture one last memory before their teenager flew the coop.

"Does your son work in the shop, too?" Keith asks.

"Nah. He has no interest in the family business. Like most of the kids around here, he took off for greener pastures first chance he got. Town's too small, not enough job opportunities unless you want to work in tourism, tourism, or tourism. As parents, it feels good to raise a child in a close-knit community. For the kids, on the other hand . . ." Bill shrugs ruefully. "Our children bolt for big cities, while we then hire the big-city kids to work our businesses. Irony, I guess."

"Who's that?" I ask, pointing to another photo of Bill shaking hands with an older gentleman in a mint-green suit.

"That's the mayor. Mayor Howard. I won Business of the Year five years back. He presented the award."

Keith and I exchange looks. To judge by Bill's expression, he hasn't heard of the tragedy at the mayor's house yet.

"Are you and the mayor close?" Keith asks.

Shrug. "We know each other, of course. I think he's a good mayor. He and Martha have done a lot to boost business in our community. Ten years ago were lean times. We suffered compared to towns like Dahlonega, which offers up old-time charm but with the benefit of spas and wine tasting and gold mine tours. Gotta say, I wasn't sure if my own business would make it. But Mayor Howard poured a lot of money into fixing up the Mountain Laurel, took it from a historic inn to a luxury getaway for newlyweds and business execs. Then he got Dorothea, the town clerk, to put together a whole new website for the town, not to mention launch all these social media platforms. Once a month she goes around to the local businesses, has us produce candid photos to lure in more tourists. Speaking of which, want to pose?" Bill produces his cell phone, eyes us hopefully.

"No, thank you."

He shrugs, pockets his phone. "Well, to answer your question, the mayor has done right by our community. Lots of people coming here now. Good for the economy. Good for the locals."

Keith and I nod, make our goodbyes.

Per our deal, Keith gets to drive today. Which puts me in charge of navigating, but also, more important, keeping an eye out for surveillance cameras and booby traps. Already, we'd identified a ridge line running along part of the property line, and a gully along another stretch, which make for natural defenses.

That leaves us with another six options, so of course we're going with the seventh—parking just off property on the ATV trail, then hoofing it in through the woods. Keith has his compass app and can't wait to use it.

I spy the first impediment almost immediately after we dismount the ATV. Barbed wire, running willy-nilly through the trees. It's old and rusted, but still plenty sharp. I have a Leatherman tool in my pocket. I inspect the tree branches above us for surveillance cameras, then the bushes around our knees for motion-sensitive game cameras. I discover two almost immediately. Walt Davies is just as paranoid as I suspected.

I indicate with my hand to keep walking. We make it another fifty feet, to a place where a thick bush obscures all from view. Several clips of the Leatherman later, and we are through the first obstacle.

We walk in silence, Keith staring at his app to determine direction, while I take point. I half expect a hidden net to snatch us up, or the ground to open into a pit of spikes, or even some old bear trap to snap off one of our limbs. Instead, we get closer and closer, sweat trickling down our foreheads, soaking our shirts. I don't have a backpack like Keith, relying once again on the myriad of pockets in my hoodie and cargo pants. Unfortunately, the day is too hot for such layers and I quickly envy Keith and his high-tech wicking fabrics.

I abruptly stop, hold up a closed fist. As if we've been doing this for years, Keith immediately pauses, drops low. I point through the trees, where we can now see the first outbuilding.

Old, weathered barnboard, rotting at the base, a slapdash roof. The windows are so caked with dirt that it would be impossible to see inside even if we were standing up close, let alone from this distance.

The building appears neglected. At the sight of it I'm struck by déjà vu, though I'm not sure why. Like the mildewed cellar where I was once held, there is something sad about this place, something abandoned.

I can imagine girls being held in this building. I can imagine bodies abandoned beneath those decaying floorboards. I can picture this being the last thing someone like Lilah Abenito ever saw.

The distance from Walt's place to the grave sites is less than six miles. Easily traveled by an ATV, with three trails connecting his property to Laurel Lane.

Except . . . why dump the bodies off his land when he has so many private acres to work with? Land where he can obviously control access and limit the chance of anyone randomly stumbling upon his handiwork?

I feel like I understand *something*, but not enough. Which, of course, is why we are here.

I resume my inspection of the perimeter where the woods thin out then give way to the hodgepodge collection of structures. I spy four or five spotlights; I would guess they're motion sensitive, but not terribly effective given the mid-morning sun. What I find interesting is that the lights appear new, with clean metal brackets attached to walls that clearly were erected decades ago.

I pause, tilt my head to the side. I can hear the rumble of an engine, followed by a distinct grinding sound.

I turn wide-eyed toward Keith just in time for him to nod his agreement. "Wood chipper," he murmurs.

"Great. How fucking *Fargo* of him."

Keith shrugs. Philosophically? Fatalistically? It occurs to me this is probably the stupidest thing I've ever done, and considering how I've spent the past six to seven years, that's saying something.

I can't make out any more cameras or signs of life. With the noise across the way offering cover for our approach, I step from the woods and onto the property.

No snarling dogs charge around the corner. No alarms sound shrilly. No bullets fly by my head. Just the sound of the wood chipper, deep and throaty as it shreds the next . . . something.

My heart is racing. We probably should've left a message for D.D. Or last wills and testaments for our loved ones. Too late now.

We creep toward the first dilapidated structure. Again I catch a whiff of decay. Is that what's triggering that intense sense of familiarity? The smell is earthy and moldy—the scent of neglect, not death.

We make it around the corner. Again, as if we've been doing this for years, I take up point, Keith ducks behind me, quickly works the lock on the door. He has to force it with his shoulder, and the screech of the rusted hinges makes us both draw up short. Whatever this building is used for, it clearly hasn't been active for a long time.

Again, the sound of the wood chipper, whirring across the distance.

Keith disappears inside the shed. I sweat through all my clothes and am just considering charging in behind him, butterfly blade in hand, when he returns.

"Nothing," he whispers, both of us tucking against the side of the building.

"Define *nothing*."

"Rusted-out equipment. Vintage glass bottles. Stuff our grandparents would love. Stacked floor to ceiling, too. Trust me, no one is hiding anything in there any time soon."

I frown at him. "We're trying to find a serial killer, and we've stumbled upon a hoarder instead?"

"Um . . . kind of."

The next building we approach is self-explanatory. A chicken coop, as Keith had suspected. Which leaves us with the two larger buildings. The one to our right appears to be an old two-story barn, the kind with a sliding wood door up high for loading bales of hay into the loft. Whereas straight ahead looms a low-slung log cabin that appears to tilt slightly to the right and has a front porch topped with an ancient-looking washer and an equally decrepit dryer.

Next to the barn is a tractor, John Deere green and clearly one of the newer items on the property. Otherwise it's open ground between us and the barn. Once again I note the relatively new spotlights.

I feel like there's something obvious that I'm missing. Cameras? Booby traps?

The barn itself appears as weather-beaten as the sheds. The roof is nearly covered in moss. The small high windows stay with the motif: dirt and more dirt.

In the distance, the wood chipper growls again. Then, abruptly, as if it can't take one more bite, the whirring stops. The engine snaps off. The entire property falls silent.

I feel Keith shudder beside me. I don't blame him. The wood chipper had been ominous. But the silence . . .

The silence is worse.

What did I miss? Because I'm reckless and aggressive, but I'm also experienced. And every instinct that has ever kept me alive is screaming. Abort mission. Retreat. Run while we still can.

I can tell Keith feels it, too. But where to go? We're tucked in the only available cover—the shady side of a dilapidated shed. Between us and the woods, there is nothing but exposed acreage.

The barn, I think. If we could just tuck inside the barn, find a place to hide.

Then I get it. What I saw but didn't register. It's not just the lighting on the buildings that's new—looped through the handles of the barn doors is a thick, modern chain and padlock, both completely devoid of rust.

The barn isn't our sanctuary. The barn is exactly what we're not supposed to see.

I'm still trying to work the trajectories, how to get out of this mess, when I swear the woods themselves come alive. One moment I'm judging the distance between the shed and trees, the next a scarecrow of a man is standing before me.

Tall, gaunt, with sparse gray hair that stands on end and a wiry strength that ripples through his too-skinny limbs.

Walt Davies, who clearly figured out he had company, and worked his own perimeter to sneak up on us.

He's holding a shotgun, pointed straight at us.

I put my hands up. Beside me, Keith does the same.

I take a deep breath, then step into daylight, advancing five feet toward him, Keith right beside me. If we go down, apparently we're doing it together.

"I'm sorry," I begin to babble. "So sorry. We're lost, our ATV ran out of gas, please, sir, can we use your phone . . ."

The old man responds in a way I don't expect at all.

He drops the barrel of the shotgun. He stares at me, wild-eyed.

"No!" he cries. "It can't be you. You're *dead*! Dead, I tell you! Dead, dead, dead!"

CHAPTER 23

KIMBERLY

AFTER SPEAKING WITH MAYOR HOWARD about his wife's alleged illegal kidney transplant, Kimberly paid a visit to the master bathroom, where—sure enough—she found a row of prescription bottles bearing Martha Counsel's name. A quick internet search revealed most of the pills to be anti-rejection meds, to be taken for the "life of the working transplant organ."

Kimberly returned to the room where the woman had hanged herself. D.D. was still there, supervising the ME's removal of the body. As with all hangings, the ME had left the noose in place. Analysis of the knot would be an important part of the final report, helping to determine if the woman's death was a suicide or a murder.

Right now, Kimberly had a suspicious death, which technically fell under the sheriff's jurisdiction, not that of the federal taskforce. She doubted, however, that Sheriff Smithers would balk at outside assistance with the case, especially as Martha Counsel's death had to be related to the bodies they'd recovered. It was impossible to think otherwise.

D.D. introduced the medical examiner, Dr. Dale Cabot, then his scrawny assistant, Arnold Cabot. Apparently, the coroner's office was a family business.

"What can you tell me?" Kimberly asked, flashing her credentials.

"I can tell you a cup of coffee every morning is perfectly good for you," Dr. Cabot replied drolly, working with his son to slowly lower Martha Counsel onto the waiting gurney. "And I can't wait to have one this morning myself."

She deserved that, asking for an opinion before the body was even on the stretcher. Even so, Kimberly held up a hand. "Hang on a moment."

She stopped beside the gurney. Martha's embroidered silk bathrobe remained open in front, but the kid, Cabot junior, had respectfully smoothed down her long white nightgown. No good way to do this.

"We're told this woman received a kidney transplant," Kimberly said. "Given the circumstances, I need to check."

Dr. Cabot stepped back, gesturing for her to do what she had to do. His son, on the other hand, stared at her wide-eyed.

Kimberly never liked this part. It felt intrusive, donning a pair of gloves then slowly raising up the hem of a dead woman's nightgown to better inspect the body. Mentally, she made her apologies as she drew Martha's nightgown above her thighs, exposing plain white underwear with discreet lace trim, then finally Martha's bare torso. There on the left-hand side: a significant surgical scar, still puckered and dark pink after all these years.

"Is that scar consistent with a kidney transplant?" Kimberly asked.

"Appears so. I can tell you more once I open her up."

Kimberly nodded, held out her cell phone with the photo she had shot of the prescription bottles. "And these drugs?"

The ME took her phone, played with the photo till he could make out all the labels. "These are all standard anti-rejection meds, consistent with someone who received an organ transplant."

He handed back the phone.

"Did you know a Dr. Gregory Hatch?" D.D. asked, coming to stand beside them.

"Dr. Hatch? He passed away years ago."

"Would he have been qualified to perform a kidney transplant?"

"As a general surgeon, yes, but UNOS—the United Network for Organ Sharing—could tell you more. They should have a record of everyone."

"Assuming the organ came through UNOS," D.D. said levelly.

Dr. Cabot stared at them. Then he looked back at the body, the red bathrobe sash knotted around Martha's neck. "I don't know why someone would go to such lengths to live once," he said slowly, "only to give up now."

"Guilt?" Kimberly offered.

"The Dr. Hatch I knew . . . I wouldn't rush to conclusions. Especially with the man not even alive to defend himself."

"Who might still have access to his medical records?" Kimberly asked.

"Dr. Hatch was a private practice physician. Upon his death, patients would have been notified and given the opportunity to transfer their records to the new doctor of their choice."

Kimberly exchanged a glance with D.D. Would a doctor even keep records of an illegal surgery? And yet, Martha had still required ongoing care, including the meds.

"Who would be in charge of transferring the files?" D.D. spoke up.

"Dr. Hatch's assistant. Sorry. I can picture her, but I can't seem to remember her name."

"Amy Frankel," his son offered immediately.

Kimberly and D.D. looked at him.

"Blond, beautiful," said the boy. "What's not to remember?"

Fair enough, Kimberly thought. D.D. was already jotting down the name. Kimberly went back to her photo of Martha Counsel's meds. There, on the lower left-hand label, she could see the name of the prescribing doctor.

"Dr. Dean Hathaway," she read off. "Do you know him?"

"No. But given the critical nature of maintaining the transplanted kidney's health, it's highly possible Mrs. Counsel was seeing a nephrologist out of Atlanta."

Kimberly nodded and moved on to the red silk sash still tied around Martha's neck.

She could just make out bruising above the fabric, from where it had ridden up on the neck from the force of the hanging. Kimberly had seen cases where someone had manually strangled a victim, then tried to cover it up by staging a hanging. In those cases, however, the distinct bruise pattern of fingers squeezing the victim's throat always gave the murderer away.

At the moment, she didn't see anything like that here. Of course, more would be visible once the sash was removed.

If this death looked and sounded like a suicide, why was she so uncomfortable?

She moved away from the gurney, thanked the ME for his time, and indicated that he and his son could go.

"I don't like it," D.D. said the moment they disappeared down the hall.

"We're trained to be paranoid," said Kimberly. "Doesn't mean they're really out to get us."

"Ah, but my new friend dropped this." D.D. held out a scrap of paper.

Kimberly looked at the hastily crayoned drawing of a hulking black figure with glowing red eyes. "Is that . . . what? Some kind of boogeyman?"

"I think it's a monster."

"The girl, the mayor's mute niece, gave you a picture of a monster?"

"She dropped it on the floor when he wasn't looking. She can't talk, but she's trying to tell us something."

"The boogeyman did it?"

"Or his friend, the devil."

Kimberly considered the matter. She didn't understand the drawing and, given the girl's young age and reported brain injury, wasn't even sure if she qualified as a credible witness. On the other hand, it's not like they had any better leads. "All right, let's talk to her."

Kimberly turned toward the door. D.D. grabbed her arm. "Wait. She's underaged. We have to have the mayor's permission for an interview."

"We'll ask for it. Denying us access will look suspicious. You know how it is; put on the spot, plenty of guilty parties consent to things they shouldn't."

"I don't want to call attention to her. I don't think we know everything that's going on here."

"No kidding."

"The picture projects fear. We may not understand it, but we have to respect it."

God, Kimberly was tired. She rubbed her temples, wished she was once more on the phone, talking to her husband, catching up with her girls. Deep breath. This was her job and she loved it. Most of the time. "All right. So our best approach . . . We'll question her without singling her out."

"Game plan?"

"We'll inform Mayor Howard that we need to interview everyone who was in the building last night. Guests, staff, everyone. I'll ask Sheriff Smithers to handle the guests, while you and I take the staff."

D.D. nodded. "I don't know that Mayor Howard will consent to us talking to his niece separately. My guess is he'll say she can't speak so he needs to be present to communicate on her behalf."

"We'll gather the staff and talk to them as a group. That will appear less threatening and make it harder for Mayor Howard to refuse without calling undue attention. His niece isn't alone and the rest of the staff must be able to communicate with her in some fashion—otherwise, how else could they have worked together all these years? I'll ask questions. You watch her fingers for your special coding system and we'll see what we get."

"I like it."

"Of course. I'm brilliant. Which is why we get along so well."

"And how we're going to nail the son of a bitch who's leaving a trail of dead women all over this town," D.D. agreed.

Mayor Howard wasn't thrilled with their assertion they needed to interview everyone present in the inn last night. He tried to argue his guests' right for privacy, his and his staff's need to mourn. The sheriff, however, stood firmly with them—and, denied local support, the mayor had no choice.

Sheriff Smithers sent an officer to rouse the four couples who'd stayed the night. Kimberly announced she and D.D. would handle questioning the staff, who were apparently huddled in the kitchen, awaiting news. In the meantime, she needed the mayor to identify which computer or personal tablet his wife might have used to write her suicide note.

The request sent another long shudder rippling through the mayor's bent frame. He bowed his head, appeared once again to fight for breath. The man seemed genuinely distraught. As if this were the worst night of his life. As if he still couldn't believe his wife was dead.

"She's gone," he said abruptly. "Martha, my wife, my partner, my best friend. Thirty years . . . There's no hope for me now." His tone was so hollow, it sent a shiver down Kimberly's spine.

She kneeled beside him at the table. "I'm sorry for your loss."

"I loved her."

"I understand."

"I did what she wanted."

"I know."

"I just wanted her to be healthy. Then she was. And God help me, I didn't ask any questions. I never considered the cost. If not from me, then how did she get the kidney in the end?"

"Mayor Howard, I need you to go with Sheriff Smithers now. He's going to help you find your wife's computer. It's important. Helping him will enable us to wrap up our investigation. I know this is hard. Just another hour or two, and we'll be on our way. Who is in charge of your staff?"

"My wife—" The mayor caught himself. "Cook. She's in the kitchen now. Prepping breakfast, I'm sure."

Kimberly rose to standing. "Sheriff," she prodded, indicating it was time for him to lead the mayor away.

Smithers got it. He put his hand on the mayor's shoulder, both men looking equally grim. Kimberly understood. Sheriff Smithers was a county sheriff, not the town sheriff, but these were still his people. He had obviously known the mayor and Martha Counsel personally. These kinds of cases, where the trouble struck close to home, were never easy.

Mayor Howard climbed shakily to his feet, then followed the sheriff out of the front breakfast room.

Beside Kimberly, D.D. nodded slightly, acknowledging a job well done.

And yet, how to explain the unease rippling through Kimberly's gut? They had an admission of guilt—a woman who'd killed herself because she was sorry for the kidney she had most likely stolen from one of their victims in the woods. They had the presence of medical supplies found in the mass grave—the IV port—which further supported this theory.

They had four victims, maybe all of whom had been used the same way: unwilling donors for illegal surgeries performed by a doctor dead eight years past. Illegal surgery explained the bodies, explained their timelines. Probably even explained the mass grave—three operations performed at once. Which made the victims what, medical waste?

Human nature never failed to disappoint. If there was a worst-case scenario out there, some person someplace had done it.

But the coroner's words haunted her: Why would a woman who desired to live enough to resort to an illegal surgery decide to end it all, suddenly, just like that?

"Ready?" D.D. asked.

"Ready enough."

D.D. indicated the swinging door connecting the kitchen. "No time like the present." She shoved her way through, Kimberly at her heels.

"Hey, Cook. We have some questions for you."

CHAPTER 24

FLORA

DEAD.

The word that Walt Davies shouted hangs in the air. I glance at Keith, who looks as confused as I feel.

"How'd you get here?" Davies asks now. He no longer has the pump-action shotgun pointed at our chests, but is swinging it around in a manner that's hardly any safer.

"Our ATV . . ."

"Clipped your way through the barbed wire, then. Been meaning to add more cameras. Damn land. Got too fucking much of it. But my great-granddaddy would come back from the grave if I sold an inch." Walt jerks his head to the side. I think he might actually be talking to his great-granddaddy. Whatever risks Keith and I thought we were taking, the reality seems far worse.

"Who sent ya?" Walt demands now.

Again, I peer at Keith. I'm not sure how to answer. We came on our own? Does that comfort a loner or seal our doom? Maybe we should say the police are right behind us.

I feel a rising bubble of . . . something. Hysteria? I don't get hysterical. I'm Flora Dane, with universal handcuff keys tucked in the knot of my hair and a butterfly blade in the top of my boot and homemade pepper spray in my pants pocket. Time to end this—

"Sir," Keith says. "Do you recognize her?"

Walt's rheumy blue eyes fly to my face. "You're dead," he whispers.

"No, sir," Keith speaks up before I have a chance. "But she needs your help. Immediately. We're in danger. They're coming. Please. Help us."

Appealing to the paranoid? The enemy of my enemy is my friend, and Them and They are such powerful enemies, of course we must be very good friends?

"Quick," Walt says. "Follow me."

He strides toward the log cabin and just like that we've gone from being his latest victims to his newest charges.

"How did you know?" I murmur to Keith as we jog behind a shotgun-wielding lunatic.

"Took my best guess."

"If he has lampshades made of human skin inside there, I'm going for him."

"I'll be right behind you."

"Are we on a date?" I ask Keith, as Walt clatters up to the front door, grabs the barely attached screen door, and throws it open.

"I hope so," Keith tells me. "Because let's face it. This is one helluva story to tell our future children."

WE CROSS THE THRESHOLD INTO Walt Davies's home, which may just be our final resting place.

No lights are on. Given the sunny day, it shouldn't be an issue, but—no surprise—thick dusty curtains have been pulled tight. I whack my shin, then my knee, as I realize stuff is everywhere.

Walt is already sidling up to the nearest window. He pulls back the edge of the curtain, which appears to have been fashioned from layers of army surplus blankets, and peers out. He mumbles something, then crosses quickly to the other side of the cluttered room. More squinting and muttering. Then he disappears down the hall, leaving Keith and me to stand alone in the cabin.

Now that my eyes are adjusting to the gloom, I can make out details. We are in the main room, with a massive stone fireplace before us and a significantly smaller dining space to our right. The kitchen features a pump sink and old-fashioned cast-iron stove. It appears to have been installed a hundred years ago and never updated since.

The entire space is low ceilinged, which I understand once upon a time made it easier to heat. Now it makes me feel claustrophobic, especially given that every square inch is filled with broken furniture, jumbled piles of bound newspapers, and of course a massive moth-eaten deer head mounted over the mantel.

"Again, *one sign of human skin . . .*" I murmur to Keith.

He squeezes my hand.

Walt returns. "Don't see 'em. So far, so good. Why are you here? What did you see? Where did you go?"

He's still carrying the shotgun, now down at his side. I should make a move to disarm him, but I've dealt with his kind of scary strength before. It won't be easy. And for the moment at least—when we are part of Us, hiding out from Them—maybe it's better to play along.

"They were chasing us," I say vaguely. "Our ATV ran out of gas. We ran here for help."

Walt nods somberly, as if this makes perfect sense. "Mountains are no place for a girl," he says seriously. "Not even one with a boy-friend. These are dangerous times. Daytime's hard enough. Don't get caught out after dark."

"What happens after dark?" Keith asks.

"The hills come alive," Walt whispers. "It ain't safe. T'ain't safe at all." He stares at me so hard I have to resist the urge to fidget. Slowly, he reaches out an age-spotted hand, as if to brush my cheek. Or assure himself that I'm real and not some ghost from his past. I recoil automatically, hitting the box behind me and sending half the room's contents tumbling to the floor like a chain of dominoes.

Keith belatedly tries to right whatever he can reach. I'm still staring at Walt Davies, who I swear has tears in his eyes.

"It don't matter," he says, as Keith tries to pick up. "I'll get to it later. Gives me something to do at night."

"How long have you lived here?" I ask.

"My whole life."

"You have any family?"

"Had a sister. Gone now. Had a woman. Son. Gone, too. These woods aren't safe."

"Is that why you have all the new spotlights?"

"Can't be too careful."

"When was the last time you saw *Them*?" I venture now. "They approached your property?"

Walt narrows his eyes at me. There's a particular kind of cunning there. Once more: a dreadful feeling of déjà vu.

"Why should I tell you?"

"I'm dead?"

Now there's no denying it: Walt Davies's rheumy eyes fill with tears. Two track down his bristly cheeks. "I came back for you," he says hoarsely. "I swear it!"

Before I can even think it through, I say: "I know." I don't understand what he's telling me, but his agitation pains me. "I should've waited for you."

"I made a promise. I meant to keep it."

"Mr. Davies," Keith speaks up, "what's in the barn? I couldn't help noticing . . . that's quite some lock."

"Why? What'd ya hear?" That fast, the cunning is gone, replaced by rampant paranoia.

"I, um, I'm wondering if that might be a safer place to, uh, you know, hide. From Them."

"You know, don'tcha? Someone talked, someone told. You want what I have." Before either of us can blink, the shotgun is pointed at Keith's chest. "You can't have it!"

"Please, Walt, please!" I place my hand on his arm without thinking, making my voice as high and feminine as possible. It works, his attention pinging back to me. I am someone to him. I'm not sure who. Sister, wife, girlfriend? But I am someone important, maybe even someone he loved, now back from the dead.

The most basic tenet of survival: Use what you've got.

"I'm scared . . ." I whisper. I feel like the scantily clad heroine in a slasher film. Walt focuses entirely on me, while Keith draws a ragged breath.

"It's so dark in here," I continue. "I don't like the dark."

Walt hesitates, shotgun still pointed at Keith, but his attention on my face. I can't read any of the thoughts running through his sad eyes, across his hollow cheeks. I wonder how long ago his woman and child left. How long he's been alone on this giant property, stringing barbed wire, hanging floodlights, and waiting for the mountains to attack.

I don't feel afraid of him anymore. We are kindred spirits. Two people lost in the shadows, preparing for the worst and never feeling safe again.

"They all want it," he says seriously. "If I show you . . . you can't tell. Can't share what you see. Everyone wants my secrets. What makes it grow so fast. So green."

Grow? I finally get it. What had brought us here in the first place. Walt is the local dope farmer. Chances are, that's what is in the barn. His growing operation. Which would also explain all the roads exiting the property—for middle of the night shipments.

Walt leads us out the front door. Glance here, glance there, then he hustles us across the open yard to the massive barn. We press against the side of the building, staying out of sight of . . . Them? Drones? The ghosts of the mountains? He undoes the padlock with a key he wears on a long chain around his neck.

He has to set down his shotgun to push back the heavy sliding door. Neither Keith nor I make a move. We are holding our breaths, preparing to encounter a jungle of dope plants that will only add to the surrealness of our day.

Which makes it all the crazier when Walt steps inside the warm, humid space, flips on a bank of overhead lights, and proudly declares, "Yes, sir. I grow the purest crop in all of Georgia. Behold. Davies's Microgreens."

"THE TRICK IS COCO MATS," Walt explains proudly. "No soil, no pesticides. Just plenty of love and water. I got four different crops, from micro mustard plants to pea shoots. I harvest every ten to fifteen days. Just me. Load it up, head to Atlanta. Gotta real following among the swanky chefs at high-end restaurants. Microgreens are very healthy, you know. High in vitamins, some even fight cancer."

I honestly have no idea what to say. Standing beside me, I can tell Keith is equally stunned. We are staring at row after row of metal shelving units. Each holds eight shallow trays of densely packed, tiny green shoots, like a parade of Chia Pets escaped from the 1980s.

I walk closer, inspecting the setup. There are tubes running from each tray.

"Hydroponics," Walt explains. "Makes for faster growth."

I get it, the watering system. While hanging from the ceiling above are huge banks of lights, emitting a whitish glow.

"LED lighting," Walt volunteers again, clearly proud. "Provides the best balance of light and heat. I got 'em digitally programmed.

Different growth stages have different needs. You don't gotta be too fancy about it, but I take care of my own. Best damn microgreens in Georgia," he boasts again.

"How long have you been doing this?" Keith asks. Like me, he has started wandering the aisles.

"Three years."

"How did you learn all this?" I ask, waving my hand around. Because digital lights, the automated watering system . . . With his unkempt hair, tattered jeans, and stained flannel, Walt doesn't exactly look like an advertisement for sophistication, and yet this is clearly a high-tech operation.

He shrugs. "Here and there. I've always been good with my hands. Running a farm, fixin' buildings, maintainin' equipment, takes more know-how than people think."

"Clearly."

"Plus," he adds matter-of-factly, "I grew dope for years. This is easier. More profitable and I don't gotta worry about being arrested."

"Of course."

"I wasn't always a good person," Walt says abruptly. He's standing near the door. For the first time, I realize I don't know where the shotgun is anymore. Still leaning against the outside of the barn? Or tucked somewhere behind him? For that matter, is there a second egress to this place? Or if he wanted to, could Walt take three steps back, jerk closed the heavy sliding door, and lock us in with his precious microgreens?

I don't know why he'd want to do such a thing. And yet, the hair is standing up on the back of my neck. Farther down the aisle, Keith turns and I can tell he feels it, too. A certain wrongness. A change in the air that doesn't bode well.

Maybe a guy like Walt doesn't need a reason. Maybe Keith and I have allowed ourselves to be lulled by trays of tiny green shoots while forgetting the obvious—crazy is crazy, and Walt Davies has spent decades earning a reputation as the town lunatic.

"I drank," Walt whispers now.

Has he moved? I shift slightly, trying to calculate my distance to the open door. If I bolt now, maybe I could cut him off.

"I doped and drugged and drank my way through life. If there was an illicit chemical around, I injected it. If there was a fight to be had, I picked it. I hit my girl. Smacked around my kid. Then beat them more for making me feel bad about it. I was a mean son of a bitch."

Keith and I don't say a word. Walt doesn't seem to be paying attention to us anymore. He's telling his story, and the confessional air once again makes me shiver.

"Then, I got lost. In the mountains. The very hills where I had lived my whole life. I'd gone hunting, and 'course, packed more booze than common sense. I was on a trail. Then I wasn't. Night came and it grew cold.

"I don't know how long I staggered about. Day after day. Till my beer was gone, my flask dry. I'd packed a sandwich. Ate that the first afternoon. Then, with no booze, I started to get the shakes. Can't exactly hunt when you're too weak to hold a rifle. Hell, I couldn't even manage to light a match for a fire. But the night sweats, hunger pangs, bone-deep thirst, they weren't the worst part."

"What was the worst part?" I drift toward the open door.

"The woods." Walt speaks in an almost reverent tone. "They came alive. The trees whipped at me. The bushes clawed at my feet. And the night screamed. Of every wrong I'd ever done. And there were so many.

"I screamed back, that first night. I shook my fists at the moon. I howled like a goddamn animal. The mountains wanted a piece of me? I was angry and mean and I wasn't going down without a fight. But then, every time I closed my eyes, I saw them. All the people I'd hurt. The wrongs I'd done. My boy's bruised eyes. My woman's shattered cheek. The woods, they showed me the darkness of my soul."

Walt pauses, he looks at us for the first time, and his eyes are not completely sane, and yet, the pain in them feels real. I know something about the darkness of a person's soul. Of spending long nights facing your sins.

"By the third night, I had no rage left in me. I was a broken man, destroyed by my own evil ways. I dug a hole with my bare hands. Long, deep. Tremblin' and sweatin' and out of my mind with the fucking pain. I prepared my grave and readied myself to die alone, with only the screaming trees for company. I deserved it. Lord, I deserved it.

"I prayed that final night. No atheists in a foxhole, right? I laid myself down in the earth, folded my arms over my chest, and out of my mind with the need for booze, I begged and cried like the fool I was. One more chance. Lord, give me one more chance." Walt raised his gaze heavenward. "And you know what happened?"

Keith and I shake our heads.

"Nothin'. I sweat it out. The withdrawal, the pain. I lay in the earth and shook till I thought my bones would break.

"Then . . . I slept. When I woke up, I was thirsty. Parched down to the core. But not for beer or whiskey. For water. Good, plain, clean water. So I climbed out of my grave and I staggered my way forward till eventually, I came to a stream where I drank my fill. Then I followed that stream till it led me to a trail and I finally found my way home. I'd been gone six days, with nights that dropped below freezing conditions. But I lived."

"You sobered up," I say.

Walt nods, but it's not a triumphant gesture. His shoulders are bowed and I realize now his cheeks are damp with tears. Did the mountains save him or break him? I wonder if he knows.

Walt clears his throat. He has moved toward a rack of microgreens. He strokes the velvety shoots now.

"When I got back," he says, "my woman was gone. Boy, too. Cleared out. Maybe they thought I was dead. Maybe, they just saw a chance to escape and took it. I couldn't blame 'em. I woulda run from me, too. Course, you can't escape yourself. So I stayed. I dumped out the booze. Every damn drop. I cried, like a sniveling little boy. And I walked. Every night. I had to listen to the woods. I needed the trees to talk to me. I had to learn what they needed to say.

"Maybe I went a little crazy. Locals say I am. They cross the street when I come into town. The store owners take my money but they keep their distance. I'm sober now, been clean for well over four decades. But all that drinking . . . It's possible I pickled my brain. I don't know. I still hear the woods at night. I still walk among the trees, listening to the wind tell its stories.

"And sometimes, I hear screaming. There are ghosts in these mountains, and they're not all in my head."

"What do you hear, Walt?" I ask gently. Because whether he knows it or not, he's crying again, silent tears running down his bristly cheeks. And there is something so mournful about him, I'm sorry I was ever scared of him, even as I wonder if this is just a different shade of crazy.

"I hear you," he says quietly. So quietly, I'm not sure I heard correctly. He looks up. "I hear you crying in that box. I hear all my sins, all the things I can't undo, including my biggest sin of all."

I can't speak. I can't breathe. Keith has moved closer to me. What Walt is saying doesn't make sense, and yet, I already know it does.

My pervasive sense of déjà vu.

"I told him to let you go. I told him it wasn't right."

"Who did you tell to let her go?" Keith, his voice strong and even, which is good, because at any moment I'm going to collapse.

"I was a mean son of a bitch. The things I did to my family . . . But I still didn't understand the full awfulness of what I'd done. Till he came back. Reap what you sow. I don't want to grow that kind of anger ever again."

I try to open my mouth. Nothing comes out.

"I begged him," Walt murmurs. "I begged him to be better. But I could tell. The booze, the drugs, they had him, too. Or maybe, blood simply runs black in this family.

"My boy, showing up as a grown man. Strutting around these woods. If the trees screamed at him, he liked it. If the wind fought, he yelled back. I thought I was something terrible, unnatural, evil. Then, I met my own son."

I have to put out a hand. I find a metal rack, grab on for dear life. Then Keith is there, taking my arm, shoring me up.

"He took me to the cellar," Walt whispers. "He showed me what he'd done. He was proud. So damn proud. I heard you, whimpering like a kitten. A poor broken girl who just wanted out.

"I'm sorry. I'm so so sorry."

I'm shaking my head. At least, I think I am. His words are too much, bringing back the unforgiving feel of the hard wood against my head, the stench of urine as I lay in my own waste, and the gleeful sound of Jacob's voice.

"I came back for you," Walt is saying. "I knew he'd never let you go. I couldn't bear it. I knew it wasn't enough for me to do no evil. I had to save you, too, or the woods would never let me sleep at night. So I waited till I knew he was away. Headed out on a delivery with his rig. I was gonna rescue you. Break apart that damn box with my own two hands if I had to." Walt took in a deep, ragged breath. "But I was already too late. The cellar was empty. You, the box, my boy, were gone.

"I never saw him again, till one day, I heard he died in some motel raid by the feds. I didn't cry. Not then, not now. I raised evil, my biggest sin, my deepest regret. My own son, Jacob, who I'd turned into the meanest son of a bitch of 'em all."

CHAPTER 25

D.D.

COOK TURNED OUT TO BE a burly woman wearing a grease splat-tered apron and hairnet. She had rounded up the other two work-ers, Mayor Howard's niece, wearing her light-blue maid's uniform, and another young woman with exotic features and gorgeous brown hair. The second woman also wore a maid's uniform and kept her gaze fixed on a spot slightly above D.D.'s shoulder.

"This here is Hélène," the cook said, pointing at the dark-skinned beauty. D.D. would peg the maid's age somewhere between eighteen and twenty-three. Not as young as the niece, but still . . .

"This is Girl." The cook pointed to the mayor's niece.

"Girl?" D.D. interrupted. "You call her Girl?"

"She don't mind." The cook stared D.D. right in the eye. She had her thick arms crossed over her chest. A show of aggression. She also remained standing, while having the younger helpers sit. A show of power. She was in charge and she wanted everyone in the room to know it.

Beside D.D., Kimberly cleared her throat, a subtle hint for D.D. to move on. Why start with open warfare when you could build up to it?

D.D. pulled out her small notepad. "I'm going to need your full legal names and photo IDs."

"Why?" Cook asked.

"Because I said so."

"I got breakfast to prep."

"Don't worry, once the guests hear the news, they won't be hungry."

The cook glared at D.D. The two younger girls sat in silence on the wooden bench. D.D. didn't like it. In her experience, employees talked. Especially the younger generation who barely recognized authority figures and had plenty to say about anyone who thought they were above them.

This . . . this was creepy.

Kimberly moved away from D.D.'s side. She drifted along the edge of the massive stainless-steel prep table, which was covered in flour and a pale mound of dough. The FBI agent conducted a brief inspection of the heavy door for the walk-in fridge, followed by a cursory exam of the commercial-grade dishwasher, complete with a stainless-steel hood and plastic conveyor belt for marching lines of dirty plates quickly and efficiently through boiling-hot spray.

She was drawing attention away, making it difficult for the cook and her younger charges to know where to focus.

"Legal name," D.D. spoke up sternly. She bore her gaze into the cook. As the boss woman did, so the others would follow.

"I like Cook. Been Cook for thirty years and four marriages, God rest their miserable souls."

Four marriages, D.D. thought. Four men had endured this delightful attitude?

"Well, *Cook*, I hear they're always looking for help in county lockup. Though I don't think you get to start out running the kitchen.

You'll have to work up to the position. You may find the auditioning process . . . different . . . than what you're used to."

The cook glared at her.

"I have all day. Do you?"

"Mary!" she said at last. "My legal name is Mary Theresa Josephina Smith."

"Seriously?"

"Shut up!"

The older maid, Hélène, shifted slightly, the first sign of life from the woman. Repressing a smile at her boss's expense or flinching from fear of future reprisal? Too hard to tell.

"Photo ID?" D.D. demanded.

"In my room. I'll fetch it later."

D.D. turned to Mayor Howard's niece. "Your name?"

"She can't talk," Cook said.

"Does *she* have photo ID?" D.D. hated addressing her questions back to the cook. It felt disrespectful, especially as she was convinced the girl understood everything just fine.

The cook shrugged. "No driver's license, since she can't drive. But there's probably a birth certificate. Mrs. Counsel . . ." For the first time, the cook wavered. If D.D. hadn't believed the woman was carved of granite, she would've thought the cook was upset. "Mrs. Counsel kept track of those sort of things. She took care of everyone."

D.D. wasn't sure what to make of that. Genuine care? Or control? Because employees who didn't have access to their own ID raised red flags in the law enforcement world.

"She has my papers," Hélène spoke up suddenly. Her voice was hoarse, as if she didn't use it much. D.D. realized Mayor Howard's niece had turned slightly, the side of her hand lightly touching Hélène's. Lending strength? A show of unity? D.D. quickly returned her attention to Hélène's face, before she gave them away.

"Do you know where she keeps them?" D.D. asked.

"No. My full name is Hélène Tellier," the woman delivered with an exotic lilt that spoke of faraway lands and hot, sandy beaches.

"Why did Mrs. Counsel have your papers?" Kimberly spoke up. She had moved all the way behind them, forcing the three interview subjects to twist awkwardly. The cook glowered, clearly not liking such tricks in her own kitchen.

"Our rooms . . ." Hélène didn't seem to know what to say. She glanced timidly at the cook. "Our rooms are simple. We don't have any place to store . . . valuables."

"Your rooms aren't safe?" D.D. pressed.

Hélène shook her head quickly, then gave up and stared at her feet. Another small movement: the niece covering the trembling maid's hand with her own.

"All right." D.D. squatted down until she was eye level with the silent niece. "I'm not calling you Girl. Do you have a name? Maybe we can find it in Mrs. Counsel's papers."

The girl shrugged, as if D.D.'s guess was as good as anyone's.

"Do you remember your family?" D.D. asked softly. "Your mother, your father?"

Another small shrug. D.D. glanced to where the girl's hands rested on the bench. But the girl didn't offer any fingers in coded reply. She just looked sad and hopeless. A child resigned to her fate.

"Bonita," D.D. said softly. "It's the Spanish word for pretty. What do you think? I'll call you Bonita."

Another *harrumph* from the cook.

The girl kept her gaze on D.D. She reached up and lightly touched her own face, brushing her hand across the ridged scar furrowing into her hairline, then her drooping left eyelid, sagging lip.

D.D. didn't need a code to understand what the girl was trying to say. She captured the girl's hand between her own.

"Bonita," she said firmly, then held the girl's gaze until she finally nodded.

D.D. straightened to standing. "I will need to see the records Mrs. Counsel had for all of you. This is a murder investigation. All details matter."

"Murder investigation?" The cook's arms fell to her sides in clear shock. "But the mayor—"

"What did you hear last night?" Kimberly, ambushing beautifully from behind.

"We didn't, of course—"

"The mayor and his wife fight?"

"No, never. Two most loving—"

"Did you know about the kidney transplant? Tell us about Mrs. Counsel's kidney transplant." Kimberly, her voice stern.

"What? I mean, of course. The operation was a long time ago. Afterwards, I worked with Mrs. Counsel to prepare a renal friendly diet. No pesticides, no red meats, or added salt and sugar," the cook rattled off, seeming to check off each item on her fingers. "High in fiber, lots of beans and leafy green vegetables. I'm a real cook, you know. Got a degree from a culinary institute and everything. I could work at some fancy restaurant if I wanted to. But I like it here. And the mayor, Mrs. Counsel, they take care of their own."

"So you heard nothing last night?" D.D., forcing the cook to turn back around to address her. "No sounds of disturbance, perhaps an altercation?"

"Absolutely not."

D.D. caught a movement out of the corner of her eye. The girl—Bonita—finally shifting her hand to reveal one finger. Which meant yes. As in yes, the cook had heard something and was lying? Or as in yes, Bonita hadn't heard anything either?

For this system to work, D.D. realized, she had to do a better job with the questions.

"Did you notice a change in Mrs. Counsel's behavior over the past few weeks?" she addressed the cook.

"No," the woman said.

Yes, Bonita signed.

"Were you awake last night?"

"Nope," the cook declared.

Yes, Bonita signed.

"What time did you go to bed?" D.D. zeroed in on the woman.

"Nine P.M. I have early mornings, prepping breakfast for the guests."

Bonita hesitated. Maybe she didn't know what time the cook went to bed.

"What time did you get up?" D.D. continued smoothly.

"When I heard the sirens. Four A.M.? Something like that?"

"And when did you hear the disturbance before that?"

"Two A.M.—" The cook caught herself. Too late she saw D.D.'s trap. "I'm a light sleeper," the woman corrected quickly. "Maybe something woke me around two. But I didn't hear nothin' more. I peed, went back to bed."

"You sound like you were close to Mrs. Counsel. That you cared about her."

"She and her husband are good people. Ask anyone."

Nothing from Bonita.

"Did you suspect she was a suicide risk?" D.D. asked.

"Never."

"When did you last speak to her?"

"'Round eight. She came to the kitchen to discuss the morning menu."

"Did she seem off?"

"No."

"Preoccupied?"

"No."

"What's for breakfast?" Kimberly spoke up from behind.

The cook growled, clearly tiring of this game.

"Biscuits with sausage gravy. The mayor's favorite."

"Who made that decision?"

"Mrs. Counsel."

"Who wasn't preoccupied or distracted?"

"I said she wasn't!"

"Though she killed herself just hours later."

"She wouldn't do such a thing—" Again, the cook seemed to realize the trap. "I mean, I never saw any signs."

"What do you think happened?" D.D. asked curiously.

Her change in tone seemed to catch the cook off guard. "What do you mean? I heard she was found hanging. There was a note. Suicide is suicide. What else could've happened?"

"What else indeed," Kimberly commented from behind.

"Do you believe Mrs. Counsel committed suicide?" D.D. repeated. "Just hours after talking to you and ordering breakfast."

"Sure," the cook snapped.

No, Bonita signed. While Hélène made an agitated sound in her throat. The cook glared at both maids. They immediately turned their attention to the floor.

"Who else was here last night?" said Kimberly, now by the walk-in fridge.

"Eight guests. Mayor Howard. The girls and me."

"Where does the help sleep?" Kimberly again.

"We have rooms in the basement. Nice rooms." The cook shot Hélène a look.

"Do you each have your own room?"

"Yeah, they're good rooms."

"And in the summer? Clearly this place requires more than two maids during high season?"

"This house was built in the day and age of live-in servants. There's plenty of space."

"I want to see your rooms," D.D. said.

"Ask the mayor. It's his house."

"How long have you worked here, Hélène?" Kimberly spoke up.

The maid didn't seem to know how to answer. D.D. squatted back down. "It's okay. If you have any concerns about your security, you may walk out with us right now. I will personally guarantee your safety." She looked at Bonita as she said this.

"Now see here, I don't like what you're implying—"

"Hélène."

"I started in January," the woman whispered.

"Do you have your own room?"

"Yes."

"Bathroom?"

"We share. Four girls to a bath. It is better . . . better than what I had back home."

"What did you think of Mrs. Counsel?"

"She took care of us."

"Did you talk to her last night?"

"I cleared the dinner dishes for her and the mayor."

"Did she speak to you?"

"No."

"How did she and the mayor seem?"

Awkward shrug. "It is my job to clear the dishes."

Was it D.D.'s imagination, or did the cook's posture just relax?

"After clearing the dishes, what did you do?"

"I went to bed."

"Did you hear anything?"

"Just . . . sirens. After four. I came upstairs. The mayor. He was very upset. He was . . . he was crying."

D.D. nodded slowly. So the mayor was genuinely distraught over the loss of his wife.

D.D. switched her attention to Bonita. "Did you see Mrs. Counsel last night?"

"She can't talk!" the cook exploded.

"She can indicate yes or no."

"She's stupid—"

"You will shut up or I will remove you from this room!" Kimberly clipped out sharply.

The cook thinned her lips mutinously, but fell silent.

"Bonita, did you see Mrs. Counsel last night?"

A faint nod.

"After dinner?"

Head shake.

"She took them dinner," Hélène volunteered. "She serves, I clear."

Another nod.

"Did you hear anything in the middle of the night?"

Bonita hesitated. She shook her head no, but at her side, her hand stirred. One finger, meaning yes. Hélène jolted slightly, as if realizing for the first time something might be going on. The older maid quickly glanced away.

"Did you hear any sounds of arguing?"

Another head shake. Finger nod.

"Violence?" D.D. asked intently.

Head no. Finger yes.

D.D. blinked her eyes, trying to figure out how to ask her next question. "Do you believe Mrs. Counsel hanged herself?"

"Oh for God's sake!" the cook exploded.

Kimberly strode forward, placed a restraining hand on the woman's shoulder. "One more word . . ."

D.D. kept her eyes on Bonita. The girl looked at the cook. She made a helpless sort of shrug. Playing a role D.D. was starting to recognize. They thought she was stupid and she let them. While down at her side . . .

Two fingers for no.

Bonita had heard something in the middle of the night. There had been an argument, some kind of altercation. Mrs. Counsel hadn't hanged herself.

"All right." D.D. rose smoothly to standing.

She addressed the cook. "Thank you for your time. That will be all for now. Good luck with breakfast."

Kimberly didn't say a word, simply followed D.D. back out through the kitchen doors.

"What did you learn?" Kimberly asked the moment they were clear of the room.

"Mrs. Counsel didn't commit suicide and we gotta get both of those girls out of here, right now."

CHAPTER 26

FLORA

WALT DAVIES IS JACOB'S FATHER. My mind feels shattered by the information. And yet it makes perfect sense. The way the two men move, how they carry themselves. Their shared paranoia but also their natural technical aptitude. Walt has built an entire state-of-the-art microgreens operation in an abandoned barn, while Jacob spent years custom fitting houses and long-haul rigs to hide kidnapped girls.

They are both clever; they are both crazy.

I'm aware of Keith watching me, waiting for my next move, while across the barn Walt continues to fuss over a tray of tiny sprouts. Is he afraid of me, of what I'll do next?

Is he telling the truth when he says that he tried to come back for me? That he believed what his son was doing was wrong and he wanted to rescue me?

This is a man who says the trees scream and the woods are alive with ghosts.

Then again, maybe they are.

I know what must happen next. The whole reason we came to Georgia. Because the only way forward is back. My only end, where it all started eight years before.

"Do you know where he held me?" I ask Walt.

He nods, still stroking pea shoots.

"Was it on this property?"

"Nah. I didn't know he was even in the area. Till one night, at Stickneys Pub, he found me."

"I want to go there," I say.

He knows I don't mean the tavern. "You won't like it," he says softly.

"Take me anyway."

WE DON'T CLIMB INTO WALT'S truck. As Keith and I had theorized yesterday, the preferred mode of travel for the locals was the ATV trails. Walt has his four-wheeler, and we fetch our own to follow him, the subterfuge of having run out of gas no longer being necessary.

Keith doesn't say anything as we approach our ride, still tucked in the bushes. Right before he pulls on his helmet, I stop him with a hand on his shoulder. I lean forward. This time, I find his lips all by myself. We kiss long and slow. Gentle.

It reminds me of the woods of Maine. Of being a girl again, with the sun on my cheeks and a winding deer path unspooling before me. It is promise and hope and a whisper of a future I once thought impossible.

When I finally pull back, his hand is covering my own.

"We'll do this together," he says, and I know exactly what he means.

Keith drives us onto Walt's property. Most likely I should call D.D. and tell her what we have discovered and where we are going. But I feel fragile, the moment too dreamlike to survive being put into words.

I'm not alone. I have Keith. And besides, whatever we learn about Walt, about Jacob, it may still not hold any relevance for the task-force. Maybe it's simply another chapter in my story, which is for me to hear first.

Walt has his shotgun. It's strapped onto the back of his ATV. It doesn't strike me as ominous anymore. Simply a tool a paranoid microgreens grower never leaves home without.

Walt unchains the main gate, opens it long enough for us to pull out on the dirt road. He locks up behind, then mounts his four-wheeler and roars around us to take the lead. We follow him for several miles, having to weave our way around deep ruts. Then a smaller trail appears on the right, heading farther into the woods. Walt guns it and Keith does the same.

Up we climb. I think we must be somewhere in the vicinity of the two grave sites, but having cut through Walt's property, I feel disoriented. I can't be sure.

The wooded trail suddenly spits us out onto a newer dirt road. I recognize the pattern from the map we'd studied yesterday—the whole ATV trail system acts as a series of shortcuts, slicing straight lines through the mountains to connect road here to road there—hence the locals' preference for moving around.

Then, in front of us: a hulking, misshapen form just now appearing in a clearing ahead.

The cabin that broke me.

The cabin that made me.

I can't help myself; I feel as if I've finally come home again.

"WHY DIDN'T JACOB HAVE YOUR last name?" I ask Walt as we climb off our four-wheelers.

We are parked on the edge of the woods. The dilapidated structure is several hundred yards ahead in a clearing. I already know Walt will recon the area before we advance. His paranoia, I can tell, is a life-style.

The old man shrugs. "He *was* called Davies when he was a kid. But his mom and I, we never married. Just two people who shacked up for a bit. I never thought to ask what might be on the birth certificate. Or maybe he changed it later. I didn't ask."

"How old was he when he and his mother split?" Keith asks, removing his helmet, shaking out his hair.

"Four or five. Little guy. Could shoot, though. I taught him that."

"After they left, you never saw them again until . . . he came back?" I ask.

"Nope."

"Never went looking?"

"Nope."

"He just . . . showed up. What, forty years later?" I'm not sure I believe this.

Walt looks at me. "The Lord works in mysterious ways."

"How did you know he was really your son?" Keith asks.

"A man always knows his own blood."

"He's your son," I state without hesitation. "Having seen you both." Then, because Walt is now unhooking the shotgun from his ATV: "Do you know how he died?"

"FBI killed him. It was on the TV."

"The FBI didn't kill him."

Walt stops. He studies me for a long while. "Did you love him?" he asks, which isn't what I was expecting at all. "Seems to me, that's what drives most women to kill."

"I didn't love him. I thought he was a monster. I thought he needed to be wiped off this earth. But toward the end . . . He might have loved me a little. If monsters are capable of such a thing."

Keith blinks his eyes at this revelation.

"Monsters can love," Walt declares. "But that don't change what we are."

Keith and I fall in step behind Jacob Ness's gun-toting father, and follow him toward the cabin.

MY FIRST IMPRESSIONS ARE MIXED. The structure isn't a house as I'd always assumed, but more like a collapsing shack. There's a tiny wooden porch with a sagging roof and rotted floorboards. The first step up isn't even attached anymore, but lies a few feet away, nearly lost in the tall grass.

"Who owns this?" Keith asks, eyeing the building dubiously.

Walt shrugs.

"Jacob said he had to leave because the owner wanted it back," I speak up.

"Nah. This place has been abandoned for decades. Mountains are dotted with shacks just like it. Old family homes, long since deserted. Custom is to let 'em be. Such things can come in handy for lost hikers, hunters, whatnot."

"But I remember lights in the basement. Running water."

"There's a well," Walt says and points a hundred yards off. "Jacob fixed the pump. Not that hard to do."

"And the electricity?"

"Tapped into a line, or was using battery-operated devices. I didn't pay much attention myself, but again, not hard."

Says the guy with an entire growing operation in his ramshackle barn.

"Why didn't anyone notice?" Keith again. "I mean, if this is an abandoned property, shouldn't someone have realized lights were suddenly going on at night?"

"Where are the neighbors to realize?"

Keith and I look around. We see trees and more trees, then a wide, heavily rutted dirt road leading away from the house.

"'Sides," Walt says, "at least when Jacob brought me here, he didn't turn on lights upstairs, only in the cellar."

I nod slowly. I hadn't thought about it, but for our entire stay in the house, we were in the basement, even Jacob. It hadn't occurred to me that might be because he didn't want to give away that he was squatting in a deserted house.

I also understand now why the FBI was never able to find traces of this place's location. It hadn't turned over ownership or gone into foreclosure, or even had a real estate identity. It was just an abandoned shack in the woods.

Again, clever and crazy.

Now Walt steps cautiously onto the front porch, skirting the massive hole in the middle. He leads with his right foot, testing each board before adding his whole weight.

I follow behind him, well aware that this is the height of stupidity. That I got out of this goddamn prison once, and now will probably plunge through some rotted piece of wood to my doom. But I can't stop myself. Already this is everything and nothing like I imagined.

The smell hits me. Mold and mildew. And just like that I'm in the basement again. I reel slightly, put out a hand. Keith catches me, while ahead Walt pauses.

"You're sure?" he asks. He's carrying the shotgun loosely at his side. Whether to protect against any nesting varmints or extract revenge for his son's death, I have no idea. I feel punch-drunk, a woman on a tightrope, peering at the certain death looming below and admiring the view.

I should call D.D., I think again. And not out of investigative duty, but because she'd kick my ass for doing this, and right now her brand of tough love is probably exactly what I need.

Instead, I follow Walt over the threshold.

———

THE MAIN LIVING AREA IS smaller than small, with a crude attempt at a galley kitchen to the left and a giant hole in the wall straight ahead where a woodstove once lived. Standing beside me, Keith sneezes, then sneezes again. Dust whirs up in disturbed clouds. If Jacob had been a squatter, apparently no one has reclaimed the space since.

"When did Jacob bring you here?" I ask Walt now.

He shrugs. "Years ago—"

"What month?" I interrupt.

He has to think about it. "August."

"You're sure? That's the first time you came to this place?"

"Pretty sure." He scratches his beard. "I mean, I don't pay much mind to the calendar."

"I would've been here, five, six months by then. You didn't know before?"

"I had no idea my son had returned to the area, let alone was living in this here cabin with some girl locked in the cellar. Like I said, he found me. Walked right up and introduced himself in the bar."

"Why?" Keith asks.

"Said he wanted to finally meet his old man."

"What was his mood like?" Keith again.

"Dunno. He shook my hand, offered to buy me dinner. I didn't say no to dinner."

"And just like that," I speak up, "he reappears, buys you a meal, then introduces you to his sex slave?"

Walt frowns at me. "I saw him around a few more times. Even brought him to the old homestead. I was growing dope back then. Jacob appreciated it. I could tell the apple hadn't fallen far from the tree. Guy that hard-looking, he was his old man all over again. Nothing he wouldn't drink or snort. I tried to warn him, but he just laughed, told me not to worry." Walt shrugs again. "Not my place to judge another man."

"Did he tell you what he did?" Keith asks.

"Long-haul trucker."

"And his mom?" My turn. "Did he mention her?"

"Nah. And I didn't ask."

"He had a daughter. Did he mention her?"

Walt looks more uncomfortable. "He showed up. Bought me dinner. We did a little talking. A little visiting. I wasn't sure why he'd returned. What he wanted. I was still figuring it out, when he brought me here one night. Told me he wanted to show me something. Told me I'd be proud of him."

Walt stares at me. "You don't remember?"

I'm honestly not sure. Multiple voices in the basement? It rings a bell, but I can't bring it into focus. I suffer an impression of incredible thirst and hunger. Of hearing footsteps and thinking desperately: *Finally, I'll be let out.* There'd be burgers or wings or whatever Jacob's most recent craving was. And water. I desperately wanted water.

Except then there'd been talking. On the other side of the box. So much talking. Me whimpering, clawing my shredded fingertips against the closed lid like a wounded animal. Why wasn't he undoing the lock? Why wasn't he feeding me? Then, the creak of the stairs. Footsteps retreating. Voices drifting farther and farther away, until I was once again alone and starving in the dark.

"He was proud of what he'd accomplished," Walt says now. "Rigging up the place, building the box, snatching himself a friend. Told me all about you, how everyone was looking for you with your picture being all over the news. And still, no one suspected him, knew what had happened, where to look. Like he'd stolen some treasure from right beneath everyone's noses. Guess he thought I'd be proud of him, too. Cuz that's what he remembered from being a little boy. That's what his mom had told him. That I was that kind of man."

Walt doesn't look at me anymore. "I felt shame that night. The trees screamed and raged at me. Wouldn't let me sleep. That's when I knew what I had to do. But I was too late."

"Maybe that's why he brought you over," Keith offers. "He already planned on taking off. He just wanted one last moment to brag."

"Maybe," Walt says. He turns toward the basement stairs.

"Wait." I hold out a hand. "Did Jacob mention being in the area before, say, fifteen years ago?"

I glance at Keith. The time frame of the other graves, and Lilah Abenito's murder.

That shrug again. "Forty years of past is too much to cover. We stuck to the present. That was hard enough." He hits the stairs, rat-a-tat-tat, down to the cellar.

I follow much more slowly, testing each tread, my head pressed against the cool wall for support.

Walt is correct about the cellar. What I'd considered a basement was really little more than a single, dark moldy room. Walt finds a lantern, lights it, and the infamous shit brown carpet once more comes into view. I realize now it's just a remnant tossed upon an earthen floor. The sofa I hated so much is shoved against a wall, stuffing coming out in giant chunks. I remember a coffee table, cheap, compressed wood, but it's nowhere in sight. Maybe I imagined it. Maybe some lost hiker broke it down for firewood. I don't know.

The bathroom in the corner is barely as big as a closet and every bit as disgusting as I remember. I can just make out a moldy bar of soap. Same as the one Jacob let me use to wash my hair? It looks like a separate life-form; I can't even bring myself to touch it.

In my mind, this place is every bit as foul and smelly and awful as my memories. Yet, I recall it somehow being bigger, even nicer. Or maybe that's just how it seemed after being released from a pine box. Hell, Jacob probably could've stuck me in an outhouse after that damn prison, and it would've seemed like a luxurious master bath.

I'm shaking. I don't even realize it until Keith puts his arm around my shoulders. I'm covered in goose bumps and shivering uncontrollably.

Walt, shotgun still in hand, eyes me worriedly. Does he think I'll scream hysterically, break down?

Am I going to scream hysterically and break down?

I can't wrap my mind around it. I'm here at last. Ground zero. And it's the same, but it's different. It's just as horrible and horrifying . . . and yet it also seems smaller, less significant, less scary.

I'm no longer the girl in the box.

I am Flora Dane.

I left this place.

I survived Jacob Ness.

And right now, if his father turns on me with that shotgun, I will have him facedown on this floor with his own shotgun pressed against the back of his head so fast, even Keith won't see it coming. And if he twitches, I'll pull the trigger without thinking twice.

Something must show in my face, because Walt takes a nervous step back.

Fuck this entire damn shack. And thank God Jacob Ness is already burning in hell.

"I'm done here," I state. Then without waiting for either Walt or Keith to respond, I head straight up the rickety stairs, out of the collapsing cabin, and right to the middle of the clearing till I can feel the wind on my face.

I am free, I tell myself.

And for the first time in years, I almost believe it.

CHAPTER 27

Bonita, the blond woman has *named me. I try it on in my head. I wait to hear my mother's voice whisper it to me. I do not feel beautiful with my scarred head and sagging face and dragging foot. Can a Stupid Girl really be Bonita?*

I am humbled the blond woman gave me such a gift. As well as scared.

I am Stupid Girl. I can't work my lips or tongue to tell the detective what she needs to know. I'm too weak to stand up to Cook, who will make Hélène and me pay for talking to the police.

I am nothing. Bonita, Girl—they are both the same. Broken. Though in my differentness, I do know some things others don't. That the house has memory, feels pain. That colors are not just crayons, but moods and powerful expressions of their own.

That my mother is standing beside me, right now. I feel her presence as strongly as the scent of biscuits wafting from the oven. My mother is here, a sliver of silver gliding in and out of the light. She appears when I need her the most. When the worst is about to happen.

I hold my breath, rolling out more biscuit dough, then cutting it into rounds for the waiting cookie sheet. Like Cook, I pretend I don't hear the argument raging on the other side of the kitchen door.

"DO YOU HAVE DOCUMENTATION FOR *either of your maids?" the blond detective is demanding.*

"What do you mean?" Mayor Howard. His voice is hollow with guilt. If I drew him, I would use reds and golds, with a core of darkest night. He loved his wife, but it couldn't save them from the corrupt ambition at the center of their marriage.

The Bad Man is pure black. Mayor Howard . . . he has more color, though the end result is not so different.

"Birth certificate for Bonita—"

"Who is Bonita?"

"Sorry, your niece."

"Her name is Bonita?" The mayor, genuinely confused.

"I don't know," the detective replies crisply. "But I'm pretty sure her birth certificate doesn't list it as Girl."

Silence. The stove timer chimes. Cook is stirring sausage gravy on the gas range while also eavesdropping shamelessly. She's clearly distracted. I put on oven mitts, check the biscuits.

They are fluffy and golden on top. I pull the tray out of the oven, place it on the top to cool. I can't speak. I can't read. The entire world outside this house is terrifying to me. But maybe if I ever did leave, I could be like my own mother, making people sigh happily over plates of food. Cook has taught me enough, and maybe I have some of my mother in me after all.

I feel her again, brushing my shoulder. Does she like the name Bonita? Maybe I could use it instead.

My eyes burn, though I am much too old to cry.

From the other side of the doorway: "Of course we have the paperwork. My wife . . ." The mayor, choked up and angry. "My wife just died! For God's sake, I don't have time for this right now. Have you no compassion?"

Another male voice. The sheriff. I would draw him in shades of deep purples, blues, and reds. Big, like the Bad Man, but softer around the edges. Deeper. For good or evil, I'm not sure yet. But I like his voice. It sounds like a warm blanket, and our rooms in the basement are much colder than anyone thinks.

"Maybe we could wait," the sheriff starts now. "We did find record of the suicide note on the office computer. Here   "

"No." The blond detective again. She is a burst of oranges, yellows, reds. There's no dark in her. Only searing light that will either blind or save. I both fear her presence and lean toward the flame.

My mother brushes my shoulder again. She is agitated today.

Something worse looms ahead. The mayor's wife is dead, the police are still here, and more will be made to pay. Because I can't tell the truth about the Bad Man, what really happened to the mayor's wife, what happens to all of us.

I'm not Bonita.

I'm Stupid Girl once again.

The other female voice speaks up. I don't understand the two female police. The blonde I met first has a hard, Northern clip. This one has a softer voice, rounder vowels. Of here, but not from here. I would color her in the shades of the forest, with sparks of fireflies. She is of the earth. Quieter, but sparkly in her own way.

"Mayor Howard," the other police lady says now, "we understand this is a difficult time. But when you start talking about an illegal organ transplant, I don't care how many years back, the safety of your staff becomes our primary concern."

Total silence. I hastily cut out more biscuits. At the range, Cook is

listening so hard she's forgotten to stir the gravy. I smell it burn before she does. Or maybe she doesn't care.

Hélène is gone. She must tend beds, start the daily cleaning regi-
men. Or she's made the mistake of returning to her room—in which
case, the Bad Man probably already has her, and is playing with his
knife, wringing her neck.

When painting, black is not the absence of color. It is the presence
of many colors. Which makes pure evil hard to predict.

"Does your wife have a personal office in addition to the inn's?"
The blonde again, sounding as if she's offering the mayor a break.

"No. Just the one office. For the business."

"All right. I'll go through it myself. We find the proper paperwork
for your staff, then all is well."

"You need to leave. The night has been long and hard enough.
The guests are headed downstairs. I need to pull things together."

"With all due respect, sir," says the other police lady, "that's not
an option."

"My wife committed suicide—"

"Your wife died a suspicious death."

"What?" The mayor, sounding bewildered.

"That's the current classification." The Southern cop again.
"Suicide is an official ruling. The ME hasn't made it. Meaning currently, your wife died a suspicious death, and your entire lodging
establishment is a crime scene. Be happy Sergeant Warren only wants
paperwork."

Another pause. Then a sound I don't completely understand. Sup-
pressed sobbing. Mayor Howard is crying. In all my years, through all
that's happened . . .

The death of his wife has caused him suffering. Does that make
me happy, ease my own pain?

The sausage gravy is smoking now.

I don't care that the mayor is crying. I have heard so many girls cry and what did it ever get them? I'm happy he hurts. So happy, I slam my round cookie cutter through the biscuit dough and shake the prep table.

Cook eyes me sharply at the unexpected display of emotion, then seems to realize she's failed in her own cooking duties. Belatedly she snatches the cast-iron skillet off the burner, then curses a blue streak.

I smile maliciously at her back.

My mother, my beautiful mamita, brushes my shoulder again. "Chiquita," I can almost hear her whisper, as if to soothe.

If I draw her, what colors would I use? Fire like the blond detective? Earth like the second? Or have I become what made me, bright and shiny on the outside with a dark, soulless core?

I don't have the answer.

I worry again about Hélène. Where is she? Why hasn't she appeared again? She should be as eager as Cook and me to learn what's happening next. Pulling some sheets doesn't take that long. And she's not allowed to start the vacuum cleaner till all the guests are up. Meaning she should be back in the kitchen by now, inventing busy-work while eavesdropping on the cops grilling the mayor.

Unless she did go downstairs.

Unless the Bad Man did take the opportunity to silence one more weak link.

Something terrible: That's what my mami's presence always means. Danger ahead.

I can't take it anymore. I set down the biscuit cutter. And with my hands and apron still dusted with flour, I limp determinedly for the swinging door.

Behind me, Cook makes a strangled sound. I feel the air move. Maybe she tries to grab me. Maybe, the silvery spirit of my mother blocks her. I don't look back. No time for looking back.

I burst into the breakfast room.

I don't pay any attention to the mayor, or the burly sheriff, or the FBI lady. I grab the hand of the blond detective.

I play with fire.

As I drag her wordlessly from the room, toward the servants' quarters below.

CHAOS BEHIND US. THE MAYOR *hastily pushing back his chair, scrambling to follow. "Wait. Stop!"*

The Southern cop: "This is a crime scene."

The purple sheriff: "Mayor Howard, you will sit down. Right now!"

I don't pause. I'm slow, my right leg dragging, but I'm also sparking with energy. The blond cop questions nothing. She grips my hand as tightly as I hold hers. I lead her to a small door off the back hallway. The few rooms in this section are administrative—Mrs. Counsel's office, the filing room, housekeeping supplies. But this door. This unmarked door . . .

I wrench it open, and as always the first thing that hits me is the whiff of decay. While the house sighs in agitation. Buildings have feelings, too, and what has happened in the levels below has hurt it. I understand these things, though from what I can tell, others don't.

I risk a glance at the detective. Her face is impassive. If she catches the odor, feels the house shift nervously, she doesn't show it. Maybe she's like the others, deaf to such things.

Maybe there's no one like me.

The stairway light is on. I don't wait. I can feel a relentless pressure building in my chest. Hélène. Something is wrong. Toward the bottom of the stairs, I trip and nearly go down.

The detective catches me. "Easy," she murmurs.

I'm so strung out I think I might vomit.

This is it, I realize now. I've taken my last stand. Without the killing rage and heroic drama I'd always envisioned. I was going to feel my real name flood through me. I was going to gather my mother's spirit close. Then I was going to unleash myself like an atom bomb through the black rot of this house, searing away the mayor, his wife, the Bad Man. Reducing them to ash.

Now I'm down to a frantic race. To find Hélène. To find something, anything, that might communicate all the words I can't say. If I can make the detective wonder, arouse her suspicions about this place . . . She's fire, not easily doused. She might leave today, but she'll question, she'll gather more information. She'll know enough not to be put off by the mayor's fancy ways.

She'll leave after this. Then I'll wait. Because given this stunt, my fate is sealed. Tonight, the Bad Man will return. He'll step inside my room, lift his knife, and prove what a Stupid Girl I've always been.

Maybe my death will finally give the blond detective what she needs to make the Bad Man pay.

She is fire.

And this whole place needs to burn.

I start throwing open doors. I don't even know what's behind some of them. The Bad Man? Rooms of whips and chains and instruments of torture? Given the sounds I've heard over the years, I've always wondered.

The detective is still holding my hand, but I notice now she's unsnapped her holster. I nod approvingly. She squeezes my fingers.

The first few rooms are empty. Bare cots, blank walls. These spaces are bigger than mine and hold two to four beds. Hélène's is farther down the hall. Small like mine. Once she was in a big room with roommates, but when they left, she was sequestered. She doesn't talk about it. None of the girls ever talk about it. For the past few weeks it's just been her, me, and Stacey. But then Stacey found the knife and I cleaned up the mess and now it's just Hélène and me.

Which is also not good.

The basement never stays empty for long.

I come to my little room on the left. I throw open the door, stumble in before the detective can stop me. Is he here? Is he waiting?

For an instant, I think I see his hulking shape loom ahead. My eyes widen. The Bad Man is here to kill me. But my detective and her fire will get him first.

Except when I flinch and press back against the wall, the dreaded demon turns out to be only a shadow after all.

The detective is at my shoulder, breathing heavily. My fear has spread itself to her.

I try to pull it together. Communicate, communicate—how can I explain?

Pictures beneath my mattress. I grab the thin mattress, toss it up. I should have a drawing or two. But the floor is bare, the pictures gone. The Bad Man got here first.

I whimper in sheer frustration. I need to talk, I need to tell. Hélène, Hélène, Hélène.

Once again, I think I'm going to be sick.

"Is this your room?" the detective asks.

I nod, rub my forehead. It hurts so much. The jagged scar feels like a red-hot poker, searing across my skull.

"Where are your clothes?"

I shake my head, still massaging my temples.

"You don't have any clothes?"

I point to a small blue pile at the end of my cot, my old, threadbare uniform, which I wear at night.

"Personal possessions?"

I hold up two fingers. No.

"It's freezing down here."

Nod.

"Bonita, this isn't right. How they're treating you . . . this isn't family taking care of family."

I stare at her hard. I try to tell her with my eyes that they're not my family. My mamita was my family. But the Bad Man shot her, and the bullet hit me—and when I woke up again, here I was. With a cracked skull and a drooping face and no voice.

Mrs. Counsel, standing over me. "She's awfully young. Are you sure she won't grow out of it?"

The Bad Man, hulking behind her. "The doctor said something about speech aphasia; the bullet damaged the speech/language center of the brain. She'll never be able to speak, read, or write."

"Hmmm. A mute housemaid. I don't know."

"Please, Martha. It's perfect and you know it."

I stare all this at the detective. I try, as hard as one person can, to beam my life story from my head into hers.

The detective takes my hand again. "Shhh," she says. "Shhh," and I realize I'm finally making a sound, from deep in my chest. Keening. I am keening and rocking and crying for the little girl who was gone before she ever had a chance. I'm mourning the life I've been trying to return to ever since.

I need the detective to understand. For someone to see me. For someone to hear me, and all the words that were stolen from my throat.

"I'll take you upstairs," she begins.

I jerk away. Shake my head furiously. Hélène, we must find Hélène. She doesn't get it. No one gets it. I'm on my own.

I limp once more for the hallway. I hear noise on the stairs behind us. The others coming to help—or maybe the mayor, having won the battle, coming to interrupt. I can't worry about him or what he'll do. Hélène should've appeared by now. Something is wrong and I'm the only hope she has.

Stacey. We never really knew each other. But I watched her die, and in that instant, we were sisters. I have such little family left. So I must do this for her, for Hélène. My sisters in death.

More doors, flinging them open wildly. I don't know where the Bad Man is. If he appears, I hope the detective shoots him. If not, I will grab her gun and do it for her. But maybe one of these rooms has Hélène. She's hiding, she's frightened. She's dead.

It's all crashing in on me now. My last stand. My final chance. If I can't make the detective realize what is going on . . .

Please, please, please . . .

The pair of heavy wooden doors at the end of the hallway. Guarding the big room, the awful room. Brimstone and blood.

I shiver. Then I grab the heavy handle and pull with all my strength. But it won't budge. Locked. Of course. The room where Mrs. Counsel died. The room no one is ever allowed to see.

I whimper in sheer frustration.

"Hey now." The detective, standing beside me again. "It's okay. I can help. This room, it's important? You need in?"

I nod frantically.

"I'll get the key. This house is a crime scene. As a detective, I have the right to search."

I feel fresh moisture on my cheeks.

"Are you scared?"

I nod.

"Do you want to go back upstairs?"

I shake my head.

She reaches out, touches my cheek. Her blue eyes are clear, her features hard. I know she means it when she says, "No one is going to hurt you, Bonita."

I can't help myself. I smile, my crooked, awful smile, all my drooping mouth has ever been able to manage. She doesn't understand.

And I'm still just a Stupid Girl. I take her hand. I press it against my cheek. I let her feel my tears. I let myself experience one moment of human kindness. Probably all I have left.

I'm going to die tonight. I fear for Hélène. But I mourn for myself and who I might have been.

Then, I take a deep breath. I straighten my spine. I pull away. I hold up two fingers.

No. She will not be able to save me. No one can defeat the Bad Man.

I turn back down the hall, and stumbling over my own dragging leg, continue my search for Hélène.

CHAPTER 28

KIMBERLY

MAYOR HOWARD WAS CLEARLY AGITATED. "You can't go down there! I am the homeowner. I deny you permission. For God's sake, my wife is dead. I'm the victim here!"

He tried to rise from his seat. Sheriff Smithers used his massive hand to force the man back down.

"Interfere in our investigation again, and I will arrest you," Kimberly informed the red-faced mayor. She turned to Sheriff Smithers. "You got him?"

"He's not going anywhere."

"Good."

Kimberly didn't know where the silent maid was taking D.D., but the look of determination on the young girl's face had been enough to tell her it wasn't good. D.D. could handle it, though. Meaning they had another issue that required immediate tending. Martha Counsel's office.

Kimberly wanted first crack at all the woman's correspondence, business diaries, and official documents. Especially any related to their "niece" and their other workers.

Here was a fact: Where there was one crime, there were generally dozens more.

Basically, if Martha Counsel was the kind of woman willing to accept an illegal organ, and her husband was the kind of guy willing to turn a blind eye to such a major scam, what else were they involved with?

Kimberly was hoping to find answers in the woman's office, as apparently Martha Counsel had been the brains of the operation—or at least the head administrator.

First surprise when she entered the space: Someone had been there first. The left-hand drawer of the cherrywood desk had been yanked open and files spilled across the top and down onto the floor. Further inspection revealed the lock had been forced.

Kimberly scowled, snapped on gloves, and kneeled down to survey the damage.

Mayor Howard had been accompanied by Sheriff Smithers at all times, and the sheriff hadn't mentioned this, meaning it had most likely happened after they were done checking the office's desktop computer. From that moment on, the mayor had been sequestered in the nook. Which left the cook in the kitchen? It was possible she'd snuck down the hall. Or the maids, Bonita and Hélène. Given Bonita seemed to have a task only D.D. could handle, Kimberly felt it was safe to rule her out.

Unless, of course, there was someone else in the house.

Kimberly got that prickly feeling in the back of her neck. Sure, they'd been treating Martha Counsel's hanging as a suspicious death. But they hadn't gotten too serious about considering the inn's guests as a threat.

Kimberly rose to standing and hurried back to the front room.

Keeping her gaze on Mayor Howard, who sat in distressed silence, she pulled aside Sheriff Smithers.

"Where are we with interviewing the guests?"

"Four couples. I sent a deputy up to fetch them. They were getting dressed, given the early morning hour, then coming on down."

"How long ago?"

"I don't know." He glanced at his watch. "Been thirty minutes or so."

"No one needs thirty minutes to get dressed. Have your deputy escort them down, right now. Verify everyone's photo ID, take all vitals. The office has been burglarized. Something more is going on here. Or someone else is in this hotel."

Sheriff Smithers thinned his lips, nodded curtly. He activated the radio clipped to his shoulder, murmured some instructions low enough for the mayor to remain oblivious, then resumed his oversight of the dining room.

Kimberly hightailed it back to the office. Now she noticed a painted door ajar just beyond the office. It produced a draft of cold air. Stairs to the basement, she realized. That's what Mayor Howard had been talking about. He didn't want them going "down there." More power to Bonita and D.D., then. Kimberly hoped the girl was giving D.D. the grand tour—deadly family secret here, evil doings there. That would be perfect.

In the meantime, Kimberly had the office.

Each of the files strewn across the floor bore a name of an employee. The paperwork inside seemed standard: copies of W-2s, photo IDs. Martha Counsel had said her paperwork was in order—and at first blush, she hadn't been lying.

But then Kimberly noticed what wasn't present. Hélène's file. Anything identifiable with their niece. Furthermore, there was an empty folder. *Stacey Kasmer* was inked across the top. But Kimberly couldn't find any trace of a photo ID or other paperwork.

Next, she booted up the desktop. Password protected. Meaning she'd have to return to the mayor for info, which she didn't feel like doing right now, or wait for Keith, who could probably learn more from the machine in ten minutes than she could in ten hours. She wondered what he and Flora were doing for the day. Hopefully keeping out of trouble.

She turned around, noticing one of the volumes was slightly askew on the bookshelf. Kimberly ran her fingers carefully up and down the spines of the old history books. She tugged one. Sure enough, the rest came out to reveal a squat black wall safe tucked behind.

Roughly the size of a hotel safe, the rectangular unit probably didn't contain large treasures. But important passports, documents, a detailed confession of the kidney operation fifteen years ago—Kimberly could only hope.

But how to get the combination?

She rocked back on her heels, considering. Dates of birth were always possible, but also predictable. In her experience . . . She inspected the inside perimeter of the shelf, seeking for a taped slip of paper. When that revealed nothing, she crawled under the desk, clicked on her pocket flashlight, and repeated the same careful scrutiny of the underside of the desk. Still no dice.

Everyone wrote down combinations as everyone feared forgetting. Furthermore, they kept them close because no one wanted to slog halfway across a house when they did forget. Meaning there had to be the combination somewhere. She just had to think like Martha Counsel.

Kimberly took a seat in the desk chair. Black executive leather. Too big for her slender form, but nice. An instant appearance of corporate power. She pulled the chair up to the desk, took in the view. Computer monitor front and center. Keyboard mounted beneath. Mouse pad to the right. Three beautifully framed photos to the right. The mayor and Martha's wedding photo. Then a faded, vintage print, maybe Martha Counsel's mother.

The final photo was a woman with a brilliant smile and shiny black hair. Kimberly didn't recognize her at all.

But all in all, a tidy space. Everything in its place.

Kimberly swiveled the chair till her back was now to the desk and she was directly facing the safe. The code would be within reaching distance. She was certain of it. Martha was a woman who clearly didn't like clutter and was much too efficient to want to spend time digging around to find a forgotten string of numbers. Elegant yet personal. Subtle but easy access.

Then Kimberly got it. The first crumbling novel, a dated history of the area. Kimberly grabbed it off the floor and sure enough, discovered three numbers, written in pencil lightly across the inside top cover.

Kimberly spun the dial. Right. Left. Right.

Click.

She opened the door.

THE SAFE MIGHT NOT BE tall, but it was surprisingly deep. First thing Kimberly encountered, a gold box. She drew it out, took one sniff, and knew what it was: chocolate. Judging by the packaging, very high end. And clearly valued enough to keep in the safe, away from greedy staff members.

Kimberly had to smile. She could respect a woman who kept imported chocolates under lock and key.

Next up: a brick of one-hundred-dollar bills, totaling ten thousand dollars. This was stacked on top of three more bricks, with rows of three going back, back, back.

Kimberly pulled out a hundred thousand dollars. All in cash. Significant funds for an inn operator, she thought. And yet more evidence that nothing in this place was as it seemed.

Next, she found passports. Martha Counsel. Howard Counsel.

Then two more sets from Argentina. Photos matched Martha and Howard. Names were not the same.

Cash and fake IDs.

"Now we're getting somewhere," Kimberly murmured.

After cash and fake IDs, next up would be a gun. But instead, feeling lightly into the dark depths, Kimberly felt a different shape completely. Several inches long, flat, with narrow grooves and jagged teeth. She figured it out just as she drew it from the felt-lined safe: a brass key. Old and heavy, like they used to have in historic hotels and grand manors.

She looked around the updated office with its modern computer, printer, and scanner. The filing cabinets all contained traditional locks, the door to the room, as well.

Then, she had an idea. Holding the key close, she descended down into the basement.

SHE FOUND D.D. WITH THE girl.

D.D. stood in front of a pair of heavy wooden doors at the end of the long, cold hallway. The girl was moving frantically from door to door, her agitation making it clear that whatever she was looking for, she hadn't found it.

Kimberly felt like she'd entered a dungeon. If the upstairs of the B&B was the stately Victorian, then this was the dark dank cellar, hastily retrofitted with rooms for the staff. The corridor was narrow, the floor tiled with stone worn smooth from decades of use, the walls lined with old-fashioned-looking sconces that added more shadows than they dispelled.

Bonita appeared in front of Kimberly. She was stumbling worse than usual, nearly lurching on her feet. She took one look at Kimberly with tear-streaked cheeks, then literally shoved her aside and grabbed the next doorknob.

Kimberly looked askance at D.D.

"She's looking for something, but I don't know what." D.D. shrugged, clearly as miserable as the girl.

Kimberly held up the brass key. "Would this help?"

Immediately the girl was in front of her, eyes wide. She grabbed the key, then careened down the hall to the heavy wooden doors.

Even from here, Kimberly could tell the huge brass lock appeared to be the perfect match for the key. The girl inserted the old key and gave a hard twist. A resounding click echoed down the narrow hall.

The girl shoved both doors open, nearly falling into the room. A fresh rush of cold air greeted all of them. Then D.D. and Kimberly moved forward.

COMPARED TO THE CORRIDOR, THE room was enormous. Old. Again the smooth stone floor, colored somewhere between gray and black. A massive stone hearth, which dominated the side wall and featured giant slabs of granite.

Kimberly could smell ash, so the hearth had recently been used— and thank goodness. Given the pervasive chill, she couldn't imagine staying in this room during any season without a fire.

They were beneath the earth, so there were no windows. Just more of the old brass lights, which she flicked on with a switch. In the back of the room loomed a huge oak table, large enough to seat twelve if not sixteen. Before it sat a long dark leather sofa with half a dozen wingback chairs arranged around it in a semi-circle.

A gathering space. But for what? Kimberly couldn't see any evidence of a TV, or electronics of any kind. What would make a dozen people want to sit in this room in the bowels of the earth?

The girl stood in front of the sofa. She pointed at the floor. Stomped her foot.

D.D. had moved closer to her. Now the detective reached down, inspected the stone floor. "I don't see anything."

Another foot stomp, the girl clearly frustrated.

Kimberly spoke up, "You gave Sergeant Warren a drawing. Of a demon. Was that from you?"

Frantic nod.

"That demon, was he here?"

Very fast nodding now.

"He's a man," D.D. said.

Yes yes yes yes yes yes.

"Is he here now?" Kimberly asked.

Shrug. Fear plain on her face.

"What about last night?"

Yes!

"With Martha and Mayor Howard?"

Yes yes yes yes yes yes.

"Bonita," D.D. said slowly, "is he the one who hurt Mrs. Counsel?"

Yes!

Kimberly drifted closer. She peered at the floor, then around the room. She couldn't make out any obvious signs of blood or violence. Then again, the only way to fake a hanging was to actually strangle the victim. A relatively clean death. She would have to bring in an evidence team. There were chemicals that could be sprayed that would reveal traces of blood. Of course, the older the residence, the harder it was to prove that blood was a recent event. It seemed most buildings had stories of violence to tell.

She walked the space, sniffed the hearth, held out her hands for warmth. It had definitely been used recently—though again, that didn't prove anything. And their interrogation of Bonita wouldn't be enough. By definition, they had to ask her yes-or-no questions. Technically, that was leading a witness—and given she also was a minor, it wouldn't hold up in court.

They would have to call in some kind of forensic interview special-ist, because this was clearly outside Kimberly and D.D.'s wheelhouse. They were simply doing what good investigators did—making it up as they went along.

Kimberly glanced at the doors. The very large, very heavy, very solid oak doors, kept locked at all times, with a key hidden in a safe. What was it about this room that demanded such security?

Mostly, she thought it was cold and drafty, and even with the fur-nishings, too dungeony for most tourists' tastes. Dinner theater? But then, why lock up the set?

Bonita was tugging on D.D.'s arm, clearly agitated again.

"Are you looking for the demon man?" D.D. asked.

Quick no, eyes wide with fear.

"But you're looking for someone?"

Yes.

"A guest?"

No.

Pause. D.D. clearly trying to figure out how to most efficiently ask the next question. "Is it someone I've met?"

Yes.

"Mayor Howard is still upstairs with Sheriff Smithers," Kimberly provided. "The cook is in the kitchen. Smithers's deputies are round-ing up the guests. Someone broke into Martha Counsel's office. I'm wondering if there isn't a fox in our midst. Or maybe," she consid-ered, looking at the girl, "a demon."

The girl sighed. Tugged D.D.'s arm again.

"Hélène!" D.D. declared suddenly. "The other maid."

Yes yes yes yes yes yes!

"Are you worried about her?"

Yes!

"Do you think something bad might have happened?"

Furious head nod.

"The demon?"

More nodding.

Kimberly and D.D. exchanged a glance. "Hélène's personnel file was missing from Martha Counsel's office," Kimberly murmured.

"Top-to-bottom search. Entire place. Between a suspicious death and now a missing woman, we have cause. Let's tear this place apart."

"The mayor is going to have a fit," Kimberly said.

D.D.'s smile was feral. "Let him."

She took Bonita's hand. "You stay with me, all right? We're a team. Where I go, you go. You don't leave my side; I don't leave your side."

The girl looked up at her. In the shadows, her expression was hard to read. Something between longing and fatalism, Kimberly thought. And being a mother herself, that expression on a child's face broke her heart.

"You're not staying here anymore," Kimberly spoke up.

The girl startled. Clearly she hadn't expected this.

"As of now, you are a witness. We're taking you away and keeping you safe."

That look again: wanting to believe but fearing to hope.

"Bonita," D.D. said softly. "We got you. I swear it. We got you."

The girl took a breath. She nodded slowly. But as she followed D.D. out the door, still holding the detective's hand, Kimberly could see nothing but fear in the slump of the girl's shoulders.

They climbed the basement stairs back to the main lobby.

D.D. took Bonita to a separate room in the inn, so the girl wouldn't be exposed to the mayor or the cook for one moment longer.

While Kimberly instructed Sheriff Smithers to have his officers tear apart the inn. Which left Kimberly to interview the gathered guests, four ordinary-looking couples who clearly had no idea what was going on, and were rapidly losing whatever initial excitement they'd felt over the situation.

The mayor sat slouched in the corner, lost in a world of grief and guilt.

They didn't find Hélène.

And by the end of the afternoon, it was clear the cook had vanished, as well.

Kimberly declared the entire inn a crime scene. The guests gathered their bags and were transferred to other hotels, officers logging their IDs and personal contact information. After a bit of discussion, Sheriff Smithers made the decision to take the mayor into custody, charged with failing to provide proper paperwork on his employees. Most likely, the mayor would be out on bail in the morning, but his arrest kept the B&B clear for the evening, enabling the crime scene techs to descend and perform a much more thorough exam. It also gave some teeth to their future warning for the mayor not to leave town.

Mayor Howard didn't respond. Now devoid of his morning bluster, he'd journeyed to a remote place deep inside himself. Sheriff Smithers informed Kimberly he'd be putting the mayor on suicide watch. Kimberly thought that was an excellent judgment call.

Then it was done. The Mountain Laurel B&B devoid of guests and staff. One set of investigators leaving, another set—including forensic techs—arriving, while the gathered locals finally grew bored of the show.

Kimberly and D.D. walked Bonita down the front steps. They waited patiently for the girl to get her bearings as she stood in the middle of the sidewalk and looked around in a daze. Had she even been allowed outside the inn before?

And the day had been long. They were all exhausted and there was still the taskforce debriefing to come.

They loaded Bonita into Kimberly's vehicle and headed for the team's motel, never noticing the shadow draw away from the window across the street.

CHAPTER 29

FLORA

KEITH AND I ARE EXHAUSTED by the time we return to the motel. I'm not even sure what time it is anymore. Six P.M.? Seven? We should probably shower and prepare for some kind of team meeting. I don't want to shower. I don't want to move. I want to sink down on the bed and stare at the ceiling till my vision blurs and reality falls away.

After our visit to Jacob's shack, Walt brought us back to his property. He fed us. Wood-fired fresh fish, topped with lemon slices and microgreens. It was better than anything I've eaten in a restaurant. So we sat on the front porch beside the washer and dryer and ate a meal any five-star chef would've been proud of.

Keith ate two plates. Given that I was suffering an out-of-body experience at the time, I stuck to one.

"You don't like it?" Walt asked me anxiously.

"I don't eat much."

"You should eat. A girl needs her strength."

Which of course, completely killed my appetite. Keith got Walt to talk. About his precious microgreens. About all the time he now spent in fancy Atlanta restaurants and the trade secrets he'd picked up along the way. About his plans for expansion, his paranoia about rivals.

He still wasn't aware of Jacob being in Niche fifteen years ago—or any time prior to Jacob showing up in the bar and introducing himself. Then again, Walt didn't get out much himself. Townspeople didn't like him and the feeling was mutual.

What was Jacob driving the time Walt had seen him?

Walt had to think about it. A pickup, he thought. Nothing special. Good enough for getting around on dirt roads.

Did Jacob own the truck? Had he rented or borrowed it?

Walt had just stared at Keith. Now why the hell would he ask questions like that?

License plates, Keith insisted. Were they Georgia, or out of state?

He thought Georgia. And oh yeah, definitely local.

This is enough to rouse me out of reverie. "How do you know Jacob's vehicle was local?"

"Town sticker on the windshield. You know. For the dump."

So Jacob had been driving a locally owned truck. Maybe something he stole? Or borrowed from a friend? Keith looks at me. I can tell already what he's thinking: We should get a photo of Walt's vehicle, including plates. I nod faintly. Keith excuses himself, disappearing quickly off the porch and on mission.

Keith really is good at this stuff.

Walt insists on cleaning up after the meal. I roam the tiny cabin, searching for photos, personal mementos, anything that might tell me something. Mostly, I sneeze at the thick piles of dust and feel increasingly claustrophobic in the dark, musty space.

If Jacob had ever lived here as a little boy, I can find no trace of it. Any remnants of Walt's family are long gone and all that remains of family photos are the faint outlines where they'd once been hung on the walls.

Keith returns. Clearly, it's time for us to be on our way. What do you say to the father of the man who kidnapped you? The father who swore he came back to save you, only to discover he was too late? The father who greeted you at gunpoint, before giving you a tour of your greatest nightmare, then feeding you a perfectly lovely meal?

I go with a simple handshake. My mind isn't working anymore. I've gone down some rabbit hole where nothing feels real.

Keith, once again, has held it together. He thanks Walt for his time, the tour, the meal. Wishes him the best with his microgreens—why not? Mentions we'd probably visit again soon. Might bring an associate or two—such as the police.

Walt nods nervously, wiping his hands again and again on the legs of his jeans. He agrees to all.

We regard each other for a long moment. I can tell he has no more apologies in him, and I know I have no more forgiveness in me, so I guess that makes us even.

"Thank you for the fish," I manage.

Then I follow Keith out the door and let him drive us back to the hotel.

"I'M SORRY," THE MOTEL ATTENDANT says the moment we walk through the lobby doors. "You must leave."

I stare at Keith. I haven't been of sound mind for hours now, so maybe I'm mishearing this.

Keith: "Excuse me?"

"We cannot have you as guests anymore. You must go." The attendant is the same man from yesterday. Small of stature, slight build, thick dark hair, and very nervous hands. He's clasping and unclasping them now, as if he's not quite sure what to do with himself.

"I thought these rooms were reserved for a week." Keith, taking charge.

"Yes. But there has been a change. Please get your things. I can give you a list of other properties."

"Is there a problem with our rooms?" Keith asks.

"Yes. That's it." The tiny man brightens. I stare at him intently. He is the worst liar I've ever encountered.

"Then we'll take another set of rooms."

"You can't."

"We can't?"

"The problem . . ." The man purses his lips, clearly thinking hard. "The problem is with all the rooms!" Fresh smile. He believes he has saved himself. I'm wondering if there are any straws in the small breakfast nook. I've used them to kill before. I'm sure I can do it again.

Keith takes hold of my hand, clearly sensing my mood. "So you're kicking everyone out? All of your guests?"

"Yes!"

"The entire assembled law enforcement team? FBI agents, county police? You do not want these fine and upstanding officers in your establishment?"

Dark rounded eyes. Fresh hesitation.

"There's a problem with all the rooms," the attendant repeats again. His voice sounds squeaky.

Keith perfectly composed, "I demand to speak to the manager."

Finally a normal reaction. The attendant pulls himself together, puffs out his chest. "I am the manager!"

"Then I demand to speak to the owner."

"I am the owner! This is my establishment! Now you must leave. Go!"

Behind us, the lobby doors open. Kimberly comes striding in with D.D. Some young girl dressed as a maid follows in their footsteps. The girl has a slight limp and drooping face and she's staring about in complete bewilderment.

"I met Jacob Ness's father," I hear myself say.

"The motel is kicking us out," Keith adds at the same time.

Kimberly and D.D. stop. The girl gazes at me wide-eyed.

"Give me thirty seconds with this guy," I announce, "and we'll have our rooms back."

"D.D." Kimberly instructs dryly, "Get your dog back on her leash."

"One more word," D.D. informs me, "and I'll call your mother."

I growl low in my throat. The sound of frustration. But she has me and she knows it. Because then my mom will call Dr. Samuel Keynes. And once my FBI victim advocate is involved . . . things get complicated. As D.D. well knows.

"So, about our rooms." Kimberly turns to the manager. Her voice is softer when she wants it to be. With a trace of the South that's been her home for a decade now. D.D. and I will always be true North. Kimberly, on the other hand, can pull off local charm. "What seems to be the problem?"

The tiny man is eager to talk to her. He pulls his gaze quickly from me. "Um . . . mechanical. All rooms must be evacuated. Everyone. Everyone must go."

"Even though we paid for an entire block of rooms for the week? Arranged through the county sheriff's department?"

"Sorry. So sorry. Nothing can be done. Everyone must go."

"Do you have a list of places we could try instead?"

"Yes!"

"Except . . ."

The manager—or owner, or whatever—flushes.

"My memory," Kimberly says calmly, "is that this was one of the only places that could accommodate a group of our size. Furthermore, given that we're about to go into the weekend during the busy fall season, what are the chances of any of these new places having rooms available?"

"Maybe you'll get lucky."

"I don't think we will. I think you're trying to kick us out of town. Split up the taskforce group. Or maybe force us all back to Atlanta. Now why would you want to do that?"

"The motel has a mechanical problem," the man squeaks again.

"You certainly are about to," I mutter.

D.D. glares at me.

"What *exactly* is the problem?" Kimberly again.

"Umm . . . No hot water! Can't have rooms without hot water."

"Perfect. I'll make a call. We'll get that fixed for you right away. Consider it a sign of our appreciation."

The manager stands there, stupefied. "And . . . and . . . my computers are down. I can't check anyone in. No computers, no service."

"I can fix that," Keith speaks up.

The man looks like he wants to cry. Or flee. Or both. "Please?" he tries.

"No."

D.D., who has been quiet this whole time, finally speaks. "Who asked you to send us away?"

The man's face twists. His hands return to their frantic clasping and unclasping. "I don't know what you're talking about."

"Then consider this our real gift to you." Kimberly touches the man's arm. "We won't press, for now. You can tell whoever demanded our departure that the police pulled rank. There was nothing you could do. And you can also tell your boss if he has a problem with our presence, feel free to contact us directly. Now, I'm going to go shower." She pulls out her room key. "Debrief in an hour." She stares at me. "I'm sorry, did you say you met Jacob Ness's *father*?"

"Yes."

"Well, you'll have much to share at the meeting."

"Wouldn't miss it for the world," I inform her.

Kimberly heads down the hall. I wait for D.D. to follow, but she and her new charge just stare at me.

"You two have adjoining rooms?" D.D. asks Keith and me.

Of course, she would know that.

Keith nods.

"I'm taking them. For Bonita and me. She can't be alone. She's a material witness."

"Bonita?" Keith asks.

D.D. gestures to the girl. "She used to work at the Mountain Laurel B and B. Now she's with us."

"Where do Keith and I go?" I ask, still processing the room change.

"You two can have my space." She smiles knowingly. Meddler.

"I can get a cot," Keith offers.

"No, no, no," the owner protests immediately. "No cots. You shouldn't even have rooms!"

Fuck Kimberly and her dog-on-a-leash comment. I reach down, pull out my butterfly blade, and make a show of flipping it open, closed, open, closed.

"You may have a cot!" the man squeaks.

But then I glance at the young maid. Her face has gone bone white. Her eyes are round with fear and she is staring at my knife in horror.

I quickly put it away, but not before I see her touch her forearm, where the cuff of her sleeve has ridden up, and an intricate pattern of scars dances across her exposed skin.

I don't feel strong anymore.

I feel shame.

For being what a monster made me.

I head down the hall before any of them see me cry.

CHAPTER 30

KIMBERLY

No LASAGNA OR CHOCOLATE TRIFLE from the church ladies tonight. Instead, the sheriff's conference room featured trays of deli sandwiches, a couple of neglected salads, and a table full of assorted beverages, most heavy on the caffeine. Franny bustled about, clearing empty plates onto a giant serving platter she effortlessly hefted from table to table, while smiling so brightly she looked like a cross between June Cleaver and a mental patient. Around the U-shaped tables, investigators booted up computers while shoveling food into their mouths.

Kimberly took a moment to gauge the overall mood. Tired but wired, she decided. She walked through the door, Flora and Keith in tow. She went with a turkey sub, a pile of green salad, and a Diet Coke. Then she took the open chair next to Sheriff Smithers. Of all of them, he looked the worse for wear. Kimberly and her crew had no ties to this area, whereas for the sheriff this was all personal.

He gave her a nod, chewed absently.

"Howard Counsel settled?" Kimberly murmured.

"Got him in a holding cell, deputy on watch."

"I'm sorry," she offered.

The sheriff looked at her. "Bad things happening around here. *Bad* things. Feels like I don't know this place anymore."

"We'll figure it out."

"Phone's starting to ring off the hook. People want reassurances that their community is safe and the problem solved. Hell, I'm more confused than I was yesterday, though of course I can't tell them that."

"Lying is part of policing," Kimberly assured him.

"Except, I want to know my county is safe, as well. Only a matter of time before the press arrives. I can't believe we've been lucky this long."

"With the ME returning to Atlanta with three more bodies, our time is probably running out," Kimberly agreed.

The sheriff closed his eyes. "You really think Martha Counsel hanged herself?"

"No."

"Someone else did it. Not her husband. I don't believe that for a moment. Meaning there's another threat out there. One we haven't identified yet."

Kimberly eyed the man with genuine sympathy. She understood his stress and strain. Their current situation had just gone from one body to five, from a cold case to a fresh murder. Nothing about this was good, especially for the local cop.

On impulse she reached over and squeezed the sheriff's meaty hand. "We're on this."

He didn't appear convinced, but at least he squeezed back.

Fresh activity in the doorway. Kimberly's fellow ERT agents arriving, dirt still smeared across their clothes. With Dr. Jackson en route to Atlanta with the recovered skeletons, the team would provide the update on the burial sites.

Kimberly waved at Harold, his lanky frame looming above his

teammates. As always, their leader, Rachel, headed the charge. She nodded at Kimberly in greeting, her sunburned face streaked with sweat and grime. Franklin and Maggie filed in after their compatriots, and they all made a beeline for food and water. Harold, after a moment of hesitation, helped himself to three different subs. The man might be built like a beanpole, but he could eat like a sumo wrestler.

Flora and Keith had already taken seats, Flora with a bottle of water, Keith with pasta salad. Kimberly let the Evidence Response Team take up positions, then it was time to start. She rose, moving to the front of the room.

"It's been a big day. Looks to me like many of you have findings to report. I'm going to start with our early morning callout to a suspicious death at the Mountain Laurel B and B." Briefly, she recapped the discovery of Martha Counsel's body, the accompanying suicide note, and Mayor Howard's revelation that his wife had had an illegal kidney transplant approximately fifteen years ago. She noticed Franny stopped fussing at the food table and stood silently, the sorrow tangible on her face. Like the sheriff, she'd probably personally known the Counsels. Nothing in this community would be the same again.

Rachel raised her hand. "Hang on. We recovered medical supplies connected to one of the bodies in the mass grave. Are you saying that victim might have been the source of the illegal kidney?"

"We don't know yet. The doctor who performed the operation passed away eight years ago. We're working on tracking down his former receptionist now to gain access to his old files. But knowing a member of this town underwent an illegal medical procedure right about the same time four bodies were buried in the woods hardly seems like coincidence."

"Meaning there could be other locals who visited this same doctor," Rachel said evenly.

Kimberly nodded. "Absolutely."

More hands shot up, but she held up her own.

"Hang on," she said. "We learned other news at the Mountain Laurel, as well. It would appear at least some of the staff isn't legal. And given that most are young women, it's highly possible our four victims in the woods have a connection to the bed and breakfast. Unfortunately, because they weren't all documented, I'm not sure how we can go back fifteen years and search for their identities. But at the very least, we know there's some kind of human trafficking going on at the Mountain Laurel, whether it's for low cost help or, worse, organ donor candidates."

The revelation rippled through the room.

"Mayor Howard has been taken into custody for now and is on suicide watch. We also have a . . ." She hesitated. She didn't want to give away much about D.D.'s new charge, Bonita. The girl was alone, voiceless, vulnerable. "We have a source," Kimberly said at last, "who has led us to believe there is another player in this operation. An unknown male, can't tell you anything more than that at the moment. It's highly possible he's the one who killed Martha Counsel, so whoever he is, he clearly has a stake in things. We believe the cook may also be complicit, and she has disappeared. Sheriff Smithers has issued a BOLO with her description. Also missing, another maid, Hélène Tellier. We have reason to believe her life is in jeopardy. Maybe even the cook, or the UNSUB, kidnapped her."

Around the room, eyes widened. Hearing it all spoken out loud, even Kimberly was startled by just how much had happened in the past twelve hours.

One of her fellow FBI agents raised his hand. "We have news that might be relevant."

"Go on."

"We've been running background on all the names of hotel guests we've been able to gather for the past sixteen years, looking for registered sex offenders, individuals with criminal histories, et cetera."

Kimberly nodded.

"A good ten to fifteen percent of the names registered at local hotels—they don't exist. The names appear to be aliases. Nor can we find corresponding credit card charges to go with these reservations, which suggests the individuals paid cash. Cross-referencing the names with restaurant credit card receipts, also nothing. We have dozens of room reservations at multiple lodging establishments that appear to belong to ghosts."

Sheriff Smithers stirred.

"Ten to fifteen percent, you say?" he spoke up.

The agent nodded. "We're talking dozens of people a year, going back a decade."

"There's always some people who prefer to pay cash. But that number seems mighty high. All lone individuals? Male, female?" the sheriff asked.

"No discernible pattern. Some reservations are for couples, some for males, females. Some names imply ethnicity, though who knows?"

"Time of year?" Kimberly pushed.

"Follows the seasonal trend. Most of the names are from the summer, when Niche is busiest. Then weekends in the fall, that sort of thing."

"So our 'ghost' tourists are arriving with everyone else. Blending in."

"Correct."

"Across multiple lodging establishments?"

"Also correct." The agent hesitated. "Though it's worth noting we didn't get any names from the Mountain Laurel inn. They claimed their computer system didn't go back far enough. I'm wondering now . . ."

"If you *did* have access to those records, just how many more 'ghosts' that would add to the list," Kimberly finished for him.

The agent nodded.

"What would draw dozens of people to one small town each year, all operating under fake names?" Kimberly asked slowly. She looked at the sheriff, but it was Keith who spoke up.

"Human trafficking, drug distribution, illegal organ transplants or other medical procedures," he rattled off. "Maybe even a pornography ring, though most of those perps prefer to stay at home with their computers. A sex ring, on the other hand, that would do it."

Kimberly stared at the computer analyst. "Thanks," she said finally.

"In all of those scenarios"—Keith leaned forward, clearly warming to his topic—"the constant is that Niche is serving as the hub. The participants come here, using fake names, then go home again. Given the amount of tourists passing through, they have the perfect cover, right? A stranger spending the weekend hardly stands out. While the location of Niche—tucked up in northern Georgia, where you have drive time to four bordering states as well as easy access to Atlanta and a major airport—makes it ideal. Finally, the small size and limited economy makes it easier for coercion. Pay off your neighbors, threaten them into silence, either works. Frankly, I'm surprised more quaint mountain towns aren't used for illegal enterprises."

Keith sat back. Sheriff Smithers rubbed his face. The poor man looked like he was about to keel over, while in the back of the room, tall, built-like-a-brick Franny appeared positively faint. She was clutching the delicate gold cross she wore around her neck and shaking her head slowly, as if to ward off words that couldn't possibly be true.

"Jacob Ness was here," Flora spoke up, her voice perfectly toneless. "We met his father today, Walt Davies, and he took us to the abandoned shack where Jacob first held me eight years ago."

"Walt Davies?" Sheriff Smithers roused himself in disbelief. "He's Ness's father?"

"He grows microgreens," Flora said.

Keith covered her hand with his own.

Kimberly stared at the whiteboard beside her. For the first time, she realized she hadn't written anything down. Because it was that kind of debriefing. So much information, so little that made any sense.

"Okay, let's take this point by point. Jacob Ness *does* have ties to Niche." Kimberly uncapped the dry-erase marker and wrote Jacob's name across the top of a column. Then she added *Ghost Guests* as a column head. Then *Mountain Laurel B&B,* where she drew multiple lines down for *Martha Counsel, Mayor Howard, Male UNSUB,* and *Cook*.

Flora was staring at the table. She didn't just look ragged, Kimberly realized. She appeared shell-shocked. The adrenaline of her momentous discovery had faded, and now the woman was crashing.

Keith did the honors. "Yes and no. Walt is Ness's father, but he claims Jacob and his mother disappeared forty years ago. Walt didn't even know if they were still alive. Then, one night, Jacob shows up in a local tavern and introduces himself to Walt. That was right after Flora's abduction—so, around eight years ago."

Kimberly nodded, and added a timeline to the board.

"According to Walt, if Jacob had been in town before then, Walt didn't know about it."

"Walt's a recluse," the sheriff said.

Kimberly got his point. "Meaning Jacob could've been in town before without Walt's knowledge."

"Jacob took Walt to where he was holding Flora," Keith said. "An abandoned cabin in the woods. That's why no one's been able to find it before. It's not a registered property at all."

Kimberly added *abandoned cabin* beneath Jacob's name. She'd never even considered such a thing. But given Keith's point that Niche was perfectly situated as a distribution point, well, abandoned cabins in the woods would also make excellent meeting sites for handoffs.

"Did Walt know what Ness was driving?"

"An old truck. It had a dump sticker, so a local vehicle."

Kimberly frowned. Jotted away. "Borrowed or owned?"

"Unknown. Walt claims he objected to what Jacob was doing. He even came back to rescue Flora. But Flora and Ness were already gone."

Sheriff Smithers spoke up. "You believe him?"

Keith was slower to reply. "I think so. But Walt . . . he's definitely a character."

"Did he know anything else about Jacob? Where he'd been for the past forty years, what he'd done?" Kimberly asked.

"Walt claimed they didn't get into the details. He was too taken aback at seeing his son after all these years to ask many questions."

"But he was sure Jacob was his son?"

"A man knows his own blood," Keith said solemnly.

Kimberly glanced at Flora. The woman's face was completely expressionless, though at least Kimberly now understood why.

"Walt took you to the cabin where Flora had been held."

Keith nodded.

Kimberly didn't really need to ask the next question to know the answer. Flora's face said it all. "And it really was the right place?"

"Shit brown carpet and all," Flora murmured. She spun her water bottle in her hands.

"Okay." Kimberly returned to the whiteboard. Though once again, she wasn't sure what exactly to document. They had a serial predator who'd been in Niche at least eight years ago. Not the same timeline as the four remains they'd discovered, but who was to say Jacob hadn't been coming and going for years before deciding to personally pay a call to dear old Dad? He'd been born here. He knew

Niche, Georgia. They had their first definitive link. Except . . . where did that leave them?

"When we had Ness's computer last year," Keith spoke up, "it was clear he was chatting with others on the dark web. A loner in real life, but an online socializer."

Kimberly waited.

"Maybe one of those contacts was here. Or, given Ness's interest in porn, there is some kind of clandestine sex ring in this area. Jacob would pay a visit for that."

"We're not choosing between a criminal enterprise theory versus a lone predator theory, we're saying maybe the lone predator was part of the criminal enterprise?"

"Exactly." Keith beamed.

Kimberly had to hand it to the computer analyst. It wasn't a bad theory, especially knowing that Jacob had been networking with other predators.

"But I didn't see anyone else," Flora whispered. She sighed, seemed to make the effort to pull herself together. "If Jacob had joined a . . . sex ring . . . why didn't others come to the basement? Why was it always just him?"

Keith shrugged. "Just because Ness was willing to play well with others for some kind of perceived personal gain doesn't mean he stopped being himself. Or that he was willing to share his own toys."

"I'm a toy?" Flora asked.

"You're the woman who destroyed him," Keith said softly. "You're the woman he went to his grave sorry he'd kidnapped."

Something passed between the two of them. Kimberly found herself looking away. Most of the room seemed to share the impulse.

Kimberly found herself studying the sheriff, then Franny again at the back of the room. Both appeared stunned. The scenarios Keith was describing couldn't possibly be happening in their backyard. She wondered if they would ever get over the shock.

Especially the sheriff. It was his job to know better. And now Kimberly found herself thinking thoughts she didn't like. All criminal enterprises required protection. The first logical person to buy off—the county sheriff.

But studying Sheriff Smithers, his haggard features, she didn't want to believe such a thing, even as she knew it was her job to remain suspicious.

This damn case. Everything was going to get worse before it got better.

Kimberly took a deep breath, waited a second, then cleared her throat, calling attention back to her.

"Before we get too far along with unsubstantiated theories," she counseled, "let's talk burial sites. What does the ERT have to report?"

Team leader Rachel did the honors. "We finished excavation of the mass grave today. No new discoveries in terms of medical debris, clothing, anything useful, but Dr. Jackson now has all of the skeletal remains for analysis. We were also able to study the walls of the crude grave. It would appear a tool similar to a pickax was used to hack into the ground, digging a shallow trench. Franklin and Howard also continued the search for missing bones from the first grave. They found dozens of small bones. Some of which, according to Dr. Jackson, might actually belong to a rabbit." Rachel skewered both of her teammates with a glance.

"I am not a forensic anthropologist," Harold said archly. He turned to Franklin. "Are you a forensic anthropologist?"

"No, sir."

"There you have it." Harold sat back, content with his argument.

Rachel rolled her eyes. "Originally, our plan was to return to Atlanta tomorrow. However, one of the reasons for our, um, current appearance, is that on one of Harold's side trips, he made a discovery. Harold."

"I can't be sure," the lanky fed said cautiously. "It was end of day, we were headed down, and the lighting wasn't good. We need to return tomorrow for further examination. Depressions can happen naturally in the woods, of course."

In the front of the room, Kimberly froze. She already knew what Harold was going to say next. And she was just tired and overwhelmed enough to wish he wouldn't. But of course, there was nothing she could do about it as Harold straightened slightly, then announced: "It's possible—probable, actually—that I just found yet another grave."

CHAPTER 31

D.D.

D.D. WATCHED AS HER NEW charge carefully checked out the motel room. Bonita, still dressed in her maid's uniform, appeared exhausted but also curious as she hobbled around the space, running her hand across the queen-sized mattress, opening the closet door, playing with the faucets in the bathroom. D.D. had a feeling the cheap brown lodging was nothing compared to the grand guest rooms at the Mountain Laurel B&B. Then again, Bonita had never been allowed to stay in those rooms. She'd slept in a closet in the basement.

Finally, the girl stopped playing with the lamp, inspecting the alarm clock. She sat down on the edge of the bed, staring at D.D. expectantly. She had a tilt to her chin. Defiance, D.D. thought. Or sheer determination not to give in to the terror and fatigue that had to be washing over her.

"Okay," D.D. said out loud. "I guess I get to do the talking for both of us."

Bonita nodded.

"First order of business. I think we should get you something to wear other than a maid's uniform."

Bonita looked down at her pale blue dress, plucked at her skirt.

"It's late for shopping, and I have no idea where to go anyway. If you don't mind looking like a detective, I have an extra BPD T-shirt and a pair of sweatpants you can use."

Bonita simply gazed at her.

"Speaking for both of us, I'm going to say, 'That's an excellent plan, D.D.' Now if only I had real luggage and not just my go bag."

D.D. rose out of the chair in the corner of Bonita's room, which was really Keith's old room, and crossed through the adjoining door to Flora's former space. Had Keith and Flora left the connecting door open when they'd stayed in neighboring rooms? Somehow, D.D. doubted it. Keith certainly wouldn't have minded. But Flora? Only time would tell.

D.D. hefted her black travel case onto the bed. She rummaged through till she found a navy-blue T-shirt and gray sweatpants. When she turned, Bonita was standing right beside her.

"Clean clothes. They'll be a bit big, but better than nothing. Do you want to take a shower, clean up first?"

Bonita didn't immediately indicate a reply. She took the clothes from D.D., studying them much the way she had studied the room. Whatever was going on in the girl's head, D.D. had no idea.

Bonita looked up again. Her dark eyes were so huge in her face. Sad, D.D. thought. Or maybe more like resigned. She had gone from the devil she knew to a complete unknown.

"You're safe," D.D. said softly. "I promise you."

The girl turned and walked back into her room. A moment later, D.D. heard the sound of a shower running.

She let out a breath she didn't know she'd been holding and collapsed on the edge of the bed. Okay, shower and clothes. Food sounded like the next logical step. She could order pizza. Who didn't like pizza? Then bedtime, most likely. Both she and Bonita were running on fumes. And in the morning?

Good God, she had no idea what she was doing.

She unearthed her phone and dialed home. Alex picked up on the second ring.

"How's it going?" He sounded cheerful, even happy. In the background came barking. Kiko, playing with Jack. The sounds of family. For a moment, a pang of homesickness swept over D.D. She clutched the phone tighter, and was startled to discover tears in her eyes.

"Hey," she said at last. Her voice came out rough. Her husband wasn't fooled for a moment.

"That good, huh?"

"We now have a current murder to go with four cold cases. And some mystery man on the run, and a vanished evil cook, not to mention a possibly endangered young woman, and oh yeah, I have a new project. A teenage girl. She can't speak or read or write. But I think she knows things that are very important. I think, right now, she needs someone she can trust."

Pause, as Alex absorbed the news. "How can I help?" he asked at last.

"Do you know anyone at the Academy, or from your own days on the job, who might be an expert in interviewing nonverbal minors?"

"Honestly, I'm not sure that category exists. But what if we break it apart? What about an expert in a nonverbal child, or an expert in interviewing children?"

"I think the nonverbal part is the biggest hurdle," D.D. said. She took a deep breath, released it. This was good. Alex had always been the calm to her storm.

"What about an expert in autism? Aren't many autistic children nonverbal?"

"She's not autistic. She suffered some kind of traumatic brain injury when she was young. It left her without communication skills, plus she has a few other physical issues."

"But nonverbal is nonverbal, right? The cause doesn't matter. It's how to bridge the gap."

"Fair enough."

"Hang on. I'm Googling."

D.D. could Google. But it felt nice to sit here and let Alex do it. She heard a crash in the background, then Alex muttering, "Slow down," to their son. Based on the ensuing noise, no decrease in activity actually happened, which made it just like usual. God she was homesick. When had she, a proud workaholic, become such a sap? But yes, she'd give anything to be with her husband and son right now.

"Picture boards," Alex announced abruptly. D.D. pulled herself together, hastily wiping at her eyes. "Or really, apps on iPhones and tablets with pictures grouped by category. Skimming quickly, it sounds like some people who can't recognize or speak words can still identify pictures. So, just because your girl can't say 'apple' doesn't mean she can't point at a picture of an apple."

"Pictures," D.D. murmured. She closed her eyes, feeling like an idiot. "Of course. She gave me a drawing of the demon. She can communicate with pictures. How do I get one of these apps?"

"You can order them, but the site I'm on wants you to log in as a speech pathologist or something like that. You know what, start with your smartphone. The emojis on the text screen."

"Which are already grouped by emotion, object, food, animal. Interesting."

"Then load up on paper and markers. I *know* you can't draw."

D.D. nodded. She didn't have an artistic bone in her body.

"But maybe *she* can," Alex finished.

"That makes sense. At least it will get us started." She tilted her head, considering. "How do you conduct a forensic interview of a minor utilizing only pictures? First, you have to establish competence. Give me an example of a truth. Give me an example of a lie. Then there's the matter of not leading the child, meaning I can't ask yes-or-no questions. Again, how do you do that when pictures are the only form of communication?"

"I'm afraid I can't help you with that, love. Now you are going to need an expert. But remember, there're many ways to use witness testimony. Maybe, given the limitations, conducting an interview that meets the highest legal bar of court testimony is impossible. But she's hardly the first witness who, for whatever reason, can't. A judge might still be willing to accept yes-or-no answers from a nonverbal witness as adequate grounds for, say, a search warrant. Something of that nature."

"Which might lead us to evidence we can use in court." Okay. D.D. was starting to get a plan together in her mind. "How's the home front?" she asked wistfully, just as another crash sounded in the background.

"Pretty much the same as always," Alex observed.

"Sorry I'm away for so long."

"You kidding? Quality time with the wild child? I'll have you know Jack and I have perfected our burps and moved on to farts. Be glad you're away."

"Well, when you put it that way."

"Sounds like you're onto something major," Alex said more quietly.

"I think so. Certainly much more than a single cold case involving a single predator."

"You have a current murder, you said?"

"Last night."

"In other words, your investigation is starting to spook someone."

"I think more than someone. I think someones." D.D. looked around the room the motel owner hadn't wanted them to be staying in anymore. For a reason she couldn't explain, the hair prickled at the back of her neck. "Whatever's going on here, I think it's been going on a long time, maybe even longer than fifteen years. And it's not Jacob Ness. Or at least, not *just* Jacob Ness. It involves this entire community in one way or another. Town this small, even those who claim they don't know, know something."

"They just haven't wanted to see," Alex finished for her. "Except now there's a squad of outsiders, poking the bees' nest."

"Exactly."

"Be careful," he warned.

"Always."

"Come home safe."

"Always."

"Love you."

They said their goodbyes. D.D. ended the call. But she still found herself studying the shadows in the corner of the room and shivering.

SHE HATED TO LEAVE BONITA alone in the room. She didn't want the girl to come out of the bathroom and feel abandoned. But D.D. needed some info, and hopefully supplies, from the reluctant motel owner. She found him seated behind the counter. He appeared to be studying his cell phone, but D.D. was positive he'd registered every sound of her footsteps coming down the hall.

Someone didn't want the taskforce staying in town. Mayor Howard was in county jail. Which left . . . Bonita's mystery demon? Someone even higher up the food chain? D.D. was not prone to nerves, but she'd give anything to have Flora's new toy—that butterfly blade—tucked in her pocket right now.

Instead, she made a show of keeping her right hand on the butt of her service pistol as she approached.

"Good evening," she said with false cheerfulness.

The man didn't put down his phone, just eyed her sullenly from beneath his helmet of thick dark hair.

"So as owner, you get the night shift?"

"My motel. My responsibility."

Or, D.D. figured, he'd been ordered to keep an eye on the outsiders.

"I could use a recommendation for pizza delivery," she said.

"I don't know."

"Now, now, this motel is your responsibility. Meaning your guests are also your responsibility. I can't believe you've been running this place for . . . how many years?"

"Twenty."

"Without a single pizza delivery."

"We're a small town—"

D.D. leaned over the counter, got up close and personal so he could see the dead seriousness in her eyes. "Little man, don't make me hurt you. Because the things I know how to do with just my thumb . . ."

The man glared at her. Finally, he reached out, grabbed some pamphlets from the desk in front of him, and slapped it on the raised counter between them. A brochure for a Dahlonega pizza parlor, with the promise of delivery to anywhere within thirty miles. Perfect.

"I could use blank paper and a pen. Printing paper will be fine. Any pen will do, though if you have colored markers, that would be excellent."

"I don't have colored markers."

D.D. sighed heavily. Made a show of wiggling her right thumb.

"I have crayons. For kids. Activity packs."

"How extraordinarily kind of you."

More shuffling around on the desk. A small pack of five crayons was tossed on the counter. Then the man swiveled his chair toward the printer behind him and extracted the tray to grab paper.

D.D. picked up the crayons. She knew these packs from her own family's attempts at dining out. When Jack was two, he used to eat the green crayon. Only the green. She and Alex had never figured out why. Now at the age of six, Jack had more self-restraint when it came to munching on wax. He wasn't much into coloring, though, being on the active side. He did, however, enjoy a rousing game of tic-tac-toe while they waited for their food to arrive.

Again, she felt a pang of homesickness. Was she growing soft in her old age? Or maybe it was just that she was standing in a deserted motel, across from a man who'd already made it clear they weren't welcome here anymore, and she had no idea if any establishment would accept them, or who in this small town they could trust.

They were outsiders. Cops always felt that way. But after a day at a mass grave followed by an early morning at a woman's hanging, and now this . . .

Bonita hadn't drawn a man. She'd drawn a demon.

D.D. didn't like it.

The owner returned with a meager stack of paper. Maybe five sheets. She gave him a look.

"Passive-aggressive much?" D.D. asked.

"Please," the man said.

And the way he said it caught her attention.

The owner licked his lips, glancing around the empty lobby. "Please, whatever you are doing. Just get it done. And leave. Just leave. It's better that way."

"Better?" D.D. pushed. "Or safer?"

The man just stared at her. "Please," he repeated softly.

And if D.D. hadn't been spooked before, she was now.

RETURNING TO THE ROOM—AND making sure she worked the bolt lock behind her—she discovered Bonita standing next to the bed,

her long black hair dripping down D.D.'s T-shirt. Bonita had rolled
up the sweatpants at the waist and the ankles. They were still big on
her, though D.D. herself was hardly huge.

The girl trembled slightly when D.D. first appeared. She had her
arms wrapped tightly around her torso, as if for comfort. Immediately, D.D. felt terrible. She should've told Bonita where she was
going. She should've . . . Many thoughts ran through her head. She
barely knew how to parent Jack, let alone take on a frightened, damaged teen. She was going to have to proceed with more care.

"I ordered us some pizza. It will be delivered here. Are you hungry?"

Bonita shrugged.

"I also got us some supplies." D.D. held up her hard-fought treasures. "Paper and crayons."

Bonita's whole face brightened. She stepped forward, taking the
crayons from D.D.'s hand with near reverence. For the first time,
D.D. could see the girl's exposed forearms. One held an intricate pattern of scars. As if she'd thrust her fist through plate glass and cut
herself in a dozen places. Except her hand was completely unblem-
ished. Just her forearm.

It was a pattern, D.D. realized at last. Like lacework. A pattern
that had been purposefully carved into the girl's skin.

Bonita caught her staring. She quickly covered the scars with her
other hand, still clutching the crayons.

"Do you like to draw?" D.D. asked at last, to break the ice.

Quick nod.

"I have paper, too. Not a lot, but I can get more." D.D. crossed
to the empty space on the TV console and set down the sheets of
paper. There was no desk in the room. D.D. usually sat with her laptop in the middle of the bed. But Bonita didn't seem to mind. She
kneeled down in front of the console, a bit awkwardly with her right
leg, then opened up the crayon pack.

She took out the crayons one by one, running her fingers up and down the entire length, exploring the paper wrapping, the sharpened tip. The girl liked to feel things, D.D. was starting to realize. Maybe because she couldn't speak, she had become more tactile instead?

"Can you draw me a picture?" D.D. asked. "Anything you like."

Bonita turned and regarded her for a long moment. Again, those dark eyes, like vast pools and impossible to penetrate. The girl was beautiful, D.D. thought. Even with the thickly ridged scar burrowing into her hairline and the droop of her mouth. Her delicate features and smooth almond skin stood out in contrast to the jagged scar. The mark didn't make her less, but proved she was more. Stronger, tougher. A survivor, like Flora. If D.D. could break down the communication barrier, perhaps Flora could reach out to her. She ran a support group of sorts back in Boston. From surviving to thriving, Flora liked to quote.

Bonita looked like someone who'd learned the hard way how to survive. She did not know yet, though, how to thrive.

The girl turned her attention back to the first piece of paper. She picked up a crayon and got to work.

Her strokes were sure and fast. Definitely, the girl had experience sketching. Maybe the mayor and his wife had granted her art supplies as a reward for good behavior? Or she had secreted away crayons when no one was looking?

D.D. took a seat in the nearby chair. She let the girl have at it, using the time to check messages on her phone and wonder how the debriefing was going.

A knock.

D.D. glanced at the door immediately, her hand going to her gun. Then she realized Bonita stood in front of her. The girl rapped the top of the console again, demanding D.D.'s attention. Bonita held out the first piece of paper.

D.D. blinked her eyes in surprise.

It was beautiful. Bonita had filled the entire page with greens and blues and browns. A forest scene, D.D. realized. Or the essence of a mountainside. It appeared her new charge was an impressionist. Close up, the colors blurred together into an abstract swirl. Lean back, however, and shapes slowly emerged. Trees, bushes, maybe a running stream.

Then, holding the picture farther away, shadows. Between the trees, behind the bushes, tucked beside boulders. So many shadows. Again, D.D. felt a ripple of unease.

She found a wavy black column, pointed at it. "Is this a demon? Are all these shadows bad people?"

Bonita shook her head. She gazed at D.D. sorrowfully

The girl took the drawing back. She stroked her finger down one blur of black, then another. Her touch was gentle. Not angry, or fearful. Sad.

"Bonita, are those ghosts? Are those . . . other girls? Girls like you?"

A single, solemn nod.

D.D. stared at the picture again. She couldn't speak. There had to be at least a dozen slender shadows tucked into the portrait. Maybe even more.

"Do you know what happened to Hélène?"

Head shake.

"But you fear for her."

Nod.

"You think the demon has her. Is he the one . . . Is he the one who did all this?" D.D. pointed to the picture again, the dozens of dark lines interspersed within the beautiful shades of blue and green.

Another solemn nod.

"And your arm?" D.D. pointed, but did not touch the elaborate scarring. "Did he do that, too?"

Nod.

D.D. swallowed thickly. "How long? How long has this been going on?"

The girl shrugged. As if to say, how could she know such a thing? Or as if she had never known any differently?

"Can you draw me his face?" D.D. asked. "The man who did this?"

Bonita sighed heavily. She appeared genuinely distressed now. She picked up a crayon, then another. She gazed at D.D. pleadingly, as if she needed help, but D.D. didn't know what to do.

"Just try," D.D. said. "Do your best. Anything you can show me will be of help."

The girl gave her a last look. More reluctantly, she kneeled down, got to work. D.D. sat back again. But this time she didn't pick up her phone. She held Bonita's first drawing and studied it over and over again.

This time when the knock came, she was prepared.

Bonita held out the new picture. Her hand trembled.

At first glance, D.D. was struck by a sea of roiling black. Hard strokes, swirling onto one another. More than just black. Reds, blues, and browns, but all topped by black again. She had layered the colors, probably had already worn the black crayon down to a nub.

D.D. held the picture farther away. Bonita visualized in terms of colors and moods, not details. Hence her reluctance to do a portrait, D.D. assumed. Because this wasn't really a face of a man as much as a capturing of a spirit—violent, dark, oppressive.

A demon.

The rendering was very good at communicating fear, but not so helpful as an investigative tool.

D.D. lowered it to her lap. "Thank you for doing this. I know it can't be easy."

Bonita nodded. She had one hand self-consciously clasped over her scarred wrist, forearm turned in. Both maids had worn long-sleeved uniforms, D.D. realized now. She wondered what other damages they had to hide.

Whatever had happened to Martha Counsel, D.D. wasn't feeling very sorry about it anymore. Nor did she have any sympathy for the mayor's show of crocodile tears. Best she could tell, they'd both made a deal with the devil. Apparently, last night the devil had come to collect his due.

Reap what you sow, she thought. Except how did a demon man with a penchant for knife games and torture figure in to Martha's illegal kidney operation?

They had learned much in the past twenty-four hours, but it still wasn't enough.

Bonita had returned to the console. She was drawing again. Slower now. Her posture had changed. Her shoulders slumped, her black hair falling around her like a curtain. There was sorrow in every line of her body. If D.D. didn't know differently, she would've sworn that the crayon was crying in the girl's hand, weeping tears of wax across the page.

Blue, then red, so much red.

D.D. braced herself as Bonita finally rose, produced her third rendition.

A flowing river of blue into a sea of red. D.D. felt her throat close up just looking at it. Pain, suffering, and sorrow.

Bonita might not be able to talk, but her artwork communicated volumes.

D.D. took the paper, her fingers trembling. She held it back, let her eyes blur, then focus, then blur again.

The river of blue had a form. Slowly but surely, she could see it. A woman's body in a blue dress, sprawled across the floor. Into the pool of red. Blood.

D.D. looked up. "Is this Hélène?"

Head shake.

"Is this what you're afraid will happen to her?"

Another head shake.

D.D. paused, considered. "Is this another girl? Another maid?"

Nod.

"She died."

Nod.

"You saw."

Double nod.

"The demon did it?"

Head shake.

"Mrs. Counsel, Mayor Howard?" Head shake, head shake. "The cook?" Head shake.

D.D. pursed her lips, running out of ideas. Good God, how many killers were they talking about in this community? "But you saw her die?"

Nod.

"Recently?"

Vigorous nod.

"Past few days?" D.D. attempted.

Definite nod.

D.D. paused again. So they had another murder. This time of a maid from the B&B. But before Martha Counsel. So first a maid, then the owner. All in the past few days—meaning, right after the taskforce arrived.

She held this picture on her lap. She traced the blue form as gently as Bonita had traced the shadows.

If these pictures were to be believed, this town was a graveyard of young women. How many bodies now dotted these woods?

And how many killers? How deep did this kind of coercion run?

"Thank you, Bonita," D.D. said softly. "I think now . . . I'll check on our pizza. Then both of us need to sleep."

CHAPTER 32

FLORA

KEITH AND I DON'T TALK on the way back to the motel.

Kimberly is behind the steering wheel. Night has fallen thick and dark, but staring out the window, I swear I see the outline of towering trees. The woods scream at night, Walt had said. I wonder if he knows more than he realizes. Or if he's playing us completely with his crazed loner act and barn full of greens. Jacob had always been scarily clever; there's no reason to think his father is any different.

Kimberly parks, and we walk inside the motel. Sitting at the front desk, the owner eyes us sullenly but doesn't try to kick us out again. Which means Keith and I do have a room for the night. The same room, now, thanks to D.D.

Kimberly nods at us in departure, arriving at her door first. Her expression is distracted, her thoughts clearly a million miles away. Trying to find the missing maid, trying to make sense of two, possibly three graves—and oh yes, some dark, dangerous UNSUB, as the FBI liked to say, on the loose around town.

Maybe the motel owner wasn't bowing to local pressure when he tried to evict us. Maybe he was simply trying to keep us safe.

Keith arrives at the door first. He unlocks it. We both step inside. Before the taskforce meeting, we'd just had time to pack up our stuff and throw it in this room. No sign of the promised cot, which doesn't surprise either of us. Now we are confronted by a single queen-sized bed with two bags sitting on top. Keith's is the silvery hard-case spinner that looks like it belongs on the space shuttle. Mine is a simple black duffel bag that's clearly seen better days.

We are nothing alike. Keith has his upscale, sixties-retro-meets-cutting-edge-modern town house. I live in a third-floor walk-up high on old-world charm, short on space, and covered in bolt locks. He always dresses like he stepped out of a men's clothing catalogue. I look like something a homeless person threw up.

Keith crosses to the bed. He lifts off both bags, sets them neatly on the floor.

"You must be exhausted," he says.

I gaze at him. He's steady. He's solid. I don't know that I can live in his world, but he has proven that he can hold his own in mine. Is that enough for a relationship? Do I even want a relationship?

"I'll take the floor," he says.

I don't answer.

"Not a problem. You need your sleep the most."

I don't answer.

He clasps and unclasps his hands. I realize for the first time that he's nervous.

"Sometimes," I hear myself whisper, "I feel my entire life is about Jacob."

Keith stills. "No. You were a person before him—"

"I don't remember that girl."

"You're a survivor after him."

"I am what he made me."

"No, Flora. That's the point. He tried to break you. Who you are now, you made yourself. You didn't give up. That's all you. Not one single bit of that is him."

"Will you kiss me?" I whisper.

"Okay." But he doesn't move and neither do I.

"I don't know what I will do. How I'll respond."

"You haven't . . . since your return?"

"No. Others do. Others get over it. I . . . I can't even stand my mother's hugs."

He nods, clearly thinking. He is always thinking. Do I love or hate that about him? I can't decide.

He takes a step forward. Then another. A final stride and he's right in front of me. Close, but not touching. I can feel the heat of him. Smell the soap of his quick shower before the meeting. I can see the faint lines bracketing his rich blue eyes, anticipate the silky feel of his hair.

He's staring at me like I'm the only thing he's ever wanted. No one has ever looked at me like that. As if I matter that much. As if I am that worthy.

He's not going to kiss me, I realize. He's waiting for me to kiss him. Another act of thoughtfulness, I suppose. Let me set the pace. Put me in control.

I place both hands on his thin blue shirt. It feels cool to the touch and forms perfectly to his long, sculpted torso. This space-age fabric probably cost more than my monthly rent, I think, but then I'm happy he bought it, because it feels good beneath my fingertips, as if I'm already touching bare skin.

He inhales sharply, but doesn't move. Waiting, waiting, waiting.

Exquisite waiting.

Has anyone ever waited for me before?

I have to stretch up on my toes to bridge the gap between us. I move my hands from his chest, to his shoulders, to the back of his neck. Then I bring his lips down to mine.

His fingers find my waist as our lips brush, brush again. Slowly, carefully, I explore his mouth. I taste him, feel him, let the sensations wash over me. And when no dark, ugly shadows rear in the back of my mind, I go deeper, hungrier, until I feel something ignite inside me. A spark long dead.

Maybe that girl I used to be, the one with the bright smile and cute little dresses and flirtatious glances, wasn't so far gone after all. Because suddenly I'm pushing Keith back, till his legs hit the bed and he collapses onto the mattress. What am I doing? What is it I want?

To not think, I realize. To escape from my head, to have one moment when I'm not Flora Dane, victim-survivor-vigilante.

I don't want to be.

I want to feel.

I pull off my gray sweatshirt. I remove my faded T-shirt. I start working the button of my cargo pants, then realize I must pause, kick off my boots.

Keith doesn't move off the bed. He remains half reclined, watching me hungrily.

I stare him in the eye. Boots off. Outer clothes. My boring panties, workout bra. There is nothing sexy about my underwear. But the way Keith is watching me, right now, I can almost believe I'm intoxicating.

Do I look good naked? I have no idea. Once I stood in front of a mirror, admiring my summer tan, my taut stomach. Now I'm probably pale and bony, covered with fresh bruises and old scars. A past-her-prime prizefighter, who's gone too many rounds in the ring. I should cover myself, turn off the light, something.

But I don't move. I stand there, totally exposed, and let him see me. Let him see all of me.

He rises slowly off the bed. Ready to flee? Already changing his mind now that he's seen the damaged goods?

His fingers find the hem of his shirt. He pulls it up over his head, then tosses it on the floor. Next, he removes his shoes, socks, pants. He does wear Calvin Kleins. I knew it. Then those are gone, too, and it's just him and me, both completely naked, separate, waiting.

He's beautiful. All rippling muscles, long, lean limbs. His skin is smooth, his chest paler than his arms after the past few days in the hot Georgia sun. He has a smattering of dark hair across his chest, leading to a thin line running down his stomach to where . . .

To where he definitely finds me as appealing as I find him.

I have a moment. Other pictures rise before my eyes. Other memories. An odious man, fat, smelly, vile. Grabbing my hair. Do this, do that. Myself, gagging, repulsed, revolted.

I shiver slightly. Close my eyes. Will the memories away.

When I open them again, Keith is still standing there, buck naked, watching, waiting.

And just like that, I'm over it. I will not be weak. I will not be a victim. I will not live in the past.

I'm alive. I'm whole. And this man . . . my fingers itch to drift across his bare skin. To feel the heat of him. I want to kiss his neck, drag my leg up his own. I want his hands on my body, clutching tight. I want his blue eyes black with hunger, his body wild with need.

I want to know I have that kind of power. I want to *feel* again.

I am Flora. He is Keith.

And I want both of us to burn.

I step forward. Lift one hand. Push him back onto the bed again. He falls willingly and I climb on top of him, my legs straddling his hips. I feel heat. So much of it. An inferno, already threatening to consume us. And damn he's gorgeous. A perfectly sculpted male. Mine, I think, all mine. Then I find his lips and his hands grip my waist frantically, and the spark combusts.

We're young. We're healthy. We're wild.

We roll and tussle, fighting in our fever to connect. I feel him, everywhere. My hips move on their own and for the first time in so long, I want one thing and one thing only.

I want this man.

His lips on my lips, throat, breasts. We roll again, then I'm on top. He accepts and gives. I take, take, take. My head arching back.

And for one moment, I am myself again. Confident, beautiful, sexy. I am the girl who should've met Keith years ago, and is so grateful to have found him now. Then he moves his hips. I gasp. He moves more, and all thoughts fly away.

I grip his shoulders and feel us both explode.

AFTERWARD, WE BOTH SPRAWL NAKED in the middle of the bed, panting hard. I'm not sure what happened to the covers. I'm not sure I care.

I have my head on Keith's shoulder. His arm is curled around me, his fingers idly stroking my arm. It's so soothing I can feel my eyes drift shut. Then I force them open. Maybe I should sleep. But I'm too afraid that when I wake up, this will be gone. We'll have the awkwardness of the morning after. Or maybe, the magic will be gone for Keith. He finally got what, for years, he wanted most.

The lone survivor of an infamous predator.

I can feel myself withdraw. Keith does, too.

"Stop," he orders.

"What?"

"Whatever you're thinking."

"What am I thinking?"

"I don't know." He tilts my head up. "You think dark thoughts, Flora. I understand. But there's nothing dark about my interest in you. There's nothing dark about my feelings toward you."

"You have feelings toward me?"

"Yes."

"Are you a serial killer?"

"I don't think so. And given that true crime is my hobby, I think I would know."

"You've always wanted to meet me."

"True."

"Because you're a true-crime aficionado, and what true-crime enthusiast wouldn't want to talk to someone like me?"

"I wanted to meet you. Then I did. And then . . . I want more. Which has nothing to do with your past and everything to do with who you are right now. And how you make me feel right now."

"Can we take this right now to right now?"

"Most relationships happen that way."

"Okay," I say.

"Okay," he agrees. Then a moment later. "Do you need to rest, or shower, or eat, or anything at all?"

I shake my head against his shoulder.

"Good. Because the first time, while great, was a bit on the rushed side. Now . . . I think we can do even better."

My eyes widen slightly. Then he's moving, shifting his weight above. I gasp. No talking, no thinking, just feeling, as he proves his point: The second time is even better.

Right before I drift off to sleep, I have a realization.

I'm not surviving anymore.

Finally, I'm thriving.

I BOLT AWAKE. I REGISTER a foreign weight on the bed, an intruder in the room. Instinctively, I lash out. Thumbs, elbows, knees. Women might not be as strong as men, but there are ways we can still do damage.

"Shit! Flora, Flora, it's me!"

A hand grabs my arm. I roll into the hold, inside my attacker's strike zone, where I can gouge my thumb into eyeballs.

"Flora, wake up!"

I'm naked. He's naked. Both of his hands clasp my arms. I should, I should . . . Keith. I had sex with Keith. I fell asleep with Keith. I am with Keith. Dear God, what have I done?

As fast as I attacked, now I retreat, yanking my arms free, spinning away.

"Stop!"

A bedside lamp snaps on. Keith's features emerge. "Flora Dane, don't move another inch."

I glare at him. "You sound like my mother."

"Really? You attack your mother in the middle of the night, too?"

"A couple of times. It's not safe to wake me."

"I didn't."

"Then it's not safe to sleep with me."

"I wasn't."

"You weren't?" Now I scowl. "I was asleep."

"I know. And you're ridiculously cute when you sleep. But I wasn't sleeping. I was thinking."

"You're always thinking!"

"Isn't that the pot calling the kettle black? Come back. Relax. You promise not to kill me, and I promise to tell you what I've been thinking."

I blink my eyes, unsure. Really, this whole situation is mortifying. Leave it to me not to be awkward the morning after, but homicidal. Yet Keith appears completely unruffled. He sits up against the headboard, then holds out his arm expectantly, wiggling his fingers in silent command.

I ease back toward him. He wiggles his fingers more. I slowly take up position beside him, bare skin to bare skin. He sighs, rather happily, I think.

"For a serial killer, you sure are nice," I grumble.

"You really think I'm a serial killer?"

"You look like Ted Bundy and you're obsessed with crime."

"Oh. When you put it that way . . ."

We both fall silent. "We're going to have to work on the sleeping arrangement," he says at last. "One more inch with that knee of yours, and this whole new excellent adventure would've been over before we even had a chance."

"Sorry."

"In the future, I'd rather you go after my eyes. If you think about it, it's in your own best interest, as well."

I close my eyes, mortified again. He strokes my arms. "It's okay, Flora," he says softly. "We all have demons. We'll figure it out. It's only the first night."

I don't say anything, but I turn my head into him, feel my cheek against his shoulder. His skin is very smooth and warm. He smells amazing. I don't want to think it, but I have to: Keith is nothing like Jacob. He's not old and fat and disgusting. Keith is exactly the kind of guy, once upon a time, I would've taken home with me. And I realize I'm incredibly grateful, if not a little choked up, to finally feel this way, have this moment, again.

"Do you ever sleep?" I ask.

"Not much. I don't have night terrors like you. But from the time I was young, my mind is always going. I'm restless that way. And I'm a bit of a night owl. It's when I get my best work done."

"At least we have that much in common."

"Do you want to hear about my incredibly brilliant thought or not?"

I roll my eyes. I like being curled up with him. I like his arm around my shoulders. Which is good, because—oh yeah—my not-a-serial-killer almost-boyfriend is pretty damn arrogant.

"Tell me your brilliant thought."

"The more we learn about this town—from the multiple victims spanning years, to the involvement of the mayor and his wife, to the presence of Jacob Ness and his father, even the motel guy trying to kick us out—I'm convinced we're looking at some sort of criminal enterprise. Not one crime, but many. Not one perpetrator, but perhaps as many as a dozen."

A sobering thought. "Okay."

"Now." Keith warms to his subject. "Think about what we learned last year about the dark web. You can't just log on to some criminal chat room. First, you have to have some other disgusting pervert vouch for your pornographic addiction, or you must provide explicit proof of your own evil doings, making you just as guilty as everyone else in the room. Basically, you have to prove you are a criminal before you can hang out with other criminals."

"Okay."

"Martha Counsel, her illegal kidney transplant. That made her guilty. Which also made her eligible for the organization. Jacob Ness, serial rapist. No problem establishing his criminal bona fides. Then there's this mystery guy who may have killed Martha Counsel, maybe even those girls in the woods. Definitely, he's earned his membership."

I nod against his shoulder. In this day and age, more and more predators were seeking each other out. Maybe not always in person, but at least on the internet, via the dark web. Even Jacob, a complete loner, had clearly been learning tricks of the trade from various chat rooms.

But yes, any time predators interacted with one another, they took the risk of exposing themselves. Hence an elaborate system of personal referrals and/or proof of deviousness, such as compromising images that would make the new person just as vulnerable as everyone else in the network.

"So, first requirement of membership: a history of evil. But a criminal operation is really no different than a business. You don't just want miscellaneous employees, you want skill sets. Which brings us to the second requirement for membership: You need to have something to offer the group."

I think about it. "Martha has the hotel. A way station for other group members to come and go without anyone noticing. Jacob . . . he could've provided transport. Maybe even provided girls. Lilah Abenito, maybe he did kidnap her. Except not for himself. He brought her here, for the group instead." I tilt my head up. "So why didn't he do that with me? Why did he keep me instead? Especially, having brought me to his new friends' backyard."

"I've been considering that. Socially speaking, Jacob was a loner. You never saw him with others."

"Never."

"So I'm wondering if he didn't play around on the dark web, perhaps become involved in whatever is going on around here, as a sort of master class. He helped them, and in return, he learned how to cover his tracks on the computer, how to utilize abandoned cabins in the woods, that sort of thing. You said he accepted that he was a monster. That he had no interest in reform."

"No. He was who he was, and he was proud of it."

"Then I think this was his education of sorts. And for that, he gritted his teeth and dealt with others. But a loner is a loner, right? So once he learned what he needed . . ."

"He went back to his loner ways."

"Confident in the fact he could now get away with an even more elaborate crime, such as not just kidnapping a girl, but holding her for over a year."

I nod. It makes a crazy kind of sense.

"Here's the deal. A business is a business and everyone has a role. Using that as a model, we should be able to start homing in on individuals around town to question. Transport. With Jacob gone, they'd need someone else to provide girls for illegal labor, organ transplants, whatever."

"Walt Davies," I murmur. "His trips to Atlanta to sell micro-greens. Maybe that's all just a cover for what he brings back."

"I thought of that. We're going to need to speak to him again."

I nod.

"Howard and Martha Counsel are lodging. The mystery man . . . I'm thinking he's muscle. Like, the enforcer of the operation. A girl gets out of line, a member of the organization appears on the verge of talking—"

"He takes action."

"Exactly. Now let's consider other roles. Marketing. Which I'm guessing takes place over the dark web. These ghost tourists who are coming into town. Who is reaching out to them, or how do they know to come here? Gotta be a dark web interface. Only way it could work."

"Agreed."

"Meaning we need to start asking around for someone with computer skills. That person will be the gatekeeper of a massive amount of information. Find him or her, we could blow this thing wide open."

I look up at Keith. "Didn't the ATV guy mention something? A town clerk who was working with the mayor starting ten years ago to boost Niche's profile, lure in tourists?"

"Dorothea," Keith murmured. "I think that was her name. And yeah, she fits perfectly. Raising the town's profile could very well be a euphemism for advertising goods on the dark web. Lodging packages could refer to all sorts of things. Yes, let's start by interrogating the town clerk. Perfect!"

"You're good at this."

"Remember that tomorrow when SSA Quincy and Sergeant War-ren tear my theory to shreds. But, Flora, there's an even bigger role we haven't discussed yet." Keith sits up straighter, peers down at me earnestly. "Who's running this enterprise? The missing cook? She doesn't sound smart enough. The missing maid? Quincy has already said she's most likely a victim, not a perpetrator. That leaves us with this UNSUB they've talked about—but again, he sounds more like brawn than brains. Meaning . . ."

"We still don't know who's in charge."

"Meaning, we still don't know who to trust."

We stare at each other for a long time in the glow of the bedside lamp.

"I'm really glad I brought my knife," I say.

"And I'm really glad I travel with you by my side," Keith answers

CHAPTER 33

MY MAMI IS COOKING AT *the stove. I watch her raise lids, stir pots. I listen to her hum happily. I am not here. Even in my dream, I know that. She is not here either. But I'm so grateful to see her, I don't care.*

My mamita.

As if she heard, she turns and smiles at me. "Chiquita," she whispers, and the love in her eyes fills my chest with such bittersweet pain, I think it might burst.

Her face is softer. Her cheeks no longer gaunt, the shadows gone from beneath her eyes. She is radiant in her white blouse and red peasant skirt, topped by her favorite apron. I see bits of crumbled cheese smudged near her pocket.

Then I look down and realize I am sitting at the kitchen table, a block of queso blanco in my hand.

A shadow drifts across the kitchen. I know then what will happen next.

"No," I try to tell her.

"It's all right, my love."

The shadow, growing darker . . .

"She calls me Bonita. Did you name me Bonita?" My voice is urgent, frantic. Any moment the door will explode open. Any second, the Bad Man will appear again.

"You have always been bonita to me. Muy bonita."

"Don't leave me."

"I'm still with you. I'm always with you. But you know that, chiquita. For everything that is lost, something is gained. Your words are gone, but you have other gifts in their place."

She smiles. Wipes her hands on her apron. Before I can get up. Before I can fly across the room and wrap my arms around her waist.

The door slams open.

The Bad Man appears.

Now we are outside, my mother kneeling on the red earth. She does not cower or beg. There is no pleading this time as the Bad Man looms before her. Her voice is simple and composed as she tells me, "Run."

But once again, I can't do it.

"Chiquita. It's okay. For everything that's lost, something is gained."

The Bad Man levels his weapon.

Now, I'm the one who begs. "Let her go. Take me. I'll be your servant forever. Just take me."

"She must pay," the Bad Man snarls.

My mother merely smiles at him. She appears serene as she says, "I do not repent. I would do it all again. They deserved the chance I gave them. And you will never get them back. I am but one. They are many. So do what you must. We both know, in the end, I won."

A howl, like the coyotes in the distance, except worse.

"Chiquita, run."

"No!"

"Remember, for everything that is lost, something is gained."

The Bad Man's finger squeezing the trigger. My mamita, staring right at him, daring him to take her life.

"I love you," I cry out frantically.

"I know, my chiquita. I know."

Then the trigger is pulled. The bullet explodes. I'm too far away to protect her. I can only watch as the bullet rips through my mamita's pale white throat.

Except suddenly she is no longer my mamita.

It is the blond lady detective, pitching forward into the red, red earth. It is Hélène, it is Stacey, it is girl after girl after girl.

And the Bad Man is not snarling anymore; he is laughing darkly.

"It will be your turn next," he tells me. "There's no one to save you anymore."

"I will save myself," I tell him.

Which only makes him laugh harder.

"I am Bonita and I have my mother's love and my sisters' pain and we will burn you to the ground!" I try to sound fierce.

He doubles over with mirth. "You know what outruns even fire, Stupid Girl?" he says as he straightens.

I shake my head.

"A bullet."

Then he reloads the gun and very calmly aims it at my head.

"Chiquita, run," my mother whispers in my ear. And I feel her again, wrapped around me like a warm embrace. Chiquita and mamita, our pack of two. She is mine and I am hers, always.

Which makes it all the more agonizing when the bullet slams into my temple and tears me away from her again.

I WAKE UP SHARPLY. THE clock reads six A.M. Dawn still an hour away. I'm surprised I slept that long, especially on a bed that feels so *soft and foreign. I take a moment to get my bearings. The strange room with a sharp chemical smell. A sound of gentle snoring across the way. The lady detective, who has appointed herself my new protector.*

I listen for the sound of footsteps in the hall. The Bad Man coming. Then I close my eyes and simply feel for him. My mother is right: For everything lost, something is gained.

This motel is not like the house. It does not sigh with pain, shift restlessly in discontent. It is just a building. Maybe it's too young to know any better. Maybe it hasn't encountered enough human horror to know how to mourn.

I do not feel the Bad Man. I don't feel anything at all.

I climb out of bed, cross to the console. I have two pieces of paper left. I snap on the lamp. I pick up my crayons, and with the image of my beautiful mamita in my mind, I draw and I draw.

Red earth. Black hair like a river. Brown eyes soft as an embrace. I draw my mother's love. Then, I draw her pain.

"No, chiquita," she whispers at my shoulder.

But I keep on going. Pouring our story onto the page. No longer dreaming. Now completely wide awake.

Which is why I'm the one who hears the screaming first.

THE BLOND DETECTIVE BOLTS OUT *of bed. One moment she is snuffling in her sleep, the next she is upright, yanking on her clothes, grabbing her gun from the bedside table.*

"Stay here," she orders me. Then she's gone.

I hear more noise now. Footsteps, hammering down the hall.

"What is it?" The FBI lady's voice.

"I don't know. Flora, stay with Bonita."

"Like hell."

"Dammit."

More screaming, shrill and high pitched. The voices and footsteps pound down the hall.

I rise to standing, place my crayons on the console. Then I do as the detective did. I pull on my clothes, open the door, and I follow, slowly, painfully, down the hall.

I encounter the first person in the lobby. It is the motel manager. The one who said we must leave last night. He's staring out the glass doors in horror.

He glances over at me. "Do not go out there," he says.

But he doesn't know all the things I've seen.

I limp my way forward. Resolute, even as I feel the silver shimmer of my mother dance in front of me.

Outside, the sun has just broken above the horizon, bathing the parking lot in rosy color. A crowd of people has gathered. I make out the detective, the FBI woman, Flora who carries a knife, and the man who is always beside her. There are others. Hotel guests roused by the noise. Strangers passing by. I have no idea.

Then I look up, and what I see finally stops me in my tracks.

Hélène. Poor, scared, lovely Hélène. She is still wearing her maid's uniform. And now her body dangles lifelessly from a tree planted at the edge of the parking lot. I have a sense of déjà vu. Blue running as a river into a pool of red.

He has cut her. Blood drips down her hands, both legs. It is not enough for him to kill. The Bad Man, he likes to destroy first. Until when he goes for the final blow, his victims lift their chins in gratitude.

Beside me, my mother is very still.

I look around the parking lot, but I don't sense him. He came. He staged this gruesome scene. He left.

"I'll call Sheriff Smithers," the FBI lady is saying to D.D.

"We need to cut her down."

"The ME won't be happy about that. Destroys evidence."

"I know, but this isn't just about the murder of a young woman. This is a message."

"Another hint we should get the hell out of town? Because frankly, the more bodies that drop, the longer we stay."

"No," D.D. says, turning to the FBI lady. "It's a message to the locals. Look what happens if you talk to us."

"Shit," the FBI lady murmurs.

"Bonita can communicate with pictures. She can't do a literal rendering of our UNSUB's face, but she did reveal another girl had been killed at the B and B, probably the day before Martha Counsel."

"Good God, and where is that body?"

D.D. looks around. "It's a big, big mountain range, with how many hundreds of miles of trails?"

Flora has moved closer to them. "I can cut her down," the woman says softly. She is holding her fancy knife, with an intricately carved pattern that both fascinates and repels me.

"I'll help," D.D. says. "It's important to preserve the knot for forensic analysis. We're going to need a ladder."

"I can hoist Flora up on my shoulders," Flora's companion says. "Then she can lower the body down to you."

"We need to get this circus under control," the FBI lady mutters.

"We need to find the motherfucker who did this," D.D. states. She turns and spots me. Her eyes widen. She looks around frantically, as if the Bad Man is here, as if he'll see.

But I already know he's not. He is gone; Cook is gone. It's just Hélène and me. Again.

I hobble forward. I ignore the detective who is hissing at me to stop. I ignore the gawkers who are staring at a woman who was never my friend, but my sister in pain.

I move till I'm right beneath her body. Till I can look straight up *and see what he did to her. Poor Hélène. Beautiful Hélène who was so afraid. If she hadn't fled the kitchen yesterday. If she'd just stayed with me.*

I stretch up now. I don't mind the blood. I have seen it, cleaned it, felt it running down my own wrist. Blood is nothing to fear. People are.

I place my hand gently on Hélène's bare foot—all I can reach.

And I promise her, as I have promised the others, I will not rest, I will not retreat.

I'm going to kill the Bad Man. I don't know how. I'm weak and gimpy and small. I don't know knives the way he does. I've never held a gun. I have no idea how to fight. I'm just me. Wordless and helpless.

But I do have one thing on my side. I don't care if I live or die. What future is there for me, really? I don't need to survive. I just need to take him down with me.

For my mother. For myself. For all of us.

I will make him pay.

CHAPTER 34

KIMBERLY

KIMBERLY PROWLED THE MOTEL RESTLESSLY. While the ME and his assistants had arrived to whisk the body away, she'd grilled the lodging owner relentlessly.

Were there cameras?

Yes, but they captured activity only at the front door, not at the edge of the parking lot.

Had he heard anything, registered any kind of disturbance?

Absolutely not!

But the man had been sweating profusely. Their UNSUB's tactic to intimidate the locals was clearly working.

She went at the man for another ten minutes, then gave up. He was too terrified to speak.

The maid's death tore at her. She'd talked to the woman just yesterday. Had agreed when D.D. said they needed to get both Bonita and Hélène out of the inn. Yet somehow, while Kimberly and Sheriff Smithers and D.D. were all still in the establishment, Hélène had been taken. Whisked away right under their noses.

Goddammit.

This case had started out as an exercise to bring closure in a fifteen-year-old missing persons case. Now? They had bodies dropping everywhere, and Kimberly couldn't shake the feeling it was all her fault.

The motel's glass doors opened. D.D. entered, her expression a mirror for Kimberly's own. Behind her came Bonita, her face pale but otherwise composed. The girl had known Hélène, but she didn't appear grief-stricken, just grim.

Next came Flora, Keith, Sheriff Smithers. That was enough for Kimberly.

"Meeting. D.D.'s room. We need a new plan of attack."

They all filed wordlessly down the hall, leaving the rattled motel operator in their wake.

D.D. held open the door to the double room. No one spoke till she closed it and bolted it behind her. Even then, Flora crossed to the window, peered out intently, then shuttered the curtains.

Siege mentality, Kimberly thought. Yet wasn't that exactly what they were in?

"We can't keep reacting to whatever the hell is going on in this town," Kimberly began.

"Damn straight," Smithers said.

The sheriff wasn't looking good natured anymore. Or exhausted or overwhelmed. Or for that matter, guilty or shifty. He appeared pissed off, which was good. In Kimberly's experience, angry cops got things done. It was one of the reasons she respected D.D. so much.

"Keith has an idea," Flora spoke up.

Kimberly stared at the computer analyst. He flushed slightly, then straightened his spine and launched into a lecture on criminal enterprises, the dark web, and the key roles of the local cabal they had not yet identified but given the required skill set, they might have a shot at locating.

No one spoke right away. Kimberly was thinking hard, as were D.D. and the sheriff. Flora kept peering through a slight crack in the curtains, as if their UNSUB might magically appear on the other side of the window. Or was lying in wait for them there.

Only Bonita appeared composed. She was sitting on the edge of the bed, watching Flora. No, Kimberly realized a moment later—gazing at the silver handle of the butterfly blade peeking out of Flora's boot.

Kimberly turned to the sheriff. "I'll buy Keith's analysis. The FBI's bread and butter is organized crime, and Keith's right—they function along the same lines as any large business enterprise. Given that, let's start with our so-called mastermind. Always best to cut off the head of the snake. Who are key influencers and leaders around here?"

The sheriff rocked back on his heels, considering. "Mayor Howard," he supplied at last. "But to look at him yesterday . . . man's genuinely distraught. Plus, he's got no motive to order the murder of his own wife, especially given her own level of involvement."

"Did you check on him this morning?" D.D. asked.

"Nah, came straight here when I heard the news. But I visited his cell around eleven last night."

"How'd he look?"

"Like a broken man."

"I don't think he's our mastermind," Kimberly said. D.D. and the sheriff nodded their agreement. The mayor's emotional response yesterday had been too genuine.

"What about our UNSUB? Our mystery killer?" Kimberly turned to D.D. "You said Bonita drew a picture."

The girl looked up at the sound of her name, then went back to her study of Flora's boot.

D.D. crossed into the second room, returning momentarily with three drawings in one hand, and a lone drawing in the other. She held out the first three, kept the fourth.

The rest of them gathered around to study.

"I'll be damned," the sheriff said first. "If that ain't a picture of pure evil, I don't know what is."

Kimberly had to agree. In terms of specific features, the coloring didn't help them. In terms of sending a shiver down her spine, however . . .

"I never thought to draw Jacob," Flora murmured softly. "But if I did, it would be something like that."

Kimberly moved to the second picture. Blue into red. It took a moment to get it. D.D. was right: Bonita was a gifted impressionist.

"That's another maid," D.D. supplied. "She died right before Martha Counsel. Bonita saw it, but said the demon didn't do it."

"The cook?" Kimberly glanced up at Bonita.

The girl shook her head.

"Do you know this woman's name?"

Nod.

Kimberly thought about the files she'd discovered in Martha Counsel's office. One had a name, but was empty. "Stacey?" She attempted to remember. "Stacey . . ." She couldn't quite get the last name.

Two quick nods.

Kimberly pursed her lips, then sighed.

A sharp clap. They all glanced up. Bonita clapped again.

"What is it?" D.D. asked.

The girl was frowning, moving her hands. She clearly had something she wanted to communicate, but didn't know how to do it. Finally, she pointed at Flora's boot. The butterfly blade. She wanted the knife.

"Are you sure?" Flora asked her.

Curt nod.

Flora appeared skeptical, but she pulled out the folded up blade and handed it over. Bonita took a moment to examine it. She shifted it from hand to hand, clearly feeling the weight, then traced the intricate dragon design etched across the surface.

"She's very tactile," D.D. volunteered.

Apparently, D.D. was doing a good job of bonding with her new charge. Now, Bonita tried to pry open the closed sides with her fingernails. She was frowning hard, one corner of her mouth pinched.

"Give it back. You're going to hurt yourself." Bonita reluctantly relinquished her new toy back to Flora. With a flick of her wrist, Flora transformed the instrument from a closed fan to a deadly knife. Bonita's eyes widened in appreciation. She took the blade back, closing her fingers around the handle gingerly.

"The blade is sharp, do not cut yourself," Flora ordered.

The girl glanced at her, then looked up again to make sure everyone was watching. Slowly, she placed the knife just above her thigh. Then, with a short, violent jerk, she pantomimed slicing open her leg.

"Someone cut open the woman's femoral artery," D.D. said.

Nod. Bonita held out her hand again. This time for the drawing. Kimberly handed it over, still confused.

Bonita's fingers danced gently over the form she'd colored in blue. Then she tapped the image once, and gazed at them expectantly.

"She cut open her own leg," Kimberly filled in softly. "She killed herself, that's what you're trying to say."

Bonita nodded sadly.

"To escape them," Flora said, because she of all people would know. More nodding.

"Do you know what happened to the body?" D.D. asked.

Nod.

"Is she in the woods?" D.D. gestured to the remaining drawing, which Kimberly now realized was a mountainside filled with subtle slashes of black lines.

Shrug.

D.D. turned to Kimberly. "Those black lines, they all represent other deceased victims."

"But . . ." Kimberly couldn't speak. There were dozens of them.

The sheriff and the others crowded close, inspecting the image, as well.

"Holy mother of God," Sheriff Smithers exhaled. "How . . . for how long . . . Holy mother of God."

"Bonita, could you lead us to where you last saw Stacey's body?" D.D. was asking.

Another nod.

Kimberly was starting to feel overwhelmed. Harold believed he'd discovered another old grave, plus they now had this new grave. She was going to have to call Atlanta, demand half the office report for duty immediately. Not to mention her supervisor would be in the next vehicle headed up.

"Plan," Kimberly directed out loud, to herself as much as anyone. "We will find Stacey's remains. We will process Hélène's body, we will send the ERT to start exhuming Harold's possible find. But all of that is *reacting*. We're chasing past damage, when what we need to do is get ahead. If we don't have any ideas for the so-called mastermind, and no leads on our current killer, where to focus next?"

"Marketing," Keith spoke up immediately. "Group like this has to be operating on the dark web. Meaning they got a computer nerd somewhere."

Kimberly contemplated it. "Except, of all the business positions, as you call it, that one doesn't have to be local. Their internet support could live anywhere and still manage shop."

"True," Keith acknowledged. "But Bill Benson—who runs the ATV rental—he mentioned a town clerk, Dorothea, who now runs the town's website and social media platform."

"That's right." The sheriff nodded. "She's been doing that . . . long time now."

"Ten years," Keith volunteered.

The sheriff stared at him. "If you say so."

"It's quite possible that whole thing is a front. Remember the ghost tourists the agent was talking about last night? Those may be customers of the cabal, brought here by that website, which has a back door to the dark web, where the real transactions are taking place."

"I'll pick up Dorothea," the sheriff said immediately.

"No!" Keith exploded, then seemed to realize he'd come on too strong when the sheriff puffed up in size. "I'm sorry. But the worst thing you can do is let a site manager know you're onto them. Plenty of computers have a kill switch—a single code that the administrator enters twice, and everything is automatically erased. We need to find the portal for the dark web, access the business enterprises site, and download all the information we can before alerting anyone to our game."

Sheriff Smithers still didn't appear happy. "How do you do that?"

"The mayor and his wife had a couple of computers at their inn, right?"

"Two desktops, a couple of tablets, and a laptop," Kimberly rattled off.

"Okay. The Counsels are part of this organization. We're sure of that. Which means they must be accessing the group's portal from at least one of their computers."

"I could get Su Chen to come up," Kimberly began.

"You don't have time. Let me at them. You know I can do it."

Keith stared at her, unwavering. He could do it. Kimberly had personally watched him in action last year when he'd worked over the copied hard drive from Jacob Ness's old laptop. But he was still a civilian.

"I can do this," Keith repeated. Then, not waiting for her reply, he turned to Sheriff Smithers. "The quickest way to access the group's dark web site will be with the Counsels' username and password. I can hack it, but that will take time. Or . . ."

"You want me to go back to Mayor Howard. Get him to cough it up."

"Tell him if he wants revenge for his wife, this is his way to do it."

The sheriff nodded slowly.

"While you're at it, you could just ask him for the name of their leader," D.D. spoke up dryly.

Sheriff Smithers gave her a look. "Man's terrified. Asking him to provide a name is a big ask. Provide some computer mumble jumble, maybe not so much."

Keith was nodding.

So apparently Kimberly's opinion wasn't needed after all.

"I want to speak to Walt Davies," Flora announced.

"Good God, is this a complete mutiny?"

"Think of it. All his trips bringing microgreens to Atlanta. Maybe what he's bringing back is girls."

"And you think he's magically going to confess this?" Kimberly quizzed.

"I think I have the best chance of spotting a lie, and pushing for the truth."

"Because you knew his son?"

"Something like that. He's also . . . I don't think his crazy act is completely an act. I think Walt is paranoid and prone to voices in his head. Too many cops show up, he'll go to ground, locking himself in his barn and never coming out. But if I go . . . He wants to talk to me. I'm the only connection to his son he has left."

Kimberly considered the matter. "You can't go alone. And not just because it's dangerous, but because if he does confess something useful, you need corroboration. Given that Keith is going to attack the computer and Sheriff Smithers needs to return to county lockup to pressure Howard Counsel . . . I'll go with you."

"Do not dress as a fed! Walt will shoot you on sight."

"Thank you, I'm not a total idiot." Kimberly turned to D.D. "Maybe you can work with Bonita on more details. The whereabouts of Stacey's body, other girls. Sheriff Smithers has deputies guarding the Mountain Laurel."

The sheriff nodded.

"If it's not too much"—Kimberly gazed at Bonita—"would you be willing to return to the inn? Help Detective Warren understand what you witnessed while you were staying there."

The girl studied her for a long moment. Then she nodded.

D.D. held up the final drawing, the one she still had in her hand. "Bonita, did you do this today?"

Nod.

"Who is this?"

D.D. extended her arm for all of them to see. Red, was Kimberly's first impression. Followed immediately by a pang of grief so real, so powerful, she nearly lost her breath. A blur of white against a dusty red ground. A halo of black around a fallen form, leading to a pool of darker red.

Another fatality. But not a fellow maid. Someone else. Someone Bonita had clearly loved.

Then, Kimberly had no doubt. She could tell D.D. understood, as well. No mother could look at that picture and not know.

"This is your mom, isn't it?" Kimberly asked softly.

Single, sorrowful nod.

Flora studied the picture with fresh interest, her features darkening into an expression Kimberly knew well.

"Did the demon do this?" D.D. asked.

Nod. A slight pause, then Bonita lifted her hand, fingered the scar burrowing into her hairline.

"He did that, too?" D.D. was clearly surprised.

Another nod.

"It's a gunshot wound," Flora provided. "Look at the path. The bullet missed its mark, grazed her left temple instead."

Causing lifelong damage.

D.D. squatted down till she was eye level with the girl. "How old were you?"

Shrug.

"Were you a baby?" Kimberly asked. Shake. "What about, were you this tall?" She placed her hand above the floor, around toddler height. Another shake. "This tall?" She moved up a foot.

Bonita contemplated the spacing for a bit. Single nod, as if that seemed about right.

D.D. and Kimberly exchanged a glance. So, older than a toddler, younger than preadolescent. Maybe five? Seven?

"And you've been with the Counsels ever since?"

Yes.

"I'm sorry," Kimberly said. Because someone owed this girl an apology. Life had failed her early, and no one in the system had ever figured it out. First she'd watched her mother die, then she'd been shot, and then she'd gotten to spend the rest of her years as a servant.

Kimberly glanced over at Sheriff Smithers, who appeared angry beyond words. She didn't need him to speak to know how he felt. All of this, in his own backyard.

"Don't kill Howard before you get the password out of him," she warned him.

"I'll work on my restraint," the sheriff promised roughly.

Kimberly inhaled deeply, took in their assorted group. Flora had her knife back, was tucking it into her boot.

"We all have our tasks."

Nodding.

"It goes without saying, our missing killer is armed and danger-ous, we have no idea who in this town we can trust, and clearly this criminal organization doesn't plan on going down without a fight."

More nods.

"Watch your backs. Be on alert. We've racked up at least three new bodies in as many days." Kimberly took another deep breath. "Let's make sure the next one isn't one of us."

CHAPTER 35

D.D.

D.D. DROVE BONITA AND KEITH back to the Mountain Laurel B&B. Kimberly had found an FBI hat in her bag, which they'd squashed as low as possible on Bonita's head to obscure her face. It wasn't much of a disguise, but it was something.

Of them all, Keith was the most relaxed. But then, from what D.D. could tell, the computer analyst regarded most of this as a grand adventure. Though he was also humming this morning. If she didn't know any better, she'd suspect . . .

Sitting behind the wheel, D.D.'s eyes widened. She decided it was time for her to stop thinking about other people's personal lives and focus on work.

Approaching the main road where the beautiful Victorian graced the corner, D.D. slowed. She could see one deputy out front, next to the yellow crime scene tape that blocked off the patio steps leading to the wraparound porch. D.D. pursed her lips, considering. She didn't like approaching from the front. Too exposed, especially given the local climate.

———

D.D. SWUNG AROUND THE BLOCK, where she discovered a second county sheriff's vehicle. Except when they pulled in, no deputy was in sight.

Immediately, she felt a prickle of dread. The back door was partially obscured by a giant mountain laurel, hence the B&B's name. Meaning that if their UNSUB had chosen to return, this is exactly where he would strike. Sneak up on an overworked, sleep-dulled officer and then . . .

A man in uniform walked into full view. He was stubbing out a cigarette and glanced up self-consciously when he noticed D.D.'s car.

She released the breath she didn't realize she'd been holding. They were on edge. Too much so. But now, she thought, they were gonna shake off their jitters, and get these assholes.

On that note, she swung open her door. Keith and Bonita followed suit.

D.D. flashed her creds at the deputy, who appeared completely chagrined at being caught taking a smoke break. Given all the thoughts that had been racing through D.D.'s head, she could care less. She let him open the door, escort them inside, then told him to resume guard. Last thing she needed was Bonita's demon breaking in when D.D. had two civilian charges.

Entering the grand old inn was disorienting. For one thing, the lights were off, casting the rear hall into shadow. For another, the silence. The Victorian sat, as if waiting.

D.D. noticed that Bonita placed her hand on the wall. If she didn't know any better, she would've sworn the girl was patting the wainscoting reassuringly.

D.D. couldn't get her bearings. The place was a labyrinth and she'd never approached from this angle before. She turned to Keith. "You need the computers, correct?"

"Yes. Step one is to figure out which of their computers has the Tor browser. That's the one they'll be using for the dark web."

"Okay. Bonita, can you guide us to the office?"

The girl nodded, limped away. If it felt scary or uncomfortable to return to this place, none of it showed on her face.

They rounded a corner and the grand entryway appeared straight ahead, with the sweeping stairs to their right and another hallway veering to their left. Down that hall was the room where they'd discovered Martha Counsel's body. And apparently, the first door on the right was the woman's office.

D.D. looked around, noting file folders on the floor, an empty safe. The edges of the room and the desk were covered in fingerprint powder. Whatever had been in the safe had been bagged, tagged, carried away.

The room still carried a faint metallic tang of chemical residue. Forensic tests for blood, body fluids, God only knows what. She noticed a section of carpet that had been cut up and removed, as well as a giant piece of fabric from a once gorgeously covered silk-striped wingback. Meaning maybe some of those test results had been positive.

Keith didn't seem to notice. He went straight to the desk, snapped on the fancy stained-glass work lamp, and contemplated the computer monitor.

"Gloves," D.D. ordered.

Faint blush. The computer analyst nodded, then pulled out a pair from his pocket. Not cheap latex, but thin black fabric. Exactly like what some wealthy true-crime enthusiast might order from the internet. D.D. resisted the desire to roll her eyes. Keith might have questionable bona fides, but his work spoke for itself. If anyone could trace the activities of their secret criminal operation, it would be him.

He fired up the desktop, already in his geek zone.

"When I hear from Sheriff Smithers with the username and password, I'll let you know," D.D. informed him.

Keith nodded absently, gloved fingertips already racing across the keyboard.

That left her and Bonita.

Once in the hallway, D.D. asked, "Do you have a favorite place in this hotel?"

Bonita seemed to consider it. Finally, she pointed to the stairs.

"Show me."

It took a little bit. Stairs slowed the girl down, and they had to go up two flights. On the top floor, Bonita led D.D. down a wide, crimson-carpeted hallway. She grew more tentative as they progressed. Finally, they reached a door at the end.

Bonita glanced at D.D., then knocked softly. When no sound came from inside . . .

The girl gently opened the door and crept forward.

The room was gorgeous, the top floor of the turret and stunning in its own right with its curved wall of windows and its yawning ceiling. The Counsels had obviously turned it into a honeymoon suite, with a king bed topping a circular rug while beautifully appointed antiques framed the space. Above, the pointed ceiling had been painted dark blue with a burst of stars at night, while the walls around them held the deep blush of sunset.

Bonita slowly shuffled into the space. D.D. thought she would go to the windows or take a seat on the beautiful sofa. Instead, the girl headed to the middle of the carpet, where she awkwardly lowered herself onto the floor. Then, after arranging herself in a straight line, her hands clasped on her stomach, she looked up.

What the hell. D.D. took up a position on the floor beside Bonita, and did the same.

Now, she could see the painted stars weren't random. With a bit of concentration, D.D. could make out the Big Dipper, the Little Dipper, the North Star, some other constellations.

Bonita pointed up. At first this pattern, then another. D.D. angled her head to mirror the girl's line of sight, but still didn't get it.

"What do you see?" she asked.

Of course, it was an open-ended question, and Bonita couldn't answer it. She turned her head till she and D.D. were nearly nose to nose. Her eyes were mournful. The expression of a young girl who'd already lost too much.

D.D. couldn't help where her thoughts took her. Would Jack like an older sister? It wasn't her place to ask. It would be grossly over-stepping to assume custody of this girl. But when this was done . . . Bonita's mother was dead. Her life had been one of forced servitude. Was D.D. really supposed to just hand her over to child services? She already couldn't bear the thought.

"Are you thinking of your mother?" D.D. asked softly.

A nod. Bonita had painted her mother in a desert. The stars at night were generally very clear in such places. Maybe looking at these stars here made her feel closer to her former home.

"Are you thinking of the other girls?" D.D. asked.

Another nod. Then more pointing. Here, here, and here.

D.D. thought about it. "You've named each star after a girl? Some-one who was here, then went missing."

A fresh nod. So the turret ceiling was Bonita's accounting system. Given how little she had, it made sense.

Bonita reached over. She took D.D.'s hand, squeezed it lightly, and D.D. felt her heart break all over again. She was supposed to be pro-fessional. But all she wanted to do was wrap this child in her arms and keep her safe.

"I would like to hear about your mother," D.D. said softly. "After we've figured out a better communication system, maybe you can tell me about her."

Nod.

D.D. smiled. "Thank you for showing me this room. I can see what it means to you. But for now, honey, I think we have to return to the basement."

D.D.'S PHONE RANG AS THEY were headed downstairs. She recognized the county sheriff's number and picked up. Immediately she heard sounds of commotion in the background.

"We got a problem," Sheriff Smithers announced grimly.

"Howard Counsel?"

"Just found him dead in his cell."

"I'm so sorry, sir." D.D. could hear the receptionist, Franny, in the background: "But the gentleman was making such a commotion and he wouldn't go away. I had no choice but to call for Deputy Chad . . ."

"I understand, Franny," said the sheriff. "I understand." But D.D. could hear him sigh heavily.

She figured she knew what had happened: A diversion at the front of the sheriff's office had lured the on-watch deputy from Howard Counsel's cell.

"Can Franny give you a description of the man who caused the commotion? Any detail at all. Set her down, make her visualize."

"You think it was a setup?"

"I think it would be too much of a coincidence to be otherwise. Housecleaning, remember? First Martha, then Hélène, now Howard. For all we know, the cook is dead, too."

Though D.D. doubted that last statement; that woman was too mean to die. If anyone could hold her own with some evil UNSUB, even work as his right-hand person, it would be her.

"How'd he get the damn blanket?" Sheriff Smithers was now asking someone.

"He said he was cold, sir. I didn't think. I'm sorry, sir. I'm very,

very sorry." A young man's voice, most likely Deputy Chad. It was the kind of mistake that haunted an officer.

Another sigh, then more noises from the background.

"I never got to talk to Howard." Sheriff Smithers returned to the phone. "By the time I got here, the deed was done and bedlam already erupting."

"You don't know the username or password," D.D. filled in.

"No, ma'am."

D.D.'s turn to sigh. "I'll let Keith know. But, Sheriff, don't be too hard on yourself. I've seen Keith in action before. Howard's death slows us down, but we're not out."

"I'm very sorry, ma'am."

Which was echoed by more apologizing from the background. Franny again, probably wringing her hands or clutching her golden cross.

"We already knew they were one step ahead of us," D.D. said. "All the more reason to keep moving forward. Maybe you should join us at the Mountain Laurel. Usernames and passwords are often based on personal information. It's possible there's something written down or a key photo in the office or bedroom that might help us out."

"I'll help," Franny was saying in the background. "Please let me do something. I feel terrible!"

D.D. rolled her eyes. She didn't care who came, as long as it was someone.

"Give me an hour or so," the sheriff said. "Gotta sort out the body here, then we'll be by."

"Thank you, Sheriff." D.D. ended the call. Bonita was gazing at her expectantly. "Howard Counsel is dead," D.D. told her.

A flicker of expression crossed the girl's face, then nothing. Had she hated the Counsels for treating her like a maid? Or had she been grateful that they'd taken her in when she had nothing left? Maybe a bit of both. It was possible to love and hate your captors—just ask Flora.

Bonita finished leading the way down the stairs. They stopped at the office long enough to give Keith the news.

He was no longer working the desktop, but had a laptop open in front of him. Now, he shrugged philosophically. "Found the Tor browser. This is the machine."

"At least we have some progress for the morning. The sheriff will be by to see if he can help search for the username and password."

Another shrug. "Lotta data in this office. I can start with birth dates, anniversary dates, name of their favorite cat, that sort of thing. I'll get it eventually."

"Exactly what I told him."

"Where are you going?"

"Down to the basement. It was where the servants lived."

Keith frowned. "In these grand old homes, the servants' quarters were generally in the attic. Homeowners needed the chillier temps in the cellar for storing root vegetables and other perishables. Add to that a large enough space to hold all the coal and wood used to heat a home of this size, plus a much smaller, contained room for dumping kitchen offal, other . . . waste products." Keith wrinkled his nose. "Basically a nice cool cellar was too valuable to waste on servants."

D.D. had no idea. "This basement has a dozen tiny rooms and hallways. Maybe the Counsels did it later."

Keith clearly didn't like her answer. "I have to back up the original hard drive before I can start working," he said slowly. "While I wait, I think I'll go with you."

"You really want to tour the basement?"

"Yes. I really do."

CHAPTER 36

FLORA

I HAD SEX LAST NIGHT.

It brings a surreal quality to my morning. After so many years of believing I would never be that woman, never have that experience again . . .

Do I *look* different?

Am I different?

I'm grateful to partner with Kimberly today. D.D. would study me. She'd know. Kimberly and I don't have that kind of relationship.

Keith kissed me lightly before departure. Then stood with his forehead pressed against my own, a quiet moment that said even more. No awkward morning after for us. Instead, we'd gone from bedroom to crime scene. I'm not sure how many couples do that, but with Keith, it doesn't feel extraordinary at all. Just another day in the life.

Now, I try to pull myself together. Maybe I had a sublime night. Maybe I'm even more excited for this evening. But some things haven't changed. The pile of dead bodies. A town where nothing is as it seems. And now a morning call on a man who probably isn't right in the head and will be greeting us with a shotgun.

We'd switched vehicles with D.D., giving her the official fed car while we commandeered the rental. Kimberly had taken to heart what I said—Walt isn't the type of guy who'd take kindly to police on his property. Kimberly had ditched her credentials as well as her sidearm. I don't believe for a moment, however, that she's weaponless. I'm guessing ankle holster. Fits well with my knife.

Just two armed, paranoid women paying a visit to an even more paranoid man. What could possibly go wrong?

Walt's gate at the edge of his property is locked up tight. Kimberly pulls over to the side and we both get out. Given Walt's propensity for cameras, I already have an easy expression pasted on my face. Kimberly appears faintly bored, wearing a tight-fitting black tee with jeans. She appears wiry and athletic. In a fight, I wouldn't bet against her.

I walk up to the gate, pick out the camera mounted on the post. I stand right before it, wave, then wait.

A minute passes. Then another. The gate doesn't magically open, but it's not that kind of mechanical beast. Walt's property is an odd mix of new security technology with old buildings and fence lines. He's going to have to walk down and unfasten the padlock himself. The question is, will he?

Kimberly yawns, stretches. Again, playing the role of my disinterested friend.

We never hear Walt coming, but in an instant he appears on the other side of the metal gate. Both Kimberly and I startle.

For the first time, I see a flicker of unease in Kimberly's expression. Especially once she takes in Walt's pump-action shotgun.

"You're back," he says.

"I have a few more questions."

"Got a new friend."

"This is Kimberly."

"ATF, FBI, Statie?" He stares at Kimberly. "You ain't no civilian, that's for sure."

Kimberly regards him coolly. "FBI," she says at last. "But this morning, I'm here for Flora."

Walt, however, is no dumb bunny. "I've seen you before."

I remember just as Walt connects the dots.

"You were on the TV. You led the raid that killed my boy."

Kimberly doesn't say a word.

"You rid the world of a beast," Walt tells her flatly. Then he works his key in the padlock, and lets us in.

We follow Walt through the woods to his cabin, with its cluttered front porch harvest of dried wood and moss. He keeps his shotgun loose at his side. I can't help but stare at it suspiciously. Did Keith and I survive this man once, just so I could deliver up both myself and the federal agent who'd been involved in Jacob's death the next day?

Walt has a lot of reasons to use that shotgun. Though Kimberly and I are hardly defenseless, his property, his gun, his motives, give him the clear advantage. I straighten my shoulders, force myself to pay attention, focus on every line of his body. If there's anything I've learned over the years, it's that all predators telegraph their intent right before they attack.

Walking beside me, Kimberly is doing her best to mentally note all the various outbuildings, while appearing to look at nothing at all. Neither Walt nor I are fooled. We are a curious little trio of mutual suspicion. Plus, we all share Jacob. And I guess, if Walt is truly to be believed, we all had our reasons for wanting Jacob dead.

Walt takes up position in a hard wooden chair on his front porch. It seems to be his vantage point of choice—where he can sit and survey his kingdom. This forces Kimberly and me to perch on the broken-down love seat wedged across from him, with our backs to the yard. Kimberly is definitely uncomfortable. I didn't like it yesterday, and I don't like it now.

Most serial predators are eventually caught due to their own arro-gance. The more misdeeds they survive, the more careless they grow. I wonder if the same is true for vigilantes.

"Do you know Howard and Martha Counsel of the Mountain Laurel inn?" I ask Walt.

He shrugs. "Mayor Howard? Everyone knows him."

"Martha was found hanged yesterday. And today, one of the maids from the B and B was left hanging outside our motel. She hadn't just been murdered. Someone worked her over with a knife beforehand."

Walt's expression doesn't change. Neither do his hands move from the shotgun resting on his lap. "These woods are a scary place," he says at last.

I lean forward, stare at him intently. "The trees might scream at night, Walt. But trees don't murder young women. Men do. Men like Jacob."

"Jacob's dead."

"But this town isn't settled. These mountains, the forest, the com-munity. There are bodies and bones everywhere. You're not living in the wild, Walt. You're living on a graveyard."

Walt gazes off. I can't tell what he's thinking. Or maybe what he's hearing—the wind howling, girls screaming? Clever and crazy. An old man who by his own admission fried his brain with drugs and alcohol years ago. Still, I think he knows more than he's telling. But I'm also willing to believe even *he's* not sure what's real anymore.

Isolation can play tricks on the mind. Something Walt and I both understand well.

"Talk to me," I murmur. "You and me, Walt. Talk, and I will listen."

Beside me, Kimberly doesn't move. If she approves or disapproves of my approach, I have no idea. But she's still letting me take the lead, and I appreciate the show of confidence.

"Counsels are high and mighty," Walt says at last.

"You met them?"

"Town this small? Can hardly avoid knowing each other."

"The Counsels are the ones who told us to look you up. They said you were crazy, maybe even violent. They blamed you for the bodies in the woods."

Walt shrugs. "People blame me for a lotta things. Makes it easier on them."

Kimberly spoke up for the first time. "Do you think Mayor Howard is the violent type? Could he have killed his own wife?"

"Nah. Howard's just a talker. Doesn't have the stomach for real action."

"Someone is killing people around here."

Again, Walt doesn't speak right away.

"You deliver your microgreens to Atlanta yourself, Walt?" I ask innocently.

For the first time his hand twitches on the barrel of his shotgun. "Most times."

"Ever bring anything back?"

"Like what?"

"You tell me."

"I don't do bad things anymore. Told you that yesterday. Woods set me straight."

My turn to shrug. "Lots of people swear to reform. To give up violence, rage, the need to just . . . tap off some of that darkness inside. It's hard to do. I know, Walt, I know."

"My boy was evil."

I don't speak.

"When he came back, showed up in that tavern . . . I didn't believe for a moment he came back to see his old man. No good reason, not after all these years."

"Maybe he wanted to check out his hometown."

"Boy was five when he left. You remember much when you were five?"

I shake my head. Then, a moment later, I think I understand. "I always assumed he brought me here because he felt comfortable. Knew the area. But you're saying he couldn't have known these mountains, this town. He was too young when he left."

Walt nodded.

"So how did he know about the abandoned cabin? How did he know to bring me here?"

Another shrug. But I understand now Walt isn't being obtuse. He doesn't know the answers to these questions, and he's wondered about it himself. What truly brought Jacob back to Niche, Georgia? Because in Walt's own estimation, it couldn't have been homesickness, or a sudden desire to connect with dear old Dad.

Kimberly's turn. "Jacob wouldn't be the type to hang out with the Counsels. At least I can't picture it."

"Nah."

"So who would he hang out with? Who would bring him here, Walt?"

"I don't always drive to Atlanta," Walt says abruptly.

Kimberly and I both wait.

"Late spring to early fall, temperatures can be very hot. My old van, the AC doesn't work so well. I worried about my plants wilting before I got there."

I nod encouragingly.

"One night, I'm sitting in the tavern—"

"You spend a lot of time in bars for a guy who claims he doesn't drink."

"Man's gotta eat. So I'm sitting there. And a fellow comes over. We get to chatting. He tells me he has a delivery business. Runs flowers, fresh fish, whatever, in his refrigerated truck up from Atlanta to local inns and restaurants. Man was bragging about his rig."

"Okay."

"We chat a little more, and it comes to me. Hot months, he could take my greens down, bring his fish and flowers back up. Good for me, good for him. We shake, and that's it. Done deal for the past several years."

"You trusted this man, some stranger, with your microgreens?" I already don't believe him.

"That's the thing. I shouldn't have. No good reason to. But this guy, he had a way of speaking. Later, I got to thinking. Seems to me, he already knew. About my greens. My business. He knew everything before I ever sat down. Wasn't some kind of coincidence. More like a setup."

"But you continued the arrangement?"

"No reason not to. Man picks up, delivers, without missing a date. I might be half-cracked, but I ain't stupid. And business is business."

"Who's the man, Walt?" Kimberly now, her voice a tad impatient.

"Clayton. Grew up around here. Not sure where he calls home now. One of those guys, comes and goes as he pleases."

"Is Clayton a first or last name?"

"Didn't bother to ask."

"How do you pay him?"

"Cash." Walt stares at her. "Like I'm trusting my money to some bank."

"What does Clayton look like?"

"Big guy. Dark hair, brown eyes. Not that young, not that old. Hell, we don't exchange pleasantries."

There's something he's still not telling us. "Come on, Walt."

After a moment's hesitation: "He carries a knife. Big ol' thing with an ugly-ass serrated blade. But he doesn't keep it tucked away. He wants everyone to see it. He wants you to know."

"Know what?"

"He's one of us. Like Jacob. Like I used to be. A mean son of a bitch who makes no apologies. That knife, it's not just for show. And all those runs to Atlanta with his fancy refrigerated truck . . . Lots of things you can carry in a rig like that."

"Where do we find Clayton?" Kimberly asks.

"Around. Like I said, he doesn't exactly have an address. But sooner or later, he shows up again."

"How do you get in touch with him when you have a delivery?"

"I don't. He comes by. Every two weeks. Can't fault the man for reliability."

"When is the next pickup?"

"Five days."

"We don't have five days, Walt," I say honestly. "I'm not even sure we have five hours."

"Name of the tavern where you first met him?" Kimberly presses.

That faint hesitation again. Then a sigh. Long, uneven. It reminds me a bit of a death rattle, but maybe I'm just letting the conversation spook me.

"There's something I should show you," Walt says. He stands up, shotgun held before him. Belatedly, Kimberly and I rise to our feet. "You know I talk about the woods. You know what I believe. About the dark. The trees. That all that moaning and shrieking ain't just the wind ripping through the forest."

I nod.

"People think I'm crazy, talking like that. I know. I've heard them. For years now." Walt stares at me. "I didn't save you."

It's not a question, so I don't answer.

"Never saved anyone really. Just inflicted my share of violence, then fathered a boy who did even worse. That's my legacy. Death and microgreens."

I still don't say anything.

"I know why the woods scream at night," he murmurs. "And if you don't mind going for a little hike, I can prove it."

CHAPTER 37

D.D.

D.D. LET BONITA BE THEIR guide upon leaving the office. She expected the girl to head straight for the basement stairs, but instead she veered into the foyer, then crossed the pretty breakfast room into the kitchen. Bonita halted in front of the long, stainless steel commercial dishwasher. She pantomimed picking something up, then once again slashed at her leg.

"This is where Stacey got the knife, killed herself," D.D. filled in.

Brisk nod.

Bonita moved to the far right, opened up a door to a utility closet, pointed at a mop sitting in a bucket.

Keith's turn. "Someone used the mop to clean up."

Bonita tapped her chest.

"You had to clean it up?" D.D. felt ill at the thought.

Another brisk nod, then Bonita was shambling out of the kitchen. This time, they headed for the cellar. D.D. and Keith adjusted their pace to match Bonita's, as she worked her way slowly down the narrow staircase to the cool, dark space below.

At the bottom, D.D. found the light switch, though once again the old sconces did little to illuminate the space.

Bonita hobbled forward and they followed. This time, the girl went directly for the heavy wooden doors at the end of the hall. The intricately carved double doors remained open from yesterday, the same chemical scent from the upstairs office emitting from this stone-forged space. D.D. wouldn't be surprised if the forensic techs had spent the night dousing the room's floor in luminol to reveal blood patterns. Kimberly would get the official report. D.D. already bet the findings included things gory and macabre.

In this room, Bonita moved less certainly. She shifted from hobble to shuffle, her shoulders up, her chin ducked low. She had assumed a defensive position, as if the shadows might attack at any moment. She moved to one of the stone walls and pressed her hand against it. Grounding herself? Something more?

Keith found the light switch in this room. It lit up a dangling over-head light, a wooden wheel suspended by dark metal chains and topped with flickering candelabras. Again, it did little to fight off the dark.

"What is this?" Keith breathed quietly.

"I don't know. I'm guessing a meeting space."

"You mean worldwide headquarters of Evil Enterprise?"

"Certainly looks it."

Bonita hobbled to the massive stone fireplace. She peered inside, ran her hand along the collection of heavy, wrought iron pokers, then wandered closer to the huge oak table, appearing pensive. Finally, she pointed at a spot on the stone floor between the table and the far wall.

She gazed up at D.D. expectantly.

"Is that the last place you saw Stacey's body?"

Nod.

"Do you know what happened to it after that?" Because why would you bring a body to the basement?

Shrug.

D.D.'s turn to inspect the fireplace. "Did they try to burn it?" she wondered out loud. A normal fire would never get the job done. A crematorium had to burn at over a thousand degrees to reduce bone to ash. Even a large hearth such as this one, she'd be staring at a pile of blackened bones, let alone still catch the scent of cooked flesh. Work too many burn scenes in a row, and detectives had a tendency to give up barbecue.

D.D. glanced back up at Bonita.

The girl shrugged again. Apparently, this was as much as she knew. D.D. crossed to the spot on the floor. Farthest point from the double doors, let alone the trek Bonita's demon man would have had to make from the kitchen, across the very exposed foyer, down the stairs, and through an incredibly large cellar, while carrying a body. It didn't make sense. Criminals were lazy by nature. Why not just cart the maid's body out the back door under the cover of night? Bringing a body here entailed so much extra effort—and risk.

D.D. didn't like it.

Keith was walking around the room, running his hands from one wall to another and frowning intently. Geeks, D.D. thought, just as her cell phone rang.

She held up her phone, surprised she had reception in the basement. She didn't recognize the number, but the area code matched Kimberly's.

"Excuse me for a sec," D.D. said, then moved from the stone room into the hall. "Sergeant Detective D. D. Warren."

"Sergeant Warren? This is Special Agent Rachel Childs. I'm leading the ERT."

"I remember."

"I've been trying to reach SSA Quincy, but she's not answering her cell."

"Okay." Maybe Kimberly didn't feel comfortable answering her phone in front of Walt? Though for a taskforce leader to not take a call . . .

"We have news to report," Childs said. "Since I can't reach Kimberly, I felt it was best to inform you."

"I heard you guys had discovered another possible grave?"

"We've found five more graves."

The team leader's tone was curt. Even after seeing Bonita's drawing, even knowing there had to be more bodies in the woods, D.D. felt shocked.

"Given the number," Childs continued now, "I need to contact HQ for reinforcements. We're going to need multiple teams, perhaps even multiple forensic anthropologists, to work a scene of this size."

"There may be dozens of graves," D.D. managed to say.

A moment of silence. "Then I'm going to recommend bringing in search dogs again."

It wasn't really D.D.'s call, being an out-of-state cop, but she still said, "I would agree."

"These remains, they appear more recent than the first ones we found. We're not experts, but based on some flora, fauna, something"—Childs's voice was dry—"Harold is thinking the past five years."

"I have a feeling we're going to find remains from all sorts of time periods."

That pause again. But D.D. didn't clarify. She was keeping Bonita's role to herself. The girl was in enough danger. The fewer who knew about her, even among the taskforce, the better.

"I texted SSA Quincy and left a message," Childs said now.

"But you still haven't heard anything back? Not even a text?"

"Negative."

"I'll reach out."

"I appreciate it. I'll be in touch later this afternoon. We're going to cordon off and secure what we've found thus far, while Harold and Franklin continue to search."

More graves, thought D.D. More bodies. "Sounds good."

"I'll be in touch. If you do hear from Quincy—"

"I'll be sure to let you know." D.D. hung up the phone. She moved back into the meeting room. "Keith, when you and Flora were at Walt's yesterday, did you have cell phone coverage?"

"Oh yeah. Wi-Fi, too. His security system depends on it."

D.D. nodded absently. "Mind texting Flora for me?"

"Why?"

"Just . . . touch base. I'll do the same with Kimberly."

Keith wasn't fooled. But he followed D.D.'s gaze to Bonita, who was standing near the table, arms wrapped tight around her waist. "Okay."

He pulled out his phone, tapped away. D.D. sent her own message. She had a hollow feeling in the pit of her stomach. But whether that was the effect of this dungeon-like space or a legitimate investigative instinct, she couldn't be sure.

Keith had put away his phone and was inspecting the walls again.

"What are you looking for?" D.D. asked finally.

"I'm not sure. But this space, it isn't right."

"What do you mean?"

"Old homes generally have cellars with earthen floors, and with pillars of piled rock in the middle to help support the home above. This basement, with its narrow hall, tiny room, and now this . . . This is quite elaborate."

"Maybe the Counsels did this after the fact, so they would have extra space for their staff. I mean, at some point they clearly added plumbing and electricity."

"To the small rooms, sure. But this space." He moved near the fireplace. "This wall is clearly part of the original foundation." He ran his fingers along the jagged lines of giant chunks of stone, piled tight. Clearly an engineering feat back in the day when they'd had no heavy equipment. "If only these stones could talk."

D.D. arched a brow. "From computer analyst to stone whisperer?"

"Nah, just a nerd who read about the history of this town while we were driving up."

"Dahlonega started the gold rush. 'There's gold in them thar hills.' That's what you told us."

Keith nodded. "Guess what else is in these hills?"

"Well, gold mines." D.D. paused, said more slowly, "Tunnels. These hills would be full of tunnels, where various miners searched for gold."

"And after the gold rush, guess what else this area became known for?"

"I haven't a clue."

"A major hub along the Underground Railroad. Wealthy abolitionists took in escaping slaves. Where they could secret them away in their cellars, then spirit them along a vast network of underground tunnels."

D.D. got it. "You think there's a tunnel down here. This room, it's a meeting point for a reason."

"If the same people were always appearing at this inn for some clandestine meeting, people might notice. And we probably would've heard about it. Local gossip and such. But what if they didn't have to ever enter the inn? What if there was another way?"

D.D. looked around. What Keith was saying made some sense. "Your wall, the fireplace wall, is original," she noted slowly. She turned to the left. "That wall, also clearly old stone." Behind her were the double doors, framed into drywall. Which made sense. A cellar was generally open, whereas the Counsels had clearly enclosed this space after the fact. Which left her with the wall behind the oak table, where Bonita stood.

That wall wasn't old, dark stone. It was drywall, covered in some historically patterned wallpaper of deep crimson with tiny gold diamonds. The dark color absorbed the light, made the wall that much harder to see. As if the wallpaper wasn't just decoration, but camouflage.

Keith was back at the fireplace, running his fingers along the upper ledge of stone. A lever, D.D. realized. He was looking for some hidden latch that would reveal the secret doorway. Which didn't feel so far-fetched after all. And certainly would explain bringing a dead body down here.

She took up a position on the other side of the fireplace, just as they both heard footsteps thunder overhead.

D.D. froze. Keith, too.

Heavy wooden doors, D.D. thought. They could barricade them with chairs. Then keep looking for the escape tunnel while waiting for a hulking demon to break in from the other side?

Why the hell hadn't Kimberly texted back yet? Or Flora?

D.D. experienced that hollow, edgy feeling again.

She needed to take action. Identify the threat, then neutralize it.

Except all she had was the sound of heavy footsteps and a room ringed in black.

"Detective Warren?" a voice suddenly called out from down the cellar corridor.

The sheriff's voice. D.D. nearly sagged in relief. Of course, he was coming over to help.

"Yoo hoo?" Franny's voice, echoing her boss's.

D.D. cleared her throat. "We're down here, in the basement!" she called out.

Keith had finally relaxed, returning his attention to the fireplace's intricate stonework.

The sheriff finally appeared in the doorway. His eyes were wide. "Never been down here before. Never would've even known such a room like this exists."

"Welcome to headquarters for Diabolical-R-Us," Keith said.

Franny had followed the sheriff into the room. The older woman was wearing a pale blue sweater set, which she now clutched at her chest. "I don't . . . I'm not sure . . ."

She caught sight of Bonita, in her oversized sweats and FBI cap. "You have a child down here? That's terrible!"

Franny gave D.D. a clear look of disapproval.

"We're about to go up," D.D. said defensively, even as she prepared to go on the attack. "So what exactly happened at the jail this morning?"

Franny promptly flushed. "I don't rightly know. Mr. Benson came in, claiming some taskforce officer had taken advantage of his business."

"Who's Mr. Benson? What's his business?"

"Bill Benson. He runs the ATV rental operation."

"Wait a minute." Keith drew up short. "Flora and I talked to Bill Benson twice. We rented ATVs from him, but we paid, fair and square. I still have the receipts!"

Franny spread her hands. "I tried asking him what he meant, but he just grew angrier and angrier. Next thing I knew, he was shouting at me."

Keith frowned. "Really? He didn't strike me as the shouting type."

"Can't say that he's done that before," Franny agreed. "Can't say that I'd like for him to do that again. But he grew so agitated . . . I had to call for help. I didn't know what else to do."

"You called for the deputy who was watching Howard's cell," D.D. filled in.

"Deputy Chad was the only one in the building. It was still pretty early, you understand, and everyone's been working such long hours . . ."

D.D. got it. The cabal had needed to take out Howard, and once again they'd moved strategically. Appointed this Bill Benson, who'd probably learned about at least some of their investigative efforts from Keith and Flora, to head to the police department first thing in the morning. He'd provided the distraction, while a second person had slid by to encourage Howard to do the deed. Or, for all they knew, person number two had already been in the station. Hell, maybe even worked at the county sheriff's department, which employed dozens of civilians as well as officers. At this point, anything was possible.

D.D. found herself eyeing the sheriff again. On the one hand, the corrupt local sheriff seemed too obvious. On the other hand, clichés always started with a kernel of truth. Sheriff Smithers put on a good show as the local father figure, genuinely concerned for his community. But he was also one of the few people who knew they needed a password from Mayor Howard. No one else in the sheriff's department, not to mention the town, had been in on that discussion. Just D.D., Kimberly, Flora, Keith, and Bonita. D.D. trusted her team implicitly. Which left her with . . .

"I'm sorry," D.D. said at last, given that Franny was clearly distressed and the silence growing strained.

The older woman nodded stiffly. "I apologized to Sheriff Smithers. I'll add my apologies to you, too. This is my mistake and mine alone. We haven't ever had such a . . . situation before. I'm afraid I saw Mr. Benson as my neighbor, never even crossed my mind he might be a threat. Shame on me for that. But what's done is done. I'm here, and I want to help. What can I do?"

D.D. looked over at Keith, who was working the fireplace.

"What are you looking for?" Sheriff Smithers asked, clearly noting Keith's effort.

"A secret tunnel."

"A secret tunnel?"

"He's not lying," D.D. assured the sheriff.

"And I'm not wrong either," Keith stated triumphantly. "Look at this." His fingers closed around the edge of one of the stones. He tugged. It moved. And at the far end of the room, just beyond the huge oak table, the crimson-covered wall slowly rumbled to life, a panel emerging, then sliding right.

Bonita jumped back, hobbling quickly to D.D.'s side.

D.D. couldn't blame the girl. A draft of cold air blew into the room, striking her across the face. It carried the scent of dirt and pine, but also something fainter, more troubling.

The smell of death.

The secret doorway rumbled all the way open, and they stared into the abyss.

CHAPTER 38

KIMBERLY

KIMBERLY FELT UNEASY. AFTER WALT'S pronouncement that he could prove the trees really did scream at night, Walt had walked across his sprawling property and disappeared into an outbuilding.

"Does he always carry the shotgun?" Kimberly asked Flora the second he was gone.

"Yes."

"I have a backup twenty-two. You have what, your bright shiny knife?"

"It's a good knife."

"One butterfly blade plus one small caliber handgun hardly equals adequate protection against buckspray."

"Then let's not get shot."

"Do you believe him?" Kimberly asked seriously. "That he really did try to save you? That he's not as evil as Jacob Ness and now he's magically going to compensate for an entire life of reprobation by leading us to the bad guys?"

"I don't know. It sounds funny to say this, but . . . Jacob had some good in him. He liked to play games. He brought me DVDs of my favorite TV shows. He could be nice. On occasion. Maybe his father has some good in him, too."

Kimberly was not convinced, but then she heard the sound of a four-stroke engine firing to life. A moment later, Walt reappeared, driving a mud-splattered red ATV with monster tires. He parked the beast in front of the porch, then headed back, ostensibly for another. Their modes of transportation, Kimberly deduced. Flora and Keith had said the locals preferred the network of forest trails to county roads. Better access—and better cover.

As in, Walt could lead them just about anywhere, and who would know?

Kimberly dug her phone out of her pocket to text D.D. No bars, dammit. Funny, because she could've sworn she'd had coverage earlier.

Walt roared around the corner on a second ATV, this one even filthier than the first. He gazed at them expectantly. Kimberly took that as a hint to follow Flora to the first four-wheeler. Flora was already climbing on, wrapping her fingers around the handlebars.

"You know what you're doing?"

"Easy peasy. Only hit four or five trees yesterday. Hang on tight."

With a lurch, they were off. A short pause as Walt dealt with the gate guarding his property, unlocking, opening, closing up, relocking. Waiting, Kimberly thought she saw a flash of light in the woods. A glint of metal? But then it was gone and Walt was pulling away in a spray of gravel.

Kimberly had a prickly feeling at the back of her neck. As if the trees did have eyes, and were anxious to keep their secrets.

Walt veered off the road onto a narrow, rutted trail Kimberly wouldn't have known existed. Flora had no problem following him; maybe this was what they'd done yesterday.

Right, left, right, left. Sharp turn, sharper turn. Then the whine of the engines as they chugged up, up, up and Kimberly had to clutch Flora for balance.

Abruptly they tore into a grassy clearing. Walt killed his engine. Flora did the same.

The old man climbed off his ATV, picked up his ubiquitous shotgun. "Now, we walk."

Flora and Kimberly once more fell in line. And once more, Kimberly could feel unease snaking down her spine.

CROSSING THE MEADOW WAS HOT work. None of them had water, but Walt didn't seem to notice. He led them to the far line of bordering woods, slipping back between the trees with the ease of a mountain man who'd been doing this all his life.

Kimberly appreciated the shade. She used it to check her phone again. Still no signal. She noticed Flora doing the same. They exchanged glances, but didn't say a word.

Whatever happened next, they were on their own. Two of them, one of him. In a fair fight, Kimberly would put her money on her and Flora. But Walt didn't strike her as the kind of guy who fought fair. She was already noting how he held his shotgun, one finger always near the trigger. First order of business would be getting that weapon away from him. Because as long as he could whirl at any second, pump, shoot, pump, shoot . . .

She didn't have a good feeling about their afternoon anymore.

MORE TWISTS AND TURNS. BY Kimberly's estimation, Walt could disappear at any moment, and she and Flora would be just as dead as if he'd used his weapon. They looped around and around, the trees growing tighter and thicker around them.

Walt slowed.

Flora nearly bumped into him before realizing the death march had ended. Kimberly came up beside Flora. Straight ahead of them appeared to be a pile of boulders. Except, as Kimberly let her eyes adjust, she could make out various rusted-out objects nearly lost in the overgrown meadow grass, weedy shrubs.

Flora advanced first, going from a rusted-out shell of an old wagon, to a pile of discarded wooded crates, to what appeared to be an old pickax.

"Kimberly," she called.

Kimberly walked over, followed the line of Flora's finger to the pickax. The handle appeared old, aged to the weathered gray of wood long exposed to the elements. The metal head on the other hand . . .

"Didn't your friends say the graves had been carved with a pickax?" Flora murmured.

"Yep."

"Looks like this one could do it."

Kimberly nodded, squatting down for further inspection. The metal head didn't just look new, it bore signs of dried mud and something . . . darker. She pulled out her phone, shot a quick pic. Still not enough bars to share the photo, but at least it gave them a start of documentation.

"What is this place?" Flora asked Walt.

"Old mine. These hills are riddled with 'em."

Kimberly followed Flora over to the rock pile, where—sure enough—she could now see an opening set back from the first few tumbled stones.

"Is it safe?" Kimberly asked Walt.

He shrugged. "Are the mountains safe?"

Fair enough.

Flora was already exploring the opening. Up close, it was surprisingly large. It appeared some of the rock face had collapsed over the years, creating a jumble of large boulders that partially obscured the opening. But even those rocks had fallen a good ten feet away, meaning an ATV or other vehicle could navigate the opening.

Perhaps pulling a small trailer loaded with a lifeless body, the driver stopping to add the pickax to the pile, then continuing down the mountain to a place where no human would think to look again. Unless, of course, you were an inexperienced hiker with terrible blisters and a need for a walking stick.

A faint moan came from the mine entrance. It built in intensity, before dying off again.

"The wind," Flora murmured. "The way it cuts through the rocks."

"Sure," Kimberly muttered. "The wind."

Kimberly turned to Walt. "Who knows about this mine?"

"Locals. Mountain folks. Ain't secret."

"Do people still go inside?"

"When I was a kid, we'd come here to drink. But then, twenty, thirty years ago, a group of teens headed in and only two came out. County blocked the entrance after that."

"It's not blocked now."

"Nope."

Kimberly studied the ground. She was no expert, but she thought she could just discern what appeared to be wide tire tracks, close together, such as what an ATV would leave behind.

"Why did you bring us here, Walt?" Kimberly realized for the first time he wasn't holding the shotgun at his side anymore. He'd positioned it before him, loose but at the ready.

"I followed the screams," he told her. "I thought if I could find the trees, tell them I had repented, they wouldn't haunt me no more. Took me a long time. Walking the woods, night after night.

"Eventually, I followed the cries here. But when I came back during the day, the woods had fallen silent again. I had to keep waiting. Then last night, the trees started again. I could hear them, clear as a whistle, standing here."

"Who's screaming, Walt?"

"People I hurt. Maybe the girls Jacob hurt. Just wait. You'll understand what I mean soon enough."

A noise above them, followed by a small shower of falling rocks. Kimberly jumped as half a dozen pebbles careened down the mine entrance. Flora, already standing in the pile of boulders at the opening, leapt to the side.

Walt's gaze jerked up. One second he was standing relaxed, the next he was raising his shotgun to his shoulder, screaming, "I see you, devil! I see you standing there!"

Kimberly dropped into a crouch, going for her ankle-holstered .22. Walt was pointing that damn shotgun right at her and Flora. Yelling at shadows, lost in some haze where he looked ready to shoot first, question later.

She was aware of Flora, twenty feet away, reaching for her butterfly blade. A fresh shower of rocks, then a particularly large rock dropped from above, smacking Flora on the head. The woman went down hard, a blur of blood and shadow.

As Walt continued waving his shotgun wildly toward Kimberly, the only person who now stood between him and the mine.

"Begone with you, I say. Begone!"

Shit. Kimberly jerked out her .22, lifted it up from the crouched position.

Pump, kaboom.

Walt let loose with his first load. Too high.

Kimberly honed in on the target. Except, just as she was about to squeeze the trigger . . .

Crack.

The ensuing noise was no shotgun blast, but a rifle. Coming from somewhere above and behind Kimberly as she ducked her head reflexively, then fell back toward Flora, a fresh avalanche of debris crashing upon the mine opening.

Before her, Walt staggered. Bright red blood bloomed across his dirty T-shirt. He pumped his shotgun for a fresh load, aiming it up, up, up. The air cracked again. A second flower of blood joined the first across his chest. He still worked to aim his weapon. Then, his knees buckled. His grip on his shotgun loosened. He sank to his knees.

His lips were moving. A last prayer to God, or to the ghosts that haunted his nights?

Then Kimberly got it. Walt Davies wasn't pleading for mercy. He was giving her a command.

Go.

His blood-frothed lips moved again.

Get away, get away, get away!

More noise from overhead. Footsteps scrabbling down the rock face.

Kimberly looked ahead to the sunny clearing, where Walt was now collapsed in the grass.

She looked behind to the gaping maw of the dangerous old mining tunnel, where Flora was collapsed, bleeding heavily.

It wasn't much of a decision. She raced for the entrance, aware of the danger descending rapidly from the rock pile above. She zigged right, then left, jumping over one pile of fresh debris, then another as the rifle cracked again. Dirt sprayed her ankles, slivers of rock slicing at her pants.

She stumbled behind the first stone massive enough to provide cover, breathing hard. Flora had slipped behind a neighboring boulder, where she now appeared to be unconscious from a head wound, which coated her face in blood. No time to check for further injuries. Now or never.

Kimberly darted forth, and using all her strength, hoisted Flora up and over her shoulders in a fireman's hold.

Then Kimberly staggered into the belly of the beast, acutely aware of the armed man, scrambling through the boulder field behind her and much too quickly, closing the gap between them.

CHAPTER 39

THE HOUSE IS AGITATED.

The others don't feel it. They stare at the secret panel sliding open to reveal a sudden, gaping wound in the cellar. They are shocked and amazed.

The house is scared.

I place my hand on the wall closest to me. I try to tell the building it's okay. I know bad things have happened here. It's not the mansion's fault, any more than it is mine. We're both victims.

The house is ashamed.

Once more I try to soothe, but the house doesn't believe me. "Go," it shifts, groans. "Go, go, go."

The house shudders deep on its foundation. An ominous cracking sound emits from its old timber joints—this, the others hear.

"Sudden temperature change," Keith says. "Just causing the beams to contract."

Smart people are often stupid, I think. But then I worry my lower lip. The building must be very upset. I've never heard it do that before.

"Someone should go in." Keith again. His voice isn't scared, more like uncertain.

D.D. takes an automatic step around the huge table between us and the tunnel. Then she pauses, glancing at me. I don't need words to understand what she's thinking. She can't walk into that tunnel. She has a responsibility to me; she must keep me safe.

"Go," the house moans again, and I can feel a small shudder rumble beneath my fingertips.

The sheriff moves forward. "I'll do it." He unclips a flashlight from his duty belt, snaps on the beam.

"I'll go, too," Keith speaks up. His decision doesn't surprise me. I would draw him in shades of orange and green and yellow, with a faint shadow of black. He could have more dark around him, but his curiosity won't allow it.

He has his phone out, fiddling with it.

"Any word from Flora?" D.D. asks sharply.

He shakes his head. They don't say anything out loud, but I can tell they're worried.

The older woman glances at me in concern. Mrs. Counsel wouldn't approve of the woman's shockingly large build, but would like her pretty blue sweater. As for me, I'm not a fan of strangers. I need to stay with D.D. It's very important to stay with D.D. I know it, even if I don't know why I know it. "Maybe we should go upstairs, dear," the woman says soothingly. "Let them do what they need to do. Wouldn't you like a glass of lemonade?"

I shake my head, while the house shudders unhappily.

The sheriff steps around the oak table, approaching the secret doorway. The beam of his flashlight punches through the pitch-black gloom, illuminating the tunnel of darkness that waits beyond. Keith joins him, his phone glowing more weakly than the sheriff's high-powered flashlight. The opening is broad enough for them to stand shoulder to shoulder. Tall enough for them to remain upright.

And yet, even with two beams of light . . .

Nothing but deep shadows ahead, as they take the first step, then another. I reach for D.D.'s hand, but she's already left my side, rounding the table to where she can better monitor the sheriff and Keith's progress.

"Tunnel's not bad." The sheriff's voice echoes from somewhere ahead. "Reinforced with wood timbers. Recently used, too. Some of these beams aren't that old."

"A secret entrance to a secret club," D.D. murmurs.

Near the fireplace, the sheriff's department lady twists the gold cross she wears around her neck. She doesn't like the tunnel any more than D.D.

I run my fingers down the wall next to me. A gentle touch, meant to soothe.

I'm waiting, I realize. The house is waiting, too.

Then the sheriff's voice again, more distant. "We found the cook," his voice booms grimly.

"Do you need help?" D.D. has to cup her hands around her mouth to amplify her question.

"Nothing to be done now. Tunnel goes on for a ways. We're gonna follow, see if we can discover the end."

"I'll call for backup."

D.D. reaches into her back pocket for her phone.

The older woman moves. Reaches down. Lifts up. Suddenly she has a fire poker gripped in her man-sized hands.

D.D. remains focused on her phone, tapping away.

I open my mouth, but of course, no sound comes out.

The big woman closes the gap between them.

D.D. hits another button on her phone.

The big woman raises the poker over her head.

Too late, I realize her colors aren't blue and gray. Instead, she swirls with voids of black, screams of red. She is sadness, pain, rage.

She and the demon, they have the same colors.

I try to scream. Silent. Horrified. At the last second, my brain fires to life. I stop wasting effort on my useless throat, rap on the wall instead. Three knocks. Hard, urgent.

D.D. glances up. Just as the fireplace poker whistles down.

D.D. throws up her forearm, tries to twist away. A sickening crack as metal meets bone, then her right arm falls limply to her side.

The poker rises back up, the grandmother woman not looking anything like a grandmother anymore.

I move. I throw myself against the edge of the huge oak table, ramming it straight into D.D. and the woman, because there's no way to hit one and not the other.

D.D. gets knocked forward, straight into the tunnel, while the hulking sheriff's lady tumbles sideways, poker clanging to the floor as she tries to catch herself.

Then I feel it. Something cold and dark gathering behind me.

The house tried to warn me. Go, it had moaned. Go, go, go.

But of course, I didn't listen to it any more than I listened to my mother so many years before.

And now . . .

I turn. He stands in the middle of the wood-framed doorway. He holds his favorite serrated blade in front of him.

He grins.

And I know exactly what's going to happen next.

CHAPTER 40

FLORA

'M DREAMING OF JACOB. *I know it's a dream, because he's smiling at me.*

"So you met my old man, huh? Tough ol' coot. Guess the apple didn't fall far from that twisted tree. Microgreens, huh? Never woulda thunkit."

We're sitting outside the cabin where he held me. In the meadow, on a red and white checked tablecloth. Before us is a fast-food buffet. Fried chicken, hamburgers, pizza, waffles. Jacob isn't eating, though. He looks younger, more relaxed, with his favorite ketchup-stained T-shirt barely covering his flabby gut.

"Home sweet home," he says, gesturing to the dilapidated cabin behind us. "Miss it?"

I open my mouth, but no words come out. Then I realize I'm not sitting on the picnic blanket. I'm back in the box, daylight filtering through the crudely bored air holes, taunting me.

"Now, now, I told you what would happen if you disobeyed. You got away once, Flora. You shoulda stayed away."

No, *I'm not in the box. Because I can see him, which would be impossible. But all around me is dark, with just specks of light. I try to lift my hand to the lid, then discover I can't move my fingers. My arms. My legs. I'm trapped. Weighed down, a terrible pressure crushing my chest.*

I'm in a grave. A shallow grave with just my face exposed, watching Jacob from the edge of the picnic blanket.

"You always thought you'd die here," this new, happy Jacob tells me. "I used to hear you whimpering to yourself in the box. 'Gonna die, gonna die, gonna die,'" he mocks. "You never were a strong one."

I try to wiggle my toes, lift a single finger, turn my head. Nothing. I feel a whimper building in my throat, just as he said. Then, I feel moisture on my face. A single tear tracking down my cheek.

Jacob moves till he's leaning right over me.

"Never shoulda come back."

I can't move.

"But you missed me, didn't you, Flora? You had to see, you had to know. Because the more you learn, the closer to me you become. And now you're gonna die in my backyard. Just the way I planned it."

He grins at me.

I hate him. All over again, even as he leans down and gently wipes the tear from my cheek.

"I loved you," he whispers. "And you'll always be mine, cuz deep down in your heart, you know you love me, too."

Then Jacob is gone and Kimberly looms above me. "Wake up! Wake the fuck up!"

She slaps me across the face.

I wake up.

THE WORLD IS DARK, AND once again I'm disoriented. I can't see, but I realize I *can* move. Arms, feet, head. Dear God, what the hell happened to my head? I moan, and Kimberly nearly slaps me again.

"Shhh!"

The urgency in her tone brings me around as much as my throbbing temple. She's crouched behind a considerable boulder, peering at something before her. I'm lying in the dirt, where I've apparently been dropped like a sack of potatoes. My face feels wet and sticky. I touch my cheek gently. Not tears. Blood.

I have a vague memory of rocks falling and a rifle cracking. I'm not sure which of them got me, but at least I'm alive. Mostly.

I try to sit up. The world swims, then my stomach. Concussion, most likely. Kimberly has her .22 in her hands and is clearly on guard against some immediate threat. I'm going to have to do better than lounge at her feet.

"Knife," she mutters, not a question, but an order.

I fumble around till I find my butterfly blade. I flick my wrist to snap it open, but my effort is so pathetic, I nearly drop the folded handles instead.

I register footsteps for the first time. Heavy and coming from the other side of the boulder where Kimberly has brought us—carried me—to cover. Someone is making a slow and stealthy approach. Stalking us.

This time, I snap my dragon-handled blade open successfully. The dark swims before my eyes, and I still feel the vague presence of Jacob pressing down on me.

The sensation brings me strength. I'm not a fresh-out-of-captivity survivor anymore, and Dream Jacob isn't nearly as compelling as he thinks. I belong to me. And I came here by choice to help other people, including this hodgepodge team of investigators I've come to trust.

Now I'm going to have Kimberly's back, as she clearly had mine. Then we're both going home safely tonight. At which point I'm going to find Keith and spend more quality time exorcising demons.

The footsteps are closer. I'm not sure who's on the other side of that boulder. I'm guessing, due to the relentless dark, that we are now in the mine. Kimberly grabbed me and made a strategic retreat. Had Walt turned on us in the end? Like father like son?

Except I remember the crack of a rifle, and Walt favored his shotgun.

Then I have an image of something else, Walt falling back in the grass, his chest stained red. That makes me remember a particular motel room, where I held a gun to his son's head one moment, and felt the hot spray of blood and brains the next.

I wonder if Jacob had any idea when he snatched me off the Florida beach that he'd be dooming himself and his family. That one drunk foolish blonde, spinning on the sand to music only she could hear, would one day kill them all.

Kimberly grows tenser beside me. The sound of approach has stopped. Meaning our attacker is where? Right on the other side of the boulder, waiting for the rabbits to bolt? Or finding a ledge that would give him higher ground, the perfect sniper's perch? He could shoot us dead in the space of twin heartbeats.

We should move. But to retreat would give up our position. Not to mention, I'm propped up like a four-day drunk against a boulder, and currently have just about as much coordination. We could go on the offensive, but how? The moment Kimberly pops up to fire her weapon, she's exposed to return fire. And as for my knife, well, it really *is* stupid—a knife in the middle of a gunfight.

I have an idea. It's not the best, it's not the worst. It's classical me, making the most of the resources on hand. I dig my fingers around in the dirt beside me till I find a decent-sized rock. Then I whack Kimberly against the leg till I have her attention. I pantomime my intent. If she's dazzled by my brilliance, she certainly doesn't show it. She shrugs, more like *what do we have to lose?*

Exactly.

Deep breath. My head hurts. My stomach churns. My heart . . . A piece of Jacob lives there; he's not wrong about that. But he isn't me, just a sliver of the past I'm finally learning to let go. All the more reason to survive into the future.

I toss the rock as hard as I can down into the dark void behind us. I aim for the wall on the other side of the tunnel, a long diagonal. There is a faint thump in the distance, nothing more.

Not enough for our stalker to take the bait.

So I grab another rock, then another and throw them in quick succession. One must hit hard, and the ensuing spray of pebbles makes just the right noise—two people scrabbling away in the dark.

The footsteps resume. Closer and closer.

Kimberly steadies her .22.

We both wait.

CHAPTER 41

D.D.

ONE MOMENT, D.D. SWAM IN a sea of black, disoriented. The next, her eyes snapped open, just in time to see a fire poker smashing down toward her skull for the second time. Instinctively she tried to raise her right arm, but the responding lance of pain took her breath away. She rolled to the side, just as the poker crashed against the stone floor next to her shoulder.

A fierce voice above her: "Die, dammit. Just die!"

Franny, the sheriff's receptionist, loomed above her. The delicate gold cross still dangled around her neck, but the rest of her was barely recognizable. Her carefully styled ash-blond hair had unraveled into a mad scientist's cap. Her pale blue sweater set was covered in dirt and soot, and a line of black smudge marred her hip where it appeared something had hit her. Some things remained the same, however. Her broad shoulders, surprisingly tall build, impressive upper body strength.

Fire poker, lifting back up.

Move, Sergeant, move.

Flat on her back, half in the tunnel, half out, and with a right arm that still throbbed angrily, D.D. was out of options. Continue worming frantically into the dark tunnel might give her cover, buy her some time, but . . .

Bonita.

What had happened to Bonita? She needed to protect Bonita. With a quick twist, D.D. jerked her torso through the passage door, into the stone chamber. Her arm said no, but the rest of her demanded yes, and she rolled beneath the giant oak table, hissing in pain.

Scream of outrage as Franny realized she'd just lost her target.

Don't think. Don't feel. Move.

D.D. popped up the other side. Her right arm was clearly injured. She could twist her wrist, wiggle her fingers, so maybe not broken, but currently useless for drawing her weapon. She knew something, however, that Franny didn't: D.D. had suffered a major injury to her left arm years ago. And as part of her recovery, she'd taught herself to shoot one-handed, versus the required two-handed grip. She'd started with her uninjured right arm; then, out of sheer paranoia, when her left arm had recovered, she'd perfected left-handed shooting as well, so she'd never be at a disadvantage again.

The older woman glared at her now, her grip still tight on her makeshift weapon, but the vast table blocking her from her target. Franny narrowed her gaze shrewdly, obviously, just like D.D. moving on to plan B.

Kimberly had mentioned some things about the woman. She was tougher than she looked, a born survivor who'd had to rebuild her life after losing her newborn child, and highly skilled at overcoming obstacles. Which explained how determined the massive woman looked right now, staring at D.D. across the table, fire poker at the ready.

Shit.

Quickly, D.D. glanced around the room. No sign of Bonita. Hopefully the girl had headed upstairs and tucked herself someplace safe. Now, D.D. made a show of clutching her right arm, wobbling unsteadily on her feet. In a showdown of brawn, no way D.D. was coming out on top. Not against an opponent this large and aggressive. Which left her with . . . stalling. Buying time for Bonita to escape, for reinforcements to arrive, for D.D.'s field of vision to clear enough so she could successfully get off a shot.

"Why?" she asked. It didn't require any acting to make her voice rough with pain.

"None of you should be here. We had everything under control!"

"Importing young girls for hired help? Organ donors? Sex slaves?"

"We offer only the best product to the best customers," Franny answered matter-of-factly. "No shipments of sickly immigrants for us. We take orders, and personally acquire what would best suit our clients' needs."

D.D. could read between those lines. Most human-trafficking operations involved importing container loads of girls who were then shuttled out to "massage parlors" and the like. Mass product for mass distribution.

Tucked this far north in the mountains, dozens of foreign girls would stand out. But specific individuals, brought in as housemaids till the right fit could be made . . . D.D. felt ill.

"But *why*? After everything you've been through . . . the loss of your own child . . . why kidnap someone else's?"

"I didn't lose him."

D.D. stared at the woman. Franny smiled—it was not a nice expression on the woman's face.

"I knew I had to give the baby up once he was born. Back in those days, it was the only option for an unmarried woman like me. Especially in a small town like this. Bunch of close-minded, judgmental asses. Looking down their noses at me because what, I was *only* a waitress, and a young, stupid, pregnant one at that. I heard their whispers. I took it. I told myself what must be done. But then, I held my baby in my arms. And I . . . I couldn't do it."

"You kept your baby . . . but told everyone he'd died?"

"I've always been smarter than people assumed."

"You can't hide an infant," D.D. said.

"You can if the father is willing to take him."

"Wait, who's the father?"

Franny still had her poker raised in a batter's stance, but with the enormous table lodged between her and D.D., they were currently at a stalemate. The older woman's gaze, however, kept darting past D.D.'s shoulder. Expecting company? Bonita's demon man? D.D. was killing time, looking for the right opportunity. Was it possible Franny was doing the same?

D.D. shifted slowly to the right, closer to the fireplace, where she'd have at least a partial line of sight on the gaping wooden doors.

"Who raised your son, Franny?" D.D. asked quietly, though she thought she might have an idea. Franny knew all about the taskforce team's activities these past few days, being part of the meetings. But there was one other person who'd had a front row seat. Keith and Flora had included him, with neither of them being the wiser.

"Doesn't matter," Franny replied stiffly.

So D.D. said it for her: "Bill Benson, the owner of the ATV shop. He kept talking with Keith and Flora. And today, you said he was the one who came into the station and raised the fuss to distract the on-duty deputy. You two were in on it together. You told him when to arrive, when there would be only one deputy around. And while Deputy Chad dealt with Bill, you were the one who paid the visit to Mayor Howard. Good God, you're behind all this. But *why*?"

"I love him. I've loved him most of my life," Franny said simply. "And he loves me, too."

"Then you should've gotten married. Raised your son together.

Instead . . ." D.D. gestured with her good hand in the empty air. "You built an entire life out of lies."

"It's complicated."

"Seriously?"

Franny frowned at D.D. Her gaze returned to the open doorway behind D.D.'s shoulder. No doubt about it, the woman was waiting for someone. Shit, D.D. thought again. Because even if she could shoot with her left arm, she could still only aim in one direction at a time.

"Bill's married. His wife, however, isn't well. Schizophrenia. Sad really. Most days Bill keeps her locked in her room."

"Because that's kinder than having her hospitalized?"

"Have you seen those places? Terrible. Just terrible."

D.D. took another step to the right. Something was up. Franny's willingness to talk, buy time of her own. D.D. could feel the impending threat. She just couldn't see it. "So your married lover with a mentally ill wife raised your son. And you what, visited as a family friend, monitored your own kid growing up?"

"Aunt Franny," she provided. "But my son figured it out, being such a smart boy. Not to mention he doesn't look anything like that frail, haunted woman in the house. One day he wanted the truth. Bill and I gave it to him. Of course he was grateful to realize I was his mother, not the crazy woman locked in the rear bedroom."

"I wouldn't be so sure there was only one crazy woman in that house."

"You don't know anything," Franny replied flatly.

"I know your son's a monster," D.D. countered. "Bonita drew him as pure evil. That's the son you denied, gave away, then tried to reclaim. And now you excuse his behavior even as it grows worse? He killed those girls, didn't he? Then Bill disposed of the bodies."

"Martha needed a kidney. Bill and I were talking about it one night when Clayton was home. He said he could help."

"He kidnapped girls to be human organ donors!"

"He ran a domestic services business in New Mexico. Lots of hired girls. It wasn't too hard to see if one of them had the right blood type."

"He was a *pimp*!" D.D. shouted. "And twenty to one, Bonita's mother was one of his first victims."

"He saved Martha's life!"

"Except it didn't stop there. He had a thing for girls. He liked to acquire them, he liked to torture them. Living in a small town, that might stand out. But if he imported them, shared them with others . . . Dear God, your son turned his violent obsession into a business, and you *helped* him!"

"This community needs him! Our town was dying. Businesses failing, good people on the verge of losing their homes. Clayton is smart. He saw the opportunity. He started supplying a cheaper work-force, which people certainly appreciated. Then there was a guest here, a guest there, who wanted extra services. Martha and Howard—well, they couldn't very well say no, could they? And with the increase in offerings came more and more people arriving into the community, willing to spend money."

"Such as Jacob Ness?"

"It was my idea to have Dorothea build the website, with its portal to the dark web, where even more important business could be done.

"Once word got out, well . . . The past ten years have been a boon for this community. Everyone has benefited. Everyone!"

"How many bodies are we going to find in the woods, Franny? How many!"

"We were doing just fine—"

"With Bill digging graves and you managing things in the sheriff's department so no one ever connected the dots on all the girls who appeared and disappeared? You're going to jail, Franny. And your son, as well as Bill, Dorothea, and every single person in this town if that's what it takes. You're all going down."

The woman snorted. "Now who's crazy? The sheriff and that young man aren't coming back. Those tunnels go on forever. You need a guide. Not to mention, Bill is already closing in from the other side. I shut this secret door, and no one will be the wiser."

"I will. And you're in no position to stop me."

Franny smiled. Again, it wasn't a nice look on her face. "Clayton will take care of you. Right after he's done with the girl."

"Your son is here?"

"Way ahead of you."

"That's why Bonita ran."

"She doesn't stand a chance."

"Franny," D.D. said coolly. "You severely injured my right arm. It means you attacked a police officer. It means I can respond with deadly force."

"With the table between us, I'm hardly a threat to you now."

"And where are the witnesses to testify to that?"

The woman paused. She still held the poker, but for the first time appeared uncertain. Her gaze once more flicked to the open doorway. Looking for her son, waiting for her son. Which was why she'd been willing to talk as much as D.D.

But D.D. couldn't afford to stall any longer. Not with this Clayton monster chasing Bonita.

D.D. raised her sidearm with her left hand. All those years of practice . . . She had nothing to doubt. Nothing to fear.

Her left finger on the trigger. Slight squeeze. She fired.

The bullet smacked Franny's right shoulder. The poker clattered to the floor as the woman staggered back, clutching at her injury, surprise written all over her face.

"I would have aimed for your heart," D.D. informed her, "if I thought you had one."

The older woman collapsed to the floor, still staring at D.D. in shock.

"You won't immediately die from that wound. Then again, without prompt medical treatment, plenty of things could go wrong. I suggest you start atoning for your sins sooner versus later."

D.D. took a second to check out her right arm again, rotating it slowly, flexing her fingers. It hurt like a son of a bitch, but didn't seem to be broken. Bone bruise maybe. Hardly mattered. She could handle the pain. She would do whatever necessary to keep her promise to Bonita. Now, she leaned over the table till she could look Franny in the eye. Already the woman's brow was beaded with sweat, her body starting to tremble as shock set in.

"Hey, Franny," D.D. said in her nicest voice. "I'm going to go find your son. And then, I'm going to kill him."

CHAPTER 42

THE BAD MAN STANDS IN *front of me in the stone room.*

No, he's sitting at my mother's table, shoveling her home-cooked food into his mouth. He leers at me from between the elaborately carved twin doors, twisting his favorite blade.

No, he looms in the desert, firing a bullet through my mother's throat.

He is now. He is then.

He is here.

And I'm just me: no gun, no knife, no magical powers. I can't scream. I can't run. I can only stand in place as he approaches.

The Bad Man and the older woman go together. And now, that woman stands over D.D., poker ready for a fresh strike. D.D. is on the ground next to the tunnel opening, not moving.

I need to do something. Protect my friend. Escape the Bad Man. Make him pay.

So much anger and frustration well up inside me. Always, it's been him. He killed my mother. Robbed me of my voice. Enslaved me into a life of servitude where I was forced to watch him destroy other girls.

There's no good in this man. Just layers of evil.

"Clayton, hurry up!" the grandma woman urges. "I don't think she's dead."

So maybe D.D. will be all right. If I can find a way to get the Bad Man away.

He smiles again. He knows I'm a cripple, but it doesn't inspire compassion in him. Just contempt.

I try to cower back, but my hip makes contact with the wall. I'm trapped, no means of retreat. So I try something else. He thinks I'm helpless—and I let him.

I take a small step sideways onto uneven stone. Grunt as I pretend to twist my ankle. Fall crouched to the floor.

One, two, three, four . . .

He strides forward, sure of himself, as he whirls his hunting knife. Five.

He reaches me. I rear up awkwardly, and lash out as hard as I can with my good leg. I hit the side of his knee. He roars in surprise, and staggers slightly, pulling the woman's attention away from D.D. Good.

I kick him again, nailing him in the balls. He screams, clutches himself, and drops.

"Clayton!" the grandma woman screams in clear distress.

I head for the doorway.

At the last second, he slashes out with his blade, slicing open my exposed ankle. In sheer rage, I turn on him again. I kick his head, watch it bounce against the hard floor. I do it again, spraying blood from my ankle. My blood onto the stone. My mother's into the red earth. We have both bled too much for this man.

"Stop it!" the grandma woman shrieks, but she is stuck behind the table. She can't get to me, and seems to have momentarily forgotten D.D.

I don't want to leave the blond detective, but if I go, the Bad Man will follow. I want to believe D.D. can figure out how to handle the giant woman. Whereas the Bad Man . . . No one has ever fought him and won.

Wake up, wake up, wake up, I think in my mind to D.D. Then simply: Survive.

Because I don't think I have it in me to bear another loss. Then again, I don't think I have it in me to still be alive by day's end.

I struggle out of the room, limping badly down the hall. I've had years to learn how to hobble with speed. I'm not giving up now.

Behind me I hear cursing, then crashing. The Bad Man staggering to his feet.

He will come for me.

I can't scream. I can't run.

I limp as fast as I can into the dark.

CHAPTER 43

KIMBERLY

CROUCHED BEHIND THE ROCK, KIMBERLY held her breath in the dark tunnel and focused on the sound of approaching footsteps. Flora remained propped up awkwardly beside her, in no condition to run or fight. This was it, then. One pistol versus one rifle.

As her FBI instructors liked to say, this is why we train.

The shadows beside the boulder started to shift, take shape. They formed into the faint silhouette of a man. Come on, she thought, *two more steps*. She had only one chance to get this right.

He stopped and Kimberly nearly groaned.

Flora dug in the dirt beside her, obviously searching for another stone to throw. Except.

The shadow pivoted sharply. He'd figured out their little game. One quick step sideways, the rifle leveled in front of him.

Pop, pop, pop.

Kimberly didn't hesitate. Three to center mass. The man dropped. The rifle dropped. Then Kimberly darted forward, kicking the rifle clear, before collapsing herself, shaking uncontrollably from adrenaline and belated terror.

"That was a little close," Flora said, just as more footsteps sounded in the dark behind them. Not walking this time. Running.

"Shit." No time to find new cover. Kimberly fumbled around in the dirt, grabbing the rifle their first opponent had tried to use against them. Flora once more held up her blade.

A light burst into view. Then a second.

Kimberly was just settling her finger on the trigger, when a voice called out:

"Sheriff! Drop your weapon."

A light hit her between the eyes. The second beam found Flora with her feral grin and bloody forehead.

"Are you okay?" Keith called out of the dark—and forget Flora, Kimberly could've kissed him.

KEITH EXAMINED FLORA'S HEAD WOUND while Sheriff Smithers explained about the secret door that had led them into the old mining shaft. Keith and the sheriff had spent the past twenty minutes or so roaming a warren of tunnels while searching for an exit. Then they'd heard the gunshots and started running.

Now, Sheriff Smithers flashed his light on their stalker's body.

"That's Bill Benson," Keith spoke up in surprise. "The ATV rental guy. Why is he trying to kill us?"

"He already shot Walt," Kimberly provided. "He's dead, at the other end of the passageway."

"But why?" Keith asked again.

Sheriff Smithers appeared troubled. "Bill doesn't have a criminal record that I know of. Quiet man, really. Married Penny Johnson forty years ago. Pretty thing. Unfortunately, she turned out to be not quite right in the head. They had a son together, but Penny's condition grew worse. Last I knew, Bill tended his business, then went home to take care of his wife."

"Walt led us here," Flora provided. "He said he could prove that the woods really did scream at night. I assumed he figured out the sounds were coming from this mine entrance. Which, if it's connected to the B and B, makes sense."

"We found the cook's body fifty feet beyond the secret door," the sheriff said grimly. "Died hard. At least one set of screams that won't be heard again."

Flora was still frowning. "But why was Bill Benson here? How did he know we'd be coming? Because clearly that was one hell of an ambush, and Keith and I never talked to him about us coming here. We didn't even know this tunnel existed."

Kimberly shook her head. She didn't understand either. "You said Bill and his wife had a son?" she asked the sheriff.

Smithers nodded slowly. She didn't like the look on his face. "Big guy," he confirmed. "In his younger days, was known for brawling and drunken disorderlies. Not the kind of guy you wanted to cross. But after high school, he moved out West. Last I heard, he was running his own business in New Mexico, someplace like that. Sounded like he was doing all right for himself. I know he's been home more lately. I figured to help out with his mom, maybe see about taking over his father's business. But Clayton's always been a hard one to pin down. Being his own boss, he can come and go as he pleases."

Flora glanced at Kimberly. The woman's forehead really did look awful. "As in he has plenty of opportunity to kidnap girls, network with others, then return here with the new merchandise."

"Honestly, I haven't seen the man in years. Didn't even really give him much thought. But then . . ." The sheriff suddenly closed his eyes, shoulders sagging. "Shhhh-rimp."

"Spit it out, Sheriff," Kimberly demanded.

"I normally don't pay much mind to gossip. But Bill . . . rumor is he and Franny have been having an affair for years. She's single and it's not like he has a real marriage."

"Your receptionist, Franny, is dating our dead rifleman?"

"She said Bill came to the department today. Raised such a fuss, the deputy who was watching Mayor Howard had to assist." The sheriff's voice had grown hoarse. "Howard hanged himself. Then Franny . . . Franny came to the inn with me."

"Franny is at the Mountain Laurel?" Flora spoke up sharply, then promptly winced. "With D.D.? And *Bonita*?"

"Super tall, surprisingly broad-shouldered Franny?" Kimberly asked more pointedly, staring at the sheriff. "Because it's not like Bill Benson is a big guy. Where according to Bonita, her monster is huge."

It was hard to tell in the dark, but it was possible the sheriff's face had gone white. "Bill's wife is a wisp of a woman."

"We saw her picture at his store," Keith confirmed. "Not exactly a giant among women."

"You said Franny was pregnant, that Franny lost her baby," Kimberly continued. "What if that's just a story she told, and the real reason she stayed in town, got a job at the sheriff's department, was to remain near her son?"

"That poor boy," the sheriff murmured. "Stuck at home all day with a crazy woman."

"Given up by another crazy woman," Flora added dryly.

"We have to get back." Keith was already standing up. "Bill and Franny must be working together. That's why Bill knew to be outside the tunnels. He was waiting for Franny to lead us out. He was going to pick us off one by one."

"Help me up," said Flora, still propped awkwardly against the boulder. Blood caked half her face. She raised an arm, but even that appeared halfhearted. Keith moved immediately to her side, offering his shoulder for support as she struggled to her feet.

Flora winced, almost toppled, but Keith caught her again. "Why are there two of you?" she asked.

"Twice the fun?"

"Good God, that's awful. But thanks for cheering me up." Kimberly checked her phone. "I don't have a signal. You?" she asked the sheriff.

He shook his head.

"Try your radio. We need backup. Every officer in the damn county, state, I don't care. And circulate the description of Bill Benson, Jr.—"

"Clayton."

"Armed and dangerous. Approach with caution. I'll handle FAA. Get out a notice to apprehend anyone matching Franny's or Clayton's description, ground charter flights, whatever it takes. Given their access to the dark web, there's no telling how many resources they have available. Certainly, they must've had some kind of escape plan in place for life after ambushing a federal taskforce."

"Agreed."

"Uh, guys." Flora again. "I think you two should go ahead. I'm not, um, I'm not moving so well."

Even with Keith's arm around her waist, she was swaying where she stood. Now, the vigilante held out her butterfly blade to Kimberly. "For good luck."

"You keep that. We don't know how many people are roaming these tunnels yet. Besides, at the rate things are going"—Kimberly eyed Flora and Keith grimly—"you may be our cavalry."

"Deal," Keith said.

Last nods all around. Then Kimberly stepped forward briskly, the sheriff already at her side.

"Stay safe," Kimberly ordered Flora and Keith.

"Back at you."

Kimberly and the sheriff raced into the gloom.

CHAPTER 44

AM SILENT. I AM SLOW. *I am weak.*

What I need to be is smart.

As I hear the Bad Man's roar behind me, I think, I will turn, I will take a stand. I'll summon my mother's love and my slaughtered sisters' anguish, and we'll incinerate him with our rage.

I recognize now, as I lurch down the hall, that these fantasies are only that—the vivid dreams of a girl too weak to fight back.

He's coming. He'll grab me by the shoulder, twist me about. And in one second of searing pain, it'll be done. I'll be with my mamita. Surely that won't be so bad. Our pack of two, together again.

Footsteps, pounding closer.

The hallway is too long. I won't make it.

I could veer off into one of the many rooms, but then what? They're small and barren. I'll be nothing but a mouse, trapped in a corner. I need to get upstairs. The kitchen. It has knives and rolling pins and all sorts of weapons for a little thing like me.

The footsteps grow louder. Yet the hall goes on and on.

I send out my best plea to the house. I know it's sad and unhappy. I know it never wanted to be used this way. "Help me now," I beg of it. "I see you, I hear you. Please, please, help me."

And just like that, the hall lights flicker, then wink off, casting the entire hall into gloom.

A fresh roar of frustration. The Bad Man lurches to a stop somewhere in the dark, disoriented by the sudden pall.

Whereas me . . . I've been roaming these halls under the cover of night for years. I'm the mouse, scurrying along, keeping out of sight. I don't need light to see. I know every inch of the hall by the feel of the stones against my feet.

Faster now. As much as a gimpy girl can do.

The Bad Man surges forward again. Slower, with an occasional thump and curse as he hits a wall, a doorjamb. His legs are longer than mine. Even slowed, he'll eat up the distance between us in no time.

The stairs. I sense them before I make out the first riser. In my mind, I'm whimpering with relief. In real life, I'm just as silent as always.

Creeping now. Up, up, up. The door, just there, I can nearly reach.

"Stop, police!" I hear a new voice boom behind me. D.D. is alive!

I twist just in time to see a beam of light slice across the hall. D.D. has a flashlight tucked between her ribs and her injured right arm.

Meaning D.D. is holding her gun in her left hand. None too steadily.

The Bad Man turns. The beam of light catches the side of his face. He is grinning as he beholds an injured cop, swaying on her feet, daring to defy him.

The Bad Man charges the detective.

Bam. Bam. Bam.

D.D.'s gun. But the Bad Man doesn't seem to care. He smashes D.D. to the ground as if she were nothing more than a paper doll.

I see the knife flash up.

Then, I can't look anymore.

THE HOUSE GROANS WITH AGITATION *as I finally burst through the cellar door. I stumble into the carpeted hall, falling to my knees, then scramble up again. I'm crying. Snot drips from my nose, tears coat my cheeks.*

I'm terrified and pissed off and emptied out. So many years, so many ambitions, and here I am again, watching the Bad Man take it all away. I hate him beyond all rationality. I hurt beyond all possibility.

Why are so many dying for a Stupid Girl like me?

I careen wildly toward the kitchen. The building moans again. Wind whips the mangled knots of my hair, though the doors are closed and the house shuttered tight. The girls, my mother. I can feel them all. The Bad Man is feasting. And they are as angry as I am.

I make it across the marble foyer into the breakfast room. Through the window I see a police officer standing guard. He catches the shadow of my movement, bobbing up and down as I drag my right leg. His eyes widen.

I try to shake my head, warn him away, but he doesn't notice.

He runs down the porch, bursting through the front doors behind me.

"Hey there—"

Just as the basement door flies open, cracking against the sidewall. The deputy turns, caught between a sobbing little girl and a hulking fiend with a knife. He doesn't need any help figuring it out.

"Stop! Police!"

Does he pull his weapon? Does he manage to fend off the first blow or two? I don't have it in me to turn and look, as once again the Bad Man charges. The officer goes down.

I hear a gurgle I know too well. The young man dying. Alive one moment, gone the next. The Bad Man isn't just a monster. He is the devil himself.

I crash through the swinging door into the kitchen. More wind whips around my face, tears at my hair. I want to be angry at them. Stop picking on me. Attack him instead.

But I get it. Even in death, they are afraid. I would be, too.

I snap on the commercial dishwasher. Once it reaches temperature, it'll fill the kitchen with steam as boiling hot water sprays from inside the hood. I've worked with the dishwasher. I know how to withstand its spray. Does he?

I want a knife, but I've already been through that. Waving a butter knife at him. Only to have him attack, disarm, then carve me up with his much larger blade.

He's so big, so strong. He stood behind Mrs. Counsel and squeezed the life out of her without breaking a sweat. He took out my blond protector in a single tackle, leaving her broken on the floor. Then dashed upstairs and killed a second armed deputy in a matter of minutes.

I feel a fresh hitch in my throat, panic rising, choking me. In desperation, I yank open the door to the broom closet. The mop sits inside, long handle protruding from its rolling yellow bucket. Maybe I can use the wooden handle to hit him, like the older woman attacking D.D. with the poker. The handle is long enough, maybe I can stay out of reach of his blade.

Then I see the bottle of bleach and am seized by a second idea.

I grab the bottle, unscrew the cap, douse the mophead liberally. I just finish emptying the bottle when the kitchen door bangs open. The Bad Man looms before me, his face flecked with blood, his hunting knife still dripping.

The room goes still. No more wind, restless spirits. We are all, living and dead, equally terrified.

"Did you miss me?" he asks.

I tighten my hands on the mop handle, and prepare to make my last stand.

CHAPTER 45

KIMBERLY

"WHAT THE—" KIMBERLY ARRIVED AT the stone chamber first, the sheriff on her heels. Somewhere behind them, Keith and Flora still labored through the tunnels.

It took Kimberly a moment to absorb the scene. The secret doorway was now partially blocked by the giant oak table. And propped up against the doorframe was Franny, her pale blue sweater covered in blood. She was gripping her right shoulder. Then she saw the sheriff and promptly moaned.

"Sheriff, Sheriff, please help. That Yankee detective went crazy. She shot me."

Kimberly ignored the woman, picking up the fire poker that lay at Franny's side. She made out blood and a blond hair.

She turned to Sheriff Smithers, pointing to the single hair in the room's dim light. His expression was equally grim.

"Franny," said the sheriff sternly. "What did you do?"

"Why, nothing at all. I was just standing down here, waiting for your return, and the detective, I swear she went a mite wild—"

"Bill Benson's dead."

"I shot him myself," Kimberly volunteered.

Franny paled. Her lower lip quivered.

The sheriff shook his head. "You did this, Franny. You and Bill. Why?"

The woman looked up. "I'm just a mom, Sheriff, doing whatever it takes to protect my son."

"Told you so," Kimberly informed the sheriff.

Just as *bang, bang, bang.* Gunshots. From the hallway.

"You got her," Kimberly ordered the sheriff. Then she was sprinting out of the room, .22 in hand.

CHAPTER 46

D.D.

D.D. HAD BEEN STANDING. SHE remembered that much. She'd been upright, holding her firearm at her left side, with her bruised right arm tight against her torso.

The hallway was dark, but she could hear plenty. A scuffling sound she bet was Bonita, hobbling ahead. Followed by harder, angrier footsteps stalking in her wake.

Then her flashlight had found its target. A huge shadowy figure that looked as wide as a cement truck and as tall as a grizzly bear. A demon—Bonita had been exactly right. Something less man, more beast. D.D. had widened her stance, issued her first warning. Then the monster had turned and charged her.

She'd fired her weapon. A good officer reacts on instinct. But she had no memory of aiming before she was slammed against the hard stone floor, the air leaving her body in a giant whoosh, as the flashlight rolled free, and her firearm . . . Was she holding it, not holding it?

No time to think before a large serrated blade flashed down

toward her chest. She twisted enough to take the first strike in her shoulder, the blade skittering across her bone. Then the knife jerked up, spraying blood, her blood, before preparing for a fresh descent. D.D. brought up her left hand to beat at him, fingers digging for his eyeballs, the soft part of his throat. He was straddling her body, pinning her in place. She couldn't move, couldn't breathe.

The knife flashed down.

A gun fired. Not D.D.'s but from somewhere behind her. Sheetrock exploded on the wall. The second round sprayed stone chips in her face.

Abruptly, the demon man sprang to his feet. Except he had both hands wrapped around D.D.'s shirt, dragging her up with him as if she were no more than a doll, her feet dangling inches off the floor. He held her directly in front him. A human shield.

"I will kill her first," the beast whispered in her ear. She knew he meant Bonita. "The way I should have killed her, in the desert years ago. Her mother thought she could get away, as well. But they never do. I always win in the end."

"This isn't over yet," D.D. gritted out. Pain radiated from every line of her body. Her arm, her head, her back, her bloody shoulder.

"You're right, because when I'm done with her, I'm going to find you again. And your friend, as well." He jerked his head to whomever stood behind her—Kimberly, Flora, someone who cared.

D.D. tried to open her mouth. She wanted to yell, "Shoot him," even if it meant the damn bullet had to travel through her body first. Just shoot the beast and put him down like the mad dog he was.

Except then she was flying through the air. The brute had tossed her down the hall, where she slammed into her rescuer and both tumbled to the floor.

"Are you all right?" Kimberly asked breathlessly, trying to untangle from D.D.'s splayed form.

"Thank you for breaking my fall."

"Jesus, D.D., you're covered in blood."

"Knife wound. Shoulder. Mostly bone."

"*What?*"

"Shut up. He's going after Bonita. She's upstairs, I think. *Move!*"

"I've got him."

"Not if I get there first." D.D. heaved herself up, swayed once, then snatched her sidearm off the floor.

Oh yeah, she hurt. But she was pissed off even more. That demon son of a bitch . . .

Now, she really was going to kill him.

CHAPTER 47

FLORA

IN THE TUNNEL, FLORA REGISTERED the sound of gunshots. She paused, gritting her teeth through the sea of nausea. "That doesn't sound good."

"Maybe that means Kimberly and the sheriff have already caught him."

More shots. One two.

"Then what's that sound, the monster getting away?"

Keith didn't have an answer.

"We need a plan," Flora said.

"You need a doctor."

"Plenty of time to rest when I'm dead. What happens if we go right up here?"

"We roam around in the dark forever until years from now someone finds our skeletons?"

"That's the spirit. Got your compass app?"

Heavy sigh. "You're going to be the death of me."

"It's okay. No one wants to live forever."

"I love you, Flora Dane."

"I love you too, geek boy. Let's get going."

CHAPTER 48

THE BAD MAN PAUSES INSIDE *the doorway. I retreat slowly, putting as much of the prep table between us as I can. The space is now filling with steam as I'd hoped, the dishwasher chugging through its cycle, empty dish rack rolling through boiling hot spray before arriving at the end, then wrapping down and around to do it all over again.*

He eyes the dishwasher, then me.

"Hoping to escape in a cloud of smoke?"

He smiles again. I can't answer back and he knows it.

"Do you miss it? Being able to talk? Tell people things? Including what I did to your stupid mama so many years ago?"

I don't move, just watch as he steps farther into the room. I've had years to study him, view him in action. I know he's as powerful as he looks. I know he can take down fleeing girls in a single leap. I know he smiles so broadly when he uses that knife, there can be flecks of blood in his teeth.

"Your mother was a whore. She ever tell you that?"

Three steps into the room. At the edge of the prep table now. Soon, my back will be pressed against the giant range. I'm trying to think, through my own pounding heartbeat, if there's some way I can use that.

"Maid service, my ass. She could never make enough money to support you cleaning sheets. Dancing between them, however . . . She did it for you. So her daughter could have something more than rice and beans for dinner."

I decide the range is a bad idea. If he leaps now and pins me against it, he'll use those gas burners on me.

I need to get to the dishwasher. But for me to slide left, he must move right. I'll have to move closer to him before I can drop back.

No time like the present.

I lift the soaking mop head. It's heavy and my arms shudder with the strain.

He laughs. "Gonna fend me off with a mop?"

I snap it in the air before him. Bleach sprays out. Maybe my mother lends a guiding hand, because some droplets nail him in the eyes. He yelps, jumping back, and I slide quickly into the steam of the dishwasher while I have the chance.

"You little shit! I'm not just going to kill you, I'm going to take my time with it. Cops are dead, you know. Neither put up a fight. Now your mom, she was interesting. Bitch had started intercepting girls on the way to my office, waving them off. Sometimes she even gave them money to board another bus, get out of there. She thought she could save them from her fate.

"I couldn't let that continue, of course. The defiance. The disruption of my inventory. In my line of work, freshness of goods matters."

He wipes at his eyes with his free hand. They appear red and swollen, but he doesn't seem bothered. A man who has inflicted so much pain, maybe he likes it himself. Maybe, after all these years, he doesn't feel it anymore.

The room starts to stir. He can't sense it, but I can. His words, his voice, his presence—he's making them angry. Reminding them of how easily he destroyed them.

The mist swirls around the dishwasher, seeking substance. I feel a silvery presence at my shoulder. My mamita. She is sad. Because he told me the truth? It wasn't anything I hadn't figured out these past years. This man, his line of work, the days we had meat on the table.

She is my mamita. I am her chiquita. I don't care about the rest. The Bad Man is evil. And the rest of us suffered for it.

As if listening, the room grows heavy. The house has opinions, too. Not that the Bad Man understands. Like so many, he ignores what he can't comprehend.

"Shooting you was one of the best things I ever did," he gloats now. "Gave me an excuse to bail on that godforsaken desert and come home once and for all. I needed the local doc to patch you up. There's good money in young girls, you know. But unfortunately, the bullet did too much damage to your face, lowered the value. Once he diagnosed you as mute, however, I convinced Martha to take you in. What could be better than a servant who can never talk back? I moved my operation to the mountains and business exploded, especially after I found some other 'specialty' suppliers who were only too happy to help. We've had a great run for over a decade now. If that damn hiker had never gone off trail . . ."

I tilt my head, listening despite myself. I don't know this story. The whole of it. I only know the bits and pieces myself and the others have lived. My curiosity allows him to close the gap between us without me realizing it.

His flash of smile in the steamy air is the only warning I get.

He pounces. Instinctively, I swing up the mop. I can't see where I hit. Enough to earn a startled oomph, then he's on the move again.

I jab the air with the mop. I twirl it to spray more bleach. I target his groin, knees, any point of weakness, while the dishwasher's steam builds thickly, and the house groans its distress, and I feel my mother's spirit suddenly snap around me, as if she would hold me tight.

He grabs the wooden handle. I try to tug back. He jerks the mop toward him. I have no choice but to release my only weapon, or be tossed against him.

He steps through the steam, and there's no mistaking the triumph in his face. He brings up his bloody blade, waving it almost lazily. A click, somewhere to the side. It sounds familiar, but I can't place it.

Whap.

Something nails him from behind. I can't see what in the mist. But he jumps to the left, glancing quickly behind him.

Whap.

The mop handle whacks him in the shoulder, moved by hands that aren't my own.

"What the fuck?" he growls at me. "What are you doing?"

I can't answer, of course. I can't tell him that his rage and wickedness trapped them here. They died hating him. They died screaming and begging for mercy. Until their souls were doomed to haunt him, or maybe his presence haunts them. I've never been sure. But he has harmed and killed and hated. And now, he is joined with them, all of his victims, and they've waited a long time for this moment.

Across the kitchen the gas range flares on. All six burners raging hot. A low shadow darts through the mist, shockingly close.

The Bad Man leaps back from the stove, closer to the dishwasher. I understand what I must do next.

I feel power. I feel peace. I'm not a towering inferno of rage or vengeance.

I am a daughter, a sister, a friend.

I'm a girl who doesn't want anyone to suffer anymore.

Cabinets shake. Pots rattle. Glass suddenly sweeps off a distant shelf and shatters to the ground. The mist seems to come alive. Shadows, crouching black forms, here, there, everywhere.

The Bad Man backs up again, deeper into the boiling mist. He's forgotten about his knife. He doesn't know how to fight what he can't see. But he feels the threat now. I can see it in the growing rage and horror on his face.

He thought he could destroy us. He thought he could snuff out our lives as carelessly and callously as he wanted. He thought he could get away with anything, because who was to stop a man as wicked as him?

He thought wrong.

My mother strokes my cheek. Soothing. Encouraging.

The shadow darting by again. An oomph as something lashes out against the Bad Man's legs. He howls in frustration.

Then, it's all very simple.

I step toward the Bad Man. I pick up the mop at his feet.

The backs of his legs are pressed against the churning conveyor belt, as he stabs the mist with his knife, slashes at the thick steam.

"Now." I hear the voice as clear as day.

And I follow its command, lifting the heavy mop all the way up, till the head is level with his chest.

AT THE LAST MINUTE, THE *Bad Man turns the blade toward me.*

As the kitchen door slams open, the FBI agent races through, D.D. lurching in behind her, covered in blood.

"Bonita, duck!"

I understand that they want to shoot him but I'm in their way. I should step back, let them do their jobs. But this isn't about them. This is about me and my sisters and my mother.

Because I can feel them, even if no one else does. I can see them, even if no one else wants to. And I know them, my sisters in pain.

Together, we shove the mop head into the Bad Man's chest. To- gether, we drive him back with superhuman strength until he topples onto the conveyor belt, and the sanitizing cycle once more kicks to life.

"No, no, no!" he tries to scream.

But we hold the mop. We pin him against the rolling dish rack as others lift his feet, helping him along. His face disappears into the spray of boiling water. We listen to him scream and scream. We don't let go.

I keep my grip until he is so deep inside the scorching spray, the mop can't reach him anymore.

Then I let it clatter to the floor.

THE GIRLS SIGH THEIR GRATITUDE,

The house shudders back into silence.

Kimberly finally steps forward. She snaps off the machine, looking at me in concern as the steam clears.

D.D.: "Are you okay? Bonita, nod, something!"

"Great job!" Flora's voice, from the side entrance. The click I had heard earlier had been the door opening. And the shadow in the mist? Definitely not Flora, who looked like she could barely stand. On the other hand, Keith was covered in a sheen of sweat and appeared pleased with himself.

"How the hell did you beat us here?" Kimberly wanted to know.

"Took a shortcut. Who knew?"

"Sorry," Keith tells me. "I'm not a knife or gun kind of guy. But I knew Special Agent Quincy and the sheriff were on their way here. I figured if I could keep the monster man distracted, buy us some time . . . Except, then you took care of everything. Brilliantly, I might add."

I don't deny him his moment of triumph. Keith can take the credit, but I know he wasn't the only one distracting the Bad Man. Just as I know I wasn't the only one who finally shoved him into a spray of *boiling water. There are others here who needed their revenge. And we are all happy they finally got it.*

D.D. steps forward. I still haven't moved. Now she uses her left hand to brush back my hair, peer at my face.

I finally meet her gaze, smiling tentatively. D.D. looks terrible, blood on her face, her shoulder, her hands. Then there's Flora, who can barely stand up and appears to have part of her skull cracked open. These are tough women, though. Both of them appear satisfied.

"You did good, Bonita. You did good," D.D. tells me.

"With some help from my man," Flora says proudly, pointing at Keith, who promptly blushes.

I smile again. I let them think what they want to think. While around me, I feel the soft caress of my mother's spirit enfold me in a final embrace. Her silvery shadow gathers in the upper left-hand corner of the kitchen, now joined by purple, then green, then orange. Dozens of colors. Dozens of lost souls finally moving on.

They will wait for me, and watch over me. As I will always wait and watch for them.

A last kiss on my cheek. I feel it like the brush of butterfly wings. Mamita and chiquita. Together again.

Then, D.D.'s arm wraps around my shoulders. She half hugs me, half uses me to hold herself up. I welcome both as I listen to the grumbles and laughter of my new family, easing into the aftermath.

I close my eyes.

I send my love to my mother. I promise her I will live, I will love, I will find a way to be happy.

Then, I let her go.

EPILOGUE

BONITA

HER NAME IS FLORA DANE. Once, she knew a bad man, too. He kidnapped her and hurt her and tried to break her. But she held strong. She survived him. She rebuilt her life. She found people to love, people who love her.

She is not surviving anymore, she explains to me. She is thriving.

And she is going to teach me how to do it, too.

During the day, a new lady comes to visit me. Her name is JoAnn Kelly and she knows the magic of speech. She works with lips and tongues and how to make them do what you want. She is teaching me noises. Puh, puh, puh. Hah, hah, hah.

I haven't heard myself in so long, the first noise shocks me. The second makes me cry.

Later, when D.D. comes to check on me at lunch, she cries, too.

My new friends are busy.

I can't tell them where the other girls are, but there is another woman, Dorothea, who works in the town offices and runs some kind of website; she talks enough for everyone. D.D. tells me Franny, the Bad Man's mother, refuses all conversations. Her man is dead. Her son, too. She doesn't care about the police, our town, what she did. She sits in silence.

But Flora's boyfriend, Keith, can make computers do whatever he wants. With some information from Dorothea, he finds everything D.D. and the others want. Now, the FBI agent Kimberly is gone every day, overseeing the dozens of law enforcement experts pouring through our mountains, unearthing sad piles of bones, and helping them find their way home.

I'm called Bonita now. I like this name. I don't think it's the one from my mother, but it is the one from my new life with my new family, and I will keep it.

Eventually, D.D. says I can come to a big city called Boston. There is a place there that specializes in injuries like mine. My new therapist tells me they can help me make some progress. Maybe not speech, but I will learn to communicate with pictures and some words and maybe things like sign language. It turns out there are many kinds of talking in the world. I will find a way in the end.

D.D. says I can live with her and her husband, Alex. Her son, Jack, already wants to meet me. He has a dog named Kiko who eats shoes and runs like the wind. I want to meet Alex and Jack and Kiko, even if it means leaving this tiny place that has been both my prison and my home for so long.

Flora tells me it's okay to be scared. She says I must talk about it and not hold it inside. Fear is natural, but I should always remember that I am strong. All survivors are strong, and no one can take that from us.

People have vanished.

Not girls this time. Townsfolk, business owners. Here, then— when the FBI goes to raid their homes—gone.

Dorothea's computer includes names, D.D. explains to me one day. Many are local. Some are from around the world.

She and Kimberly are not concerned about the ones who've fled. D.D. tells me they will catch them all in the end. The ripples from this case—bodies in the woods, names in the computer—it will take years to unravel.

But that's the FBI's job. I don't have to do anything. They have Franny and Dorothea and other guilty parties and piles of evidence to help them out.

It's my job to be a girl now. Not a stupid girl. Just . . . a teenager. One who will go to school, and study speech and maybe make new friends, like Alex and Jack and Kiko.

I've never been a child before. I don't know if it's hard or not, but I would like to try.

I cry at night. I have bad dreams. I wake up, maybe trying to scream, but of course there is no sound.

Flora tells me she does the same, and she's been rescued for seven years. She assures me it gets easier. I will learn about me, and what I need to get to the other side.

I have never been me before either.

Flora loves Keith. They never say anything, but we all know. They blush when the other walks into the room. I like how they smile radiantly. It brings a lightness to my chest.

I think I understand what Flora is trying to teach me. It won't be all better right away. But someday, it will be all better.

We have been staying at our same motel. After the Last Stand at the Mountain Laurel and the string of arrests, the motel manager has been very nice to us. He swears he never wanted us to leave, but had received a threatening note. It turns out many people knew Clayton, and most were scared of him.

D.D. must return to Boston soon. She misses her family and needs them. I can't go just yet. There is paperwork that must be in order. I don't know how you put paperwork in order, but Kimberly assures me it can be done. In the meantime, Flora and Keith will stay with me.

Flora is arranging the burial of a man named Walt Davies. I didn't know him. I don't really know most locals, just the guests that stayed at the hotel. Apparently, Walt was the father of Flora's bad man. But she says Walt was good in the end and tried to help her, help me.

She is sad when she talks about him, but then her mood shifts and becomes sharp. I can't decide on colors for Flora. Sometimes, I think she's all different shades on different days.

Maybe because she is still learning to be herself. She says if she can do it, anyone can.

I talk to Flora and Keith with pictures. Which is to say, I don't talk much. I listen a lot. I like to listen to people who are actually speaking to me. Who look me in the eye and care about my reaction. We're all getting good at charades; plus I get to draw. As much as I like, as often as I like.

The speech lady tells me my pictures are very good. She has a friend who displays artwork. She would like to introduce me to her.

I want to find my mother.

The Bad Man killed her. I know that. I was able to draw that for my friends. But I don't know what happened after that. I have a special picture in my photo boards. The therapist lady helped me make it. It's like one of the emojis I have learned about, except I designed this one with my mother's eyes and my mother's hair.

I touch it first thing in the morning and last thing before I go to bed. And I feel her, silvery and warm in the air around me.

I show her picture often to Flora and D.D. I make my questioning face. We are all getting good at this.

D.D. figured out first what I wanted. She says they haven't been able to find any records. Of my birth, or my mother. But they have been retracing the Bad Man's life. They know he ran a business in New Mexico. There are legal records. Now they are working on the illegal stuff. He is dead, and witnesses will come forward. She tells me they will have information soon.

The FBI out there have already started hunting. Sooner or later, they will find a stretch of desert, dotted with bones just like in the mountains. My mother will be one of them. They will carefully lift her from the red dirt and bring her home to me. Her name is Flora Dane. She is a survivor and my mentor.

Her name is D. D. Warren. She is a detective and my protector.

Her name is Kimberly Quincy. She is an FBI agent and the person who will bring all my lost sisters justice.

My name is Bonita. I am pretty. I am strong.

I am my mother's daughter. Always.

ACKNOWLEDGMENTS

I started this book with barely a wisp of an idea—what would it be like to be an abducted child with no ability to speak, read, or write? I contacted my dear friend and gifted speech therapist, JoAnn Kelly, MS, CCC-SLP, from Children Unlimited Inc. She walked me through the basics of speech aphasia, then introduced me to storyboards and other communication techniques for nonverbal children. It is due to her that Bonita is such a gifted artist and D.D. figured out text emojis. Thank you, JoAnn!

This puzzle then led me to Executive Director Liz Kelley-Scott, and forensic interviewer Beth D'Angelo of the Child Advocacy Center of Carroll County, in order to learn how to conduct a forensic interview of a nonverbal witness. According to them, I'd just created their worst nightmare. Yay, me! But they had some excellent ideas on the subject, which I fully appreciated. Thank you, Liz, Beth, and of course, therapy dog extraordinaire, Westin. They provided hope for D.D. and Kimberly in dealing with their new charge, Bonita.

Of course, no book would be complete without some fun forensics.

Thank you Dr. Lee Jantz, associate director of the Forensic Anthropology Center of the University of Tennessee (home of the Body Farm!), for educating me on the latest practices for determining time since death of skeletal remains. I also appreciate all the information on mass graves. Things I never knew and now can't get out of my head. Remember all mistakes in this novel are mine and mine alone, because Dr. Jantz is clearly brilliant, not to mention very patient with overenthusiastic thriller writers.

Next up, Lt. Michael Santuccio from the Carroll County Sheriff's Office. Cold cases, current cases, this guy knows it all. Every time my taskforce got stuck, I'd call him for fresh investigative tactics, which he never failed to deliver. Oh the amount of data out there and the things a savvy detective can learn. Again, all mistakes are mine and mine alone. Thank you, Lt. Santuccio, for being D.D.'s brains and my savior.

My deepest admiration and appreciation to my editor, Mark Tavani, for the long phone calls and brainstorming sessions that finally brought my kernel of an idea to fruition. Then kept me on track till I got it done! Also, complete adoration to my agent, Meg Ruley. An author couldn't have a better advocate on her side.

To my friends, thank you for keeping me sane. To my family, thank you for understanding when I'm insane. And to my amazing three dogs plus an entire mountain range, thank you for keeping me going. Nothing like a walk in the woods for figuring out where to hide more dead bodies.

Finally, what you've all been waiting for: the winners of the Kill a Friend, Maim a Buddy Sweepstakes. Stacey Kasmer must have some excellent friends on her side. With nearly sixty of them nominating her for death, Brandon Salemi came through with the win, and got Stacey her grand demise. Hope it was worth it, Stacey, and that all of you enjoy! On the international side, Hélène Tellier nominated herself for literary immortality. Enjoy the novel, and the thrill of your own fictional adventure! Everyone else, the contest is up and running again at LisaGardner.com. Don't be shy!

Writing is a solitary business, but publishing is a team sport. Thank you to my amazing team in the United States and abroad. And a huge shout-out to my readers, who are almost as excited to see my characters again as I am.

This one's for you.

ABOUT THE AUTHOR

Lisa Gardner is the number one *New York Times* bestselling, author of twenty one previous novels, including her most recent, *Never Tell*. Her Detective D. D. Warren novels include *Find Her, Fear Nothing, Catch Me, Love You More,* and *The Neighbor,* which won the International Thriller of the Year Award. She lives with her family in New England.